SHERRYL WOODS

THE
CALAMITY JANES
Gina & Emma

MIRA

MIRA

ISBN-13: 978-0-7783-1778-4

The Calamity Janes: Gina & Emma

Copyright © 2015 by Harlequin Books S. A.

The publisher acknowledges the copyright holder of the individual works as follows:

To Catch a Thief
Copyright © 2001 by Sherryl Woods

The Calamity Janes
Copyright © 2001 by Sherryl Woods

For questions and comments about the quality of this book, please contact us at CustomerService@Harlequin.com.

www.MIRABooks.com

Printed in U.S.A.

Praise for the novels of
Sherryl Woods

"Sherryl Woods writes emotionally satisfying novels about family, friendship and home. Truly feel-great reads!"
—#1 *New York Times* bestselling author Debbie Macomber

"Woods is a master heartstring puller."
—*Publishers Weekly* on *Seaview Inn*

"Woods's readers will eagerly anticipate her trademark small-town setting, loyal friendships, and honorable mentors as they meet new characters and reconnect with familiar ones in this heartwarming tale."
—*Booklist* on *Home in Carolina*

"Once again, Woods, with such authenticity, weaves a tale of true love and the challenges that can knock up against that love."
—*RT Book Reviews* on *Beach Lane*

"In this sweet, sometimes funny and often touching story, the characters are beautifully depicted, and readers…will…want to wish themselves away to Seaview Key."
—*RT Book Reviews* on *Seaview Inn*

"Woods…is noted for appealing character-driven stories that are often infused with the flavor and fragrance of the South."
—*Library Journal*

"A reunion story punctuated by family drama, Woods's first novel in her new Ocean Breeze series is touching, tense and tantalizing."
—*RT Book Reviews* on *Sand Castle Bay*

"A whimsical, sweet scenario…the digressions have their own charm, and Woods never fails to come back to the romantic point."
—*Publishers Weekly* on *Sweet Tea at Sunrise*

For a complete list of all titles by Sherryl Woods,
visit www.sherrylwoods.com.

Look for more of The Calamity Janes
The Calamity Janes: Lauren
available soon from MIRA Books

Dear friend,

When I first conceived the idea for the Calamity Janes series years ago, I knew I wanted to write about a group of friends who'd been a bit of a disaster back in high school, then taken very different paths. Now they're back in Wyoming for their class reunion and the chance to catch up on their lives. In a lot of ways, these women were the predecessors of the Sweet Magnolias. I'm so delighted that new readers will have a chance to get to know them.

Back then, in addition to writing about strong friendships, I also wanted to attempt a group of books set in a parallel time frame. In other words, even though these are very separate stories, the plots overlap during the big class reunion. Only the final book continues past the last dance. It was an interesting writing challenge. As you read the five stories, you'll have to decide if the experiment worked.

I hope you'll have as much fun with the Calamity Janes as you've had through the years with the Sweet Magnolias and that you'll enjoy the Wyoming setting as much as I enjoyed visiting that part of the country to do research for the series.

With all good wishes for lasting friendships in your life.

Sherryl

CONTENTS

TO CATCH A THIEF

Prologue

The office at Café Tuscany on Manhattan's Upper West Side was little bigger than a broom closet, large enough for a desk, a chair and a bookshelf crammed with cookbooks, nutrition reports, menus and file boxes of handwritten recipes. It could only hold one person at a time, but at the moment Gina Petrillo's feeling of claustrophobia had more to do with the court document in her hand than the size of the space.

"I'm going to kill him," she muttered, fingers trembling as the summons to appear for a deposition slid to the desk. "If I ever get my hands on Bobby, I am going to kill him."

She had met Roberto Rinaldi when they were both studying cooking in Italy. A passionate enthusiast of fine food, Bobby was an intuitive genius in the kitchen. They had struck up an instant rapport that had more to do with ingenious blends of sauces and inventive uses for pasta than lust.

Truthfully, Gina wouldn't have trusted Bobby anywhere near her bed. The man was more fickle about women than he was about ingredients. He was constantly experimenting with both. He got away with it because he was charming, impossible to resist when he tempted with either delectable dishes or devilish kisses—at least according to his many conquests.

Gina had ignored his romantic overtures and concentrated on his skills in the kitchen. He was the most creative chef she had met during all of her studies, which was saying quite a lot. After forsaking college, she had studied at some of the finest culinary institutes in Europe. Though she had loved French cuisine, from the gourmet recipes of Paris to the simpler fare of Provence, Italian cooking spoke to her soul. Maybe it was genetic, maybe not, but the first time she had walked into the kitchen in Rome with its aromas of garlic, tomatoes and olive oil, she had felt at home.

It had been the same for Bobby, or so he had claimed. His recipes were both bold and adventurous. She doubted he'd ever tasted plain old pasta and tomato sauce, much less eaten canned ravioli, even as a child.

Five years ago, when the year-long course in Italy had ended, they had agreed to form a partnership, seek out investors among Bobby's financial contacts and open a restaurant in New York. It had taken another year to put the deal together, but it had been worth all of the scrimping and sacrifice, all of the long nights scraping paint and sanding floors. Café Tuscany had been a dream for both of them.

Apparently, it had also been Bobby's personal get-rich-quick scheme.

According to the summons she'd been handed an hour ago, Bobby had not only embezzled restaurant funds, but stolen from their backers, as well. A check of the café's account, made just minutes ago, confirmed the worst—the coffers were empty. And the rent was due, as were payments on invoices from most of their vendors.

Gina had no one to blame but herself for this disaster. She had allowed Bobby to keep track of their finances, because she was more interested in cooking and marketing than calculating. The fact that an outsider—an attorney representing the supposedly swindled backers—knew more about the state of the business's finances than she did was humiliating. It didn't seem to matter that she had done her part to make the business thrive. She was as much at fault as the man who'd run off with the money. At least, that was the implication in the summons.

Gina thought of all she had sacrificed to put Café Tuscany on the map, including a personal life. But it had been worth it. With a promotional push by one of her old high school classmates, superstar Lauren Winters, Gina had launched Café Tuscany as the hottest restaurant in a town where five-star dining and excellent neighborhood eateries were a dime a dozen. Prime tables were booked weeks in advance, and special events were sold out. Celebrities liked to be seen here, their presence always noted in the next day's papers. In the past year, their brand-new catering division had been booked for a dozen of society's most important charity events. With each success had come new bookings that kept her on the go morning till night.

So where had all that money gone? To finance some new scheme of Bobby's, no doubt. Or perhaps to freshen his designer wardrobe of Italian suits. Or maybe to buy diamonds for his latest lover. All Gina knew for certain was that none of it was in the bank, and that second notices for unpaid bills were stuffed into a drawer of the desk that Bobby had kept under lock and key. She'd broken into it an hour ago, right after she'd read through the damning words in the summons.

When she'd called Bobby's home—an expensive brownstone on the Upper East Side—she'd discovered that the line had been disconnected. His cell phone had gone unanswered. The man was gone.

The man was slime!

And because of him, this lawyer—she glanced at the summons again—this Rafe O'Donnell was on her trail, apparently convinced that she was in on the scheme, rather than another one of its victims.

Sitting there, stunned, Gina realized that her dream was not just ending, but crash landing. Unless she could come up with money—a lot of money—she would have to declare bankruptcy and close Café Tuscany within months, if not weeks. She might be able to stave off creditors for a while, but not indefinitely.

"I have to think," she muttered.

And she wasn't going to get the job done sitting in this closet. She needed fresh air and wide-open spaces. She needed to go home to Winding River, Wyoming.

She could leave the restaurant in the capable hands of her assistant manager for a week or so. She could call this O'Donnell person and postpone the deposition until, say, sometime in the next century.

With her high school class reunion in a few days, the timing couldn't be better. Her friends—the indomitable Calamity Janes—would be there to bolster her spirits. If she decided to ask, they would offer advice. Lauren would write a check on the spot to bail her out. Emma would give her expert legal counsel. And Karen and Cassie would find some way to make her laugh.

Gina sighed. They would do all of that and more *if* she decided to tell them just how badly she'd messed up.

In fact, she thought with the first bit of optimism she'd felt all day, they might even offer her a shotgun she could use if she ever spotted Roberto Rinaldi again.

1

"Gina Petrillo has gone *where?*" Rafe O'Donnell's head snapped up at his secretary's casual announcement.

"Wyoming. She called an hour ago and rescheduled the deposition," Lydia Allen repeated, looking entirely too cheerful.

If Rafe didn't know better he'd think she was glad that this Gina had escaped his clutches. He scowled at the woman who had been assigned to him when he'd first joined the firm, Whitfield, Mason and Lockhart, seven years earlier. At the time, she'd been with the firm for twenty years and claimed that she was always assigned to new recruits to make sure they were broken in properly. She was still with him because she swore that, to this day, he was too impossible to foist off on a less-seasoned secretary.

"Did I say it was okay to reschedule?" he inquired irritably.

"You've been in court all day," she said, clearly unintimidated by his sharp tone. "We reschedule these things all the time."

"Not so some crook can go gallivanting off to Wyoming," he snapped.

"You don't know that Gina Petrillo is a crook," Lydia chided. "Innocent until proven guilty, remember?"

Rafe held on to his temper by a thread. "I do not need to be lectured on the principles of law by a grandmother," he said, deliberately minimizing whatever legal expertise she might legitimately consider her due.

Typically, she ignored the insult. "Maybe not, but you could use a few hard truths. I've eaten at that restaurant. So have most of the partners in this firm. If you weren't such a workaholic, you'd probably be a regular there, too. The food is fabulous. Gina Petrillo is a lovely, beautiful young woman. She is not a thief."

So, he thought, that explained the attitude. Lydia was personally acquainted with the elusive woman and disapproved of Rafe's determination to link Gina Petrillo to her partner's crimes. As softhearted as his secretary was, she'd probably called Gina and warned her to get out of town.

"You say she's not a thief," he began with deceptive mildness in his best go-for-the-jugular mode. "Mind telling me how you reached that conclusion? Do you have a degree in psychology, perhaps? Access to the restaurant's books? Do you happen to have any evidence whatsoever that would actually exonerate her?"

"No, I do not have any evidence," she informed him with a huff. "Neither do you. But, unlike some people, I am a very good judge of character, Rafe O'Donnell."

Rafe was forced to concede that she was…usually.

"Now that Roberto," she continued, "I can believe he's stolen from people. He has shifty eyes."

"Thank you, Miss Marple," Rafe said snidely. "Roberto Rinaldi was not the only one with access to the money."

A good chunk of that money happened to belong to Rafe's socialite mother. She had been taken in by the man's charm. Rafe hadn't explored the exact nature of the relationship, but knowing his mother's track record, it hadn't been platonic. He was no more oblivious to his mother's faults than his father had been before the divorce, but he did his best to keep her from getting robbed blind.

"But Roberto is the one who's missing," Lydia pointed out. "He's the one you should be concentrating on."

"I would if I could find him," Rafe said, not bothering to hide his exasperation. "Which is one reason I want to talk to Gina Petrillo. She just might know where he is. Now, thanks to you, I don't even know where *she* is."

"Of course you do—I told you. She's gone to Wyoming."

"It's a big state. Care to narrow it down?"

She frowned at him. "There is no need to be sarcastic."

Rafe sighed. "Do you know where she is or not?"

"Of course I do."

"Then book me on the next flight."

"I doubt that Winding River has an airport. I'll check," she said, her expression unexpectedly brightening.

"Whatever," he said, not one bit happy about the images of Western wilderness that came to mind. "Just cancel everything on my calendar and get me out there by tomorrow night."

"Will do, boss. I'll go ahead and cancel everything through next week. You could use the time off."

Lydia's sudden eagerness, the spring in her step as she started to leave his office, had him frowning. "I don't need time off," he protested. "I'll take care of this over the weekend and be back here on Monday."

"Why don't you just play it by ear?"

His gaze narrowed. "What are you up to?"

"Just doing my job," she said with an innocent expression.

Rafe seriously doubted her innocence, but for the life of him he couldn't figure out why Lydia was so blasted anxious for him to jet off to Wyoming. She was not the kind of secretary who used the boss's absence to sneak out and shop or even to take long lunch hours. No, she was the kind who meddled, the kind who took great pride in making his private life a living hell with her well-meant pestering.

And she liked this Gina Petrillo, he thought, suddenly making the connection.

"Lydia!" he bellowed.

"You don't have to shout," she scolded. "I'm just outside the door."

"When you book my room in Winding River, make sure I'm all alone in it."

She feigned shock. "Why, of course I will."

"Don't look at me like that. It wouldn't be the first time some hotel mixup had me sharing a room with a woman you thought I ought to get to know better."

"I never—"

"Save it. Just make sure of it, Lydia, or you'll spend the rest of your career at Whitfield, Mason and Lockhart doing the filing."

She shot him an unrepentant grin. "I doubt that, sir. I know where all the bodies are buried."

Rafe sighed heavily. She did, too.

When the Winding River Wildcats did a class reunion, the festivities went on for three solid days. There was a welcome barbecue on Friday night, a rodeo during the day on Saturday, a dance Saturday night and a farewell picnic on Sunday. It all flowed right into the town's annual Fourth of July celebration.

Gina was less interested in all of that than she was in spending a few quiet hours with her oldest and dearest friends. For just a little while she wanted to forget all about that slime Roberto Rinaldi and the financial mess he'd left her to clean up.

"Couldn't we just go down to the Heartbreak, have a few beers, listen to some music and chill for a few hours?" she pleaded, even as the others were coaxing her off her parents' front porch and toward a car on Friday night.

"There will be beer and music at the barbecue," Emma told her. "Besides, since when have you ever turned down the chance to party? The only one in our crowd who was any wilder was Cassie."

At the mention of Cassie, Gina's spirits sank even lower. "I wish she'd come tonight."

"She's promised to be at the dance tomorrow night," Karen reminded her. "And you know perfectly well why she stayed away."

"Because of that run-in with Cole earlier," Gina said. "She really was shaken by that. He came within seconds of bumping face-to-face into their son."

"It might have been best if he had," Karen said. "I think she's just postponing the inevitable."

"Maybe so, but as much as I wish she were here, I am not going to let it spoil tonight," Lauren said. "Now, get moving, you guys. I've been living on lettuce a long time now. I haven't had a decent barbecue in years, and I am ready to pig out, no pun intended." She herded them toward the fancy sports utility vehicle she had rented for her visit.

Twenty minutes later Lauren turned into the parking lot at the school where they had shared some of the best times of their lives. Known far and wide as the Calamity Janes, the five of them had stirred up more trouble than any graduate before or since. Cassie had been the ringleader, but the rest of them had willingly gone along with whatever mischief she devised.

Now Karen lived on a ranch, Lauren was in Hollywood, Cassie was still struggling to keep her son a secret from his father and Emma was a hot-shot attorney in Denver. Like Emma and Lauren, Gina was considered one of the class success stories. The daughter of an insurance agent and a high school secretary, in high school Gina had earned much-needed spending money by working as a waitress right here in town. Now she owned her own very exclusive restaurant in New York. By anyone's standards, it was a rags-to-riches story.

If only they knew how close it was to turning around the other way, she thought with a sigh as they approached the football field that had been turned into giant picnic grounds for the night. A stage had been set up under the goalpost at the north end, a pit for the roasted pig was at the opposite end and in between were rows of tables with every kind of food imaginable, all catered by the town's restaurants. Huge galvanized steel tubs were filled with ice and crammed with soft drinks and beer.

Classmates had already staked out spots for themselves by tossing blankets on the ground, but at the moment nobody was sitting. Everyone was milling around greeting people they hadn't seen since graduation ten years before.

Suddenly Gina felt an elbow being jammed into her ribs. "Hey," she protested, turning to face Lauren. "What was that for?"

The woman who had been declared most likely to succeed because of her brains, not her now-legendary beauty, gestured toward the bleachers, where a lone man sat, legs stretched out in front of him, elbows propped on the bench behind. He looked aloof and out of place. He also happened to be handsome as sin, but in the last few days Gina had sworn off the type. If she never met another sexy charmer, it would suit her just fine. In fact, at the moment, Bobby's disappearing act had made her view every male with healthy suspicion.

"Who, pray tell, is he?" Lauren asked. "He's definitely not one of us. Nobody we went to school with could improve that much in twenty years, much less ten."

Gina forced herself to give the stranger a closer inspection. True, he was gorgeous, in a citified, sophisticated way. Even in jeans and a chambray shirt—which looked brand-new from this distance—there was no mistaking the man for a cowboy. He was too polished, his chestnut hair a little too carefully trimmed, his complexion a little too pale, his cheekbones a little too aristocratic. He all but shouted that he was some Yankee blueblood.

"Well?" Lauren prodded. "Do you know him?"

Gina was certain she'd never seen him before, but that didn't seem to stop her heart from doing a little lurch or her stomach from taking a dip. It was possible he was someone's husband, sitting on the sidelines because he felt uncomfortable among all the strangers. She didn't think so, though. She had the uneasy sense that his penetrating gaze was locked directly on her. Not on Lauren, who tended to captivate any male in a room, but on her, Gina Petrillo, with the untamable hair, too-wide hips and a ten-year-old sundress she'd snagged from the back of the closet in her old bedroom.

Lauren, ever confident from years in the limelight, didn't seem to notice that the man's attention was elsewhere. She grinned at Gina. "Only one way to find out."

Gina wanted to tell her not to go over there, to steer as far away from the man as she could, but she knew the warning would only draw a hoot of laughter. There wasn't a person born who could intimidate Lauren once her curiosity was aroused. That confidence was something new. In high school Lauren had been as shy as she'd been brainy. The adoration of millions of fans had given her self-esteem a much-needed boost.

Gina deliberately turned her back on the scene and went in search of a desperately longed-for beer. She had just tipped up the can for a long, slow swallow when she heard Lauren say, "Oh, here you are. Gina, sweetie, this incredibly gorgeous man is looking for you. Aren't you lucky?"

Gina's stomach plummeted as she slowly turned to face them. With every fiber of her being she knew she wasn't the least bit lucky. Never had been, and certainly not lately. No, this man was not looking for her because he'd been dying to get her recipe for fettuccine.

"Gina Petrillo, Rafe O'Donnell," Lauren said, relinquishing him to Gina with a broad wink and then abandoning the two of them as if she'd just accomplished the matchmaking success of the century.

Gina recognized the name with a sense of inevitability. She forced herself to look straight into the man's unreadable topaz eyes. There was little point in pretending that she didn't recognize the name. Nor did she have to work very hard to figure out what he was doing here. She was not going to let him rattle her, though. She would remain cool, calm and collected if it killed her. She refused to let him think for a second that she was harboring any sense of guilt.

"A long way from home, aren't you, Mr. O'Donnell?"

"As are you, Ms. Petrillo."

"No, this *is* my home," she said firmly.

"And New York?"

"Where I work."

"Not any longer, if I have anything to say about it."

She gave him a wry look. "Then I guess the battle lines are drawn. It's a good thing you're not either judge or jury. I might be quaking in my boots."

"You should be, anyway. I'm very good at what I do."

"And what is it that you do, Mr. O'Donnell? Condemn people without a trial?"

"Get at the facts, Ms. Petrillo. That was the whole purpose of that deposition you skipped out on."

She regarded him with indignation. "I didn't skip out on anything. Check your appointment book. I rescheduled."

"Without my permission."

"Your secretary didn't seem to have a problem with it."

"Yes, well, Lydia sometimes forgets who's in charge."

If it had been anyone else under any other circumstance, Gina might have grinned at his resigned expression. Instead, she said only, "You must find that extremely annoying."

"Mostly it's just an inconvenience," he corrected.

"Yes, I imagine chasing halfway across the country after bad guys like me must play havoc with your schedule."

To her surprise, he chuckled.

"You have no idea," he said. "I had really big plans for this weekend."

"Oh? A ball game with the kids? Maybe a charity event with the wife?"

"No kids. No wife."

That news set off totally inappropriate little butterflies in Gina's stomach. To her deep regret they seemed to be doing a victory dance. She refused to let him see that he could disconcert her in the slightest way—especially not in *that* way.

She studied him thoughtfully. "A hot date, then?"

"Nope."

"Surely you weren't spending the weekend all alone, Mr. O'Donnell."

"Afraid so. Of course, I would have had my share of entertainment. Before I left I got a subpoena for the Café Tuscany books. I had someone pick them up yesterday morning. I understand your assistant was very helpful. Too bad you and your partner aren't that cooperative. Where can I find Rinaldi, by the way?"

Gina barely contained a groan. *That* explained the frantic messages she'd been getting from Deidre all day. Gina hadn't called back because she had vowed to take this weekend off from everything connected to the restaurant. She had figured Monday would be soon enough to return the call and face whatever catastrophe had struck. Just one more bad decision she would have to live with. They were stacking up faster than the ones the Calamity Janes had made in high school.

"I'm sure those books would have been as illuminating as anything I can tell you," she said. "You should have stayed at home with them. You could have crunched numbers all weekend long. As for Bobby, if you locate him, let me know. I have a few choice words I'd like to share with him."

"Do you expect me to believe he skipped out without telling you?"

"Frankly, I don't care what you believe. Now, go home, Mr. O'Donnell. It's not too late to cozy up with those financial records. Why not fly back tonight?"

"Because I gave the pilot on the charter jet that brought me here from Denver the night off and I hate to ruin his evening," the attorney countered. "He was looking forward to doing some line dancing at someplace called the Heartbreak."

"How very thoughtful of you. And how very expensive to go around chartering jets to get from here to there. Do your clients know how you toss their money around?"

"Oh, this trip's on me," he said easily. He glanced around at the crowded field, took a deliberate sniff of the smoky, barbecue-scented air. "I haven't been to an event like this in a long time."

She regarded him with skepticism. "For such a proponent of truth, Mr. O'Donnell, that's quite a fib. You've *never* been to an event like this, have you?"

She deliberately looked him over from head to toe. "I'm guessing some East Coast prep school, then Harvard. If you've ever been to a reunion, I'm sure it was in some fancy hotel or private country club. And my hunch is that the closest you've ever come to a horse is on a New York street corner and there was a cop mounted on its back."

"You'd be wrong," he said without rancor. "I went to public schools, then to Yale, not Harvard."

"That's not exactly a significant distinction."

"I suggest you not say that to an alumnus of either university. We do like to cling to our illusions of supremacy."

"Well, cling all you like, just do it somewhere else. I'm here to have a good time with some old friends. I don't want to find you lurking in the shadows everywhere I turn."

"Too bad. I'm not going anywhere."

His vehemence was annoying, but not all that surprising. "What really brought you running all the way out here?" she asked curiously. "Are you afraid I'm going to disappear? Are you hoping to discover I've stashed the missing money in a mattress at my parents' house?"

The idea seemed to intrigue him. "Have you?"

"Nope. No stash. No hiding place. And I can show you my airline ticket. It's round-trip. Go home, Mr. O'Donnell. I'll see you right on schedule in a couple of weeks."

"We could get this out of the way right here and

now," he suggested. "Then I could get back to New York and you could enjoy the rest of your weekend."

"Without an attorney present? I don't think so."

He shrugged. "Then I guess you'll just have to get used to having me underfoot for...how long did you say you were planning to stay?"

"Two weeks."

The news seemed to make him very unhappy, but he nodded. "Two weeks, then. I'll look forward to it."

Gina sighed. "Suit yourself. I'm going to get another beer."

He seemed to find that amusing. "Drinking won't make you forget I'm here."

"No, I imagine it won't," she agreed. "It would take a blow on the head to accomplish that. But the beer might make your presence more palatable."

She gave him a jaunty salute. "See you in court, Mr. O'Donnell."

"Oh, I'll be seeing you long before that," he said smoothly. "In fact, I'll be everywhere you turn."

If only his mission weren't to put her in jail, Gina thought with a trace of wistfulness, she might actually look forward to that.

As it was, the knot of dread in her stomach tightened. She might not be guilty of anything except the bad judgment to go into business with Bobby, but Rafe O'Donnell struck her as the kind of man who could dig up secrets, twist words and paint a very dark picture of the saintliest person on earth.

And he intended to stay right here in Winding River turning over rocks, no doubt, looking for incriminating evidence, pestering her friends. She shuddered at the prospect.

Maybe she should just get it over with. Talk to him, and send him on his way. But that idea held no appeal, either. She needed time to gather her thoughts and see an attorney back in New York. She didn't want to drag Emma or anyone else here into this unless she absolutely had to. It was her disaster and she would fix it. Assuming it could be fixed.

In the meantime the music had started and nobody loved dancing more than Gina did. She could postpone that beer for a few more minutes. She gave Rafe O'Donnell a considering look.

"Can you do a two-step?" she asked.

He looked at her blankly. "What's that?"

She regarded him with pity. "Never mind," she said, reaching for his hand. "Just follow my lead."

He caught on more quickly than she had expected. He wasn't good, but he wasn't tripping over his own feet or stepping on hers, either.

"You do rise to a challenge, don't you?" she teased.

"There's very little I won't do to win," he agreed solemnly.

"Are we still talking about dancing?"

"Were we ever?"

Gina sighed. So that was the way it was going to be. He was never going to let her forget why he was here.

"I think I'll have that beer after all," she said, even before the music ended. She started away, then turned back. "Leave my friends out of this."

"I won't say anything," he agreed, then had to ruin it by adding, "For the time being."

"Look, Mr. O'Donnell…"

"I think since we're going to become so well acquainted over the next couple of weeks, you should call me Rafe."

She shrugged off the request. "Whatever. The point is, they don't know anything about this and I don't want them to."

"Why? Your friend Lauren makes ten million a movie. She could write you a check and put an end to this right now. You could pay off all those people who've been bilked, settle up the restaurant's accounts and life would go on. You'd never have to see me again."

"She could," Gina agreed. "But it's not her problem. It's mine." She leveled a look straight into his eyes. "No, let me correct that. It's Bobby's."

"But he left you holding the bag, didn't he?"

She held up her hands. "I'm not doing this. Not now. Good night, Mr. O'Donnell."

She deliberately turned her back on him and walked away, but with every step she took, she felt his gaze burning into her. She was glad he couldn't see her face, because then he'd know exactly how badly the encounter had shaken her.

Halfway across the field, she ran into Lauren.

"What did you do with that gorgeous man?"

"That gorgeous man is a viper," Gina snapped.

Instantly her friend's teasing expression faded. "What did he do?" Lauren demanded, her gaze searching the field for the man who'd offended her friend.

Gina grinned. "It's okay. Settle down. It's nothing I can't deal with."

"Are you sure?"

"Absolutely."

But even though she managed to inject a note of confidence into her voice for Lauren's sake, Gina couldn't help wondering if Rafe O'Donnell wasn't way more than she could handle. She thought of the way her pulse had skipped in his presence, then amended the thought: he might be more than she could handle in more ways than one.

2

Rafe had been stunned when he'd realized that the woman sashaying over to him earlier in the evening was *the* Lauren Winters, an actress renowned for her beauty and her box office appeal. Who would have imagined finding such a glamorous superstar in a one-horse town in the middle of nowhere? To top it off, she seemed to fit right in. No one was gawking. No one was begging for autographs. Clearly she wasn't just a celebrity imported for the event, but a hometown girl.

But as intrigued as he was to be face-to-face with the superstar, he'd barely been able to pull his gaze away from her friend. From the moment Lauren had introduced him to Gina, he'd been captivated. That was the only word for it, and it was damned inconvenient. He didn't trust her. He didn't like her. But his body didn't seem to give two hoots about any of that.

Gina Petrillo was tall and slender with black eyes and dark hair that curled to her shoulders in sexy disarray. There was an earthy quality to her that reminded him of some of the most legendary Italian beauties. He could instantly envision her standing over a steaming pot of tomato sauce and just as easily imagine her in his bed, in a steamy tangle of arms and legs. He couldn't think of the last time he'd reacted on such a purely male level to a woman.

Of course, the fact that she was a thief—okay, an alleged thief, he conceded, thinking of Lydia's admonition—took a little of the fun away from the discovery that he was attracted to her. He had a feeling he was going to spend a lot of time reminding himself that Gina Petrillo was trouble. He would probably spend even more time in cold showers.

Holding her for that dance, watching the sway of her hips as she'd walked away from him, he'd found himself regretting the fact that she was so thoroughly forbidden. Then, again, maybe that was the real allure.

And not only was she forbidden, she didn't seem to trust him any more than he did her. That offended him. Most people considered him solid and reliable. In fact, he was one of the most respected attorneys at a firm that prided itself on its respectability. In some circles he was even considered a prize catch.

Not that he was any sort of playboy, but he was used to women being eager to see him. He seldom had time for even half the women who called asking him to accompany them to social functions. He had a hunch it would be a cold day in hell before Gina asked him to dance again, much less to join her for dinner. That made her a challenge, and as she had already guessed, he loved a challenge.

The smart thing would be to speak to a local judge, arrange a quick deposition—first thing tomorrow morning, if possible—and then hightail it out of town before he lost sight of his professional ethics.

The only problem with that was that it would leave Gina Petrillo on her own in Wyoming. She'd be able to sneak off to who-knew-where the minute his back was turned. And she was his best link to Roberto Rinaldi. The deposition was only half of what he wanted from her. He also wanted her to lead him to that sleazebag partner of hers. Sooner or later she was going to make contact with the man, if only to strangle him herself... or to get her share of the cash he'd stolen.

No, he concluded, he was here to stay. At least until Gina went back to New York, which she'd insisted would be in two weeks.

Two endless weeks, he thought despondently. Lydia would be elated.

He listened to the annoying whine of a fiddle as the band tuned up for yet another round of country songs, and shuddered. Why couldn't the woman have run off to Italy? Or Paris? Or anyplace civilized where the music tended to be classical?

"Care to dance, Mr. O'Donnell?"

He gazed down into Lauren's crystal-blue eyes and wondered why he wasn't the least bit tempted by the superstar. Because the only eyes on his mind were black as onyx and belonged to a woman who was off-limits, he made himself nod.

"I'd be honored," he told her. If nothing else, it would be a story to tell when he got back home. Maybe even to repeat to his children, if he ever got around to marrying.

They had taken only a few awkward steps to the unfamiliar rhythm when Lauren came to a stop and dropped any pretense of friendliness. "You don't know much about the Texas two-step, do you, Mr. O'Donnell?"

"Can't say that I do," he admitted. "Tonight is the first time I've tried it."

"Do you consider yourself a quick learner?" she asked.

He regarded her warily. "Under most circumstances."

"Okay, then, here's another lesson," she said. "You don't know any more about Gina than you do about the two-step. She won't tell me why you're here, but your presence is clearly upsetting her, and I don't like that. She's a terrific person and she's among friends, Mr. O'Donnell. You tangle with her, you tangle with all of us."

He grinned at the feisty defense and the warning. "I'll keep that in mind."

"I'm not saying that for your amusement," she snapped. "I mean it. People who underestimate me live to regret it."

He managed a more somber expression. "I'm aware of that, Ms. Winters. You've made your point."

She studied him intently, then nodded, evidently satisfied. "See that you don't forget it."

He watched as she went back to a cluster of three women, Gina among them. Lauren gave her friend a fierce hug, a public demonstration of support meant for his benefit, no doubt. He admired the show of loyalty, but it didn't change his mind about Gina.

Whether Gina was a thief or not remained to be seen, but her partner was, and that made her guilty of very bad judgment if nothing else. Nothing she'd said or done tonight had persuaded him of her innocence. In fact, quite the opposite.

The way he saw it, Gina was even more dangerous than he'd anticipated. She was savvy and unpredictable. She had a smart mouth. With her restaurant
under siege, she just might get it into her head that
she had nothing to lose. She could decide to run. And
she was surrounded by people who evidently would
do just about anything to protect her no matter how
guilty she might be.

He was going to have to keep a clear head, which
was doubly difficult given the effect she had on him.
Obviously, what he needed was a good night's sleep,
though he doubted he'd get it with Gina's sexy image
plaguing him. He glanced around until he found her
in the crowd.

She was dancing again, head thrown back, her gaze
locked with some cowboy's. Rafe felt his blood boil.
He wanted to stride across the field and yank her out of
the man's embrace. The depth of that unexpected and
unfamiliar streak of jealousy startled him. He hadn't
cared enough about any woman to be jealous, not ever.
This was not good, not good at all.

He definitely needed to get back to his motel room,
alone, and get his sex-starved emotions under control.
He hadn't mentioned to Gina that he'd brought the Café
Tuscany books with him. Studying those cold, hard
figures ought to put things back into perspective. And
they were a whole lot more reliable and easier to understand than any woman. His mother had taught him that.

Gina didn't get a wink of sleep all night long. Despite her cool responses and bravado the night before,
Rafe O'Donnell had gotten to her. She knew all about
the fancy Park Avenue law firm he worked for. She'd

recognized the name from its frequent mentions on the news, and some of the partners were among her best customers. They didn't take cases they didn't intend to win. She didn't doubt that he was as driven and determined as the rest of them.

Which meant he was going to make her life a living hell. Oh, in the end, she might be able to prove that Bobby had acted alone, but not without paying a high price. Her reputation would be tarnished. Between unpaid bills and legal fees, the restaurant would be forced to close. And she'd be right back where she started five years ago, working in somebody else's kitchen to scrape up enough money to open her own restaurant.

It would take longer this time, too, because she wouldn't have Bobby to draw in investors. In fact, her link to Bobby would probably prevent anyone except the most foolhardy from lending her a dime.

Sighing, she crawled out of bed, pulled on a pair of faded jeans, a short-sleeved blouse and the cowboy boots she hadn't worn since she'd left Winding River ten years ago. They still fit perfectly. Maybe there was a message there, that Winding River was where she really belonged, where people still felt a shred of respect for her.

Her parents had long since left the house. Her father worked Saturdays. Her mother spent the morning with the altar guild at church and her afternoon doing errands. Gina was used to late nights and sleeping in. She'd gotten to bed before midnight the night before, but add in a little jet lag and her schedule was completely upside down. It felt like noon, which it was in New York. The clock said otherwise.

She poured herself a cup of coffee, made two slices

of toast from her mother's homemade sourdough bread, then went onto the porch. It was already hot outside, better suited for iced tea than coffee, but she drank it anyway. Maybe a jolt of caffeine would help her think more clearly so she could decide what to do about Rafe O'Donnell.

Unfortunately, the only ideas that came to mind had more to do with discovering what his mouth would feel like against her own than they did with getting him out of town.

Too restless to sit still, she grabbed the keys to her mother's car, which had been left for her, and headed for town. She parked in the middle of the block on Main Street and considered her options. She could go to Stella's and probably find a half dozen people she knew who'd be glad to chat with her over another cup of coffee. Or she could go to the Italian restaurant down the block, where Tony would probably let her work off her frustrations over his stove.

No contest, she thought, with a stirring of antici-pation.

Tony Falcone had been her mentor. He'd hired her as a waitress while she was still in high school, but it hadn't been long before he'd discovered that her real talent was in the kitchen. He'd taught her to make la-sagna and spaghetti sauce with meatballs. He'd let her experiment with new recipes when cooking the tra-ditional dishes had grown boring. And then he had helped her to persuade her parents that she would be better off going to culinary schools around the world than to any traditional college. It had been a tough sell, especially to her father, who'd been convinced that a degree in accounting would be a lot more practical.

Given her current circumstances, Gina had to admit her father might have had a point.

A wave of nostalgia washed over her as she approached the back door at Tony's and knocked, then opened it without waiting for a response from inside.

"Anybody in here have a good recipe for meatballs?" she called out.

"Cara mia," Tony said, a smile spreading across his round face when he saw her. "Where have you been? I heard you were coming home, but then nothing. I am insulted that I was not at least the second stop on your list after your parents."

"I know, I know," she said, giving him a kiss on the cheek. "Will you forgive me?"

He studied her. "That depends."

"On?"

"How long you intend to stay. It has been too long, Gina. My customers are grumbling about the same old food, week after week. Not a day goes by that someone doesn't ask when you will be back to liven up the menu."

"What do you tell them?"

"That you are now a famous chef in New York, and that if they want to eat your food, they will have to travel there."

Gina eyed with longing the huge old stove with its simmering pots. "I could fix something for tonight," she offered. "Maybe a spicy penne *arrabiata* or a Greek-style pizza with black olives and feta cheese."

"But you are on vacation," Tony protested. "I cannot ask you to cook."

"You didn't ask. I offered. Besides, I have some

thinking to do, and I always think more clearly as I cook."

He studied her intently. "Problems, *cara mia*? Do you want to talk about them? I may not be able to solve them, but I can listen. Sometimes that is all we need, yes? An objective listener while we sort through things?"

Gina debated telling Tony everything. She knew he would keep it to himself. She also knew he would sympathize with her predicament because he, more than anyone, knew how important her restaurant was to her.

"Are you sure you wouldn't mind?" she asked.

He regarded her with feigned indignation. "How many nights did I listen to you go on and on about this boyfriend or that?"

She grinned ruefully. "More than I care to think about, but this is different."

"How?"

"Because it really matters."

"When you were sixteen, those boys mattered, too."

She thought back to the string of broken hearts she'd suffered. "Okay, you're right. I guess it's all a matter of perspective, isn't it?"

"I will fix us both an espresso and we will talk." He gestured toward the front. "Go in there and sit."

"But you have things to do," she protested. "We can talk here."

"Nothing that can't wait. Now, go. I will be there in a minute."

Gina walked into the dining room with its familiar red-checked tablecloths, the dripping candles stuck in old Chianti bottles, the wide-planked oak floor and the big picture window overlooking Main Street. An inexpertly done mural of Naples had been painted on one wall by Tony's homesick wife, Francesca.

By comparison, Café Tuscany had five-star ambience, but Gina felt perfectly at home here with the rich scents drifting from the kitchen and the sunlight spilling in the window. An astonishing sense of peace crept over her. Right here, right now, she could believe everything would be all right.

Tony joined her at a table in front. She smiled as she accepted the cup of dark espresso and took her first sip. "Still the best," she told him. "I grind and blend my own beans, but it's not the same."

"When I die, I will leave you the secret in my will," he teased. "Now talk to me. What is this big trouble in your life?"

Gina sighed and gazed into Tony's dark-brown eyes. There was so much fatherly concern there. She realized suddenly just how much she had missed this man, missed sitting here and talking about her hopes and dreams until she was certain he must be bored silly, but he had never complained. Some of the time Francesca had been with them, clucking over Gina's disappointments and offering encouragement.

"Did I ever thank you for everything you did for me?" she asked.

"You did, but there was no need. For Francesca and me, you are the daughter we never had."

"How is Francesca? I should have asked."

"Still the most beautiful woman in the world," he said, a gleam in his eyes. "She will be here soon. It will make her very happy to see you again. You can tell her everything you saw in Italy. She still dreams of seeing it again one day."

"Then take her, Tony," she said with a sudden sense of urgency. "Don't let time slip away."

He regarded her worriedly. "You aren't sick, are you?"

"No, no, of course not."

"It's just that you sounded so sad, as if there were things you wanted that you might never have."

She shook her head. "No, just things that mean the world to me that I could lose." She told him the whole story then, leaving out none of the sordid details about Bobby's betrayal of her and their investors.

True to his word, Tony listened and said nothing until she wound down. "Now, to top it off, the attorney who's filed charges against Bobby is right here in Winding River. He thinks I'm as guilty as Bobby or, at the very least, that I know something that will help his case," she concluded.

"But you don't?"

She shook her head. "I was as shocked as anyone. I'm embarrassed to say that the first clue I had of how bad things are came when I read that deposition. That's when I looked at the books."

"Then tell him that, tell this man what you have told me. Hold nothing back. He will believe you." He patted her hand. "If he does not, send him to me. I will tell him that Gina Petrillo does not lie."

If only it were that simple, Gina thought. She glanced outside and spotted Rafe standing on the sidewalk, leaning against the bumper of a very fancy car, staring right back at her.

"Speak of the devil," she muttered, resigned to the fact that the man was going to be true to his word and haunt her everywhere she went, even here in this place that had always been her sanctuary.

Tony followed her gaze. "That is Rafe O'Donnell?"

"In the flesh."

"He looks like a reasonable man."

"He's not," Gina said. "If he were, he would go away and leave me alone. I told him when I would return to New York. He doesn't believe me. He's determined to stick to me like glue until I go back."

Tony stood up. "Then we should invite him in to join us, show him that you have nothing to hide, nothing to fear from him."

"I don't know," Gina protested, but Tony was already opening the door and beckoning Rafe inside.

"Better you should sit here than loiter on the sidewalk outside," Tony told him, ushering him to the table. "I will bring you an espresso, then I must get back to work in the kitchen so things will be ready for lunch."

Rafe sat down opposite Gina, his long legs stretched out in front of him. He looked totally at ease, not one bit like a man on a mission to make her life a living hell. And, to her very deep regret, he was still the sexiest male she'd stumbled across in a very long time. She had really, really hoped she'd been wrong about that.

Rafe glanced around, surveying the restaurant with fascination.

"Is this where you got your start?" he asked.

"I worked at Stella's for a while as a waitress, then came here. Tony taught me to cook."

Rafe gestured toward the mural. "Who's the artist?"

Gina turned to look at the familiar painting, tried to imagine how it must look through Rafe's no-doubt jaded eyes.

"Francesca, Tony's wife, painted it from an old photograph," she explained a bit defensively. "She was born in Naples. She says that painting keeps her from being homesick, so I suggest you not make fun of it."

"Why would I do that?"

"Because it's probably too hokey for a sophisticated man like you," she said.

"Are you sure you're not projecting? I like it."

She studied him to see if he was mocking her, but his expression was serious. "You really like it?" she asked skeptically.

"I said I did, didn't I? I'm not an art snob, Gina." He regarded her pointedly. "Are you?"

She flushed at the accusation. "I always loved it because of what it meant to Francesca, but it's not exactly great art."

"It doesn't need to be. There's a simplicity to it that I find appealing. It gives the restaurant a personal touch, a certain charm." He met her gaze evenly. "Now I imagine your restaurant has Venetian-glass chandeliers, oil paintings you picked up in Florence, dark wood, fresh flowers and green linen tablecloths."

He was closer to the truth than Gina cared to admit. Bobby had believed that to charge the outrageous prices he intended to charge, the atmosphere had to be elegant.

"Have you been to Café Tuscany?" she asked.

"Nope."

"Then you shouldn't be making judgments."

"Which must mean I got it exactly right," he said, grinning.

"You did not."

"Which part was wrong?"

"The tablecloths are dark red," she murmured.

His grin spread. "What was that? I don't think I heard you."

"Oh, get over yourself," she said, this time very clearly. "I have to go."

"I haven't even had my espresso yet," he chided her.

"Then, by all means, stay and enjoy it. I'm sure Tony will be glad to keep you company."

Casting one last wistful look toward the kitchen, Rafe rose to his feet. "Unfortunately, it's not his company I'm after. Where you go, I go, so lead on, Gina."

She scowled at him. "You're serious, aren't you? You're going to tail me like you would some common criminal?"

"Oh, I doubt there's anything common about you," he said, but he didn't deny his intentions. "You could save me some trouble and just invite me along."

"The very last thing I want to do is save you from putting yourself out. If you want to follow me, then I suggest you get into that fancy car of yours and rev the engine, because I don't slow down to wait for anybody."

He regarded her with a resigned expression. "Suit yourself. Do your worst, Gina. I promise I'll keep up. And just in case you have any ideas about exceeding the speed limit to lose me, remember I have my cell phone with me and I'll use it to call the sheriff."

"The sheriff is a friend of mine," she countered.

"Which won't matter when I suggest to him that you skipped out on a court-ordered deposition."

"I did not skip out," she said, her voice rising. "I postponed it. You know that."

"Do I?" he asked innocently. "I imagine by the time

we get it all sorted out, you'll be late for whatever it is you're so anxious to get to."

Gina held on to her temper by a very slender thread. "I am not anxious to get anywhere except away from you," she said, gritting her teeth. "Oh, never mind. My car's down the block. You might as well come with me. I'm going to a rodeo. It might be interesting to see how you take to all that hot air and dust."

"If you want to see me sweat, I can think of far more interesting ways to go about it," Rafe taunted.

Gina felt her skin burn. Wasn't it bad enough that the man was out to torment her over the mess Bobby had created? Now he apparently intended to drive her crazy with sexual innuendoes that stirred her imagination in ways destined to leave her hot and bothered and thoroughly frustrated.

"Don't even go there," she warned him tightly. "You're probably breaking at least a dozen different rules of ethics just by hinting at such a thing."

"At least that many," he agreed, as if it were of no importance. His gaze locked with hers. "But something tells me it might be worth it."

Judging from the way her heart was thundering in her chest, Gina was very much afraid he could be right about that.

3

It had only been twenty-four hours since his arrival, and already Rafe was having a really hard time remembering why he had come to Winding River. For a man known for his razor-sharp mind and powers of concentration, it was a disconcerting experience. He'd certainly never had any trouble in the past when it came to focusing on the best interests of his clients.

Now, however, he couldn't seem to take his eyes off the woman sitting beside him in the stands at the rodeo arena. That was truly saying something, given the level of activity going on in the center of the ring and the cheers sounding all around him. His mind was drifting in all sorts of wicked directions, just as it had the night before.

Okay, he told himself, all that proved was that he was a healthy, virile male who'd been without intimate female companionship for way too long. Whose mind wouldn't wander just a bit around a woman like Gina? Pleased with the assessment of his state of mind as being perfectly normal, he gave himself permission to study her even more intently.

Gina's dark-eyed gaze was fixed on the current bronc rider with total absorption. Her cheeks were bright. Her hair, which was caught up in a red and white bandanna, had surprising auburn highlights in it. At the moment, as some man she apparently knew tried to stay on the back of a particularly wild horse, she appeared to be holding her breath. When time ran out and he was still solidly in the saddle, her cheer almost deafened Rafe. Eyes shining, she faced him.

"Did you see that? He did it. That's the toughest horse in the competition and Randy stayed with him. Amazing."

"Amazing," Rafe echoed, but his comment had nothing to do with the winning rider.

Her gaze narrowed. "Are you even paying attention?"

"Absolutely. Your friend won."

"He's leading, at any rate. There's another round of competition," she said, excitement still shining in her eyes.

It was the most unguarded she had been around Rafe since they'd met. Seeing her like that, filled with enthusiasm, her expression open, laughter glinting in her eyes, made him want things that were impossible. It had probably been safer all the way around when she'd kept him at a cool distance. The temptation to kiss her was almost too much to resist.

"Want something cold to drink?" he asked, needing to put some space between them. Being in a state of semiarousal for the past hour was beginning to get to him.

She feigned exaggerated shock. "You're willing to go off and leave me here all alone for a few minutes?

Are you sure you trust me not to steal the wildest horse in the stables and flee over the Canadian border?"

"Actually, no, but since the horses are otherwise engaged and I have the car keys, I'm not nearly as worried about it as I might be if the circumstances were different." He was still rather proud of the way he'd managed to get those keys away from her and into his own pocket.

"How do you know I don't have a spare set?" she retorted.

He gazed directly into her eyes, a look he'd perfected in the courtroom. It commanded total honesty. "Do you?"

She hesitated, then sighed. "No. And just for the record, I resent like crazy the fact that you manipulated those keys out of my possession."

He grinned. "I didn't wrestle you for them, Gina. You handed them over so I could drive."

"Right, after you gave me some very sincere hogwash about how you'd been just dying to test-drive a car like my mother's."

"You bought it, didn't you?"

"Long enough for you to get behind the wheel," she agreed. "Then I remembered that my mother's car is a very nondescript Chevy with eighty thousand miles on it."

"And what I told you was the absolute truth," Rafe insisted. "I've never driven anything like it."

Gina rolled her eyes. "Yes, *that* I can believe."

He chuckled. "Do you want something to drink or not?"

"A soda," she said finally, fanning herself with the program. "Orange, if they have it."

The action only drew attention to the perspiration beaded on her chest. Rafe's gaze seemed to be riveted to the exposed skin. He swallowed hard and resisted the urge to nab that program and use it to cool off his own overheated flesh.

"Lots of ice," she added. "I'm sweltering out here."

"Want to come with me?" he asked, forgetting all about his intention to give himself a break from her nonstop assault on his senses. "Maybe we can find some shade somewhere and cool off."

She seemed to debate that, then finally nodded. "Let's go."

Rafe let her lead the way to the refreshment stand, ordered large sodas for both of them, then glanced around until he spotted a spreading cottonwood tree with a patch of shade beneath.

"Over there okay?" he asked.

"Perfect," Gina agreed.

Seemingly oblivious to the fact that the ground was more dirt than grass, she sank down, accepted her drink, then sighed. "This is heaven," she murmured. She snagged an ice cube from the drink, held it at the base of her throat and let it slowly melt. The water trickled across her flushed skin, then ran between her breasts.

As he watched her, Rafe's throat went dry as a parched desert. Not even a long, slow swallow of his drink had a cooling effect. He was beginning to regret inviting Gina to leave the stands with him. Hell, he regretted accompanying her to the rodeo in the first place. It was testing him to his limits to keep his hands to himself.

He could have been in a nice, air-conditioned motel

room, a beer in his hand, and all those damning Café Tuscany figures right in front of him. That's where he ought to be, not out here on the verge of sunstroke and filled with more lust than he'd felt in the past twelve months combined, all directed at a woman who was totally untrustworthy, perhaps even more so than his own mother.

"Something wrong?" she inquired.

Her expression was all innocence as she let another ice cube melt, holding it a little lower, a little more provocatively this time. She'd stripped off her blouse when they'd first arrived, giving him a bad moment or two before he'd realized that she was wearing a tank top beneath. Between her deliberately provocative actions with that ice and the perspiration, the already revealing tank top was damp and clinging in a way that left very little to Rafe's overheated imagination.

"Not a thing," he claimed. "Why?"

"You look a little flushed."

"Is that so surprising? It must be ninety-five degrees out here."

"But it's a dry heat," she countered.

"Heat is heat."

Pure mischief lit her eyes. "I could help you cool off," she offered.

Before he could respond or guess what she intended, she upended her drink over his head. Fortunately, it was mostly water and melting ice by now, but the splash of frigid liquid against his burning skin was a shock.

Gina was already up and dancing away by the time he caught his breath. Rafe was on his feet in a heartbeat, fighting indignation and—to his own surprise— laughter.

"You are in such trouble," he said.

"Mighty tough words from a man who's dripping wet," she taunted. "I did you a favor. Try to keep that in mind."

"Oh, I have no intention of forgetting what you did," he said, regarding her with a deceptively lazy look as he halted his pursuit.

He waited until she stopped backing nervously away, gave her time to grow complacent, then moved so quickly she didn't have time to react. He snagged her wrist and hauled her into his arms.

He captured her gasp with his first kiss, then settled in to discover exactly how she tasted, exactly how her lips felt beneath his. There was a lingering sweet taste of orange soda to her mouth, a willing pliancy to her lush lips.

Her body fit against his as if they'd been made for each other. Between the dousing his clothes had taken, the dampness of hers and the skyrocketing heat of that kiss, he was surprised they weren't enveloped in steam.

It took a very long time—too long, by his own rigid standard of ethics—for him to discover everything he'd wanted to know about the taste and texture of her mouth. He released her suddenly and with tremendous reluctance, muttering a curse under his breath.

Wide-eyed and open-mouthed, she stared at him for a full minute and then the heat rose in her cheeks right along with a flash of temper in her eyes.

"You had no right to do that," she snapped.

"No," he said mildly. "You're right. I didn't. I'm sorry. It was a mistake."

His admission and his apology seemed to throw her off stride.

"If you think that's good enough to make me forget what just happened here, you're crazy."

Despite himself, he chuckled at that. "Yes, I imagine it will take a good deal more to make me forget it, too."

"That is not what I meant, and you know it," she said with a scowl.

"Okay, let's take a step back and reassess what just happened," he suggested reasonably.

"Oh, don't use that lawyerly tone with me. We both know what happened. You kissed me."

"You provoked me."

"I dumped water on you. If anything, that should have cooled off your libido, not inflamed it."

He shrugged. "What can I say? I obviously have a perverse streak."

"How about saying 'I'm sorry, it will never happen again,'" she suggested.

"I've already apologized." He met her gaze. "And sadly I *can't* promise it will never happen again."

"You have to," she said, sounding a little desperate.

"Why?"

"Because it's the right thing to do, because you have no business kissing me, because I have no business kissing you." She frowned at him. "You think I'm a criminal, for heaven's sake. Are you beginning to get the picture?"

Unfortunately, Rafe was, though he doubted it was the same picture she was getting. The one in his mind had him carting her straight off to bed to finish what they'd started. Given his belief that she was a thief, he figured that was a really, really lousy idea…and way too tempting at the moment. His very recent lapse in judgment was proof enough he couldn't be trusted within fifty feet of her.

He reached in his pocket, took out her car keys and tossed them to her. She regarded him with surprise.

"How are you getting back to town?" she asked.

"The old-fashioned way," he said, turning his back on her and striding away.

"Rafe, you can't walk all the way back," she protested, chasing after him. "You'll die of heat stroke."

"Thanks for your concern, but I'll be fine."

"You will not be fine. Don't be stubborn. I'll drive you back."

He faced her. "How do I know you won't try to ravish me the second we get to my motel?"

She gave him a wry look. "Oh, I think I can pretty well guarantee that you're safe."

He shrugged. "Okay, then, I trust you."

She regarded him skeptically. "Oh, really?"

"About that, anyway." He tapped a finger against the sunburned tip of her nose. "We'll have to see about the rest. I'll think it over while I'm walking."

"I don't suppose you could keep on going all the way back to New York and ponder the evidence there?" she asked wistfully.

"Not a chance."

Gina heaved a resigned sigh. "Yeah, that's what I figured."

That blistering, mind-boggling kiss was still very much on Gina's mind when she walked into the high school gym that night for the reunion dance. Spotting Rafe sitting all alone at one of the tables along the perimeter of the floor only accentuated the memory. For a man whose arrogance she had experienced firsthand, he looked surprisingly lonely. For a brief second, sympathy almost drove her over to talk to him.

"I'm not going anywhere near him," she muttered, even as she began to drift in his direction. When she realized where she was going, she added wryly, "I obviously have the willpower of a nymphomaniac."

"Who's a nymphomaniac?" Lauren demanded, startling Gina.

"Nobody, I hope," Gina retorted glumly, stopping in her tracks. She wasn't entirely sure whether she was relieved by the distraction, which was yet another fact that was worrisome. Was it moths that couldn't resist a flame and wound up dead because of it?

Lauren followed the direction of her gaze, then grinned. "Ah, yes, I heard about the kiss."

"Heard about it?" Gina asked, horrified. "How? From whom?"

"Half the town was at the rodeo. Word gets around. My source says it was more entertaining than anything that went on inside the arena."

Gina groaned. "Why did I do it? Why did I let him kiss me? And right out in public, yet! Wouldn't you think I'd learned my lesson about getting mixed up with smooth talkers after what happened a few years ago in Rome?"

"Could you have stopped him?"

"Not at first," she admitted. "He caught me by surprise, but later…"

Lauren's eyes sparkled with growing amusement. "Later? Then it did go on and on, just the way I heard?"

"Okay, yes, it went on a very long time. It was a very good kiss. In fact, it was a terrific kiss, which is why I am in more trouble than I ever thought it was possible to get into. I want to kiss a man who—" She cut herself off before she could finish the revealing thought.

"Who what?" Lauren asked, clearly fascinated by Gina's slip.

"Never mind," Gina said dismissively. "Have you seen Cassie? Did she come tonight?"

"She's here. She's busy hiding out from Cole. Seems to me she has her own problems with steering clear of intoxicating kisses," Lauren said. "And before you ask, Karen's on the dance floor, and Emma's out in the hallway on her cell phone. There's some kind of emergency back in Denver. Hopefully she's telling her boss or her client or whoever it is to take a hike. The woman is in serious need of a break. She's stretched so tight I'm afraid she's going to snap."

"Emma can take care of herself," Gina insisted. "She's always been totally levelheaded and sane compared to the rest of us."

"Take another look. I was out at the ranch with her and Caitlyn earlier. I think even that little girl senses that her mother's at the breaking point. Caitlyn's birthday is coming up, and she told me the only thing she wanted was for her mom to move here because in Denver she never, ever sees her. How pitiful is that?"

Gina glanced toward the door and spotted Emma striding toward them, her expression grim.

"What's wrong?" Gina asked, regarding her with concern.

"One of my major clients in Denver has a problem. He wants me back there tonight."

"Are you going?" Lauren asked.

"What choice do I have?"

"You could tell him that you're taking the first break you've had in years and that he can just wait until Monday," Lauren retorted heatedly. "Sweetie, if you don't start looking out for yourself, who will? Certainly not those partners who are raking in big bucks from all those billable hours you put in each month, and certainly not the clients who see nothing wrong in tracking you down when you're supposed to be on vacation. How did he get your cell phone number, anyway?"

"All my clients have my cell phone number," Emma said defensively.

Lauren removed the offending item from Emma's grasp. "Which is a really good reason for shutting it off and letting me hang on to it for the rest of the weekend. If you'd like, I can call this client of yours back and tell him that you've consulted your schedule and you are tied up in a very important negotiation and can't see him until the middle of next week. If it's a real emergency, he can speak to one of the other partners."

Emma stared at her in amazement. "You sound so convincing."

Gina chuckled. "She *is* an actress, Emma."

Emma shook her head. "Of course, she is. I just can't quite think of Lauren as anything other than the girl who used to spend the night at my house talking about boys until dawn."

"I had to talk about them. I certainly never dated them," Lauren said.

"Because you scared them to death. You were the smartest person in our class," Gina said. "That was very daunting, even to the boys with a B average."

"A fat lot of good that's doing me these days," Lauren grumbled. "Most of the people I deal with now don't even realize I have a brain."

"Which must mean that they underestimate you," Emma guessed. "Surely you can use that to your advantage."

"Maybe you two can trade services," Gina suggested. "Lauren can fend off your pushy, inconsiderate clients, and Emma, you can negotiate Lauren's deals. Nobody ever mistakes you for a pushover."

"Not a bad idea," Lauren said thoughtfully. "But we still haven't resolved this current situation. Shall I make the call?"

Emma hesitated. "Let me think about it."

Gina thought of what Lauren had said earlier about Emma's little girl. "Emma, think about Caitlyn. She's having the time of her life with her cousins and her grandparents. Do you want to spoil that by running home early?"

Emma blinked at the reminder, proof that she too seldom considered her daughter's feelings when work was involved. Then she drew herself up. "You're absolutely right. Lauren, make that call. Tell Mr. Henley that he can contact one of the senior partners if he doesn't want to wait for me to get back."

Lauren beamed at her. "Punch in that number," she said, relinquishing the cell phone temporarily to Emma.

As soon as the call had gone through, she stepped away from Emma and Gina, speaking quietly but firmly to the offensive Mr. Henley. After she'd hung up, she came back smiling.

"He'll wait. By the way, what was that big emergency, or can't you say?"

Emma grinned. "I can't say, but I can assure you that it wasn't life or death. Nor were any of his millions at risk." She reached for her cell phone, but Lauren shook her head.

"I think I'll hang on to this, at least for the rest of the night," she told Emma.

"But Caitlyn—"

"If Caitlyn calls, I know where to find you. Otherwise, your new secretary can handle anything that comes up."

Gina chuckled. "You're enjoying this, aren't you, Lauren?"

"It's actually rather nice to do something so ordinary. Maybe I should chuck it all and become somebody's secretary. I have terrific organizational skills."

Both Emma and Gina stared at her.

"Have you lost it?" Gina asked.

"Okay, maybe not a secretary," Lauren said. "Organizational skills aside, I'm a little too bossy to take orders well."

"An understatement if ever I heard one," Gina said.

Lauren sighed. "You know who I really envy? Karen. She has it all. A husband who adores her and a ranch."

"Where she works too hard," Gina pointed out.

"I guess nothing's perfect, is it?" Lauren said. She glanced behind Gina. "For example, you have this absolutely gorgeous man staring at you as if you were more tempting than a banana split, and for reasons you refuse to explain, you're avoiding the guy."

All three of them turned to stare at Rafe, who was sipping on his drink, his gaze fixed on Gina.

"He's not interested in me," she protested. "Not the way you mean, anyway."

"That kiss I heard about says otherwise," Lauren said. "In fact, that kiss speaks volumes."

Emma's eyes widened. "Kiss, what kiss? That man kissed you? Did you want him to?"

"No," Gina said. "Yes."

A slow grin replaced the indignation on Emma's face. "Not sure, are you?"

"Of course I'm sure. That kiss was totally inappropriate."

"We can sue him for sexual harassment," Emma suggested, looking a little too eager.

"Settle down," Gina advised. "Nobody is suing anybody, and you are not taking on any cases in the middle of a dance, not after Lauren worked so hard to make sure you had the night off."

"I suppose not," Emma said, clearly disappointed. "But let me know if you change your mind."

"Do you look at everything in life in terms of the legalities?" Lauren asked her.

"Pretty much," Emma acknowledged.

"That has to stop," Lauren said emphatically, then glanced at Gina. "And you and I have to see to it. Find this woman someone to dance with. Are there any eligible males in the room? Other than Gina's guy, of course."

"Rafe O'Donnell is not my guy," Gina reminded her. "I'd be glad to turn him over to Emma."

"Whatever." Lauren surveyed the gym carefully. Finally her expression brightened triumphantly. "There," she said. "He'll do very nicely." She snagged Emma's hand. "Come on. Do you know him?"

"No," Emma said, hanging back.

"Then I'll introduce you," Lauren said.

"Do you know him?" Emma asked.

"No, but that's a technicality. Don't be a spoilsport. It's one dance, not the rest of your life."

Emma cast a totally uncharacteristically helpless glance over her shoulder as Lauren dragged her away.

"I see your friend is matchmaking again," Rafe said, coming up beside Gina and startling her so badly she almost dropped her drink. "Think she'll have better luck with those two?"

"Don't do that," she said irritably.

"What?"

"Sneak up on me." She avoided his gaze, pretending that his nearness wasn't stirring up all sorts of wicked memories of the kiss they'd shared earlier. She deliberately watched the drama unfolding as Lauren introduced Emma to the stranger, then left them to their own devices. After an awkward moment the man must have asked her to dance, because Emma allowed him to lead her to the middle of the gym. Neither of them looked especially happy about being there, but Lauren stood by beaming her approval.

Apparently satisfied, Lauren came back to where Gina and Rafe were standing. Gina noticed she deliberately inserted herself protectively between them. Rafe noted her action with amusement.

"Still protecting your friend, I see," he said.

"Of course."

"Trust me, she can defend herself. Did you hear how she doused me with ice earlier today, then made me hike all the way back into town?"

Gina regarded him with indignation. "I did not! You decided to walk back. I tried to stop you."

Lauren looked from one to the other, lips twitching. "But the part about the ice was true? Did that happen before or after the kiss?"

Rafe didn't seem the least bit surprised or embarrassed by the fact that Lauren knew about that. "Before."

"Interesting. I would have thought after." She grinned. "You know, an attempt to cool you off, so to speak."

"It would have taken more than a cup of ice to do that," Rafe said.

Lauren waved her hand as if it held a fan. "Oh, my."

Gina scowled at both of them. "If you two are enjoying yourselves so much, why don't I just leave? There are a lot of people here I haven't spoken to yet."

Before she could take a step, Rafe grabbed her hand. "Not now. I was hoping for another dance lesson."

She frowned at him. "The band's not playing country-western tonight. It's playing oldies. Surely you can slow-dance. Lauren, you dance with him."

"Afraid not," Rafe insisted with a perfectly straight face. "No offense, Lauren, but Gina's a little more patient with my stumbling attempts. Dancing is one of those social graces I never had time to learn. Too much studying. It made me a very dull kid."

"Then I'm amazed so many women invite you to society balls," Lauren chimed in, drawing a startled look from both Gina and Rafe.

"How do you know that?" Gina demanded.

Lauren grinned. "The Internet is an amazing thing. You'd be surprised what you can find out. I only scanned a few editions of the New York papers, and guess whose name popped up over and over in the society columns?"

Rafe regarded her with admiration. "I underestimated you, after all, Lauren."

"Many people do," Gina said. "Lauren, I think maybe you and I need to have a little talk."

"Tomorrow will be soon enough. There's a handsome man who's eager to dance with you. My hunch is he knows his right foot from his left, despite what he says."

She winked at Rafe, then added for Gina's benefit, "Just keep your guard up, sweetie. From what I've read about him, you don't want to cross him."

Unfortunately, Gina was already well aware of that.

4

Since the whole purpose of coming to Winding River had been to clear her head and decide what to do to save her restaurant, Gina awoke at what she considered to be the unholy hour of 7:00 a.m. on Sunday morning determined to get on with that assignment. The only way she was able to drag herself out of bed was by reminding herself that it was nine in the morning in New York.

With Rafe turning up almost everywhere she went, the only way she was going to have any time to herself was to sneak out of her own house and take a drive into the nearby Snowy Range, where distractions were few and far between. And she had to do it before he turned up to accompany her or trail along behind like some sort of watchdog.

A glance outside told her it was the perfect day for going for a drive and then maybe even a hike. The sky was a crystal-clear blue with floating puffs of white clouds. The temperature had dropped overnight and promised to stay lower throughout the day. And there were no reunion events until the picnic at midday.

But before she could make her escape, she bumped straight into her parents, lingering over Sunday breakfast in the kitchen. They regarded her with surprise, no doubt because they so rarely saw her before noon.

"What on earth are you doing up so early, darling?" her mother asked. "You had a late night. It was after midnight when I heard you come in. How was the dance?"

Gina thought of the time she'd spent in Rafe's arms. For a man who'd professed to have no skill on the dance floor at all, he'd been astonishingly adept at everything from the waltz to the twist. Apparently it was only the Texas two-step that eluded him, despite his pitiful claim that he'd had no time for dances as a younger man. When she'd called him on it, he'd simply shrugged and insisted he was only following her lead.

As if, she thought dryly. She doubted he'd ever let anyone get a head start on him, much less lead him anywhere. She sighed at that. It was something she needed to keep in mind.

"The dance was fine," she said.

"Meet anyone interesting?" her mother asked, her expression just a little too innocent.

"What have you heard?" Gina asked, regarding her with resignation.

Her father frowned. "Yes, Jane, what have you heard? I'd like to know, too."

"Oh, for goodness sakes, it's nothing shocking," her mother said with a hint of exasperation. "Rose Ellen just happened to mention that Gina was with an incredibly handsome man at the rodeo yesterday afternoon."

George Petrillo seemed no more convinced by that innocuous explanation than Gina was.

"And?" he prodded.

"The man kissed me," Gina blurted, hoping to save them all the embarrassment of a long, drawn-out debate. "It was nothing."

Her mother grinned. "That's not the way I heard it. Rose Ellen said it made her toes curl."

"Jane Petrillo, I hope you weren't discussing your daughter's lack of discretion with half the town," her father said, his expression dismayed. As the owner of the local insurance company, he tended to worry first about what his customers might think. Gina had done enough outrageous, risky things with the Calamity Janes in high school to turn his hair gray. He always swore he'd taken out extra accident and liability insurance on the family just because of her dangerous shenanigans.

"No, of course not," Jane said, giving him a soothing pat on the hand. "Just Rose Ellen. She brought it up. I must say I found it fascinating." She turned to Gina. "I had no idea you'd brought a fellow home for the reunion. Why haven't we met him?"

"I didn't bring him. He's not here for the reunion. And you haven't met him because I sincerely wish that *I'd* never met him," Gina said, reaching for the car keys, even though the drive no longer held much appeal. "I'm going out."

"Where?"

"I don't know, but I won't be long."

She walked out before they could pester her with more questions. As she paused on the back steps to take a deep, calming breath, she heard her mother ask, "What do you suppose is going on?"

"I have no idea," her father said grumpily. "But I'm sure half the town will know about it before we do.

That's what comes from letting her go off and spend all that time in Europe. She's come home with a lot of wild ideas."

"Oh, she has not," her mother said, then added wistfully, "I just hope there is something more to this. Wouldn't it be nice to see her married? I can't wait till we have a houseful of grandchildren to spoil."

Gina's groan was almost as heartfelt as her father's. The speculation about her and Rafe O'Donnell was getting entirely out of hand and he'd only been in town a couple of days. Right now all he was doing was shadowing her—okay, and kissing her in public. Just wait till people around here found out what he was really after.

Rafe drove by the Petrillo house about 7:45 a.m. There was no sign of Gina, though from what he'd gathered, she was not exactly a morning person. Still, he found the fact that her mother's car was missing this early on a Sunday vaguely worrisome. Had Gina taken off in it? Would her mother conspire to help her daughter skip town? Leave the country? Maybe that remark Gina had made the day before about fleeing to Canada had been no joke.

Because he hated the way his imagination was running wild, he concluded the best way to get to the truth would be to knock on the door and ask to see her. For all he knew, the entire family might be at church, though most had services that began later.

When a woman he assumed to be Mrs. Petrillo answered the door, he understood where Gina got her beauty. Her mother was probably in her late forties, maybe even her early fifties, but she looked a decade younger. There wasn't a single strand of gray in her thick, dark hair. There was hardly a wrinkle on her heart-shaped face. But while her daughter's eyes were dark, Mrs. Petrillo's were a vibrant green, and they were studying him with undisguised curiosity.

"May I help you?" she asked, when Rafe remained speechless.

He gathered his composure. "Actually, I'm looking for your daughter, Mrs. Petrillo. Is she here?"

"Ah," she said, her expression brightening. "You must be the mysterious man everyone is talking about."

"I'm Rafe O'Donnell," he said, taken aback by the friendly welcome. Obviously, the people talking were those who'd witnessed the kiss, and not Gina herself. He doubted she had painted him in a favorable light.

"My husband and I are just having a second cup of coffee, Mr. O'Donnell. Will you join us? Gina left a little while ago, but she shouldn't be gone long."

Never one to turn down caffeine or the chance to pump someone for information about Gina, he smiled. "I'd love a cup."

In the cheerful, yellow kitchen with its warm oak cupboards and white trim, she introduced Rafe to her husband and invited him to make himself at home.

"Were your ears burning?" she asked. "We were talking about you not fifteen minutes ago."

"Is that so?" he asked warily. "What did Gina have to say?"

"Not much, which is why I'm so glad you dropped by. You're not local, are you? How do you know our daughter?"

Now there was a minefield, Rafe thought. "Actually, I'm from New York."

"So, you and Gina met there?" George Petrillo asked, regarding Rafe with suspicion.

"Not exactly."

The vague response clearly stirred more suspicion on her father's part. "We don't get a lot of New Yorkers around here. How did you happen to choose Winding River for a vacation?"

"Actually I'm working."

George's gaze narrowed. "You're not some fool movie producer, are you? They come crawling around here all the time these days, paying outrageous amounts for property. If it keeps up, the next thing we know we won't be able to afford to live in our own hometown."

Rafe chuckled. "No. I haven't even been to a movie in the last two years, and I am definitely not buying any property."

"Then what do you do?" her father asked, just as Gina's mother stepped in.

"George, you're pestering the man. Let him drink his coffee in peace."

"I'm just trying to get acquainted with a man who's got half the town talking about the way he kissed my daughter," George grumbled.

So they *had* heard, Rafe thought. That explained the interrogation. "I apologize for that," he said with absolute sincerity. It had been one of the biggest mistakes of his life, though he could hardly deny enjoying it.

"There's no need to apologize to us," Jane assured him, shooting a warning look at her husband. "Is there, George?"

"Not unless Gina objected," he said, scowling at Rafe. "Did she?"

Just then the back door opened and Gina stepped

inside. "You!" she said when she saw him. "I thought that was your rental car out front. What are you doing here?"

"Looking for you, of course."

"And grilling my parents while you're at it? What a lowdown, sneaky trick," she accused. "Did you wait until you saw me leave before knocking on the door?"

"No, I did not. And actually, I've barely gotten a word in," he said, regarding her with amusement.

"That's true, dear," her mother verified. "Your father has been doing most of the talking. I'm surprised your friend hasn't told him to mind his own business."

Gina directed a frown at Rafe, then her father, then Rafe again. "I'd like to see you outside, please."

He grinned. "Sure thing. Mr. and Mrs. Petrillo, it's been a pleasure. Thanks for the coffee."

"I do hope you'll come back and visit with us," Jane said. "Perhaps you could come for dinner before you go back to New York."

"Sorry, Mom, he won't be around that long," Gina said. "Will you, Rafe?"

He gave her a penetrating look. "My schedule is actually pretty flexible. Last I heard I'll be in town for at least two weeks."

Her mother beamed. "Then I'm sure we'll be able to work something out. You must be staying at the hotel. I'll be in touch."

"I'll look forward to it," he said, then followed Gina outside. Since she couldn't seem to stop pacing up and down, he leaned against the porch railing and waited to see what she had to say.

Finally she stopped in front of him. "I do not want you here."

"So I gathered."

"My parents don't know anything about my business. They don't know anything about Bobby. Leave them alone."

"I was not pumping them for information. In fact, I thought I was doing a darned fine job of evading all of your father's questions about how we knew each other and what I do for a living."

"You didn't tell them you were a lawyer?"

"No."

"You didn't tell them you'd followed me out here?"

"No."

"You never mentioned Bobby?"

"Nope."

That seemed to silence her. Rafe couldn't help himself. He reached out and cupped her chin, forcing her to meet his gaze. "I'm just after the truth, Gina. Nothing else. If you have nothing to hide, talk to me, tell me the truth."

"You wouldn't know the truth if it bit you in the butt."

"You have a very low opinion of my ability to judge character, don't you?"

"Can you blame me? You've come after me as if I'm some hardened criminal, when I'm as much of a victim as any of the people you say that Bobby swindled. The man has all but destroyed my business. He has turned my life upside down. And because of him, an annoyingly persistent attorney won't leave me alone."

Rafe grimaced at the characterization. He'd always considered persistence to be a virtue, but he could see her point. Moreover, he was forced to admit that he was beginning to believe in at least the possibility of her innocence, but he was a long way from having any evidence for or against her. She might not see that as much of a shift in his opinion, but in truth it was a major concession. He usually trusted his initial gut reaction in any given situation, and he rarely let go of preconceived notions this easily.

"You could go a long way toward making your case, if you would just sit down and get this deposition over with," he pointed out.

"Not without my attorney present."

"Of course not, but isn't your friend Emma an attorney?"

"Yes, but her practice is not in Wyoming, and besides, she's here this weekend because she's overworked and badly needs a break. I'm not going to get her involved in this," she said flatly. "Hell, I'm here because I need a break, but I haven't had five seconds to think with you trailing around after me. I started to take a drive, but I stopped for coffee instead. I glanced outside and spotted you heading in this direction. I had this horrible feeling this was exactly where you were going. Lo and behold, here you are, sneaking around behind my back to cross-examine my parents."

"I was not cross-examining your parents," he repeated patiently. "I stopped by looking for you. Your mother invited me in. Your father did most of the talking. That's it."

She gave him a plaintive look. "Couldn't you go away?" she asked in what had become a familiar, wistful refrain. "Go home? I'll be there in a couple of weeks and answer every single question you have."

"Much as I would like to get out of the wilds of Wyoming and back to civilization, I can't take a chance that you'll disappear. You're my best link to Rinaldi."

"I haven't heard from him. In fact, if he's smart, I will never hear from him, because if I ever get five minutes alone with him, I will wring his scrawny neck."

She said it with such heartfelt conviction that Rafe's faith in her shot up another notch. That still didn't mean he could go running back to New York the way she wanted. Unfortunately, he was here for the duration.

And gazing into her sad, vulnerable eyes was making that more and more difficult with every passing day.

"I'll tell you what," he said finally. "I'll make you a deal."

She regarded him with suspicion. "What sort of a deal?"

"What's on the reunion agenda for the day?"

"A picnic in the park."

"Is that the last event?"

"No, most of us will be here for the Fourth of July fireworks later in the week."

He regarded her solemnly. "Do you swear that you will not skip town on me?"

She sighed. "I'm not going anywhere. How many times do I have to tell you that? You can turn your back on me. In fact, it might be nice if you just forgot all about me."

Rafe grinned at her wistful tone. "I can't do that, but I will back off. I have some paperwork to do."

"Hallelujah!" she said, though her tone was less than enthusiastic.

"I'm not saying I won't cruise by the park—"

"I should have known it was too good to be true," she murmured.

"That could be just because I'm longing for a glimpse of you," Rafe suggested.

"Oh, of course," she said sarcastically. "Why didn't I think of that?"

He was surprised by her skepticism. "You don't think that could be true?"

"You are not hanging around here because you're attracted to me. You're here because you want to nail me with a crime."

"Maybe that's how it started," Rafe said quietly, regretting the admission almost before the words were out of his mouth.

She gave him a startled look. "What are you saying?"

"I've already said it. Never mind. The point is I will try to give you a little space. Just don't make me regret it. I have a lot of resources and I will use them to find you, so save yourself the trouble."

He'd taken half a dozen steps, almost made it to safety, when she called out to him. He turned back.

"What?" he asked, noting the confusion in her eyes.

"Are you saying that kiss yesterday…" Her gaze locked on his. "Did it mean something?"

Rafe couldn't help the smile tugging at his lips. Her words were too close to an invitation, way too close to a dare, or maybe he'd just been searching a little too desperately for any excuse at all to do it again.

"I don't know," he said nonchalantly. He walked slowly back to her. "Only one way to find out."

Alarm flared in her eyes just as he bent down and lightly touched his mouth to hers. He could have stopped with that. He should have. But her soft little moan, the way she swayed toward him, they were too much. The next thing he knew she was in his arms and he was devouring her mouth.

The morning had been unseasonably cool up until then, but now the temperature shot up until it felt hotter than it had under the blazing sun on his walk back into town the day before. His heart pounded and his body turned hard, even as hers went pliant, molding to his in a way that left him shaken and her trembling.

His breathing was ragged when he finally pulled away. "I guess we have our answer," he murmured, his voice husky.

She stared back at him with dazed eyes. "Answer?"

"That kiss definitely meant something."

"What did it mean?"

He took a step back before he replied. "Trouble," he said quietly. "It was definitely trouble."

Trouble? Gina echoed to herself after Rafe had wisely walked away. It wasn't just trouble. It was a disaster. If he'd asked, she would have followed him straight to the nearest bed without giving it a second thought. She would have slept with a man who wanted to put her in jail.

Okay, maybe he was beginning to cut her a little slack, but he definitely didn't trust her, not the way a man ought to trust a woman he was making love to. Of course, that kiss had been all about lust, not love. Gina supposed a man—or a woman—could have spectacular sex with somebody without worrying too much about such niceties as trust. Personally, she'd never tried it. She'd had one serious relationship in Italy, but since coming back to the United States, she'd barely had time to date, much less get involved with a man deeply enough to think about letting him into her bed. And her relationship with Carlo had taught her all about the dangers of dating a suspicious man. His lack of trust, his constant accusations that she was deceiving him had destroyed them.

Now, in just a few short days, Rafe had stirred her hormones to such a fever pitch that she was willing to toss aside everything she valued for a quick romp with yet another man who didn't believe in her.

"I saw what Rose Ellen meant," Gina's mother said quietly, slipping up beside Gina and putting an arm around her waist.

"You saw?"

"Oh, yes. So did your father."

"I'm surprised he didn't go for his shotgun."

"I think he might have, if you'd shown even the tiniest hint of displeasure."

Gina regarded her mother with a wry look. "Well, that certainly didn't happen, did it?"

Her mother chuckled. "No, which begs the question, what is your relationship with Rafe O'Donnell?"

"I wish I knew," Gina said plaintively. "It's…it's confusing."

"Do you want to talk about it?"

She shook her head. "Not yet, Mom, but I'll tell you everything when I get it sorted out. I promise."

"If you want your father to run him off, he will, you know."

Gina grinned. "I know, and believe me, the thought holds a certain appeal." She uttered a sigh of resignation. "But Rafe would just come back again."

"Your father was a persistent man, too," Jane said, looking nostalgic.

"Did you ever try to shake him?"

"For a while," she said, then grinned. "But my heart was never in it. Is your heart really in getting rid of Rafe once and for all?"

"Apparently not," Gina said. In fact, she was beginning to look forward to having him pop up when she least expected it. As for those devastating kisses, she was pretty sure she was becoming addicted.

5

Rafe had expected to be back in New York by Monday. Unfortunately, Gina showed every sign of sticking to her guns and staying in Winding River for a full two weeks. He'd hoped that his pestering would eventually wear her down, but she was clearly stubborn. Maybe that trait was also the reason she hadn't given in to the inevitable and shuttered Café Tuscany already.

He had been true to his word on Sunday. He'd steered clear of her, though he hadn't been able to resist taking a stroll through the park where the reunion attendees were gathered for their picnic. Gina had been playing baseball at the time, looking more carefree than she had since arriving in Wyoming. He regretted being the one responsible for putting a perpetual frown on her face, the worry lines between her eyes, but he had a job to do, whether he liked it or not.

Since it looked like he was stuck here, he had no choice but to call his office and have his appointments shifted to other partners or postponed until his return.

Even as he dialed, he was dreading the third degree he was likely to get from his meddlesome secretary.

"Have you made contact yet?" Lydia asked in an undertone, as if he were on some sort of secret mission.

"Yes, I have 'made contact,'" Rafe said impatiently. "How are things on that end? Any word from the investigator on Rinaldi's whereabouts?"

"Nothing. Charlie Flynn says the man has vanished. He's probably basking in the sun on a beach in the Cayman Islands by now."

"Entirely possible," Rafe agreed. "What's the deal on the restaurant? Have you been by there?"

"It was operating at full capacity last night. I checked it myself. Gina's assistant has everything running smoothly. The veal piccata was as superb as ever."

"Did I pay for your dinner?"

"No, but now that you mention it, that's a very good idea. After all, it seems I was spying for you."

"If that's what you were doing, you must not be very good at it. You're not giving me anything I can use, Lydia."

"Because there's nothing to pass along. All I can say is that it's a shame that jerk's actions might bankrupt the place."

"Is the word out about Bobby skipping town?"

"It wasn't in any of the society columns, and Deidre, that's Gina's assistant, acted as if everything were perfectly normal. If there was any buzz about their problems, I certainly didn't hear it." She hesitated, then said, "You know, if you just stopped bugging her, I think Gina could keep the place open and pay back all the money Bobby stole. Not that she should have to, if you ask me, but I suppose somebody is obligated to make good on the investors' losses. Why not at least give her a chance?"

"If she's guilty of conspiring with her partner—"

"She's not," Lydia retorted, cutting him off. "I wish you'd just use that supposedly stellar gut instinct of yours where she's concerned. Have you spent a single minute with her? If you had, you'd know she's no thief."

Maybe not, Rafe thought, but he refused to give his know-it-all secretary the satisfaction of admitting that just yet. Then there was the very intriguing question of how Gina was keeping the place afloat on her own. Assuming she wasn't involved in the scam—which he still considered to be a sizable leap—she had to be hurting financially.

Then again, Lauren Winters probably had very deep pockets. Even though Gina had insisted she wasn't going to burden her friends with her problems, maybe she had lied. Maybe Lauren was quietly bailing her friend out of her financial difficulties. Rafe wondered if he owed the actress a warning about what a risky venture she'd be getting into. Unfortunately, based on past experience, he had a hunch she wouldn't take the news well and that she'd manage to turn him into the bad guy.

"Lydia, cancel my appointments for the next two weeks. If that changes, I'll let you know."

"You're staying?" she asked, sounding more pleased than shocked. "Why?"

"Because Gina is staying."

"How are you and Gina getting along?"

"Let's just say nobody's likely to nominate us for couple of the year." He tried to keep the regret out of his voice when he said it.

Apparently he'd succeeded, because Lydia sighed heavily. "Then you're an even bigger fool than I thought you were," she said. "Romantically speaking, of course."

"Of course," he said wryly. "Sorry to disappoint you."

"You've been doing it for seven years. I should be used to it," she said with weary resignation. "But I keep holding out hope that one of these days you'll come to your senses, find a woman who can put up with you and settle down."

She paused, then added, "Now would be a good time, Rafe. You're not getting any younger, and you could do a whole lot worse than Gina Petrillo."

"So you've mentioned—more than once, as a matter of fact."

"It bears repeating," she said. "Bye, boss."

"Goodbye, Lydia. Hopefully they'll appreciate your humor in the unemployment line."

"Your threats don't bother me."

"I know. I know. All those bodies," he said and hung up. If only he could find a few of the skeletons in *her* closet. A woman as cheeky as Lydia was bound to have dozens of them.

If he was going to stay in Winding River, Rafe couldn't keep wearing the same clothes, especially since the only dry cleaner in town seemed to have a quirky disregard for customer service. Whoever owned the business apparently opened when he felt like it. If he had regular hours, they weren't posted, and Rafe had yet to see the lights on in the business.

The only clothing store in town offered Western wear. Rafe resigned himself to a new wardrobe of jeans he'd rarely have the opportunity to wear once he got back to New York. His closet was filled with practical

suits and three tuxedos for all of the charity events he
was duty-bound to attend because his partners' wives
served on the boards and the fund-raising committees.

He left the hotel, walked down Main Street and
was about to go into the clothing store when he spotted Emma Rogers accompanied by a little girl, who
looked as if she might be about six. Emma frowned
when she saw him.

"Still here, Mr. O'Donnell?" Emma asked, her tone
not especially friendly. "I thought you'd be long gone
by now."

"I'm afraid my business is taking longer than I'd
hoped."

Her gaze narrowed. "What exactly is your business?"

Before he could respond, Gina came darting out of
the café across the street and pointedly got between
them. Ignoring the two adults, she hunkered down to
give the little girl a hug.

"Caitlyn Rogers, you are getting so big I hardly recognized you. How old are you now? Ten?"

The child giggled. "No, Aunt Gina, I'm only six."

"I can't believe it." She leaned closer. "I think Stella
has your pancakes on the griddle. Do you want to run
on over there so you can get them while they're hot?"

Caitlyn looked up at her mother. "Is it okay?"

Emma regarded Gina with amusement, then turned
her attention to her daughter. "Go," she said. When the
little girl would have darted straight across the street,
Emma reached out and caught her. "Hey, what do we
do before crossing the street, even here in Winding
River?"

Caitlyn regarded her guiltily. "Look both ways," she said, then dutifully did just that.

"Okay then, *now* you can go."

All three of them watched the child's progress, then Gina beamed at Emma. "We should join her."

"In a minute," Emma said. "Rafe was just about to explain why he's still in town."

Gina gave him a sharp look. "Was he really?"

He grinned. "Emma was certainly hopeful that I might. In all honesty, I was heading for the store to buy some clothes."

"You don't look like a man who wears a lot of jeans," Emma said. "In fact, if I had to hazard a guess, I'd say you usually wear thousand-dollar suits. I recognize the type. I go up against them in court every day. In fact, again if I were guessing, I'd say you're either a lawyer or a stockbroker, Mr. O'Donnell. Which is it? Or are my instincts totally wrong?"

Rafe looked to Gina for some sense of what she expected him to do under the circumstances. She sighed.

"Oh, for heaven's sakes, he's a lawyer," she said with no attempt to hide her exasperation. "Now that we know you have razor-sharp instincts, Emma, can we please go get some breakfast? I'm starved."

"Not until we clear up one more thing," Emma said, her gaze locked with Rafe's. "Why are you hassling Gina?"

"Maybe I'm just a suitor who won't take no for an answer," he said, enjoying the flash of indignation in Gina's eyes. Apparently she liked that explanation even less than the truth.

Emma's gaze turned to Gina. "Is he?"

"He's the most annoying man I know," Gina said

with heartfelt sincerity. "And that is all I intend to say on the subject." She latched on to Emma's arm. "Let's go."

This time her friend allowed herself to be led away, but not before pointedly meeting Rafe's gaze. "I'm keeping an eye on you," she warned.

Emma and half the rest of the people in Winding River, Rafe thought with resignation. Would a thief inspire that kind of protectiveness and loyalty? He needed to ask more questions about Gina, but doing so would stir up a real hornet's nest. She might never forgive him for unfairly dragging her friends and family into this, and for reasons he didn't care to examine too closely, that bothered him way more than it should.

"So, I was telling Mommy that I think we should live here forever and ever," Caitlyn told Gina, her eyes shining. "Grandpa has already gotten me my own horse."

"Grandpa ought to know better," Emma grumbled under her breath, then smiled at her daughter. "Darling, we live in Denver. You'd miss all your friends if we moved here."

"No, I wouldn't," Caitlyn insisted. "I already have a lot of friends here." Her expression brightened. "And I have cousins here. I don't have any cousins in Denver."

"She's got you there," Gina said, grinning.

"Oh, stay out of it," Emma snapped. "I don't see you moving back to Winding River."

"You never know," Gina said. Of course, if Rafe was successful in his attempts to make her part of Bobby's scam, she might be in jail instead, but it was seeming more and more likely that she was going to have to leave New York once this mess was straightened out. Customers could be fickle. If Café Tuscany's reputation was tarnished, they would stay away in droves. Any chance she might have of paying off the old debts would vanish.

She sighed, then realized that Emma was staring at her with a shocked expression. "What?" she asked.

"You aren't seriously considering coming back here to live, are you?" Emma asked. "I thought you had your dream job in your dream city."

"I do, but things could change."

"Does this have something to do with Rafe?"

Gina nodded. "Let it alone, though, Emma. You have enough on your plate without me dumping my worries on you."

"Hey, we're friends. Friends can always share their troubles with each other."

"Then why don't you tell me why you're wound tighter than a string on Pete Sampras's tennis racket?"

"Too much work, too little time," Emma said succinctly.

"Mommy is never, ever home," Caitlyn said. "She works really, really hard."

Emma winced at the matter-of-fact assessment by her six-year-old. "It's going to get better, baby. I promise."

Gina studied her worriedly. "When? I know you're thinking about taking on a big case here with Sue Ellen. How much time will you have if you're commuting between here and Denver?"

"I'll manage," Emma said tightly.

"And Caitlyn?" Gina persisted gently. "Will she manage, too?"

"Look, I'm doing the best I can, Gina, okay?" Emma

stood up. "I have to get over to the jail. Will you take Caitlyn back to my mom's?"

"Of course," Gina said at once. She winked at the little girl. "But only if she'll go to the toy store with me first. What do you think, Caitlyn? Want to help me pick out some toys?"

Caitlyn bounced up and down on the vinyl seat of the booth excitedly. "Who're you buying toys for, Aunt Gina? Do you have kids at home?"

"Nope." She grinned. "I guess if we find something really, really special, I'll have to give it to you."

Caitlyn's eyes widened. "Really?"

Emma shook her head, looking amused. "You're going to spoil her."

"That's what an honorary aunt is supposed to do, right, Caitlyn?"

"Uh-huh," the little girl said solemnly.

"Okay then, have fun, you two." Emma kissed Caitlyn on the forehead. "See you later, sweet pea."

"Bye, Mommy," Caitlyn replied distractedly. "Aunt Gina, I was thinking. There's this really, really neat Barbie I've been wanting. Do you think maybe the toy store has it?"

"If it doesn't, we'll go find ourselves a computer and look for it online."

Caitlyn bounded out of her seat. "I'm ready. Are you?"

Gina drank her last sip of coffee, then joined the eager child. Truthfully, she was almost as enthusiastic as Caitlyn. Henderson Toys had been one of her favorite places as a child. She would save up her allowance for a whole month, then go into the store with her mother and walk up and down the crowded aisles studying the dolls and the trains and the board games before making her selection.

Sometimes, between the cost of an item and indecision, it was several months before she made a purchase. One memorable year, she bought a miniature stove, in which she could actually bake cookies, albeit very tiny ones. Her excitement over that purchase should probably have been a clue about the direction her life was likely to take.

Back on the street, they ran into Rafe standing outside of Henderson's, his gaze locked on an elaborate train display in the window. The expression on his face was surprisingly wistful for a man whose every boyhood whim had probably been fulfilled.

Caitlyn slipped up beside him, her gaze every bit as fascinated as his. "It's a really cool train, isn't it?"

Surprised, he glanced down at her, then grinned. "It sure is. Do you like trains?"

Caitlyn nodded. "But I like dolls better. Aunt Gina is going to buy me a Barbie if they have the one I want."

Rafe's gaze shifted until it met Gina's reflected in the window. "Is that so?"

"It's not an expensive toy," Gina said defensively.

He frowned at her. "Did I suggest it was?"

"No. Never mind. Come on, Caitlyn. Let's see if they have the doll you want."

The little girl gazed up at Rafe. "You can come, too, if you want," she said politely. "I'll bet they have lots more trains inside."

"Maybe I will take a look," Rafe said, ignoring the frown Gina directed at him.

Inside, Nell Henderson rushed out from behind the counter to give Gina a hug. "And this is your fam-

ily," she enthused. "How lovely that you've brought
them in."

"Actually, this is Emma's daughter, Caitlyn. You
remember Emma, don't you?"

"Well, of course. The two of you were in here often
enough, right along with Cassie, Lauren and Karen."
She beamed at Rafe. "They were some of my best customers, at least until they discovered boys. Then I lost
them to the cosmetics counter over at the drugstore."

"I can't imagine why," Rafe said. "They're all beautiful enough without makeup."

Nell chuckled. "Oh, honey, you have found yourself a jewel."

"Rafe and I are not married," Gina said irritably.
"We're not involved. We're not anything."

That threw the older woman for little more than a
heartbeat. "Well then, you should work on changing
that. A gallant man is a rarity these days. You should
hang on to him if you're lucky enough to find one."

"Something to keep in mind," Rafe said, regarding
her with amusement.

Bored with the adult conversation, Caitlyn wandered
over to the dolls. She was back in seconds, clutching a
Barbie in a fancy ball gown.

"This is the one I've been wanting and wanting,"
she announced to Gina.

Gina hunkered down beside her. "She is beautiful,"
she agreed. "You're sure this is what you want?"

Caitlyn's head bobbed, then she cast a shy look at
Rafe. "What do you think? Isn't she beautiful?"

But Rafe's gaze was locked on Gina, not the doll,
when he murmured, "Yes, she certainly is."

Gina's cheeks burned. "I thought you wanted to look at the trains," she grumbled.

"I'll come with you," Caitlyn offered, tucking her hand into Rafe's. "I've been here before. I can show you where they are."

Gina watched the two of them disappear at the end of the aisle, then sighed. When she looked up, Nell Henderson was grinning.

"Can't say that I blame you for sighing over that one. If I were thirty years younger, I'd give you a run for your money."

"There is nothing between Rafe and me," Gina repeated very firmly.

Nell shook her head. "Then that's a real pity, especially since the man looks at you as if you were the most fascinating creature he's ever come across. I haven't seen a look like that since the night my Herbie, God rest his soul, swept me off my feet."

Gina recalled belatedly that Herb Henderson had died just over a year ago. "You must miss him," she said sympathetically.

"Every day of my life," Nell agreed. "But I have my memories. That's something you ought to think about. Grab as many memories as you can, Gina. They're what carry you through during the difficult times. Otherwise, all you'll have are regrets. You don't want the last two words you whisper on your deathbed to be *if only*."

Gina heard Caitlyn's giggle, then Rafe's lower rumble of laughter. They were sweet sounds. She was already regretting that she had no claim to Rafe or to any family of her own, for that matter. Lately, she'd had no time to think about any future outside of Café

Tuscany. With the restaurant's fate so much in doubt, she was forced to face the fact that without it her life would be unbearably empty.

She gave Nell's hand a squeeze, then went after Caitlyn and Rafe. She found them both watching an intricate labyrinth of miniature train tracks as half a dozen tiny engines sped around them on what appeared certain to be a collision course. But of course it wasn't. At the last second Rafe touched the controls and switched the tracks, sending the various trains safely past each other.

"Do you collect trains?" Gina asked him.

He shook his head and shut down those on the display. "Never had one."

"Why not? It's obvious you want one."

"As a kid, there were better uses for our money. Now I don't have the time to fiddle with a hobby."

"You know what they say about all work and no play, don't you?"

He regarded her seriously. "That it gets the job done?"

She groaned. "No, that it makes for a very dull guy."

A dangerous glint appeared in his eyes. "You think I'm boring?"

She knew exactly how he intended to prove otherwise, and a part of her wanted him to demonstrate, but there was Caitlyn to consider, and Nell. "Not boring, just limited. Under other circumstances, I might be tempted to try to change that."

"Oh? How?"

"Let me think about it," she said. "Maybe one of these days I'll give you a list of my recommendations. Will you pay any attention to them?"

"I might," he said solemnly. "What would my reward be?"

"More fun," she said at once.

He grinned. "You'll have to provide more incentive than that."

"Such as?"

"Will I get the girl?"

Gina shuddered at the penetrating look in his eyes. "I suppose that depends."

"On?"

"How badly you want her."

"I'm beginning to wonder about that myself."

He said it in a way that made Gina's breath hitch in her throat. She was thankful Caitlyn chose that moment to reach for her hand and give it a tug.

"Aunt Gina, since you're buying me a toy, why don't you buy one for Mr. O'Donnell, too?"

"His toys are too expensive," Gina said.

"That's right," Rafe agreed, his gaze locked with hers. "In fact, something tells me they're priceless."

6

There had been times in her life—even after enduring Carlo's possessiveness—when Gina had deeply regretted the lack of a man who'd be there when she woke up and when she went to bed at night, a man who cared more about spending time with her than about his career. Now it seemed she had one.

It wasn't nearly as much fun as she'd anticipated.

Rafe O'Donnell was everywhere she turned, his expression remote, his gaze cool. The nonstop surveillance wasn't exactly what she'd dreamed of. In fact, it was all too reminiscent of Carlo. The fact that Rafe was so blatant about it grated on her nerves. She hated that everyone in town knew he was there to keep an eye on her for some reason that neither of them had revealed.

Other than her one conversation with Tony, Gina had refused to discuss Rafe's presence with her friends or her family. Only Lauren knew part of it—that she had to give a deposition when she got back to New York and that she wasn't looking forward to it. Cassie, Karen and Emma were studying her almost as intently as Rafe was, but their motive was concern, his was distrust.

He'd been at it for nearly two weeks now, though he'd stayed true to his word and remained mostly in the background ever since that chance meeting at Henderson's Toy Store over a week earlier. For some perverse reason Gina found that even more annoying and nerve-racking than having to deal with him. She was constantly on edge, continually reminded of the times they'd kissed and just how much she wanted him to kiss her again. For a few minutes in his arms she'd been able to forget why he was here. In fact, she'd forgotten almost everything, including her name.

His unexpected admission that he, too, had been affected by those kisses, had thrown her. Not that it made any real difference. He might be attracted to her, but he wasn't happy about it. In fact, Rafe didn't strike her as the kind of man who would violate his own ethical standards on a regular basis. Kissing a suspect, no matter how unjustly accused, was bound to be a breach of those ethics. No wonder he was keeping his distance.

Right now, for example, he was sitting in the booth next to hers at the diner, sipping coffee and pretending to read the morning paper. She knew it was only pretense, because his gaze rarely shifted away from her long enough for more than a glimpse of the headlines. She sighed heavily.

"You might as well come over here and join me," she said finally. Maybe they could discuss this like two reasonable people and find a way to peacefully coexist, since it was evident that nothing was going to make him go away.

He stared at her, clearly surprised by the invitation. "You sure about that?"

"Lately I don't seem to be sure about much of anything, but you're getting on my nerves over there, so, what the heck?"

A grin came and went so quickly she thought she'd imagined it. It was probably a good thing he didn't smile too often. She had a hunch the effect could be devastating, even more devastating than the rare hint of vulnerability she'd seen on his face as he and Caitlyn had played with the toy trains. Wondering what that was about had kept her awake for several nights, despite repeated lectures to herself that Rafe's past was none of her concern.

Carrying the paper and his cup of coffee, Rafe slid into the booth opposite her. Gina tried to pretend he was someone who'd come into her restaurant for a good meal, someone deserving of friendly conversation. She'd certainly been forced to be polite to a lot of arrogant, exasperating people over the years. What was one more?

"Still enjoying your visit to Winding River?" she asked politely, as if he were just another tourist instead of a man with an agenda.

"It's been interesting," he said.

"Finding much to do?"

He regarded her with amusement. "You know the answer to that, since I've pretty much been doing whatever you're doing. Are *you* bored?"

"I'm never bored when I'm home, especially with so many of my friends around."

"If you're so fond of this place, why did you leave?"

"I wanted to be a chef, a really good one. Tony ran out of recipes." It was a simplistic answer, but true enough.

"So you left here and went to New York?"

"Not right away. I trained all over at a series of culinary institutes here and in Europe," she said.

"Must have been expensive."

She had a hunch his interest in the cost had less to do with curiosity than with his desire to build a case that she'd needed Café Tuscany money to pay off old debts. She leaned forward and met his gaze evenly.

"I was very good. I received several scholarships," she told him.

"Is that how you met Rinaldi, at one of those cooking schools?"

"Yes," she said. "But before we go too far along that particular path, let's agree here and now to save all those nasty deposition questions for New York."

"It might not leave us much to talk about," he said, that grin sneaking back.

"Consider it a challenge. You look like the kind of man who thrives on challenges."

"I do," he agreed. "Okay then, you pick a nice, neutral topic. What shall we talk about?"

"Let's talk about you," she suggested. "Why did you decide to become a lawyer?"

"To protect the little guy from swindlers and crooks," he said readily.

Gina laughed. "Didn't take long to get back to your low opinion of me, did it?"

"That's your interpretation," he said. "Guilty conscience?"

"Not me." She regarded him intently. "Tell me something. Why did you take this case? Usually your firm is involved in much more lucrative, high-profile cases. You don't actually work for the little guys. You work for corporate America. Yet here you are up to your neck in a case that involves peanuts. Even if you recover every missing dollar that Bobby allegedly stole, your cut won't amount to much by your firm's standards. And just think of all the billable hours you're missing while you hang around out here keeping me under surveillance."

He shrugged. "I was due for a vacation, anyway."

"But you wouldn't have chosen to take it here, would you?"

"No," he admitted. "Probably not."

"So why did you take a case that was going to cost so much for such little reward?"

"It was personal," he said, his expression turning grim.

"Oh? In what way?"

"My mother was among those Rinaldi swindled out of their money." There was a dangerous glint in his eyes. "I imagine you can see why I'd want him caught."

Gina was taken aback by the admission. She hadn't thought about Rafe having a mother—or any other family, for that matter—let alone a mother who'd backed Café Tuscany. "How much did she give Bobby?"

"I doubt she viewed it as a gift. She *invested* a hundred thousand."

She stared at him, openmouthed with shock. "What? Where did she get that kind of cash? Forgive me if I'm wrong, but I got the impression the other day that your family didn't have a lot of money. Or were you just trying to play on my sympathy at the toy store?"

"We didn't. Not when I was a kid. My dad worked two jobs to keep food on the table. It was a constant source of friction between him and my mother. She was used to having the finer things in life, but she made the mistake of falling for a guy working construction on one of my grandfather's skyscrapers. Needless to say, my grandparents disapproved. They cut her off without a dime."

He regarded Gina with a bleak expression. "At first I don't think it really mattered to her. They were doing okay and they were wildly in love. Then I came along, and the finances got a little tighter. When my sister was born, every dollar was stretched to the limit. My grandfather saw to it that my dad was never hired on the best-paying jobs."

Gina was appalled. "What a mean-spirited thing to do."

"You won't get any argument from me about that. It was the worst kind of abuse of power. Eventually it took its toll on the marriage, probably just as my grandfather intended. The fights got louder and nastier. My mother found richer companions. Ultimately my father tired of being humiliated and divorced her. He's living somewhere in the Pacific Northwest. We're not in touch, though I did get a copy of the newspaper announcement when he remarried a few years ago."

"I'm sorry," Gina said quietly. "His leaving must have made things even more difficult."

"It could have, but my mother is a survivor. She remarried a little more quickly, within months of the divorce, this time to someone my grandparents approved of. The money began to flow again, so my sister has had an easier time of it, despite the fact that the marriage only lasted a year. There was a hefty settlement."

His expression turned wry. "Then came another marriage, another divorce, another settlement. Financially my mother has done well for herself, but she's never found the kind of love she had with my father. While she's looking for it, she gets mixed up with guys like Rinaldi."

Gina was surprised by the depth of compassion she felt for him. His motives in going after Bobby and her made a lot more sense now. It also explained why he was distrustful, not just of her, but of all women. "So this is your chance to get even with all the people who've taken advantage of her?"

"Something like that."

She met his gaze with an unflinching look. "I had nothing to do with any of this. Unless she's been a customer, I don't even know your mother."

"You wouldn't have to in order to benefit from Rinaldi's con," he pointed out. "But I imagine you do know her. In fact, I suspect she's been a frequent diner at Café Tuscany, usually on Rinaldi's arm."

Gina shook her head. "Bobby never brought his women to the restaurant. They would've distracted him from cooking. Whatever else can be said about Bobby—and at the moment, there's quite a lot I could say—he was a total professional in the kitchen. Nobody except employees was allowed back there, not even his investors. He gave them a private tour a few days before our official opening, but told them it was off-limits from that moment on."

There was no mistaking the disbelief in Rafe's expression. "Are you sure he wasn't inviting guests in for a little after-hours hanky-panky?"

"If you mean his women, no. We had an agreement."

Rafe grinned at that. "Yeah, he had one with my mother, too. It wasn't worth the paper it was written on."

"But—"

He held up his hand. "Don't even try to defend him, Gina. The man is a con artist."

"And you think I am, as well," she concluded.

"The jury's still out on that, but at the very least you demonstrated lousy judgment in choosing your business partner. Whose idea was it for the two of you to go into business together, anyway? Yours or Rinaldi's?"

"I'm not going to answer that," she said. "Frankly, you should know better than to ask."

"We're just chatting," he said blandly. "Getting acquainted."

"We're already acquainted. I think getting to know each other any better would be a risky business."

"You could be right about that," he agreed with apparent regret.

Before they could continue, several of Gina's friends showed up. Radiating indignation, they stood beside the table glaring at Rafe. They might not understand what was going on between Gina and him, but obviously they were prepared to leap to her defense.

"What is *he* doing here?" Emma demanded. "Is he harassing you again?"

"No. He was here all alone. Since I was killing time waiting for you guys, I took pity on him and invited him to join me," Gina admitted.

"Why?" Emma said. She gave Gina an apologetic look. "I bugged Lauren till she told me about the deposition. Sorry. He's not trying to question you without counsel present, is he?"

Rafe chuckled. "I wouldn't dream of it."

Emma drew herself up. "I should hope not. I'd have you disbarred."

Gina grinned. "As you know, Emma is an attorney."

"Yours?" Rafe asked. "Did you change your mind and hire her?"

"No," Gina said.

"But I will be if she needs me, and if she needs a New York attorney, I can arrange that, too," Emma responded, gaze narrowed. "Does she need legal representation?"

"Not if she's innocent."

"Innocent of what?" Emma asked.

"Never mind. I am," Gina said.

"Back up a minute," Lauren said. "I thought she was just some sort of witness you were trying to question. Why is there any doubt about Gina's innocence? Gina has never done anything illegal in her entire life."

"Not even when Cassie begged her to," Karen said in an obvious attempt to lighten the tense mood. "She was always the voice of calm and reason." She grinned. "Not that the rest of us ever paid any attention to her."

Gina held up a hand to prevent a recitation of the pranks the Calamity Janes had been involved with years ago. A few of them might have skirted the fringes of the law. A clever attorney—which Rafe most definitely was—might be able to use them to suggest a pattern of behavior likely to culminate in this massive swindle.

"Let's not go there," she pleaded. "Could we change the subject?"

"In a minute," Emma promised. "First, I'd like to remind Mr. O'Donnell that sometimes the innocent need better representation than the guilty, especially if some shark is out to get them." She regarded Rafe pointedly. "Watch your step, Mr. O'Donnell."

Her gaze shifted to Gina. "Stay away from him," she advised.

"I wish I could," Gina told her.

"I'm crushed," he said.

"Something tells me a freight train couldn't crush *your* ego," she retorted.

"Making judgments about me again?"

She shrugged. "I guess that makes us even, doesn't it?"

He laughed and slid from the booth. "See you around, Gina."

"I'm sure," she said with a heartfelt sigh.

Somehow, though, in the last few minutes she had discovered that Rafe was far more complex and intriguing than she'd originally guessed. That made the prospect of bumping into him everywhere she turned a lot less daunting. She figured that was a very bad sign, given that the man wanted to lock her away.

Rafe assumed Gina wouldn't be going anywhere for a while. He had a feeling these friendly gabfests went on and on once the five women got together. Just in case he was wrong, he walked down the block, leaned against the bumper of his rental car and placed a call on his cell phone to the paralegal who was doing follow-up on the case back in New York.

"Have you been able to get into the bank records of Café Tuscany or Rinaldi or Petrillo yet?" he asked Joan Lansing.

"The judge is looking over the paperwork now," Joan told him. "We should know something before the end of the day."

"I need those records. We need to see if any withdrawals and deposits match up."

"I know, boss. I think we made a good case to the

judge, though, if you ask me, that money is in some off-shore account by now, not in a personal checking account at the corner bank."

Rafe sighed. "You're probably right, but we need to know for certain."

"Anything else I can do on this end?"

"Stay on that investigator. He should have found something on Rinaldi's whereabouts by now."

"Will do. No clues from Ms. Petrillo?"

"None. I'm actually beginning to believe she might not know anything, not about the con and not about Rinaldi's disappearance."

"How is that possible? They were partners."

"We already know the man was a smooth operator. She could have been taken in by him, too."

"Uh-oh, boss. I think I hear that knight on a white horse charging to the rescue."

"Could be," he conceded. "But please don't tell Lydia. She'll never let me hear the end of it."

He glanced up just in time to see Gina and the other women emerging from Stella's. They piled into Lauren's fancy sports utility vehicle. Rafe got behind the wheel of his own rental car and started after them. His pulse began to pound when he realized they were heading straight for the small airstrip on the outskirts of town.

Sure enough, Lauren turned in, drove to a hangar operated by a charter company and parked. Blood boiling, Rafe stalked across the tarmac to intercept them.

"Going somewhere?" he asked Gina.

"You followed us?" she countered, her expression indignant.

"Of course I did. It's a good thing, too. Are you planning on skipping town?"

"Oh, for heaven's sakes," Emma snapped. "There is nothing to prevent her from going anywhere, Mr. O'Donnell. Back off."

"I can't do that."

"Then you'll have to charter your own plane, because you're not getting on board with us," Lauren snapped.

Rafe ignored them both and kept his gaze on Gina. "Why the sudden decision to run?"

"I'm not running anywhere."

"Then why didn't you mention this trip when we were talking?"

"It didn't come up. Besides, Lauren was still working out the details. I didn't know if we were going."

"Going where?" he asked.

She frowned at him, but she answered with barely concealed impatience. "I am going to Denver with my friends because Cassie's mother is having surgery. We want to be there to support her. It's not a big deal. We'll be back in a day or so, as soon as we know that everything's okay."

Rafe caught the unmistakable worry in her eyes, the hint of urgency in her voice. Because of his career, because of his mother's short-term attention span with men, he was a cynical man. There weren't a lot of people he trusted. Something told him he could trust Gina, at least about this.

Finally he nodded and stepped out of her path. "Don't make me regret this," he warned.

"I won't," she promised. Her lips curved into the beginnings of a smile. "Careful, Rafe. Someone might get the idea that you have a heart."

"They'd be wrong," he said tightly, then watched

her go. As she was about to take the final step into the plane, he called to her. She looked back. "I hope everything goes okay with Cassie's mother."

She acknowledged his words with a wave, then disappeared inside the plane. Rafe walked slowly back into the hangar, then crossed to the office.

Inside, he found a middle-aged woman chatting on the phone. She glanced up, murmured something to whoever was on the other end of the line, then smiled at Rafe.

"What can I do for you?"

"That charter you've got going out, did the pilot file a flight plan?"

"He sure did. Plus, when Lauren called, she told me where they're going."

"Which is?"

Her gaze narrowed. "Are you with the media?"

"No."

"Because I'm not doing or saying anything that's going to get that woman's picture splashed all over one of those supermarket tabloids. When she's around here, she's among friends. What she does and where she goes is nobody's business."

"Believe it or not, I don't give two hoots about where Lauren Winters goes, but I do care about her friend Gina. I need to know where that plane is headed."

Her eyes widened at his fierce tone. "Is Gina in some kind of trouble?"

"That depends on where that flight is going."

"Denver," she told him finally. "They're going to Denver to be there for Cassie while her mom has her surgery."

Relief flooded through Rafe. Gina hadn't lied to him. "Good," he murmured. "That's great."

The woman regarded him with a puzzled expression. "You think it's great that Cassie's mother is having surgery?"

"No, of course not." Any explanation he tried to give would be way too complicated and unnecessary. "Never mind. Thanks for the information."

"Sure thing."

Rafe felt lighter somehow as he drove back into town. For once in his life his trust hadn't been misplaced.

Of course, it remained to be seen if Gina actually showed up back in Winding River when this mission of mercy ended. Something told him that until she came back again, he was going to be doing a lot of pacing and worrying.

7

Rafe was not used to having time on his hands. He didn't like being idle. Worse, he realized that he actually missed Gina, and not just because he couldn't ask a few more sneaky questions in an attempt to learn something new about Rinaldi and the missing money. He also found it worrisome that her planned two-week trip was now creeping on into its third week with no sign of Gina in Winding River.

"Still in town?" a gruff voice inquired just before Gina's father slid into the booth opposite him at Stella's. "I thought you'd be long gone by now, especially with Gina out of town for the last few days."

"Unfortunately, I haven't finished my business here," Rafe said. "Can I buy you a cup of coffee?"

"Don't mind if you do," George Petrillo replied, signaling to Stella. "You never did say what your business here is, did you?"

"No."

George's gaze narrowed. "Is there some deep, dark secret to it?"

"No, it's just a confidential matter. I can't discuss it."

"Okay, then, let me think. What kind of professions take their secrets so seriously? You don't strike me as a psychiatrist. And given the way you were kissing my daughter, I doubt you're a priest. How am I doing so far?"

"Right on target," Rafe conceded, impressed with the man's deductive reasoning, if not the suspicion behind it.

"Then I'd say that leaves the law. Are you an attorney, Mr. O'Donnell? And if you are, what business could you possibly have that concerns my daughter?"

"I never said—"

"Let's get serious," George said, leaning forward. "Your being here is no accident. You're not a tourist. Your bumping into Gina way out here, when it just so happens that the two of you live in New York, is no coincidence. The way I figure it, you're either stalking her or she's in trouble. Which is it?"

Rafe admired the man's blunt assessment. He had a feeling that under other circumstances, they could get along very well. "I think you should discuss this with Gina, not me."

"The only person I'm going to be discussing anything with is the sheriff, if I don't get a straight answer in the next ten seconds."

Rafe nodded, accepting the fatherly concern and the determination he saw on George Petrillo's face. "Okay, then. I'll tell you as much as I can. I came out here because of your daughter. I'm handling a case involving her business partner. I thought Gina might have some information."

"Does she?"

"She says she doesn't."

"Then go home, Mr. O'Donnell. If Gina says she doesn't know anything, then she doesn't know anything."

"I wish I could do that, Mr. Petrillo, but I can't. Your daughter is my best link to Roberto Rinaldi. Sooner or later they're bound to be in contact."

"And when they are, I'm sure she'll let you know," her father said. "Gina's an honest, law-abiding citizen. That's the way we raised her."

"As reassuring as it is to hear you say that, it's not good enough."

George frowned. "You're not suggesting that my daughter is mixed up in whatever this Rinaldi fellow did, are you?" There was a sudden flash of alarm in his eyes. "Did he kill somebody? Gina's not in any danger, is she?"

"No, it's nothing like that, I assure you."

"Then what are you suggesting that my daughter's mixed up in?"

"I'm not suggesting anything. I'm just saying that I can't leave here until I know more than I know now."

George Petrillo sighed. "If this is all about some legal difficulty my daughter and her partner might or might not be in, what the hell was that kiss at the house all about? Was that just some sneaky tactic to try to get her to talk?"

Rafe felt his cheeks burn. He should have known better. Not only had his behavior been unprofessional, but both of those kisses they'd shared had been in plain view of Gina's neighbors or her family. The very least he could have done was to exercise more discretion.

"Actually, that was a mistake."

"Which time? At the rodeo or at the house?"

"Both times, to be perfectly honest."

"Then I suggest you keep your hands to yourself from now on. I don't want to hear any more about any so-called mistakes. This isn't New York City, where two people can get away with anything. Around here there are reputations to be considered. Eventually you'll go on your way, but Gina has to live in this community."

"I thought Gina lived in New York."

"This is her home. New York is where she works," her father said, making the same distinction Gina herself had once made. "Keep that in mind."

"I'll do my best," Rafe promised.

George bobbed his head, clearly satisfied that he'd put Rafe on notice. "See that you do," he said as he jammed his hat on his head and strolled away, pausing for a minute to share a joke with Stella before heading for the door.

After he'd gone, Rafe muttered a sharp expletive. Why was it that every time he was around Gina, her friends or her family, *they* wound up asking all the questions? He hadn't been on the defensive so much since he'd discovered in the middle of a trial that his client had been lying to him about almost everything except his name. And he didn't like the feeling any better now than he had then.

Nor was he crazy about the fact that he hadn't even discovered why Gina's trip had already lasted several days longer than originally anticipated. Just when the query had been on the tip of his tongue, George Petrillo had cleverly distracted him with his own barrage of questions.

The fragile trust Rafe had begun to feel for Gina

was already wavering. He'd give her one more day. If she didn't turn up tomorrow, he was going after her. And heaven help her if she wasn't where she had told him she would be—at Mrs. Collins's bedside in Denver.

For some reason Gina wasn't the least bit surprised to find Rafe sitting in a parked car just down the street from her house when she finally got back home several days after she'd intended to. She hadn't been on such an emotional roller coaster in years. A confrontation with him fit right in.

She watched him strolling toward her, a sinking sensation in the pit of her stomach. *One word,* she thought. Let him say just one wrong word and she would belt him. After what she and her friends had been through, she was just itching to take her anger out on somebody.

Rafe bent down to peer in the car window. "You okay?"

"No."

He seemed taken aback by her response. "What's wrong?" he asked eventually.

"Everything."

"Are you planning on sitting in there all evening?"

She scowled at him. "I might."

Rafe shrugged and walked around to the other side of the car, then got in. He sat there, staring straight ahead, seemingly perfectly comfortable with the silence.

"Caleb died," she finally murmured, barely able to get the words out. "Karen's husband. He just collapsed and died. It happened while we were in Denver. By the time we got to the hospital in Laramie, he was dead.

I've been staying with Karen at her ranch for the last few days." She glanced at him. "In case you were wondering where I'd run off to."

"Never crossed my mind," he said.

She almost managed a smile at that. "Liar."

"I'm sorry about Caleb," he said.

Gina regarded him with faint surprise. "You really mean that, don't you?"

"I do. I didn't meet him at the reunion, but I saw you and the others with him. It was obvious how close you were. It must have been a terrible shock."

"It was. I don't know how Karen's going to manage without him." Gina hoped she would never experience the kind of loss that Karen was going through. Karen was heartbroken and racked with guilt because she hadn't been there. Nothing anyone had said had been able to console her.

"She could lose their ranch," Gina whispered. "That will kill her. It meant everything to Caleb, but I don't know if Karen can keep it running on her own. I would hate to lose Café Tuscany, but it's not the same. I love it, but it's just a business. Even I can see that. That ranch meant everything to Karen and Caleb. And there's this man, Grady Blackhawk, who's just waiting in the wings to take it from her."

She shuddered at the thought. "How can something like this happen?" she asked bitterly. "Caleb didn't deserve to die. Karen certainly doesn't deserve this."

Gina glanced at Rafe to see how he was reacting to her tirade. Not until he reached over and brushed away the tears on her cheeks did she realize that she'd been crying.

"I'm sorry I'm so emotional," she apologized. "I

didn't mean to dump all of this on you. I just can't bear the way Karen looks, so lost and alone. She's one of my best friends. How can I even think about going back to New York in a few days and leaving her here to cope?"

"The others—" Rafe began.

"Will be leaving, too," Gina said. "Except for Cassie. She's staying because of her mom. At least that's the excuse. I think there's more to it. Her son's father is here and they have a whole lot of unfinished business between them. Lauren says she can stay a little longer. And Emma may be coming back and forth for a while."

"See, Karen will have people to look after her."

"I need to be here," Gina said firmly. As much as she loved Café Tuscany and her life in New York, nothing was as important as this, as being here when her friend needed her. "I have to call Deidre. Maybe she can go on managing things a little longer."

Looking resigned, Rafe handed her his cell phone. "Call."

Gina accepted the phone, but before she could dial, she remembered the deposition. "Rafe, I'm not deliberately trying to avoid the deposition."

"I know," he said with something akin to admiration in his eyes. "You're a remarkable woman, Gina Petrillo."

Startled, she stared at him. "Remarkable? Me?"

He grinned. "Yes, you. With everything that's at stake for you back in New York, your first priority is your friend's well-being. That's an admirable quality. It makes me wonder how you ever got mixed up with a sleaze like Rinaldi."

"Just lucky, I guess," she said wryly.

"Make your call."

"I could…" She hesitated, then took a deep breath. "I could talk to Emma. Perhaps we could do the deposition here. I know you can't hang around out here forever."

"We'll worry about that later. Take care of your business. After that I want you to go inside, take a shower and then I'm taking you out to dinner."

"I don't know," she protested, though without much vehemence. "I'm beat. I'll be lousy company."

"You don't have to entertain me, Gina. But you do need to eat a decent meal and get some color back in your cheeks. How can I possibly go after you in a deposition, if you look as if you might faint at any second?"

"Oh, I think I can handle you any day of the week," she retorted, feeling better already at the prospect of a good battle of wits. She handed back the cell phone. "I'll call from inside. I don't need you listening in on my trade secrets. Give me twenty minutes."

Rafe grinned. "Should I call Tony's and make a reservation?"

"Winding River's not New York. Besides, Tony always has room for me."

Rafe regarded her with suspicion. "Not in the kitchen, I hope."

"No, I imagine he'll let us sit in the dining room just this once."

He nodded. "Twenty minutes, then. I'll be waiting in my car."

"You could come inside or sit on the porch," she offered.

"No, thanks. I think it's probably best if I give your father a wide berth."

"Really? Sounds as if there's a story there."

"I'll tell you during dinner."

Gina ran inside, gave her parents a quick report on Karen, then made the call to New York. Deidre was surprisingly reassuring.

"We've been packed as usual. The guys in the kitchen are managing. Ronnie's been amazing. You'd think he'd been running the kitchen all along," she said with evident pride. "You and Bobby trained them well. The food's as great as ever. If you need to stay out there, we'll be okay. You do whatever you need to do."

Gina thought of the stack of unpaid bills she'd left behind. "Deidre, there could be problems with some of our suppliers," she said reluctantly.

"I know," the other woman said. "I saw the bills. Don't worry. You left me with a stack of signed checks. I've written a few to pay some of the suppliers who were starting to get testy, and I've spoken to the other vendors. We'll be okay, at least for a little while."

Deidre hesitated, then added, "Look, I don't know exactly what's going on, but I can tell there's a problem. If there's anything I can do, all you have to do is ask. You gave me this job when I really needed one—I owe you. I don't have any cash to lend you, but I've gotten real good at juggling creditors. I'll keep the hounds at bay for as long as I can."

"Have I ever told you how terrific you are?" Gina asked.

"At least once a day. Now let me get back to work. I've got a line of customers waiting to be seated."

"Then by all means go. Thanks, Deidre. You're a godsend."

Feeling vastly relieved by the news from New York,

she took a quick shower, pulled on a pair of jeans and her boots and added a sleeveless gingham shirt.

"Where are you going?" her father called as she passed the living room.

"Out to dinner."

"All alone?" her mother asked.

"No, Rafe's waiting."

Her father's expression darkened. "I thought I made myself clear to that man."

Gina regarded him with alarm. "Daddy, what did you say to Rafe?"

"Just that he needs to remember that this is a small town and I will not allow him to ruin your reputation."

"How terribly gallant of you, but the warning is unnecessary. Rafe and I are just…" She couldn't seem to think of a suitable word.

Friends certainly didn't describe it. And they were more than acquaintances. Given the sizzle in the air each time they met, *prospective lovers* seemed apt, but she could hardly admit that to her father. Or even to herself, under the circumstances. She was pretty sure it was unwise, at the very least, to contemplate getting into bed with a man who was about to grill her. Surely she had learned that lesson after a few months with the suspicious Carlo.

Eventually she just sighed. "You don't need to worry, that's all."

"I'll be the judge of that," her father grumbled. "Be home by midnight."

"George," her mother protested. "Gina's a grown woman."

"Maybe so, but there's not a lot to do after midnight in Winding River except get in trouble, if you catch my drift. Why do you think we have all those shotgun weddings right after graduation every year?"

Gina planted a kiss on his cheek. "I'm a long way out of high school, but I promise that Rafe and I won't go down to the river and engage in any hanky-panky after dinner."

But, of course, now that the idea had been planted in her head, that was exactly what she most wanted to do. From the moment she had watched her best friend's husband being buried, she had desperately wanted to do something—*anything*—that would remind her that she was still very much alive.

Rafe promised himself he was going to be on his best behavior over dinner. No probing questions. No sneak attacks on Gina's credibility. And most important of all, no crossing the line—which meant no kisses, no lingering caresses, no steamy looks.

Obviously, he'd lied to himself. So far he'd managed to keep the questions, at least about Rinaldi, to a minimum, but he couldn't seem to keep his hands to himself. There were a million and one excuses for touching Gina. After all, he had to help her out of the car, didn't he? And it was only polite to slip his arm around her waist when they crossed the street, right? And that stray curl that skimmed her cheek needed to be tucked behind her ear, didn't it? Could he help it if his fingers brushed hers when he handed her the menu or lingered when her hand trembled ever so slightly? She'd had a rough few days. He was only offering comfort.

And pigs flew, he thought in self-disgust.

"Rafe, is there some problem?" Gina asked, studying him worriedly.

"Nope," he said flatly, then turned his gaze to the selections on the menu. He'd expected little more than pizza and spaghetti and was surprised to find far more intriguing offerings.

"Your friend Tony has quite a menu," he noted.

"He's added a few things since I worked here." She grinned. "I send him a new recipe for Christmas every year."

"Only once a year?"

"The locals can't accept too much change all at once. You'll notice that plain old spaghetti and meatballs is still on the menu. There would be a revolt if he took it off, but once in a while he can talk his customers into trying something new."

"What do you recommend?"

"The penne *arrabiata*," she said without hesitation. "The tomato sauce has a little kick to it. I gave that one to him when I was in here the other day."

Rafe chuckled. "Yes, I can see why something spicy would appeal to you." He put the menu aside. "What about wine? Shall we order a bottle?"

"Only if you can settle for the house Chianti. I haven't been able to talk Tony into starting a decent wine cellar."

"Chianti it is, then."

As soon as the waitress had taken their order with a promise to let Tony know that it was for Gina and her friend, Rafe studied Gina. "You look better. How did the phone call go?"

"The restaurant is very busy. Deidre's holding the creditors at bay. I can stay on here a while longer."

"But not indefinitely," Rafe said. "Not if you expect

to pull Café Tuscany out of this mess. You're going to have to go back and face it."

Her cheerful expression faltered. "I know, but just for tonight can we not talk about it?"

Rafe hesitated. "Look, I know I'm probably the last person you want to—or even should—discuss any of this with, but I'm a halfway-decent listener."

"I'm sure you are, but how do I know that you won't take every word I say and twist it? Let's face it, you're not out here because you want to get to know me. You're here because you think I'm guilty of a crime."

"Not guilty, just involved," Rafe corrected.

"What's the difference?"

"I *know* you're involved with Rinaldi, and I *know* that he's done some shady financial deals."

"That's guilt by association," Gina pointed out. "Because Bobby's guilty, then I must be, too. That's what you're saying."

Rafe shook his head. "No, I'm trying to keep an open mind where you're concerned."

She regarded him doubtfully.

"Okay, maybe when I first scheduled the deposition, I made some assumptions," he conceded.

"And now?"

"I'm beginning to think my secretary might have been right, though if you ever tell her that, I'll be forced to deny it."

"Your secretary?"

"Lydia Allen. She's a big fan of yours and your restaurant. From the beginning she told me I was crazy for suspecting you of anything."

Gina's eyes brightened. "I know Lydia. I should have realized who she was when I first spoke to her about changing the deposition. She's a regular at the restaurant. And she works for you? How fascinating. You must have some redeeming qualities, then, if you can keep a woman like that on your payroll."

Rafe winced. "She might not agree. In fact, she says she stays with me precisely because I need someone to keep me honest."

"You're scared of her, aren't you?" she said, clearly enjoying the discovery. "What is she? Five-two, a hundred and five pounds? And you're scared of her. I love it."

"I am not scared of her," he insisted.

"Oh?"

He grinned. "Actually, I'm terrified. She can make my life a living hell. In fact, she takes great pride in it."

Gina chuckled. "I'll have to call Deidre and let her know that Lydia's next meal is on the house."

"Which won't do much to help your financial situation," Rafe pointed out. "Nor will it do a thing to get you into my good graces."

Her gaze narrowed. "What would it take for me to get in your good graces?"

"Some honest answers."

"I've never lied to you, Rafe."

"But you haven't told me the whole truth, either."

"I will when the time comes."

His spirits, which had been astonishingly light during their bantering exchange, sank. "And that will be?"

"When we do the deposition," she said flatly, and turned her gaze to Tony, who was crossing the restaurant, a beaming smile on his face for Gina, a cooler acknowledgment for Rafe.

Rafe couldn't help the trace of envy that filled him

as he listened to the warm exchange between these two old friends. He wasn't used to feeling shut out, all but ignored, especially by a woman. Nor was he used to the distrust that Tony made no attempt to hide.

After the man had gone to check on their meal, Gina regarded him apologetically. "Sorry about that. Tony's very protective of me, and he knows about everything that happened with Bobby and that you're here to keep an eye on me. He's worried about what's going on with the two of us."

"You mean romantically?"

She had the audacity to laugh at that. "Hardly! No, he's convinced you have ulterior motives, that you're trying to wear me down so I'll incriminate myself. He mentioned it after meeting you the other day."

"And what did you tell him?"

"That you were a lawyer. That seemed to be explanation enough."

The stereotype rankled. "Your friend Emma is a lawyer. He doesn't distrust her, does he?"

"No, but Emma grew up here. That gives her an advantage."

A few minutes later Tony returned with steaming plates filled with aromatic pasta. He served them, cast yet another suspicious look at Rafe, then returned to the kitchen.

"It's no fun, is it?" Gina asked.

"What?"

"Being regarded with distrust."

"No," Rafe agreed.

She smiled happily at that. "Good. Then you know how I feel every time I catch you watching me."

"Yes, I suppose I do," he agreed, then leaned across

the table, his gaze locked with hers. "But just so you know, sometimes when I'm watching you, it's because I find you both fascinating and stunning, and I can't take my eyes off you."

She stared at him, openmouthed, as he sat back and lifted his glass in a silent toast, then grinned. "Gives you something to think about, doesn't it?"

"Rafe, I don't think we ought to go there, do you?" she said, clearly flustered.

"Probably not," he agreed readily.

Unfortunately, he was pretty sure it was too late to derail that particular train.

8

The ringing phone woke Rafe out of a sound sleep, rousing him from a dream in which he and Gina were entangled on a feather mattress, engaging in some very slow, incredibly provocative acts. Even before he picked up the receiver, he hated whoever was on the other end of the line.

"Rafe, why haven't I heard from you?" his mother demanded in a petulant tone.

"Good morning, Mother. How lovely to hear your voice," he muttered, knowing the sarcasm would go straight over her head. "What's the problem?"

"The problem is that you are not keeping me informed. Am I or am I not your client?"

"You're one of them," he agreed, glancing at the clock and groaning when he realized it was barely 6:00 a.m. He and Gina had stayed out late the night before, doing absolutely none of the things he'd wanted most to do, which was probably why his dreams had been particularly steamy.

"The most important one, I should think," she grumbled.

"Actually you're the only one who's not paying me,"

he pointed out. "I took on your case pro bono, if you recall."

"I still think I should be getting an update from time to time. Have you found Bobby? Will I be getting my money back?"

"I haven't found Bobby. As for your money, we'll know more about that once I find out where he's gone."

"Well, if you don't know anything, why on earth are you vacationing in Wyoming, of all places?"

Rafe gritted his teeth. "I am not on vacation. I'm following a lead."

"Don't you have investigators to do that?"

"Sure I do. They cost quite a bit. Shall I put their expenses on your bill?"

Adele O'Donnell Tinsley Warwick sucked in her breath. "There's no need to be snide, Rafe."

"I'm sorry," Rafe apologized automatically. "Since I have you on the line, let me ask you again if Bobby ever said anything at all about any place he particularly liked, some country or city he might be holed up in now? Is he the kind who'd hide all his ill-gotten gains in a Swiss bank account, or would he head for the Cayman Islands?"

"Neither. When he was with me, he seemed quite content to be in New York. From my point of view, none of this makes any sense. I thought he was happy. I thought we were happy. We were together for five years. Well, most of five years. There was that period when I thought I might be in love with Mitchell Davis, but he turned out to still have a wife tucked away upstate."

"Yes, I recall," Rafe said wearily. Obviously, his mother made a habit of deluding herself about the importance of a relationship. He sighed, then asked, "What do you know about Rinaldi's business partner?"

"Gina? He rarely mentioned her," she said dismissively. "I got the sense that she was contributing very little to the business, other than a certain flair she had with the customers and preparation of some of the dishes on the menu. Bobby was the money man and the brains behind the place. I always had the feeling she was holding him back, that her thinking was far too conservative."

"Perhaps she had good reason for being that way, since Rinaldi was so irresponsible where money was concerned," he suggested.

"Bobby was a genius," she said at once.

His mother's criticism of Gina and her admiring tone when she spoke of Rinaldi, even after everything the man had done to her, made Rafe cringe. "Mother, are you anxious for me to find Rinaldi so we can put him behind bars, or are you hoping to resume your affair with him?"

"How can you even ask me such a thing?" she asked indignantly.

"Because I honestly want to know the answer," he said. "I get this terrible feeling in the pit of my stomach that you want the man back, even after everything he's done."

"Don't be ridiculous. He cheated me out of thousands of dollars. I wouldn't take him back if he begged me to."

"Glad to hear it," Rafe said, though he wasn't entirely certain he believed her.

"Now, tell me again why you're in Wyoming. Bobby certainly wouldn't go there. He hated anything primitive."

"They do have hot and cold running water here, Mother."

"You know what I mean. He was a sophisticated man." She paused, then added thoughtfully, "But that little partner of his wasn't. Is that it? Is Gina in Wyoming? Is she hiding out there?"

"Gina is not 'hiding out,' and she's every bit as sophisticated as you or I," Rafe said impatiently, aware the moment the words left his mouth that his mother would seize on them.

"Oh, dear," she murmured. "She *is* there. You're not being taken in by her, are you?"

"No more than you were by Rinaldi," he said dryly.

"Rafe, darling, do be careful," she said with a rare display of motherly concern.

"Believe me, Mother, in my profession, there are very few people I trust. And after growing up with your unpredictable serial marriages, there are even fewer women I trust."

"Well, that's okay, then," she said, sounding pleased. Clearly she'd missed the barb directed at her role in his distrust. Rafe sighed at the realization that she was as self-absorbed as ever.

Only after he'd hung up did Rafe realize exactly how pitiful his words were and how very badly he wanted Gina Petrillo to be the person who broke the pattern.

"Gina, sweetie, the phone's for you," Gina's mother called cheerfully after a tap on the bedroom door.

Gina groaned and rolled over, burying her head under the pillow. She had tossed and turned all night long, trying to escape the dream in which she was running endlessly after a shadow. Bobby's, no doubt. Not even her subconscious would let her catch him, because apparently on some innate level she knew that killing him was a bad idea.

"Gina, are you awake?" her mother called.

"Yes," she finally admitted. "I'll be right there."

For one fleeting second she allowed herself to anticipate hearing Rafe's voice on the other end of the line. She was finding it increasingly difficult to keep her guard up around him. Nor was she having much luck with keeping her hormones in check. Dragging on her robe, she picked up her pace as she went into the hallway to grab the nearest phone.

"Hello, doll," Bobby greeted her as if they'd parted only days before and on the very best of terms.

"Roberto Rinaldi, where the hell are you?" she demanded, shaking with indignation. "Do you have any idea what sort of a mess you've left behind for me to clean up? I have an attorney shadowing my every move. I believe you know his mother."

"Not Rafe O'Donnell."

"Bingo."

"Sorry about that. Not to worry, though. I'll get everything straightened out."

"How? When?"

"Soon," he assured her. "Gotta run, doll. I just wanted you to know to hang in there."

"Bobby, don't you dare hang up on me. Bobby! Dammit, Bobby!" She realized she was shouting at a dial tone and all but slammed the receiver back into the cradle. "Forget the consequences. If I ever get my hands on him, I'm going to kill him."

She looked up and realized that her mother was studying her with a horrified expression.

"Into the kitchen," her mother said quietly, but in a tone that had always meant business. "I think it's about time you told me what's going on."

Gina sighed and reluctantly trailed along behind her. She paused only long enough to pour herself a cup of coffee, then sat at the kitchen table. "Where's Dad?"

"He's gone to work, thank goodness. If he had heard you just now, it would have sent his blood pressure into the stratosphere. Whatever's going on, we'll keep it between us for now. I don't want your father upset. To tell you the truth, I'm not sure listening to you talk like that hasn't shaken me a little bit, too."

Her mother did look pale. Gina sought to reassure her. "It was just a figure of speech, Mother. I'm not going to kill anybody."

"It didn't sound that way to me. What has Bobby done? And does that have anything to do with what Rafe O'Donnell is doing here in Winding River?"

Gina slowly stirred two teaspoons of sugar into her coffee as she considered just how much to tell her mother. She finally settled on the whole truth. By the time she'd finished explaining all of the sordid details about Bobby's scam, her mother was practically quivering with outrage.

"What an awful man!" her mother declared. "And that was him on the phone? If I'd had any idea, I would have given him a piece of my mind."

Gina couldn't help it. She grinned. "As impressive and daunting as I've always found your lectures to be, Mom, I doubt they would have had any effect at all on Bobby. He's pretty much immune to criticism, and I doubt he has much of a conscience."

"That doesn't mean he shouldn't hear exactly what I

think of him. Taking money from all of those people..."
She shook her head. "It's a crime, that's what it is."

"Which is why Rafe is after him. And me, for that matter."

"Surely Rafe doesn't seriously think you could be involved," her mother said, her indignation stirring all over again. "You are nothing like Bobby."

"Thank you, but Rafe doesn't know me as well as you do. He says he has an open mind. At the very least he's hoping Bobby will contact me."

"Which he has. You have to tell Rafe," her mother said. "That will prove to him that you want this resolved as badly as he does."

"What am I supposed to tell him?" Gina asked. "That Bobby called but wouldn't say where he was?"

"That's the truth, isn't it?"

"Yes, but all it proves is that Bobby knows I'm in Wyoming and that we're in touch," Gina said, feeling despondent. She was not nearly as sure as her mother that Rafe wouldn't take the news of Bobby's call and somehow twist it to fit his own scenario, condemning her in the process.

"You have to tell Rafe," her mother repeated. "Keeping it a secret will only make you look guilty if he finds out about the call later." She gestured toward the phone. "Call him right now. That's my advice." She bent down and kissed Gina's forehead. "I have to get going or I'll be late. You have a good day. This will all work itself out, I promise. People like Bobby eventually get what's coming to them."

"I wish I shared your conviction about that," Gina said, giving her mother a half-hearted smile. "But I will think about what you've said."

If only her parents had caller ID, she thought, staring at the phone, but in this small, friendly community such high-tech equipment was viewed as both unnecessary and in many ways impolite. No one saw any need to know who was calling before picking up the phone. Heck, half the people in town, her folks included, didn't even own answering machines. People didn't have the same desire for being connected twenty-four hours a day, seven days a week that they did in New York. There was a lot to be said for that attitude, but right now Gina regretted it.

When the phone rang, Gina jumped, then scowled at the offending instrument before picking it up.

"Yes," she muttered curtly.

"You didn't by any chance wake up on the wrong side of the bed, did you?" Rafe inquired cheerfully.

"Something like that," she said.

"I know the feeling. My mother woke me out of a sound sleep, which would have been bad enough, but she also ruined a particularly fascinating dream."

"Oh, really?"

"Just so you know, you were the star attraction."

"You shouldn't say things like that," Gina chided, even though the news was fascinating. "I thought we had agreed that there would be no more crossing the line."

"Did we? My subconscious must have forgotten all about that. Now then, would I be risking my life if I suggested breakfast at Stella's in twenty minutes? That's not crossing the line, is it?"

Gina thought of Bobby's call and her mother's advice that she share that information with Rafe. "Actually, breakfast might be good. I'll see you there. Make it thirty minutes, though. I'm only half-awake, and I usually don't do mornings. It'll take me a while to jump-start my brain."

"I suppose saying that it's not your brain that interests me would be a really bad idea," Rafe teased.

Gina laughed, her mood improving considerably. "A really, really bad one," she agreed. "See you soon."

As it turned out, it took her closer to an hour to shower, dress and walk to Stella's. Admittedly, she was deliberately dragging her feet. Every time she thought of Bobby's call and his refusal to even admit where he was, she felt more and more despondent. By the time she got to Stella's, she was crankier than ever. Finding that Rafe had finished reading the paper and was drumming his fingers on the table immediately put her on the defensive.

"I thought maybe you'd stood me up," he said as she slid into the booth opposite him.

"I told you I'd be here, didn't I?" she snapped before she could stop herself.

His expression turned thoughtful. "There's that tone again. Did something happen this morning to get your day off to a rotten start?"

"You mean aside from your call?"

He winced but said gamely, "Yes, aside from that."

Gina waited until Stella had poured her a cup of coffee and taken their orders before answering with the truth. "I heard from Bobby," she admitted in a rush, before she could change her mind. She didn't feel one bit better once the words were out.

Rafe nodded slowly. "I see. And what did he have to say?"

"Not much. He wouldn't say where he was. He

wouldn't answer any of my questions. He just said everything was going to work out."

"For whom?" Rafe asked. "I don't imagine he was talking about the people he bilked out of their money."

"No, I imagine not," Gina agreed ruefully. "Anyway, I thought you should know, even though it doesn't exactly give you any new information."

"Thank you," he said solemnly. "I know it wasn't easy for you to tell me about the call."

She studied his face intently. "You don't think I'm holding anything back, do you?"

"Are you?"

"No, that's the whole story. The call didn't last more than a minute."

His expression turned thoughtful. "I wonder why. Does he suspect your phone could be tapped?"

"I doubt it," Gina said. "Bobby never has been big on prolonged telephone calls. Ironically, in his own way I think he just wanted to reassure me."

"Were you reassured?" Rafe asked.

"Hardly. I was furious. I want more than a patronizing pat on the head," she said, her fury stirring all over again. "I want answers. I want every penny of that money returned. I want to put this mess behind me."

For the first time since he'd tried to put her life under a microscope, Rafe regarded her with what appeared to be genuine sympathy. "I'm sorry," he said quietly.

"Why are you sorry?"

"Because it must be hell having everything you've worked for put at risk through no fault of your own."

Startled, Gina merely stared. "You finally believe I wasn't involved?"

He nodded. "I do."

"Then go back to New York," she pleaded. "Concentrate on finding Bobby and getting to the bottom of this. Do it for your clients and, unofficially at least, do it for me. Not that I can afford to pay you. My cash, as you know, is somewhat limited these days."

Unfortunately, before the words were out of her mouth, he was shaking his head. "I can't work for you. It would be a conflict of interest. And I can't leave. You're still my best lead. If Bobby contacted you once, he'll do it again. Next time we'll be ready."

"Ready how? You're not going to tap my parents' phone, are you?"

"No, but a caller ID could help. Do they have one?"

"No, and my father will hate it. He doesn't know what's going on. I told my mother this morning, but we agreed that he doesn't need to know. It will only upset him, and his blood pressure is already bad. I mean it, Rafe. I don't want him involved in any way."

"Then we'll find another way," he said, his expression thoughtful. "Maybe we should both go back to New York."

"No," she said flatly. "I told you yesterday, I won't leave while Karen's under so much pressure."

"Then you make a suggestion."

Gina considered an idea she'd been toying with ever since Caleb's funeral. "I need an excuse to keep hanging around," she said slowly. "Karen will hate it if she thinks I've put my life on hold because of her."

"Okay. Any ideas?"

"I could go to work for Tony," she said with a surprising lack of enthusiasm. She knew it would feel as if she was only marking time, but it was the best she could do. "I'd tell everyone I'm just helping him out for a while. Maybe he'd even take that trip to Italy he's been promising Francesca."

"That keeps you in town, but how does it help with pinning down Bobby's whereabouts?"

"We could put the caller ID on the restaurant phone. Tony would agree. He knows what's going on, and he'd want to help nail Bobby."

Rafe shook his head. "That's only a partial solution. Right now Bobby's contact number for you is at your parents' house. He can just keep right on using that. Unless…" His gaze met hers.

Gina's pulse skipped a beat at the heated look in his eyes. "Unless what?"

"Unless you moved in with me at the hotel," he said slowly.

"Oh, no," she said at once, despite the decided leap of her pulse. "That is a really bad idea."

He grinned. "I don't know. I think it opens up some fascinating possibilities."

"You would."

"Are you saying that you're not even a tiny bit intrigued by what could happen if the two of us were sharing close quarters?"

"I'm saying that your clients would be horrified to discover that you were getting up close and personal with a suspect. Not five minutes ago you pointed out that it would be a conflict just to unofficially help me out."

"I could always tell them that I'm keeping you under surveillance."

Gina laughed at that. "Is that what you call it?"

"Okay, do you have a better idea?"

She considered the question. "I'll get my own place," she said eventually.

Rafe seemed completely taken aback. "Your own place? That sounds awfully permanent."

Gina shrugged. "Who knows? Given the situation in New York, coming back here might be the smartest thing—the only thing—I can do." Ever since her conversation with Bobby, she felt as though she'd lost the will to fight.

"You're conceding defeat on Café Tuscany?" Rafe asked, studying her with a shocked expression. "I don't buy it."

"I may not have any choice. Deidre's keeping things going for now, but we can't keep playing this shell game with the creditors forever. Maybe declaring bankruptcy is the way to go."

"Surely you don't believe that! I thought you cared about that restaurant."

"I do, but isn't that what you've wanted all along, to drive me out of business?" she asked, unable to keep a trace of bitterness out of her voice.

"No. I wanted answers. I wanted Rinaldi to pay."

"And me," she reminded him.

"Only if you were involved."

"Well, involved or not, it's my neck that's in the noose. Bobby's not here to take his share of the heat."

"Dammit, Gina, we're going to find him. You just have to help me out. Don't give up now." He studied her intently. "What's happened to you? I thought you were a fighter."

"I was," she agreed, then added sadly, "but so was Caleb. Look where that got him."

"You can't compare the two situations at all," Rafe insisted.

"Can't I? An uphill battle is an uphill battle, whether it's a ranch or a restaurant that's under siege."

Rafe slammed his fist on the table. "I won't let you do this. I won't let you just walk away."

Now that she'd actually gotten the word *bankruptcy* past her lips, it wasn't nearly as scary as she'd imagined. At least then all of this would be over. Rafe would go away. She could put her life back together again.

"You can't stop me," she told him flatly.

He stared at her with an obvious mix of frustration and concern. "Don't do this. Don't give up."

"I'm not giving up. I'm merely accepting the inevitable," she said, just as Emma walked in.

Rafe regarded Emma with relief. "Thank God. Maybe you can talk some sense into her. I'm not having any luck."

Emma frowned, looking from Rafe to Gina and back again. "What's this all about?"

Rafe tossed his napkin on the table and stood up, gesturing for Emma to take his place. "She'll explain," he said, then added with a shrug, "or not."

Gina stared after him, startled by the depth of his apparent disappointment in her.

"Okay, start talking," Emma ordered. "And this time I want to know everything. I can't help you if you hold out on me."

Gina shook her head. She couldn't go through this again this morning. She felt too raw, too vulnerable. Again she saw the disappointment in Rafe's eyes, and shuddered. It seemed she was letting everyone down, including a man who hadn't had that much faith in her to begin with. What did that say about her? She was letting other people control her life, and that had to stop. She needed to take charge again, and the first step was talking to Tony. She might not know yet what she could do—or even what she wanted to do—about Café Tuscany, but she did know that she needed to stay right here in Winding River until Karen's life was more settled.

"Not now," she told Emma. "There's something I need to do."

"And it can't wait ten minutes?"

"No, it can't," Gina said.

"If that man has upset you in some way, I'll make him regret it," Emma promised.

"No, actually, that man has made me see things clearly for the first time in weeks."

She might find Rafe O'Donnell annoying and pushy and arrogant, but he was right about one thing: she was a fighter. It was past time she started acting like one and seized control of her life again, even if no one else agreed with what she was about to do.

9

After leaving Gina, Rafe was more determined than ever to track down Bobby Rinaldi and make him pay for his crimes. It was no longer just about the money. Unjust or not, most of the investors, Rafe's mother included, could afford to take their losses. Now, though, his concern extended to Gina, who was clearly paying a far higher toll than mere dollars.

The bleak, defeated look on Gina's face the day before would haunt him forever. He blamed himself for that, and for somehow leading her to the conclusion that the only way out was to declare bankruptcy and come home to Wyoming. That was the last thing he'd intended when he'd started all this.

He muttered a harsh expletive and faced facts. That was *exactly* what he'd hoped for when he'd come charging out here on his white horse determined to save the day for his clients. But that was before he'd known anything at all about Gina Petrillo and the kind of warm, decent, caring woman she was. For once in his life, he should have paid attention to his secretary. Not that he'd ever admit that to Lydia. There were some things best left unsaid to a woman who tended to gloat.

Without pausing to consider what he was about to do, he headed straight for Tony's and pounded on the front door until Tony came out of the kitchen and opened it.

"There's no need to break the door down," the man chided.

"Sorry. I should have realized you'd be in the kitchen and come around back."

"Or waited until the restaurant was open," Tony suggested mildly, though he stepped aside to allow Rafe to enter.

"This couldn't wait," Rafe said.

Worry immediately creased Tony's forehead. "It's about our Gina?"

Rafe nodded. "Yes. And she doesn't know I'm here. It's better if it stays that way."

"I imagine she would not approve," Tony guessed. "So, why did you come? I am *her* friend, not yours."

"That's precisely why I came," Rafe said. "I think she's about to do something she's going to regret and only you can stop her."

"Then we must talk." Tony beckoned him toward the back. "However, you will have to explain while I work. I am making pasta and I cannot stop without ruining it."

In the kitchen Rafe drew in a deep breath, savoring the aromas of garlic and tomatoes, oregano and basil, flour and eggs. He also took in the aging but spotless appliances, the floor that looked as if it had just been mopped to a shine. If this was where Gina had learned the basics of the restaurant business, she had learned from a man who obviously took pride in his work. The room was both cozy and efficient.

"Sit," Tony said, gesturing toward a stool. "If you would like coffee, you will have to pour it yourself," he added, already working with the dough again, stretching it with nimble fingers, then putting it through a pasta machine to form perfect fettuccine noodles.

"No coffee, but thanks."

Tony glanced at him. "What is wrong with our Gina?"

"She said she had told you about her business difficulties," Rafe began cautiously, in case she hadn't been as totally forthright with Tony as he had been led to believe.

Anger brought bright patches of color to Tony's cheeks. Rafe couldn't translate the word he uttered, but it was evidently not complimentary toward Bobby.

"If he were here, I would toss him in a pot of boiling water myself," Tony said with a huff.

"Join the club," Rafe said.

Tony seemed taken aback by the ferocity of his response. "I was under the impression that you thought our Gina shared the blame."

"I was suspicious of her, yes," Rafe admitted.

"And now?"

"I'm all but convinced that she had nothing to do with anything that happened."

"But not totally convinced?" Tony asked, scowling at him. "Then you can go. I have nothing to say to you, and you have nothing to say that I wish to hear."

Rafe smiled. "But that's why you must listen, because you believe in Gina unconditionally, because you will want what is best for her."

"Of course," Tony said at once. "But how? What help can I give her? She would never take money from me, even if I had enough to fix the problem Bobby has created."

Rafe thought of her display of pride and knew Tony was right. "Not money, but I do think she is going to come to you for a job. In fact, I think she is going to tell you that she wants to move back here and work with you."

"She came here yesterday and said precisely that."

"What did you tell her?"

"That she would be welcome, but that she should think about it. Obviously, you think the decision is as impetuous as I do. You think she made the offer not because it is what she truly wants, but because she thinks it is her only option."

Rafe admired the man's quick thinking, as well as his understanding of Gina. "Yes, that is exactly what I think. She's giving up, Tony. I think a lot of things have been piling up the last few weeks, including the death of her friend's husband, and she's throwing in the towel, taking the easy way out. She's convinced herself that she has an obligation to stay here for her friend's sake. I admire that, and in the short term it makes sense. But a permanent move?" He shook his head. "I don't think so. I just thought you ought to know that, so you don't take what she says too seriously."

Tony's hands stilled. "You want me to turn her down, even if she comes back and says she is certain it is what she wants?"

"No, of course not. Just don't count on her staying forever. She loves that restaurant in New York. She'll regret it if she gives up on it. She just needs a breather until her fighting spirit comes back."

Tony's gaze narrowed. "Is this some ploy to get her back in New York where you can drag her into court?"

"Absolutely not," Rafe said, offended, even though on some level he could understand the man's suspicion. He had not come here with good intentions toward Gina. Only in recent days had that changed.

"Then what makes you think you know what is best for our Gina? Do you care for her?"

Rafe debated lying, but Tony's knowing eyes would see straight through him. "More than I have any right to, given my role in all of this," he finally admitted.

The back door opened just then and Gina stepped inside, a look of grim determination on her face. When she caught sight of Rafe, she frowned.

"What are you doing here?" she asked suspiciously.

"He is learning how to make pasta from a master," Tony said, giving Rafe a wink.

"I had no idea you were interested in the finer points of making your own noodles," Gina said, her gaze locked with Rafe's.

"It's a recent interest," he said easily.

"I see."

"What brings you by, *cara mia?*" Tony asked.

"Do I need a reason to visit?"

"Never, but you usually have one. It has not been long enough for you to have given careful thought to what we discussed yesterday."

Once again she regarded Rafe with suspicion, but then she turned to Tony. "I still want a job."

"You have a job," he replied. "In fact, it seems to

me you have been away from it too long, all things considered."

Color bloomed in her cheeks and she whirled on Rafe. "What have you been telling him?"

Tony interceded. "I do not need anyone to tell me things where your best interests are concerned. This business of yours does not run itself. Mine certainly does not and yours is more demanding, yes? Especially now."

"Are you saying you don't want me here?" she asked, a hitch in her voice revealing just how close to tears she was. "I thought you just wanted me to think it over. Are you saying now that you don't want me at all?"

"Never!" Tony said. "You have a place here always. I just don't want you to use my kitchen to hide out from your troubles. I want you to face them like the brave woman you are."

Her gaze flew from Tony to Rafe and back again. "Is that what the two of you think, that I'm running away, that I'm hiding out?"

"Aren't you?" Rafe asked quietly. "That call from Bobby yesterday morning was the final blow, wasn't it?"

"No, the final blow was finding you in here conspiring with a man I'd always thought was my friend," she retorted angrily, then ran for the door, slamming it behind her as she left.

Tony started after her, but Rafe stopped him. "I'll go. It's me she's furious with."

Tony nodded. "The job is hers if she doesn't change her mind. You understand that, don't you?"

"Of course," he said, then went to try to undo some of the damage he'd caused, not this morning, but over the past few weeks.

* * *

Gina ran until she was out of breath and had a blister forming on her heel. She was cursing Rafe O'Donnell every step of the way, with a couple of healthy epithets reserved for Tony, as well.

She was limping and winded when Rafe caught up with her. She noticed that he was driving, not running, which meant he'd taken his own sweet time about pursuing her. He'd probably hoped that a little time and exercise would help her to work off some steam. It hadn't. If anything, she was angrier and more hurt than ever.

"Want a lift?" he asked.

"No."

"Don't be stubborn. Get in the car."

"No," she repeated, though the thought of all that air-conditioned comfort was way too tempting. "Go away. I don't want to talk to you."

"If you don't get in, I'll just be forced to park and walk with you. Then two of us will be miserable and courting sunstroke."

He would do it, too. She could see the determination in the grim set of his jaw. "Okay, fine," she said, grudgingly walking around the car to get in.

Rafe gave her a quick sideways glance. "Going anyplace in particular?"

"Away from you."

His lips twitched. "Now that you know that's out of the question, any other destination you'd care to try?"

"Home," she said finally, then added hopefully, "alone."

He shook his head. "Not an option. You don't need to be alone, Gina. You need to talk this out with someone who knows all the facts, someone who's a good listener."

"Someone who wants to put me in jail?" she added wryly.

"Not you. Bobby Rinaldi," he corrected.

She sighed and let that pass. She wasn't convinced about that yet. Catching Rafe with Tony had shaken her. She had been counting on Tony to be the one person totally on her side, the one person who would give her a fresh start, no questions asked. His refusal to do so was Rafe's doing and she wasn't entirely sure of Rafe's motives. Until she was, she wasn't discussing anything about Café Tuscany with him.

That didn't mean she couldn't enjoy his company, at least for an afternoon. Whatever else he was, Rafe O'Donnell was definitely a sexy distraction, a far cry from most of the men she'd crossed paths with lately. He was certainly an improvement over Bobby.

"Pull over," she commanded.

He regarded her with a startled expression, but he actually did as she'd asked. Pleased, she grinned. "That was easier than I'd expected."

"Care to explain what we're doing on the side of the road?" he inquired lightly as an occasional car whizzed past.

"Here's the deal. If you promise that you will not say another word about the restaurant or about my decision to stay in Winding River, I will go to Laramie with you."

He didn't immediately seize the offer the way she'd anticipated. Instead, his expression grew thoughtful.

"Why Laramie?" he asked.

She ticked off the reasons. "Because it is not Winding River, because we can go to a movie there, because I heard about a restaurant I'd like to try."

"Aha," he said, grinning at her. "That's the real reason, isn't it? You can't help it. Even when you're on some kind of break, you can't resist checking out the competition."

Gina frowned. "It's not competitiveness. I just happen to like food."

"Oh, really? When was the last time you actually ate a meal? I've been with you on several occasions lately, and though you talk a lot about food, you barely touch anything that's put in front of you."

"I haven't been that hungry," she said defensively. "Do you want to go to Laramie or not? Last chance. I can always drive myself."

"Okay. Okay. Just point me the right way," he said.

Gina gave him directions, then sat back, and for the first time since she'd talked to Bobby the day before, she began to relax as the miles flew by. Rafe flipped on the car radio and found a soothing oldies station that concentrated on ballads. By the time they reached the outskirts of Laramie, she was actually feeling pretty mellow.

"Lunch first?" he asked as he drove into downtown.

"Yes," she agreed, suddenly starved. The restaurant she'd heard about was actually a coffee house with an interesting menu of salads, some of which she thought she might be able to incorporate into the Café Tuscany luncheon selections. Even as the prospect crossed her mind, she realized the incongruity of it. One minute she was ready to shut the place down, the next she couldn't help planning for its future. Maybe she wasn't as committed to giving up as she'd made herself believe. Funny how both Tony and, more important, Rafe had seen that when she hadn't.

Gina studied the menu and found two or three different salads that sounded intriguing. She regarded Rafe hopefully. "Do you know what you want?"

"I was thinking about a burger," he said.

She regarded him with undisguised regret, which he immediately picked up on. "What's wrong with a burger?" he asked.

"Nothing, but would you mind getting a salad with it?"

"Why?"

"Because I want to sample three of these, and I'll feel like an idiot if I have to order all of them myself. Not that it would be the first time. I once ordered half a dozen appetizers at a restaurant in Paris because I knew I'd never get back there. The waiter brought them all without a single comment, but the next thing I knew the entire wait staff and the chef were standing at the door of the kitchen staring at me as if I'd sprouted two heads."

"Did that bother you?"

"No, but it kept me from taking notes," she said sorrowfully. "I tried to write everything down after I left, but I couldn't remember every ingredient the way I could have if I'd done it on the spot. It took me months of experimenting to be able to nail down some of the subtler spices."

"So what you're telling me is that I am about to help you steal some chef's recipes," Rafe said.

"I'm not going to steal them," she protested even though he looked more amused than appalled by the notion. "I'll enhance them."

"An interesting distinction." He glanced up at the waitress, then gestured toward Gina. "Talk to her. She knows what we're both having."

After she'd placed their order, Gina regarded him with a grin. "I like a man who's not afraid to let a woman take charge."

"And I like a woman with confidence," he said. "It's nice to see yours coming back. It's also good to see you thinking about the future. I'm glad we came here."

"So am I," Gina said, her gaze locked with his.

"Are we having our first official date, Gina Petrillo?" he asked solemnly.

Her pulse fluttered at the suggestion. "I don't know, are we?"

"It certainly seems that way to me."

"Dating could be complicated," she said with real regret. "Maybe we shouldn't even think about it until... well, until everything is settled."

"You're probably right," he agreed. "But that's not what I want."

"Neither do I," she admitted in a whisper.

In fact, right this second with her heartbeat skittering crazily, she wanted very much to be on a first date with this man. She wanted to get to know what made him tick, wanted to feel his lips on hers again, wanted to feel his skin heat beneath her touch. It had been a very long time since she had wanted any of that, even longer since she had needed it the way she did right this minute. In fact, the way she was feeling was more appropriate to a fifth date, maybe even a tenth.

As if he sensed her turmoil, perhaps even shared it, he reached across the table and clasped her hand in his. There was strength and warmth in his touch. As the pad of his thumb grazed her palm, there was even more—a teasing hint of smoldering sensuality. Gina swallowed hard. Her gaze lifted, met his.

"Suddenly I'm not very hungry," she said, watching closely for his reaction to the unspoken implications of that.

"Neither am I," he said without hesitation, his gaze unwavering. "Do you want me to cancel the order?"

She shook her head, then chuckled at his obvious disappointment. It gave her courage. "Get it to go."

Ten minutes later they had three carry-out orders of salad and a warm loaf of sourdough bread. Even though she felt almost giddy, Gina managed to get to the car without bursting into laughter at the waitress's knowing expression.

"She knew," she said, collapsing in the front seat with the stack of take-out boxes. "She knew exactly what had happened, that we wanted each other more than food."

"She did not," Rafe insisted.

"Oh, yes, she did," Gina argued. "She actually gave me a thumbs-up signal as we left."

Rafe seemed vaguely startled. "Oh, really? Now what do you suppose she meant by that?"

"I hope you're teasing," Gina said.

He reached over and skimmed a finger along her cheek. "Why is that?"

"Because otherwise I am about to make a huge fool of myself," she said.

"Oh?"

"I am about to suggest that we take all this food to a hotel room," she said. When Rafe remained silent, she swallowed hard. "Well, have I made a fool of myself?"

"No," he said, his voice suddenly husky. Though he'd been about to start the car, he dropped his hand away from the key and faced her. "But I want you to think about this. Is it really what you want? You don't strike me as the kind of woman to engage in casual flings."

She laughed at that. "If only you knew."

"Meaning?"

"Meaning that I have never engaged in flings of any kind, casual or otherwise."

His eyes widened. "You're not...?"

"You can say the word," she teased. "And, no, I'm not a virgin, though my experience is almost as limited. It's just that it's been years since I've had the time or the inclination to get involved with anyone. I try my best to forget about the last time I did."

"Why now?" he asked. "Why me? As you pointed out earlier, this isn't exactly an uncomplicated situation."

"No," she agreed.

"Is that part of the attraction? Because it's a little dangerous?"

She considered the question, then shook her head. "No. If anything, that would make me run the other way."

He regarded her ruefully. "I notice you're not exactly gushing with a hundred reasons why you've chosen me to break your self-imposed celibacy."

"Is that what you want? Do you want me to stroke your ego?"

"No, if there's any stroking to be done, I can think of other parts I'd prefer to have you touching."

Heat gathered low in her belly as his words sank in. "Then what is this hesitation about?" she asked.

He took her hand in his, turned it over and kissed her palm. "As much as I would like to take you to a hotel room and spend the rest of the afternoon letting you seduce me, I'm not going to do it," he said with obvious regret.

Embarrassment flooded through her. When she would have jerked her hand away, he held it more tightly.

"One of these days you and I are going to end up in bed together," he assured her emphatically. "Make no mistake about that. But when we do, it will be for the right reasons. It won't be because you're looking for a temporary escape from your problems."

"That's a lousy thing to say," she told him heatedly, but then the truth hit her. That was exactly what she'd been looking for. She'd wanted a distraction, something to make her feel alive, and a quick romp with an extraordinarily virile man would have accomplished that.

She forced herself to meet his gaze. There was nothing condemning in his expression. If anything, he looked as if he completely understood her actions.

"I'm sorry," she said in a voice barely above a whisper.

"Don't be. Having a beautiful woman find me desirable, whatever the reason, is never a bad thing. I'm just holding out until it's perfect."

"That day might never come," she said.

"It will," he replied with total confidence. "Sooner than you think." He gestured toward the boxes she was clutching with a white-knuckled grip. "Let's go find some idyllic spot and have a picnic."

"You're not afraid to be alone with me?" she teased.

"No way," he assured her.

"I could get carried away."

He laughed at the suggestion. "Now, *that* is something to look forward to."

10

Gina could have suffered from terminal embarrassment for throwing herself at Rafe, but he refused to allow it. By the time they'd shared their picnic, he had her laughing unselfconsciously again. Because of that, her feelings—and her respect—for him deepened a little more. So did the attraction, even though she couldn't seem to shut out the fact that their relationship had begun with his insulting belief that she could be a thief.

But as the days wore on with no more calls from Bobby and little for her to do in Winding River, Gina began to feel more restless than ever. She couldn't go on this way, not with Rafe looking over her shoulder— albeit with less suspicion. Cooking dinner for her parents and baking for her friends wasn't nearly enough to satisfy her urge to be back in the kitchen cooking for a whole restaurant filled with satisfied customers.

After her outburst in his kitchen, accusing both Tony and Rafe of conspiring, Tony forgave her and let her fill in from time to time, but it wasn't nearly enough. She was drifting and she didn't like it. She had to do something to shake things up, something to get her life back on track.

Maybe it was time to get some sound legal advice. No, she corrected, the truth was, it was way past time. She'd been putting it off, pretending to herself that Bobby would show up and prove that it was all some terrible misunderstanding, a mistake that could be easily rectified. She had been deluding herself that he would straighten everything out so that she wouldn't have to make any of the tough choices. Despite everything, despite all the evidence to the contrary, she hadn't wanted to believe that a man she'd considered a friend, as well as a business partner, had betrayed her.

Clearly, she admitted with a sigh, she had been wrong. Bobby's intentions weren't honorable. And Deidre's juggling act with the creditors couldn't go on indefinitely. Gina couldn't ask her to stand in the line of fire forever. This wasn't Deidre's problem to solve. It was hers.

She needed to make a decision, then get back to New York to handle the fallout herself, whether she chose to stay open and fight, as Tony and Rafe expected her to do, or to disappoint them both, sell or close the restaurant and pay off everyone she could.

Even though she hated involving her friends in what was happening, she knew that there wasn't a better lawyer—a better advocate—around than Emma. Fortunately, Emma was scheduled to drive up from Denver on Friday morning. Gina resolved to be waiting for her.

She knocked on the front door at the ranch at ten, knowing that Emma would have gotten an early start. Mrs. Clayton greeted her with a smile and a glass of lemonade, just as she had countless times when she and Emma had been teenagers. There was something comforting about it. In many ways so little had changed in the past ten years. The bonds she had formed back then were still strong.

"Emma should be here soon. Are you sure you don't want to wait inside?" she asked when Gina moved to sit in one of the rockers. "It's a scorcher out there today."

"Thanks. I'll be fine on the porch, if you don't mind. I need to have a few words in private with Emma."

"Then I'll get Caitlyn out of your hair as soon as they get here," Mrs. Clayton promised, wiping her hands on her apron and taking a seat beside Gina. "Caitlyn's going to want to get out to the barn to see her pony, anyway."

Gina grinned. "I don't suppose that pony is a bribe from her grandfather to keep her coming up here."

"Of course it is," Mrs. Clayton said unrepentantly. "Now that Emma's divorced, her father and I would give anything to have the two of them here all the time. I know Emma is very successful in Denver, but she hasn't been truly happy there for a long time. She just refuses to admit it. And Caitlyn loves it here."

"No doubt about that," Gina agreed. "And I think a certain newspaper editor might be pleased to have them nearby, too."

The suggestion brought a wistful expression to Mrs. Clayton's face. "Ford seems to be a fine young man. Emma could do worse. Of course, every time they're together for five minutes, they seem to end up in an argument."

"I've noticed," Gina said with amusement. "Don't you think all of that explosive chemistry is a good thing?"

"I don't know," Mrs. Clayton said skeptically. "I

haven't seen any evidence that they have a meeting of the minds about anything at all. If Ford said the grass was green, I think Emma would contradict him and point out every single brown patch in the lawn. I listen to the two of them and shake my head. Whatever happened to that agreeable girl we raised?"

"She grew up and became an outstanding lawyer with a passion for defending the little guy. Arguing is second nature to her. If she'd been on the debate team in high school, they would have been national champions, but back then she hated confrontation."

"Well, that's certainly changed, hasn't it?" Mrs. Clayton said. "And I'm proud of all she's accomplished, I really am. I just wish she'd give poor Ford a break every once in a while."

Gina patted Mrs. Clayton's hand. "She will. I predict that watching them will give Winding River more entertainment than any other courtship to come along in years."

"I don't know about that," Emma's mother said, grinning at her. "They'll have to work for that honor. I've heard some absolutely fascinating things about you and that young man who followed you here from back East."

Gina blushed, even as she insisted that she and Rafe were just friends.

"Maybe so, but if Emma and Ford were half as friendly, I'd be a happy woman," Mrs. Clayton said, then glanced at the driveway. "There's my wayward daughter now."

Practically before Emma pulled to a stop in front of the house, Caitlyn tumbled out of the car. "Grandma,

Grandma, how's my pony? I gotta see him right now. I missed him soooo much. Do you think he missed me?"

Mrs. Clayton winked at Gina, then reached for Caitlyn's hand. "Of course I do. Let's go to the barn. I think your grandpa's down there with him right now. He probably already has the saddle on, so you can go for a ride."

Caitlyn's smile spread. "Really? Hurry, Grandma."

Emma emerged from the car, shaking her head as the two of them went off toward the barn. "I swear that pony is all Caitlyn talked about all week. Now she's begging me to let her stay here when I go back to Denver."

"Why don't you?" Gina asked. "In fact, why don't you just pack up and move here?"

Emma's gaze narrowed. "Okay, what has Mom been telling you? Did she put you up to this?"

"No. This is my own idea, I swear it," Gina insisted.

"Yeah, right." Emma sat in the rocker next to Gina's and sighed. "That breeze feels good." She gazed enviously at the glass of lemonade Gina was holding. "And that looks wonderful."

Gina grinned. "If I hand it over, will you give me some free legal advice?"

"Absolutely," Emma said, reaching eagerly for the glass. "Talk to me. What's going on?"

"This is confidential, right?"

"You're asking as a client, then, not as a friend?"

Gina nodded.

"I don't think a glass of lemonade would qualify as a retainer. Give me a buck. That'll make it nice and legal."

Gina pulled the dollar out of her pocket and gave it

to her friend. Emma tucked it in her purse and grabbed a legal pad from her briefcase. "Tell me," she said when she was ready.

"I'm in trouble," Gina told Emma then. "I just don't know for sure how much."

"Start at the beginning and let's see if we can't get you out of trouble, then," Emma said briskly.

As Emma took copious notes, Gina outlined the mess Bobby had created, the financial disaster he'd left behind. "Right now my manager is juggling creditors, but some of them are bound to start getting impatient. Should I sell out and pay them what I can? Declare bankruptcy?" She regarded Emma despondently. "I hate this. I just hate it. If it were my mess, I'd take responsibility for it, but it's not. I'm so furious with Bobby, I'd like to see him strung up by his toenails and left to die."

"An interesting form of justice," Emma said, clearly amused. "I don't think the legal system has a provision for it, though."

"Too bad."

"Okay, here are the options I do see," Emma said. "Depending on your partnership arrangement with Bobby, you might be able to distance yourself from the problem, but that could take some very tricky and time-consuming legal maneuvering."

Gina shook her head. "As much as I would like to and even if it were perfectly legal, I can't duck out on my responsibility to make things right if I can. A lot of our vendors are small businesses. I can't just abandon them. And our investors gave us their money in good faith. I thought Bobby was paying them back with interest, but apparently they haven't seen a dime."

"It's probably not as simple as filing for bankruptcy. Not with Bobby missing, but you could start the proceedings. It would buy some time to reorganize the business. Your investors and creditors would get their money on a timetable established by the court. It's complicated, but I think at the same time you could sue Bobby for restitution of everything he stole." Emma regarded her intently. "What are the odds he still has the money?"

"I have no idea. I don't know if he stole it so he could go off to live on some Caribbean island or if he took it to pay gambling debts or if he ran off with it just for kicks."

"Well, that doesn't matter. We'll sue just in case there's anything left to get back. I have a friend, a classmate from law school, who's practicing in New York. Since I haven't passed the New York bar to be licensed there, he can handle things on that end. He'll file the papers when we're ready."

Emma's professional, no-nonsense approach gave Gina the first spark of hope she'd felt in days. "You really think we can straighten this out and save Café Tuscany?"

"Absolutely, if that's what you really want." She studied Gina with a penetrating look. "Is it?"

"Of course," Gina said without hesitation. "Why would you even ask something like that?"

"Because you're still here. Even with all this needing your immediate attention, you didn't run straight back to New York after the reunion."

"Because of Cassie's mom and then Caleb," Gina said, feeling oddly defensive.

"Is that all?"

"Yes."

"The funeral was weeks ago," Emma pointed out. "Karen's getting back on her feet. Are you ready to go back to New York?"

When Gina started to respond, Emma held up her hand. "You don't have to answer me now. Think about it. Something is keeping you here. Could be it's nothing more than a delaying tactic, because you haven't wanted to face what's going on in New York. But that's not like you. It could be that you're feeling the same pull that Cassie felt, the same pull that Lauren mentions from time to time."

"And you?" Gina asked. "Are you feeling it, too, Emma?"

"Maybe," she admitted. "Just a little. Being here is good for Caitlyn. I can't deny that. And Denver is a rat race for me, no question about it."

"Then you have been thinking about staying," Gina concluded.

"Not thinking about it, not consciously, anyway. But the possibility is just there. I can't ignore it forever," she said with a sigh, then shook her head. "But we're talking about you now. I just want you to be sure you understand why you've stayed here, rather than go back to New York to kick butt and settle all of this weeks ago. *That's* what I would have expected you to do."

"Are you saying I've been acting like a coward?"

"I'm not making any judgments. You have to figure out what you really want before you make a final decision about how you want me to handle this."

Gina nodded. "You're right. I'll think about it and I'll call you before you head back to Denver."

"Take your time. I'm actually thinking about sticking around all week."

"Oh, really? Does Ford Hamilton have anything to do with that?"

"Don't be ridiculous," Emma snapped impatiently. "It's for Caitlyn. And because this case of Sue Ellen's I'm working on is getting closer to trial. I have witnesses to depose and a ton of last-minute details to handle right here."

Gina grinned. "Whatever you say."

"That's the truth."

"Maybe you should do some thinking over the weekend, too," Gina teased. "Maybe I'm not the only one whose feelings are ambivalent these days."

Emma scowled at her. "Keep it up and I'll charge you my regular fee."

Gina shuddered. "Then I really would go bankrupt." She bent down and kissed Emma's cheek. "Thanks, sweetie. I'll call you."

Emma waved, then called out just as Gina was about to get in her car. "By the way, one piece of advice for right now—steer clear of Rafe. No matter what he says about being after Bobby, not you, you can't trust him. From now on he needs to go through me."

"I don't think that's going to work," Gina told her, thinking of the way her relationship with Rafe was progressing and just how badly she wanted it to wind up in bed.

"Why not?"

"Because we're just a little bit beyond needing an intermediary."

Emma's eyes widened. "Please tell me you're not sleeping with him."

"I'm not sleeping with him," Gina told her solemnly. "More's the pity. But I'm definitely hoping that will change."

"Are you nuts?" Emma demanded.

"Nope. For the first time in a long time, I'm finally going after something I want. I'm paying some attention to my personal life."

"Do you want Rafe more than you want Café Tuscany? Because that's what this could come down to," Emma warned.

Her vehemence took Gina by surprise, but it didn't scare her the way Emma had obviously intended it to. That was just one more thing she was going to have to think about over the weekend.

Rafe was hunkered down in his room going through a pile of papers that Lydia had faxed to him just that morning. It seemed he was destined to run his law practice from a Winding River hotel for the foreseeable future. He was so caught up in his work that the pounding on his door startled him. Finding Emma Rogers on his doorstep startled him even more.

"This is a surprise," he said.

"Yes, I imagine it is," she said, her expression as fierce as her tone. "I imagine you thought you could try all sorts of sneaky tactics to get what you wanted from Gina and no one would call you on it, but I'm here to tell you otherwise."

"I have no idea what you're talking about. Why don't you come in and explain it."

She stepped into the room, took note of the piles of paperwork. "Working on the Café Tuscany case, are you?"

Rafe sighed. "Gina told you."

"She told me everything. I'm now representing her."

"Good."

She blinked at that. "Good?" she said, sounding ever-so-slightly more hesitant.

"She needs a strong advocate. Obviously, I can't be that for her."

"I'm glad you understand a little bit about ethics. I was beginning to think you were totally clueless."

He regarded Emma curiously. "What exactly has Gina been telling you?"

"I'm not at liberty to discuss that."

"And I'm not asking for details about Café Tuscany's financial mess. I'm asking you what she's told you about the two of us."

Emma seemed to be weighing the ethics of saying anything about that, as well. "Enough that I suspect you're crossing the line," she said finally.

"Did she say anything about objecting?"

"That's beside the point. It's wrong. You have to know that. Go back to New York, Rafe. You'll be contacted by an attorney there. Gina will come in and answer all your questions, and we'll get this mess straightened out."

"I'm not convinced Gina has any answers to my questions," he said.

"Then what are you still doing here?" she demanded.

"Bobby Rinaldi has all the answers. He's been in touch with Gina once. I imagine he will be again. Why don't you convince her to let us tap her phone or, at the very least, hook up a caller ID?"

"I'll discuss it with her."

"I've already mentioned it. She refused."

Emma's expression turned thoughtful. "I imagine she doesn't want her parents involved."

"So she said, but the bottom line is, the longer she stays with them, the more likely they are going to get drawn into this. Bobby will call there again. If her mother answers, I imagine he'll get an earful. Gina says her mother's fit to be tied and ready to tell him just that. Her father, however, doesn't know a thing, and she wants it to stay that way."

"Maybe I can convince her to get her own place and her own phone, at least temporarily," Emma said slowly. "I know she wants to locate Bobby as badly as you do. If he thinks she's giving up on New York and settling here, he might even risk a visit. He owes her an explanation, if nothing else."

Rafe nodded. "That was my thinking."

"I'll talk to her," Emma promised.

Rafe glanced out the window. "Now would be a good time. Here she comes." He stood up and opened the door. "Come on in and join the party." Once she was inside, he retreated to the chair beside the desk. He had a feeling anyplace else would put him right in the line of fire. The two women were scowling at each other.

"What are you doing here?" Gina demanded.

At the same moment Emma chided, "I thought I told you to stay away from Rafe."

Gina shrugged. "I told you that wasn't going to work."

Emma looked from Gina to Rafe and back, then sighed. "Okay, here's a suggestion," she said to Rafe. "I'll make a deal with you. If you promise her immunity from all prosecution on this, she can help you catch Bobby. And I want it in writing."

"Done," Rafe said.

Emma looked at Gina. "Okay with you?"

"We won't be on opposing sides anymore?" Gina asked, her gaze locked with Rafe's.

"No. We'll be partners," he said.

A smile broke slowly and spread across her face. "Done," she agreed at once.

"If you decide to stay in Winding River for the time being, I also think you should consider getting your own place, at least temporarily," Emma said. "Unless you want to put some kind of wiretap or caller ID on the phone at your parents' place."

"I don't want them dragged into this," Gina said. "I think moving into my own place makes a lot of sense. In fact, I'm pretty sure the room next to this one is available." She glanced toward the wall and grinned. "It even has a connecting door. How handy."

Rafe groaned. "Now, Gina, we've talked about this. Nothing's changed."

"Sure it has. We're partners now. Where you go, I go, right?"

Emma moaned. "I'm out of here. I'll leave you two to work out the details. Rafe, I'll expect that agreement by the end of the day." She gave Gina a stern look. "Until I have it, could the two of you try to keep your hands to yourselves?"

"Not a problem," Rafe insisted, shoving his hands in his pockets.

But as adamant as he was, he wasn't so sure about Gina. That gleam in her eyes suggested she was not above creating a little mischief just to test his resolve. In fact, right this second she was regarding him a little too cheerfully.

"This is an interesting turn of events, isn't it?" she commented after Emma had gone.

"I suppose that depends on your point of view," he responded cautiously.

"Well, from my point of view what could be better than getting all those nasty suspicions cleared up? Now we're free to do whatever we want to do."

"Oh, really? Exactly how do you see this partnership progressing?"

"Well, for starters, you could stop lurking back there in the corner and come over here."

"Why would I want to do that?"

"So we can properly seal this deal."

He chuckled at that. "I think Emma would recommend a signed document for that."

Gina shrugged. "Emma has her way of doing things. I have mine." Her grin turned wicked. "I think you'll like my way better."

Heat shot through him. "I'm sure I would, but it's still a bad idea. Sex can really complicate a business relationship."

Her expression turned thoughtful. "Is that what we have now, a business relationship?"

"Exactly."

"That's not entirely how I see it," she said, taking a few steps in his direction.

Rafe began to feel crowded. His resolve was starting to waver. "Oh?" he said, his voice husky.

"Want to know how I see it?"

He had a feeling he'd better know exactly what was going on in that complicated brain of hers. "Sure."

She slid onto his lap and wound her arms around his neck. "The way I see it we've been given a fresh start. We're on the same side. We're partners. And for partners to work together successfully, they should know each other very, very well. You might even say, they should know each other—" her gaze locked with his "—intimately."

Rafe's breath caught in his throat as her hands slipped to his chest. She began to work the buttons of his shirt free. Each time her knuckles skimmed across bare skin, a shock jolted through him. He caught her hands and held them still as he met her gaze.

"That agreement isn't drawn up and signed yet," he reminded her.

"That's okay. I trust you."

"Do you? Emma would advise you against that."

"What does she know?"

"Quite a lot, as it happens. You hired her, didn't you? She's looking out for your best interests. You should pay attention to her."

"I'd rather pay attention to you right now."

Before he could stop her, her wickedly clever mouth settled on his. In no time at all she had his thinking muddled and his breath hitching. When the kiss ended, his resolve was in tatters, but he made one last valiant attempt to make her see reason.

Gina merely smiled knowingly and framed his face in her hands. "You have every intention of drawing up that document and granting me immunity, correct?"

"Yes, but—"

"That's all I need to know. I *trust* you." Her gaze narrowed ever so slightly. "Or is that not the problem? Do you not trust me? Do you still think I could be involved in this with Bobby? Do you think this is some ploy on my part to keep an eye on you, so I can report what you've been up to?"

"Absolutely not. I wouldn't have made the agreement with Emma, if I believed that," he assured her.

Her smile returned. "Then we don't have a problem, do we?"

Rafe gave up the battle. "Actually we do," he told her.

She regarded him with a resigned expression. "What now?"

"You have way too many clothes on, Ms. Petrillo."

It took a moment for his words to register, but when they did, her expression brightened. "If only all of our problems could be solved so easily," she said.

She reached for the hem of her T-shirt, but Rafe stilled her hands. "In good time, Gina. In good time."

This time when his mouth found hers, there was no hesitation, no restraint, just a slow, sweet, savoring kiss that rocked him like nothing had in years. Knowing that this time there would be no pulling back gave him permission to take his time and enjoy the trip. This time the final destination was never in doubt.

11

Rafe made love just exactly the way Gina had imagined he would, with total concentration and the kind of raw passion that had been missing from her life. His mouth was hot and clever, but his hands were positively wicked. Long, lazy caresses alternated with skimming, intimate touches that made her crave more. He did things to her breasts that made her cry out and arch toward him, pleading for him not to stop.

And then he skimmed away her sensible cotton panties and began yet another wicked exploration that had her writhing and begging for release.

"Not just yet," he whispered, his breath cool against the bare skin of her sensitive inner thigh.

He began a whole new assault of kisses that roved from stomach to ankle to toes and back again, until he reached the juncture of her thighs. When he touched her with his tongue, she came apart in a shuddering release.

Clutching his shoulders, she came slowly back to earth, then met his smoldering gaze. She felt a need to say something, to explain how devastating, how incredible the experience had been. "That was—"

"Just the beginning," he said, cutting off her words with a kiss that sent her senses soaring once more.

Her body was straining yet again by the time his gaze locked with hers. Poised above her, he reminded her of a proud warrior, a little arrogant, a lot masculine. She hadn't thought it was possible to want more than he'd already given her, but she did. Anticipation and yearning coupled with a building heat as he finally, at long last, entered her.

The sensation, the hard, slick slide of his arousal deep inside her took her breath away. But just beyond that incredible moment of satisfaction there was a hunger for more, a hunger that began with a sense of loss as he withdrew, then deepened as he entered her again.

The rhythm, as old as time, but new to her with this man became a torment and a pleasure. Rafe added nuances she'd never imagined, slow, fast, then slow again, teasing her, streaking toward a peak, then carrying her down, lulling her, before finally taking her to an impossible height, one that had every part of her at a fever pitch, demanding release, reaching for it.

They tumbled over the edge together, panting, clinging together, crying out in unison.

When the waves of pleasure had stilled, when heated flesh began to cool, she sighed deeply and buried her head against his neck. Then, cradled in his arms, feeling safer than she had in months, maybe even years, she slept. The very last thing on her mind was the future and what it might hold.

Rafe was a little awed, more than a little panicked by what had just happened between him and the woman who was curled so trustingly against him. He was not a man prone to making impulsive decisions. His relationships, such as they were, tended to be simple. He was definitely not a man who thought in terms of forever.

But here he was, completely sated and drained from making love with a woman who had impulsively thrown herself at him, who was about as complicated as anyone he'd ever met and who was definitely all about forever. How the hell had this happened?

Okay, he knew how it had happened. He'd been thinking about Gina in this way for weeks now. Maybe not from the moment they'd met, but certainly from the first time they'd kissed. Once the ethical barrier to pursuing a relationship had been lifted by that agreement he'd made earlier with Emma, he'd been all too susceptible.

He sighed and shifted until she was cradled even more tightly against him. Never one to transfer the blame for something to someone else when his own role was perfectly evident, he forced himself to accept responsibility for what had just happened. Gina might have initiated things, but he'd been an eager participant.

All of which begged the question, what now? If he had a functioning brain cell left, he'd leave the pursuit of Bobby Rinaldi in Emma's capable hands and hightail it back to New York and his other clients. Sticking around Winding River and carrying on a fling with Gina was a dead-end road for both of them. She would realize it once the initial physical attraction wore off. What was the expression? Their relationship was definitely too hot not to cool down. That was certainly his experience. Even relationships based on more than he and Gina had in common eventually burned themselves out. His mother's certainly had. In fact, he predicted that after today, now that he and Gina had tasted what had previously been forbidden, the attraction would be well on its way to dying.

He glanced at her, took in the rosy cheeks, the lush curve of breast and hip, the dark cloud of tousled hair, the thoroughly kissable mouth. His body stirred with all the urgency he had felt not a half hour before.

So much for diminishing attraction, he thought as he ran his hand over petal-soft skin that smelled of citrus and ginger. Her nipple peaked to a hard bud against his palm. She shifted restlessly as his caresses intensified and became bolder.

Then she was wide awake and moving against him, welcoming him, hips thrusting against hips, seeking, urgent. The heat climbed as he buried himself deep inside, withdrew, then sank into her again and again.

This time, she was the first to cry out, the first to reach a shuddering climax. As the waves washed through her, they set off his own explosion. Muscles bunched, strained, then relaxed into the demanding pleasure of it.

"Too much," she cried as their bodies mated with fierce intensity, arching together in another wild burst of sensation. Then, "More, please, more."

Her words were an echo of his reeling thoughts. Being with Gina was too much by far, and yet he knew, with soul-searing honesty, that he could never get enough.

When Gina woke from an exhausted sleep this time, there were no sneaky caresses teasing her awake. In fact she was in the king-size bed all alone. The sound of water running told her that Rafe was taking a shower.

His side of the vast mattress was cool to her touch, suggesting that he'd been up for a while now.

It was dark outside. Inside, there was only the glow from beneath the bathroom door and a digital clock on a bedside stand to light the room.

Gina heard the water shut off, the sound of off-key humming, and grinned. What would he think if she slipped into the room and joined him? Oddly, she felt more uncertain about his reaction now than she might have hours ago.

She had seduced Rafe. There was no question in her mind about that. She had done precisely what she'd told Emma she intended to do. She had wanted something and she had gone after it.

What now, though? Was Rafe happy about the turn of events? She knew he had enjoyed the sex as much as she had, but beyond that? Had all those doubts of his crowded in again? Had he succumbed to all of the sensible, rational arguments that would have kept her out of his bed in the first place? Not knowing kept her right where she was, waiting, feeling more vulnerable than she had in years.

Not that she regretted anything, not one single, amazing second. But it would be nice to know where she stood, what she could expect when he emerged from behind that door. She watched it with the same trepidation a suspect might feel awaiting a jury's verdict. Even as she made the analogy, she cringed.

When Rafe eventually opened the door, her heart slammed against her ribs. He was wearing a pair of still-new jeans and nothing more. The snap was undone and the waistband rode low on his hips. No cowboy had ever looked sexier than this. Longer now than when he'd first arrived in Winding River, his hair was damp and tousled. She wished she dared to run her fingers through it to add to its surprising tendency to curl. She gave him a hesitant smile, which he was a little too slow to return. Her pulse skittered unsteadily.

"You're awake," he said, his tone cautious and surprisingly uncertain.

"So are you," she noted, forcing a teasing note into her voice.

Looking incredibly unsettled and awkward, he dropped down on the side of the bed. He lifted his hand as if he might caress her, but then let it drop to his thigh.

"Are you okay?" he asked, studying her intently.

"Of course. Why wouldn't I be?"

"I thought you might be having second thoughts."

Her gaze searched his. "Are you?"

"Hell, yes," he said fiercely, but his expression softened to take the sting out. "And if you were the least bit sensible, you'd be scared spitless, too."

She grinned at that. "I don't scare so easily."

"We really do have to talk about this, Gina."

"Why? We're two consenting adults. Why do we need to make a big deal out of something so natural?"

"Because—"

She frowned at him. "I will not talk this to death, Rafe. I will not regret it. If that's what you're hoping for, forget it."

"I don't want you to regret it. I just want you to realize that it can't go on."

"And why is that? Because you have decreed that it can't?"

"No, because it can't go anywhere."

She began to lose patience with his oh-so-reasonable tone. "Why can't it? And who said I wanted it to go anywhere, anyway?"

"Let's face it, Gina. You don't do this sort of thing."

"Have sex?"

"Have *casual* sex," he corrected.

"And that's all you have," she shot back. "Is that what you're trying to tell me?"

He winced at the charge, but he didn't deny it.

"Well, that's just dandy," she said, taking his silence for assent. "We're agreed. This is casual sex. If I agree to those terms, I assume you'll have no objections." She gathered the sheet around her, dragged it off the bed and marched into the bathroom, spine rigid, shoulders back. She shot one last heated look over her shoulder. "Since this is all so damned casual, I don't expect you to buy me dinner. Give me ten minutes and I'll be out of here and you can get back to that paperwork."

Then she slammed the bathroom door behind her.

The roar of the shower drowned out her hot, salty tears. At least, she hoped it did. And if Rafe had a single shred of decency in his body, he would be gone when she came out.

Instead, as she leaned against the wall of the shower and let her tears flow, the curtain was suddenly yanked back. Still in his jeans, Rafe stepped into the shower with her, his expression grim and determined. She was too shocked to react.

Rafe tucked a finger under her chin and forced her to meet his gaze. His thumb brushed futilely at the mix of streaming tears and flowing water from the pounding shower. "I'm sorry," he said, looking contrite.

"For what?"

"For upsetting you. I was just trying to make sure that we were on the same page. I wasn't trying to diminish what had happened."

"But you did," she said, her voice catching. "You made it seem cheap and tawdry and unimportant."

He sighed, gathering her close. "It was anything but that. In fact, that's the problem. You caught me off guard. I never expected to feel so much, to want so much, especially with things so uncertain."

"What things? I thought everything between you and me was finally straightforward. You want Bobby. I agreed to help you in any way I can."

"It's more than that, Gina. You have to see that."

"I don't," she insisted. "You'll have to explain it."

He pushed wet strands of hair back from her face, a smile tugging at his lips. "You want an explanation here? Now?"

"You picked the place," she pointed out.

"But there are so many more interesting things we could be doing," he said, his gaze drifting from mouth to breasts, then lower still.

Gina could see the hard bulge of his arousal pressing against soaking wet denim. When he ran a finger along the curve of her breast, then skimmed a nail across the peak, she shuddered. Desire, hot and urgent, slammed through her once more. All thoughts of resolving their differences fled as she reached for the zipper on his jeans, slid it slowly down, then took the hard thrust of his arousal in her hand.

Rafe moaned, then lifted her until she could straddle him, her back braced against the wall. There, with the shower cascading over them like a waterfall, their bodies slick and hot and hungry, they streaked toward a violent, earth-shattering climax that left them panting and clinging together.

When they could move again, when they had caught their breath, Rafe lowered her to unsteady legs, then reached for the soap and gently washed her. Then he cut off the water, reached for a towel and dried first her, then himself.

"Now then," he said, his tone sounding deliberately casual. "What do you say we get dressed and go get some dinner?"

Gina knew what he was doing. He wanted to get them onto neutral turf before renewing the discussion of the future.

"I could call Tony's and have a pizza delivered right here," she suggested.

"Bad idea," he said at once.

"Why?"

"I seem to be having trouble keeping my hands to myself."

She regarded him with amusement. "And that's a problem because…?"

"Because I'm starving and you must be, too."

"A pizza would solve that," she said.

"So would a nice, quiet dinner in a restaurant where we'd be obligated to behave ourselves. We could have a little wine, a little pleasant conversation."

"Why do I think that the conversation you have in mind will be anything but pleasant?"

His jaw set stubbornly. "Gina—"

"Okay, say I agree to go out, will you agree not to bring up our relationship?"

He seemed to be torn, but he finally nodded.

"And no mention of Bobby?"

"Okay," he agreed with obvious reluctance. "What's left?"

She patted his cheek. "I'm sure we'll think of something. If not, we'll invite Tony and Francesca to join us. You can help me convince him to take her to Italy while I cover things here for him."

Rafe paused in pulling on a clean shirt to stare at her. "You're talking temporarily, right?"

"Yes. Why the resigned look?"

"Because I was hoping that now that we have this agreement, you'd be ready to go back to New York."

"If you're anxious to go home, go," she said, though her heart felt suddenly empty at the prospect of him leaving. "Emma or I will keep you posted if Bobby turns up."

Rafe shook his head. "Not that I don't trust you, but I'll feel better if I'm around to keep a close eye on you."

Something in his voice alarmed her. "Because you still don't trust me?"

"No, because we have no way of knowing whether Bobby took that money because he's desperate for some reason."

"Desperate? What on earth do you mean?"

"If he's gotten himself mixed up in something bad, something like gambling debts or big-time drug deals, he could be in danger. I don't want him dragging you into that."

The thought of there being any actual danger in all of this had never occurred to Gina. The prospect of losing Café Tuscany had been daunting enough.

"Surely, if there were any danger, he would warn me," she said slowly but without much conviction. After all, if Bobby had been concerned about her at all, he would never have put her in this position in the first place.

"We can't be sure of that," Rafe said, his expression grim.

He brushed a finger across her forehead. "Don't look so worried. I am not going to let anything happen to you."

He held out his hand. "Let's go. I recommend a big plate of pasta and some wine."

Gina sighed. Normally that was a prescription she would recommend herself. Tonight, though, she had a feeling it was going to take a whole lot more to chase away the sudden butterflies in her stomach.

She was still unnerved when they reached Tony's. Peg Lafferty, who'd been with Tony since he opened, led them to a table near the kitchen. "I know Tony's going to be running in and out to talk to you, so this will be more convenient."

"Where's Francesca tonight?" Gina asked.

"Home. She's not feeling well."

"What's wrong? Do you know?"

"I'm not sure," Peggy said, her expression filled with concern. "She's been staying home a lot lately. Tony doesn't talk much about it, and I haven't wanted to pry."

He hadn't said anything to Gina, either, but she had none of Peggy's reticence about prying. She intended to get to the bottom of this. "Tell him I'm here, okay?"

"Will do," Peggy promised. "Everyone's eating late tonight, it seems. He's got a half dozen orders going right now, but he'll be out soon. Can I bring you a bottle of Chianti while you look over the menu?"

"Chianti would be good," Rafe told her. When she

had gone, he regarded Gina with concern. "Don't start taking what she said and exaggerating it in your head. Francesca may be perfectly fine. She might just be taking some time off."

"You don't know her. She doesn't take time off, not willingly." She started to stand up. "Maybe I should go over there to check on her."

Rafe tugged her back down. "Maybe you should wait and let Tony answer your questions before you go charging over to see her."

"These are my friends," she said, "not yours."

"That doesn't make my advice any less sensible," he said mildly.

Gina sighed and relented. "You're probably right. I'm probably making a mountain out of a molehill. Tony would have told me if it was anything serious."

"Exactly," he said just as Peggy returned with the wine and a promise that Tony would join them shortly.

"Do you want to order before that?" she asked.

"No," Gina said at once. "I want answers before I want food."

"Speak for yourself," Rafe said. "How about a plate of antipasto for the time being?"

"You've got it," Peggy said, then went off to check on another group of late arrivals.

When the antipasto arrived, Gina realized that she was ravenous. Since there was nothing she could do until Tony emerged from the kitchen, anyway, she picked up a carrot stick, then a stalk of celery, then reached for the warm garlic bread that Peggy had brought with it. Rafe watched her approvingly.

"That's better," he said at last. "You've got some color back in your cheeks. I was worried there for a bit. This tendency of yours to take on everyone else's problems is not a good thing."

"These are my friends," she said defensively. "What would you have me do?"

He sighed. "I imagine telling you to maintain a little distance would be a waste of my breath."

She studied his expression, trying to gauge if he was actually serious. "Can you do that? Can you maintain a nice, safe distance when your friends are in trouble?"

Her question seemed to catch him off guard. "Truthfully, there are not that many people I consider friends."

Gina stared at him. "Surely you can't mean that."

"It's true. I have business acquaintances. There are dozens of people at my law firm who are colleagues, but friends? People I'd call up just to go out and have a drink for the fun of it? I haven't had the time."

"But that's awful," she said without thinking about her own barren social life in New York. Was she any better? "Everyone should have friends, people they can count on, people they would go the extra mile for without question."

"Well, I don't."

"Do you expect me to believe that there is no one important in your life?"

"That's the truth."

"What about your mother? You said you jumped into this case because of her," she said triumphantly. "You must care about her."

"I don't like to see anyone swindled. *That's* why I took the case."

"I don't believe you."

"It's true."

Before she could probe any deeper, they were joined

by Tony, who looked more tired than she had ever seen him. Rafe looked relieved to have her attention shifting away from him and on to Tony, but she had no intention of forgetting about his admission that there was no one in his life who really mattered to him.

"Are you okay?" Gina asked Tony.

"It's been a busy night. That's all," Tony said.

"Have you eaten?"

"I haven't had the time."

Gina jumped up. "Then you sit right here. I'm going to fix something for all of us. And if anyone else comes in, I'll handle it. Have a glass of wine. Talk to Rafe. Relax."

Tony patted her hand. "You're a good girl, *cara mia*."

"And a better cook," she reminded him with a grin. "I'll make you two a meal that will make you weep."

Rafe started to protest, but Gina silenced him with a look. "I need to do this," she said quietly. "It won't take long."

"It will take as long as it takes," Tony chided, his expression stern. "Good food cannot be rushed."

Gina pressed a kiss to his pale cheek. "Advice from the master," she teased, managing to keep a smile plastered firmly on her face as she left the two men to their wine and their conversation.

But once she reached the kitchen, she sagged against the door. Something was terribly wrong. Suddenly her own problems with Bobby, her confusion over her relationship with Rafe, none of it mattered. How sad that Rafe didn't understand the meaning of such deep and abiding friendships.

But maybe, once she'd dealt with whatever was

going on with Tony and Francesca, once Karen's life was settled again, maybe then she could take the time to teach him.

12

Rafe studied Tony's tired face and concluded that Gina was right to be concerned. He might not know the man well, but there was a general air of despondency about him that was unmistakable even to him.

"Gina's worried about you," he said.

"And I am worried for her," Tony responded. "The longer this business with her partner drags on, the sadder she becomes. I don't like it. If I knew this man, I would wring his neck myself."

"Join the club," Rafe said, though he chafed at Tony's evasive change of topic. Apparently, he really was lousy at this friendship thing. Surely a man with his skills at cross-examination should have been able to get a direct response. He considered his words, realized then that unlike his courtroom style, he'd made a statement, rather than asking a probing question. It seemed like he was even out of practice at being a decent lawyer.

"But I wasn't really talking about Gina. I was asking about you. Is everything okay?" he asked more pointedly. "Peggy said something earlier about your wife that made Gina conclude that she might not be well."

If anything, Tony looked even more dispirited. "Francesca grows more homesick day by day. Her only sister, who lives in Rome, is not well. Francesca wishes she were there with her, but she refuses to go back to Italy alone, and I cannot simply close the business and leave."

"There is a solution," Rafe said thoughtfully, hating himself for even thinking of it, much less voicing it. He needed to get back to New York one of these days, though amazingly the pressure seemed to lessen with every day he spent right here in Wyoming with Gina. He was beginning to adapt to the slower pace and friendlier lifestyle. And except for court, he was able to keep up with most of his work. Lydia kept his fax machine humming, and what was too lengthy and complicated to be faxed she shipped overnight.

"Oh?" Tony said, his expression brightening hopefully. "What solution?"

"Let Gina take over. She's insistent on staying here for the time being because of her friend Karen. It would give her something to do."

Tony seemed startled by the suggestion. "Were you not the one who warned me not to expect her to work here again?"

"I meant permanently," Rafe said, then shrugged. "Who knows, though? Maybe I was wrong about that, as well. Gina is not an easy woman to read."

Tony looked shocked by the assessment. "Gina? She wears her heart on her sleeve. Anyone who knows her can see that."

"Then maybe I don't know her as well as I thought."

"Or perhaps as well as you would like to?" Tony

inquired, looking amused. "Or is it that what you see terrifies you, so you pretend not to see it?"

Rafe glanced toward the kitchen, hoping to catch a glimpse of the woman in question, but the door remained steadfastly closed. "It's possible that you're right," he admitted, turning back to Tony. "Maybe I do see things that scare me, even though a part of me wants what she wants."

"This is a good thing," Tony said enthusiastically. "I am very pleased. Admitting what you want is always the first step."

"First step to what?" Rafe asked.

"The future." He grinned. "Now, what would you like to know about our Gina? Ask, and I will tell you."

His sudden openness startled Rafe. "Why the change of heart? You've been refusing to discuss her with me before now."

Tony's amusement seemed to grow. "Because you have changed. As has your reason for being here, I suspect. Now, tell me, what is it about Gina that you do not understand?"

Rafe asked the first thing that came to mind. "Is she a good chef?"

"Of all the things you might have asked, that is what you pick?" Tony said with a sad shake of his head. "Perhaps I was wrong about you, after all. I was expecting something personal."

"I thought cooking was personal to her. It's what she does."

"Yes," Tony agreed. "But not who she is. Besides, I cannot believe you have never eaten in her restaurant."

"Never, though my business associates dine there

all the time." Rafe thought of Lydia and added, "And my secretary loves the place."

"Because Gina has a passion for food. She understands it. She knows what will add to a meal and what will distract. She shares all of that when she cooks."

"Then why hasn't she fought harder to keep Café Tuscany afloat? I know she came here for that reunion, but I thought she would go back at once and charge into battle to save the restaurant. Instead, there have been times when I've had to wonder if she even cares whether it closes or not."

Tony looked shocked by Rafe's assessment. "You are wrong," he said fiercely. "She cares, too much perhaps. She has tried to distance herself, I think, out of fear. She is trying not to let it matter, in case she is not able to keep it open."

When Rafe would have responded, Tony stopped him with a sign. "Wait, there is more. There is one thing that matters more to Gina than food."

"Her friends," Rafe guessed.

Tony gave a curt nod of satisfaction. "Precisely. And can you see how that has affected what she's done these past weeks? She has taken their burdens as her own, but she has not shared hers with them."

"And she has stayed on because she cares about her friend Karen," Rafe said slowly. "She will stay on longer because of you and Francesca. If there is another friend with another crisis, she will extend her stay yet again."

"True, but it is more than that. She has stayed because a man she trusted, a man she believed in and counted on, betrayed her. Bobby Rinaldi is a criminal to you, but to Gina he was a friend. Think about that," Tony said quietly. "I will go and get us another bottle of wine."

He left Rafe feeling shaken. Not once had he stopped to consider the impact Bobby's actions would have had on Gina emotionally. He'd thought only in terms of dollars and cents, only in terms of the business, not the friendship, quite likely because he had never established such deep ties to another person.

Of course Gina had been devastated. To the woman Tony had described—the woman Rafe was only beginning to know—losing a friend would be far worse than losing a restaurant.

Rafe wasn't entirely sure he could understand that depth of feeling for another person. He didn't profess to understand love, either, and this was something altogether different, something he'd always assumed would be less intense, less demanding.

In his world, there were no messy, emotional connections. No long-term lovers. As he had explained to Gina, there were colleagues, business associates, casual acquaintances. Even his relationship with his mother was coolly polite, rather than loving. He'd grown too jaded over the years, first by watching his parents' marriage disintegrate, later by watching criminals—and yes, his colleagues, too—manipulate the legal system.

But when he thought of the way Lauren had rushed to Gina's defense while knowing none of the facts, when he considered how Emma was prepared to staunchly defend Gina, he could see that there were people in the world to whom loyalty and friendship were more than mere words.

A part of him wanted that kind of closeness to another human being—to Gina—but he was afraid to risk it. People who made commitments risked betrayal and hurt. He had only to look at what Bobby had done to Gina to see that.

And yet never, not even once, had he had the sense that Gina regretted her friendship with Rinaldi, only that it had come to this tragic end. Though she had never said the words, he realized that was also why she had been so slow to join forces with him, so reluctant to leap to her own defense and throw Bobby to the wolves. She hadn't been ready to give up on her friend.

Rafe wondered wistfully what it would be like to be deserving of that kind of loyalty. Bobby certainly wasn't. Was Rafe? He thought of what could still happen to take Café Tuscany away from Gina. He had set those wheels in motion with his suit against the restaurant and Rinaldi. Would Gina ultimately blame him for that, especially if it cost her the business she had poured her heart and soul into? Would she hate him for it? Or would she understand and forgive?

Time would tell, he supposed, then he shuddered at the thought. It implied far more patience than he had. But what choice did he have? None. Professionally and personally, he was going to have to see this through on whatever timetable it took. He tried to see beyond that to the future, but to his frustration it was disturbingly blank.

"Sorry I took so long," Gina said, sliding a plate of steaming lasagna in front of him. "This is Francesca's favorite, and it took a while to get all the ingredients together. I sent some home to her with Tony."

"Did he tell you about her homesickness?" he asked,

amazingly unsurprised that Gina had thought of preparing Francesca's favorite dish.

She nodded. "I told him to take her to Italy, that I would cover for him."

Rafe grinned, pleased that his estimation of her reaction had been proved right. "I told him you would do that."

She regarded him with surprise. "Did you? Do you approve, especially since it means another delay in getting back to New York?"

"You weren't prepared to go anytime soon, anyway. I'd accepted that."

"But you're not happy about it, are you?"

He lifted her hand and pressed a kiss to her knuckles. "Sticking around here for the time being is who you are. Since I seem to like who you are more and more, how can I possibly argue with your decision?"

"A wise man," she said approvingly.

"Not so wise," he said, tucking her hand against his thigh. "But I'm getting there."

There were a half dozen messages for Rafe when he returned to his hotel room. He checked them while Gina retreated to her own room next door, the room she had insisted on booking even after he'd said she could stay with him.

"Not here, where my parents will hear about it," she had told him.

"Do you honestly think being next door will be much of an improvement? People will draw whatever conclusions they want anyway."

"Maybe so, but at least I can tell them that we are not living together in plain sight of all their neighbors."

He'd been forced to accept her reasoning. At the moment he was grateful since two of the messages were from Lydia, who sounded increasingly amused by the fact that he was still in Winding River. Calling her back with Gina in the room would have been a test of his ability to lie with a straight face.

Another message was from his paralegal, Joan Lansing, and one was from his investigator reporting that there was a trail suggesting Bobby Rinaldi might be in the Cayman Islands.

"Let me know what you want me to do," the man concluded. "I could use a free trip down there. I have some scuba gear I've been dying to try out."

Rafe glanced up at the end of the message and saw Gina staring at him, her expression frozen.

"Bobby's in the Cayman Islands?" she asked, looking oddly shaken.

"Could be."

"Are you sending that man after him?"

Rafe couldn't read her tone at all. "What do you want me to do?"

She blinked in surprise. "You're asking me?"

"That's what it sounded like," he said lightly. "What do you want, Gina? Do you want him caught? Do you want all of this resolved once and for all?"

"Of course I want him caught," she snapped, then sighed. "Then again, a part of me keeps trying to pretend he's down there on some impromptu vacation and that he'll come back on his own."

"You know him better than I do," Rafe said. "Is there a chance of that?"

For a long time he thought she might not answer.

There was no mistaking the misery in her eyes, the uncertainty.

"I don't know," she whispered at last. "I honestly don't think I ever knew him at all."

Thinking of what Tony had said earlier, Rafe told her, "I know I accused you of lousy judgment in going into a partnership with him, but what happened isn't your fault. You saw what he wanted you to see, a charming man who was good at getting people to trust him, good at finding backers for the restaurant. You're not the only person he took in, sweetheart. My mother is older and should be wiser, but she trusted him. So did many others, many of them supposedly savvy businessmen."

His words didn't seem to console her. She stared at him bleakly. "What do I do, Rafe?"

"Do you want Café Tuscany?"

"Yes," she said at once.

"Enough to go back right now and fight for it?"

Her expression faltered at that. "I can't. Karen, Tony, they're depending on me."

"They would understand," he said, knowing it was true of Tony and just as certain that Karen, whom he barely knew, would feel the same way because she loved Gina, as did all her other friends.

"I suppose. But this trip is so important to Francesca. I can't go back on my word."

He studied her intently. "And there's a part of you that's happy here, isn't there?" he asked with sudden insight. "There's a part of you that is glad to have the chance to cook for friends and family, rather than anonymous strangers."

"I hadn't really thought about it, but yes," she said

slowly. "I'm looking forward to being back in Tony's kitchen, to having time, even on a busy night, to sit for a minute with my friends while they try some recipe I've been experimenting with."

"Do you think that feeling is just temporary?" he asked with an astonishing sense of dread.

"I honestly don't know. I only know that right now this is where I want to be, where I *have* to be."

"And Rinaldi?"

"Tell your man to find him. No matter what I decide for myself, the investors and our vendors need to be paid. We owe them that."

Rafe nodded. "I'll call the investigator right now."

He woke the man from a sound sleep, told him to book that trip to the Cayman Islands, but to leave his scuba gear at home. "You won't have time for it. Find Rinaldi. See if he still has any of the money. Then we'll see where we go next."

"If Bobby is there, can you force him to come back?" Gina asked after he'd hung up. "Isn't that one of the places with no extradition agreement with the United States?"

"Yes, but I'm sure he can be *enticed* back, one way or another. First things first. Let's make sure that's where he is."

"Will you stay here while you wait or will you go back to New York?"

He ought to go straight back to New York. There was no real reason to keep Gina under surveillance, certainly no reason he had to do it himself. But for a whole lot of very confusing and conflicting reasons, he wanted to stay right here.

"What do you want me to do?" he asked, unhappy

about this unexpected reluctance to leave. He'd come here a driven workaholic. He'd changed and he wasn't at all certain it was for the better.

Again Gina seemed startled that he was asking her preference. Then a smile spread slowly across her face. "Right now, I want you to forget about going anywhere and to come over here."

His heartbeat kicked up at the invitation in her eyes. "Oh? What did you have in mind?"

"If you don't know, then you're not half as brilliant as people think you are."

Rafe didn't hesitate. He took a few steps in her direction, but she met him halfway. When it came to being brilliant and clever, it turned out that Gina was no slouch herself. Her plans for the rest of the evening were far more innovative and satisfying than discussing the pros and cons of a return to New York. It also gave him a whole lot more to consider the next time the prospect of leaving Wyoming came up.

Gina was still half-asleep in Rafe's arms when the phone in her room rang. She leaped and ran to answer it. The sound of Bobby's voice snapped her awake.

"Bobby, where the hell are you?"

"If you think I'm going to tell you that, now that I know you've aligned yourself with the enemy, you're crazy."

"Why do you say that?"

"You're at the same hotel. Your parents told me where to find you. Are you sleeping with him?" he asked.

She ignored the question. "Why are you calling?"

"To tell you that chasing me down won't do you a bit of good. I'm safe."

"In the Caymans?" she asked.

From the other room she heard Rafe groan. She realized she had just given away their tactical advantage in finding Bobby.

"Why would you think I'm in the Caymans?" Bobby asked suspiciously. "You've got someone following me, haven't you?"

"Well, what did you expect?" she retorted, losing patience with him, with all of it. "You took off with the company money, ripped off our suppliers and investors. Of course you're being followed. If you have a grain of sense left in that pea brain of yours, you'll come home on your own and face the music before this gets any worse."

"It can't get any worse," he said. "Not back there, anyway. Down here I can live like a king."

She figured that was the final admission that they'd guessed right about where he was.

"Only if you can ignore your conscience," she said.

He laughed at that. "Not a problem."

"Just tell me one thing," she said. "Why did you do it? I thought we were friends."

"We were, doll. But friendship has its limits. In the end you have to look out for number one."

"That's a terrible way to live."

"No, that's the *only* way to live. Survival," he said succinctly. "That's what it's all about. Now, do me a favor."

"What? After everything you've done, you expect me to do you a favor?"

"Let's just say it's in your own best interests."

"Why is that?"

"If you call off whoever's tailing me, then I'll send you a little something to help pay off the debts. If business is still booming, you ought to be able to survive this little bump in the road. One day you might even thank me for turning a thriving business over to you."

"And if I don't?"

"You won't get a dime, and whoever shows up looking for me will run into some serious trouble down here. Gotta go, girl. You take care of yourself," he said, then laughed. "And I mean that sincerely. Nobody else will do it for you."

He hung up before she could respond. She was trembling when Rafe appeared and took the receiver from her hand. He replaced it, then took her in his arms.

"Are you okay? Come back to bed."

She went with him. "He threatened to do something to your investigator." She stared at Rafe, still struggling with shock at Bobby's cool demeanor and menacing threat. "He meant it, too. I could hear it in his voice. You need to call your man back."

"Flynn can take care of himself. He's dealt with bigger threats than Rinaldi. Did he confirm that he's in the Caymans?"

She nodded. "I had no idea he could be so cold, that he could be so totally self-involved."

"What else did he say?"

"That if I called off whoever was tailing him, he'd send me money to pay off some of the debts. He sounded as if that were such a magnanimous gesture on his part. He *owes* those people. He *owes* me."

Rafe chuckled.

"What's so damned funny?"

"It's good to see you getting angry," he said.

"I've been angry," she retorted.

"But not at Bobby," he suggested mildly.

"Of course I've been mad at Bobby," she said, confused by the suggestion.

Rafe shook his head. "Most of the time you've been mad at me."

She started to argue, then realized he was right. She'd been furious at Rafe for following her to Wyoming, for being suspicious of her, when it was Bobby who'd put her in that position.

She hadn't wanted to be mad at Bobby. She'd wanted to understand why her friend had done something so irresponsible, so criminal. She'd been upset by Rafe's distrust, because a part of her recognized that she should have been more suspicious of Bobby from the beginning. She'd seen how glib he could be, how little he took seriously. Maybe she should even have seen all of this coming.

"I was wrong," she said eventually. "You had no choice but to come after me, to keep an eye on me. I used terrible judgment, about Bobby, about running away, about everything."

He tucked a finger under her chin. "Hey, don't be so hard on yourself. The man's a con artist. He took you in, the same as he did everyone else."

Rafe's reassurances didn't soothe her at all. The only thing that helped when her mind was whirling was work. She left the warmth of Rafe's bed.

"I have to go."

"Where?"

"To Tony's. If you need me, you'll find me there."

"In the middle of the night?"

She shrugged as if the hour were unimportant. "I'll get some baking done for tomorrow."

To her relief, beyond that initial token protest, he didn't try to stop her.

Funny, she thought, as she raced through her shower, dressed and went to work. She was beginning to think that maybe Rafe understood her better after a few weeks than she understood herself after twenty-eight years.

13

"So, boss, are you ever coming back here?" Lydia inquired, her voice threaded with that superior amusement that Rafe found so annoying. "Not that I'm complaining, mind you. It's been really, really peaceful with you away, but the partners are beginning to ask whether you still work here. Your billable hours lately are the pits."

"Not so," Rafe protested, his gaze drifting to the bed with its tangle of sheets. Gina had left it far too soon last night, though after her conversation with Rinaldi, Rafe had understood her need to be alone, to bury herself in the kind of work that gave her solace.

"Then where are your billing records?" Lydia asked, snapping his attention back to the harsh reality of dollars and cents that for years now had controlled way too much of how he spent his time.

"I'll pull them together and fax them later today."

"They were due yesterday," she pointed out. "You're never late. Or at least you never were before you found a distraction like Gina Petrillo."

"I thought this was exactly what you wanted when you let her cancel that appointment. You did have an ulterior motive, didn't you? You wanted me to chase after her. You were hoping that I'd be attracted to her."

For a moment his comment was greeted with stunned silence. It wasn't often that Rafe could render Lydia speechless. He savored the moment.

"Are you saying what I think you're saying?" she asked eventually. "You're finally paying serious attention to someone?"

"I don't know how serious it is, but I am definitely paying attention," he admitted reluctantly.

"Well, hallelujah! Forget the billing report. I can do it myself."

"You cannot fake a billing report," he scolded.

"Of course not," she said indignantly. "But I ought to know how you've been spending your time—at least some of it. I am the one who sends your work out there and answers your phone and relays your messages. I'll bet I could come pretty darn close to getting it right."

Rafe decided to challenge her, though he was pretty sure she was right. Lydia was an extremely efficient woman who paid great attention to detail. "How many contracts do I have on my desk right now?"

"Thirty," she said at once. "I overnighted them to you yesterday. And you were on the phone at least three hours yesterday working on the Jackson-Waller electronics merger."

"Five," he retorted firmly. "Not three, five."

"Did you do any other work yesterday that I don't know about?"

"Not officially," he conceded. "I'm not billing my mother, remember?"

"Ah, so the rest of the time you were concentrating on Gina?" she said, managing to lace the suggestion with innuendo. "I guess we can't bill for *that,* can we?"

"You don't have to make it sound as if we were wrestling around naked in the mud."

"Is that how it sounded?" Lydia chuckled gleefully. "You sound a little defensive, boss. Why is that? Nobody expects you to put in twelve-hour days. There's nothing wrong with taking a little time out for dinner. Maybe a little socializing. Have you been doing more than that? Is your conscience bothering you?"

"Don't smart-mouth me," he grumbled.

"So, tell me," she began in a confiding tone that sounded a bit like a reporter for some sleazy tabloid, "have you slept with Gina yet?"

He wasn't nearly as shocked by the question as he probably should have been, but he absolutely, positively refused to be drawn into that particular discussion. He ignored the question and remained stubbornly silent.

"Not talking, huh?" Lydia said smugly. "I guess I can draw my own conclusions."

"Just keep your theories to yourself. And get me the file on the Whitney case. I'll need it in the morning. Joel Whitney—"

Lydia interrupted. "Mr. Whitney called yesterday with one of his usual inane questions that he could have answered himself if he knew how to read the contracts he signed. I've already put it in the mail."

Rafe laughed. "Okay, okay, you're the best secretary in the entire universe."

"Yes, I am," she agreed with no hint of false modesty. "You know, though, these expenses for moving every piece of paper in your office from New York to Wyoming are adding up. Ever thought of just staying there and transferring all the files? A moving van might be cheaper in the long run. And I hear Wyoming is great for skiing in the winter."

"I don't ski. Why would I want to stay in Wyoming?"

"Because of a certain chef."

"Who owns a restaurant in New York," he reminded her, vaguely disgruntled by the suggestion that he might be stuck in Wyoming forever if he wanted to be with Gina. "She'll be back, Lydia. So will I."

"Whatever you say, boss."

Rafe seriously doubted that, but he hung up, grateful to have gotten the woman's docile cooperation just this once, even if it had been feigned.

He leaned back in his chair and stared out the window. Summer was winding down. The observation startled him. He'd been here way too long, if he could tell just from glancing outside that the seasons were changing. The slant of the sun was different, the intensity of the heat had lessened. He opened his appointment book, looked at a calendar and realized he'd been here for over two months, from the end of June to the beginning of September. Moreover, he hadn't gone completely stir crazy. Far from it.

He looked at that pile of contracts sitting on his desk, weighed those against the chance to catch a glimpse of Gina and stood up. To soothe his guilty conscience, he stuffed several contracts in his briefcase and headed for Tony's. If there wasn't a law against working away from New York, then there certainly wasn't one preventing him from working at a restaurant table. Half the lawyers he knew conducted their business over lunch. Of course, most of them were with their clients or an opposing counsel.

The only companion he was hoping for was Gina.

* * *

Gina was so exhausted from her overnight work-a-thon she could barely see straight and the lunch hours were just getting started. Fortunately, most weekdays Tony's was fairly slow at midday. A few people came in for pizza, a few for his stromboli or meatball sandwiches, but the real rush didn't start till evening. The prospect of sneaking back to the hotel for a nap was the only thing keeping her going.

She was sitting at the island which doubled as a chopping block, her chin resting in her hands, her eyes half-closed, when Peggy came in to announce that Rafe was in the dining room.

"He wants to see you, if you're not too busy," she told Gina. "Since there's not another paying customer in the place yet, I told him you'd be right out."

For a moment Gina's heart leaped at the prospect of seeing Rafe, but during the long night when she'd been baking cannoli shells and preparing tiramisu for today's dessert specials, she'd spent a lot of time thinking about their relationship. She'd managed to convince herself it was doomed.

When she got back to New York—if she went back to New York—she was going to be faced with long hours and an uphill struggle to get Café Tuscany back into the black. She already knew that Rafe had been a workaholic. Neither of them would have ten seconds to spare once they resumed their old routines.

Relationships required nurturing. In the distant past that had been something at which she had excelled. In recent years she hadn't had time for it, not until she'd come back to Wyoming and inadvertently found her priorities shifting back to the way they had once been.

Despite the turmoil of recent weeks, her life felt more balanced now. She could actually envision a time when she might be perfectly contented to work right here, alongside Tony, surrounded by the people who meant the most to her—her family and friends. When she tried to add Rafe to that image, she couldn't.

She glanced up and realized Peggy was regarding her with puzzlement. "What?"

"If I had a guy who looked like him waiting for me, I wouldn't be sitting in here with such a glum expression," Peggy said.

"You're absolutely right," Gina said, forcing a smile and heading for the dining room. Hiding in the kitchen was no way to deal with this. She needed to tell Rafe about the conclusion she'd reached. Surely he wouldn't be all that unhappy if she suggested that he go back to New York.

Unfortunately, Rafe looked as if he was here to stay, she noted as she spotted him sitting at a table beside a window, papers spread out around him. He seemed perfectly content with his office away from home. She walked over to join him.

"If you're going to set up an office in here, I'll have to charge you rent," she said.

Rafe's gaze shot up, instantly filling with so much heat it almost took her breath away. Why had she ever left the man's room the night before? If this thing between them was destined to end, why wasn't she taking advantage of every single second it lasted?

"You look beat," he said, worry crowding out the desire in his expression.

"Just what every woman wants to hear. You need to work on your technique for flattery," she retorted.

"Your beauty is a given. You still look tired."

She grinned at that. "Better. But I'd suggest you keep practicing or you'll never get the girl."

A smile tugged at his lips. "I thought I already had the girl."

Her pulse did a little bump at that. "Oh, really?"

"Do I?"

She pulled out a chair and sat down. "Maybe," she said thoughtfully. "For the time being. In fact, we ought to talk about that."

"Uh-oh," he said. "You've had too much time to think overnight, haven't you?"

"I didn't spend it all on you," she said testily. "But when you did happen to cross my mind, it occurred to me that this is crazy."

"What's crazy?" he asked.

"This," she said, gesturing from him to herself and back. "You and me."

"Why is it crazy? You're the one who insisted on taking it to a whole new level. I'm just starting to get used to the idea. In fact, I'm just about convinced you're a genius."

"I don't think you're supposed to have to get used to the idea of caring about somebody. It's supposed to just happen."

"Not to me."

A tight note in his voice suggested he was admitting something to her that he rarely admitted, perhaps even to himself.

"You said something like that last night, but I can't believe it. You've never cared about someone?" she asked, unable to hide her incredulity. "Never?"

"Not really."

"What about your mother?"

"I told you, we maintain a polite distance."

Gina found the response appalling, but because of his forbidding expression, she let it go. "But you have been involved with a lot of women, right?"

"I've dated. I wouldn't say I've been 'involved' with any of them." He regarded her defensively. "Do we have to talk about this?"

"I think we do. Rafe, where do you see this going?"

"I don't know." His gaze locked with hers. "Do you?"

Gina sighed. "No," she said, then waved off the response as if to erase it. The truth was she had thought of little else all night long and she had vowed not ten minutes ago to be honest with him about her conclusions. "I take that back. If I'm being totally honest, I don't see it going anywhere. Not in the long term, at any rate."

His jaw tightened. "I see. May I ask why?"

She leaned forward. "Look, you and I didn't get off on the best foot at the beginning. You thought I was a criminal, for heaven's sake. Because of my past—no, just on general principle—I resented that like crazy. But there was this undeniable physical attraction between us even then. It was probably heightened because there was nothing we could do about it under the circumstances."

"But we did do something about it," he pointed out. "We made love."

"We had sex," she insisted. "And it was great. Fabulous, in fact."

"Glad to hear we were on the same page about that, at least," he retorted.

She refused to be intimidated by his sarcasm. "You asked me why I thought it wouldn't work. I'm trying to tell you."

Rafe held up his hands. "By all means, though I'm not so sure we ought to be having a discussion about sex with half the town listening in."

"Half the town?" Gina echoed, then turned in her chair to find that the restaurant had begun to fill up. Several fascinated gazes were turned in their direction. She was going to kill Rafe for not warning her sooner. Or maybe Peggy, who was just passing by with a smirk on her face. Gina snagged her hand. "Why didn't you tell me we had customers?"

"You were sitting right here. I figured you weren't either blind or deaf," Peggy responded with an unrepentant grin. "I guess something else had captured your attention."

"Have you taken their orders?" she asked, barely resisting the desire to grind her teeth in frustration.

"I'm doing that right now," Peggy said cheerfully. "Everybody's been pretty happy just to watch the floor show."

Gina caught the amusement in Rafe's eyes just then. "Don't say another word," she told him. "And don't go anywhere. This conversation is not over."

He gave her a mock salute. "Take your time. I'll be right here." He winked at Peggy. "Bring me a glass of Chianti when you have a minute, okay?"

"You've got it," Peggy said. "It's on the house. I haven't had this much fun around here in ages. By comparison, Tony and Francesca are totally boring."

"You can't give away wine," Gina snapped, losing

patience with the pair of them and their amusement at her expense.

"I'll pay for it out of my tips," Peggy said. "Something tells me they're going to be real good today."

Gina bit back the desire to respond and headed for the kitchen. It was too bad she'd done all the chopping and dicing earlier. Right now the prospect of slamming a really sharp knife down into something and cutting it to shreds held a whole lot of appeal.

It was more than two hours before she got back to Rafe. In addition to all the customers who'd seemingly been drawn in by reports of the lively discussion she and Rafe had been engaged in earlier, Karen had appeared, looking downcast and confused. She had been joined by Lauren and Emma. All three of them had regarded Gina with curiosity when she had emerged from the kitchen.

"Maybe you'd better sit down here and tell us what's going on," Emma advised. "Why are you working here?"

"Tony needed to take Francesca to Italy. I'm filling in."

"For how long?" Karen asked.

"I'm not sure."

"Are you thinking of staying here permanently?" Emma asked. "If so, we need to talk. It would change certain things."

Lauren, who was back in town again, immediately picked up on Emma's circumspect choice of words. "What things?" she asked. "I can totally understand if Gina wants to stay here."

All three of them stared at the glamorous superstar,

whose visits were more and more frequent. They had assumed it was because of Karen. Now Gina wasn't so sure.

"You can?" Gina said.

"Well, of course I can," Lauren responded. "Wherever we go, this is still home. Why wouldn't we want to come back? It's like a safe haven."

Gina stared at her. "Why would *you* need a safe haven? Has something happened we don't know about?"

"No, of course not," Lauren said impatiently. "I was just saying that if we needed one, this is the place we'd be most likely to come."

That said, she leaned toward Gina and asked in a conspiratorial tone, "So, is it true?"

Gina's composure slipped. "Is what true?" she asked, even though she was pretty sure she knew precisely what was coming.

Lauren glanced pointedly across the room. "Were you and Rafe having a very public discussion about the fabulous sex you've been having?"

"Not intentionally," Gina said, though she could feel the embarrassed heat climbing into her cheeks.

"But you were talking about it?" Lauren persisted. "There has been sex and it has been fabulous?"

"Yes," Gina admitted. "And a few people might have overheard. I thought we were alone."

The other three exchanged glances.

"Interesting," Karen said, grinning.

"Isn't it, though," Lauren added.

"I thought I told you to stay away from him," Emma said. But despite the disapproval in her tone, her eyes were glinting with amusement.

Karen and Lauren turned to Emma. "Why would you tell her that?" Lauren asked.

"Because it's inadvisable for the two of them to get mixed up at this particular moment in time," Emma said, again being very circumspect.

"Why?" Lauren repeated. "Is he in the middle of a messy divorce or something?"

"Of course not," Gina said. "Rafe has never been married."

"Then I don't get it," Lauren said. "He's gorgeous. He's interested." Suddenly her enthusiastic expression faded. "But when he came here, he was after something. A deposition, wasn't it? That's why Emma objects to you seeing him."

"I am not going to talk about this," Gina said. "The deposition is no longer an issue. We're *partners*," she reminded Emma.

"I don't have that paper," Emma said.

Gina waved that off as a technicality. "It's a moot point anyway. Rafe and I are not an issue. *That's* what we were discussing when half the town decided to eavesdrop, then spread the word."

"I'm confused," Karen said. "The two of you are having fabulous sex, over Emma's objections, but you're not going to keep on seeing each other. Have I got that right?"

"Pretty much," Gina said.

"Is Emma the reason you're splitting up, then?" Karen asked.

"No," Gina said. "There is nothing to split up. There is no relationship."

"Just that fabulous sex," Lauren said, a gleam in her eyes. "I'm beginning to get it."

Karen stared at her. "You are? Explain it to me."

Lauren nodded. "Happily. Our friend Gina is running scared. For the first time in her life, she is attracted to a man who might mean more to her than preparing succulent feasts for strangers. Her priorities are all topsy-turvy, after years and years of knowing exactly what she wanted. What better way to fix things than to get rid of the distraction?"

Gina listened to the explanation first with indignation, then with dawning shock. Was Lauren right? Was that what she'd been doing—running scared because Rafe had been a threat to her goals? Obviously it was true that he'd been a threat when he'd first come to town. But that issue was all but dead, and he still posed a very real threat. She was beginning to want him a little too much, to want what they had together. Hell, she had all but thrown herself at him, she wanted him so badly.

"Well?" Lauren demanded, poking her in the ribs with an elbow. "How did I do? Am I good or what?"

"You're good," Gina admitted slowly. "Just one question. Now that you've psychoanalyzed me and nailed it, what the heck am I supposed to do about it?"

14

Rafe watched Gina and her friends across the room with a sinking sensation in the pit of his stomach. From the surreptitious glances being cast his way, he suspected he was the prime topic on the agenda. He wasn't sure how he felt about his fate being decided by women he barely knew. Would they encourage Gina to let this relationship play out or would they warn her away? As skittish as she clearly was, it wouldn't take much to ruin things for the two of them.

When he could stand it no longer, he stood up and crossed the restaurant. "You ladies look as if you're enjoying yourselves," he said, then tucked a hand under Gina's elbow. "Mind if I steal her away from you, though? We were in the middle of a conversation earlier. We need to finish it."

"Not now," Gina said, refusing to budge. "We can finish it later."

Rafe shook his head. "Something tells me now would be better. Excuse us, ladies."

Rafe tried to pull her up, but Gina held back. "I am

visiting with my friends," she said, regarding him with mounting fury flashing in her eyes.

"I'm sure they won't object," he repeated confidently, giving each of them his most charming smile, the one that lulled witnesses into believing he was on their side.

"Will you?" he asked, all but daring any of them to protest.

When Emma started to reply, Lauren gave her a sharp nudge. "We don't mind at all," Lauren assured him. "I'm sure what you have to say is really, really important."

Gina scowled at her. "It's not that important," she grumbled. "It could wait."

Lauren beamed at her. "No, it can't. Just remember what I said."

Exhaling a deep sigh, Gina stopped fighting him then and stood up. She shrugged off his hand, but she did follow him back to his table.

"Would you care for a glass of wine?" Rafe asked when she was seated.

"No, thank you," she said a little too politely, her hands folded primly in front of her on the table, her gaze averted.

He refused to let her attitude get to him. "So, what did Lauren tell you?"

"Nothing that matters."

"She seemed to think otherwise. Come on, Gina," he coaxed. "What did she say? It had to do with us, didn't it?"

She leveled a withering look at him. "It did, but she was wrong, flat-out, positively wrong. If I didn't believe that before, I do now."

"Oh?"

Sparks lit her eyes. "I don't like being manhandled, Rafe."

For a minute he was about to laugh, but her expression suggested she was dead serious. "Is that how you see it? You think I manhandled you just now?"

"You dragged me away from my friends over my objections. What would you call it?"

He thought back over everything that had happened in the last ten minutes. He was pretty sure she had come along willingly if not enthusiastically, but then again, he was a mere male. What did he know about finesse?

"Manhandling implies more physical force than I used," he protested.

"Okay, you bullied me into coming with you. Is that better?"

Rafe winced. "Not really. And if that's the way you see it, then I apologize. I was just trying to get back to a conversation that I thought was really important to both of us."

She didn't seem appeased by the apology. Either she didn't take it seriously or there was something else entirely going on. He suspected it was the latter. "Is that really what has you upset with me, the fact that I interrupted your time with your friends?"

She looked vaguely disconcerted by the question, as if she hadn't expected him to guess that she was trying to sidestep the real problem. He watched her and waited.

"No," she said finally. "It's not that."

"What then?"

"You came over just when I was trying to get the answer to a question."

Rafe regarded her with confusion. "And?"

"I really wanted to know the answer," she said. "Isn't that obvious?"

"Ask me. Maybe I can answer it."

She chuckled, her expression wry. "I don't think so."

"Why not?"

"Because you're the problem. Well, not you," she corrected. "Me, and how I feel about you. The two of us. Together. Or not." She frowned at him. "See, it's very confusing."

Rafe was beginning to feel considerably better, but he was wise enough not to show it. "Okay. What is it you find most disturbing about us?"

"The fact that I care about you," she said, looking miserable. "Lauren accused me of running scared and, as much as I hate to admit it, she was right. I know I was the one who came on to you and all but dragged you into bed, but I didn't expect the sex to be so…"

"Fabulous?" he suggested, allowing himself a faint smile.

"Okay, yes," she admitted grudgingly. "I didn't expect it to be great and I didn't expect it to matter. I didn't expect *you* to matter."

The explanation filled in the rest of the picture. "And you were hoping your friends would clarify things, help you figure out what to do about that," he guessed.

"Exactly."

"It's just as well I dragged you away when I did then," he said.

She seemed thoroughly taken aback by his claim. "How can you say that?"

"Because they can't answer that," he told her, then held up his hand when she seemed to be about to speak. "I can't answer it, either. You're the only one who can figure out what your feelings are and what's best for you. Sorry, sweetheart, but I think we're going to have to muddle through this entirely on our own."

She was already shaking her head by the time he finished. "But I can't," she said. "Not with you here, not with everything else that's going on. I can't think. My head is spinning."

"Is there some reason why you have to decide all of this today?" he asked.

"No, not really, but I hate this uncertainty. Everything in my life is up in the air."

Rafe stood up, tugged his chair around to her side of the table then sat next to her. He cupped her face in his hands, his gaze locked with hers. The turmoil made her eyes darker than ever. His gaze shifted to her lips, but despite the temptation he resisted the desire to kiss her until she forgot all about her confusion.

"Okay, let's deal with one thing at a time. I'm no expert on relationships," he said quietly. "We've established that, but I think this is one of those things you're not supposed to think about, Gina. You're supposed to go with your gut, with what you're feeling in here." He tapped her in the center of her chest. "You said as much yourself earlier, remember?"

"But that's just it," she said wearily. "I don't know what's in my heart. How can I? First Bobby steals from the business and all but ruins me in the process. That filled me with anger. Then you spend weeks hounding me for answers, which I deeply resented. Caleb dies. One of my best friends is devastated, and I am worried sick about her. My mentor is frantic about his wife's state of mind. You and I wind up in bed together, which makes me feel things I never imagined feeling. Bobby is hiding out in the Cayman Islands and uttering barely veiled threats, which scare me and infuriate me all at the same time."

She regarded him with a bleak expression. "Bottom line? All I feel right now is pressure. It's coming at me from every direction. I just want to shut it all out."

"Including me?"

"Yes." She took a deep breath and met his gaze with troubled eyes. "I'm sorry, but that's how I feel."

Laid out like that, Rafe could understand her dismay and her confusion. "No, I'm the one who's sorry. You have been through a lot. Maybe because you have always seemed so strong, I didn't take into account that this would be too much, even for you. What do you want me to do?"

"You asked me once before if I wanted you to go back to New York." Her eyes glistened with unshed tears. "I do, Rafe. That's what I want."

He swallowed hard, fighting the surprising hurt that came with her words. But he had asked, implying that he would do whatever she wanted, and she had given him an honest answer. He had to walk away. There was no other choice.

"Okay," he said quietly. "I'll leave tomorrow."

For an instant she looked taken aback by his ready agreement, maybe even a little disappointed. He had a feeling he was going to cling to the latter in the weeks to come.

"I'm sorry," she whispered, as the tears finally spilled over and ran unchecked down her cheeks.

"It's okay," he told her. "I'm going now, but you're not getting rid of me for good. I'll be back."

"When?"

He grinned at that. "See, you miss me already, sweetheart. That should tell you something."

What it told him was that he wasn't going to give Gina one minute more than necessary before coming back to claim her. She would have her space, her time to sort through the emotional turmoil and the tragedies of the past couple of months.

But he wasn't going to give her time to forget about him, to convince herself that what they had wasn't real. In fact, now that he knew without a doubt what he wanted, he was going to do everything in his power to make sure she understood that it was going to last a lifetime.

Gina started to miss Rafe almost the instant she watched his flight to New York take off. But even as tears stung her eyes, her friends closed ranks around her.

"He'll be back," Lauren predicted.

"When?" she asked wistfully, just as she had asked him the day before.

"When the time is right," Lauren assured her. "Something tells me Rafe O'Donnell is the kind of man who has a finely honed sense of timing. Besides that, the man is crazy in love with you."

Gina was startled by the assessment. "He is?"

"Well, of course he is," Emma said with a touch of exasperation. "Even I can see that."

Lauren chuckled. "Listen to Emma. She may be oblivious to the way Ford feels about her, but she can still recognize love when she spots it in anyone else."

"Oh, go suck an egg," Emma snapped.

"Is that what you say in a courtroom when you don't like what a judge has to say?" Lauren chided. "You must be held in contempt quite a lot."

"Sometimes I am, but it's worth it," Emma said loftily. "Now, let's go to the Heartbreak and have a beer. Tony's is closed tonight, so Gina doesn't have to work. I'm not due in court tomorrow. We can live it up. Maybe there will be some handsome men around who'll dance with us and make us forget everything else."

Gina didn't hold out much hope that anything could take her mind off the fact that she had sent Rafe away, but she was willing to give it a try.

"I'm game," she said. "How about you, Lauren?"

"Count me in. I've always been a sucker for a handsome cowboy who can dance."

"Since when?" Gina asked. "You couldn't wait to get away from a whole town filled with cowboys."

Lauren shrugged. "Times change. Are we going to talk this to death or do it?"

Gina cast one more look at the sky in the direction where she'd last seen Rafe's plane heading east. "Let's do it," she said finally.

Unfortunately, though, a couple of beers and the attention of a few men she'd known since childhood didn't do a thing to keep her from thinking about Rafe and the fact that she'd sent him away.

"He jumped at the chance to leave," she said despondently to Lauren. "Don't you think he was awfully eager to go?"

"No, what I think is that he was doing what you asked him to do, even though he didn't want to. Did you see how much paperwork he loaded into that plane?

Boxes of it. That was a man who was settling in right here. If you'd asked, he probably would have left his firm in New York, opened an office in Winding River and stuck around indefinitely."

"The town could use a really good lawyer," Emma said, her expression thoughtful. "If Rafe had been in practice here, instead of a seventy-year-old man who's still living in the Dark Ages, I wouldn't be running back and forth from Denver right now to handle Sue Ellen's case."

"I like having you coming back and forth," Gina protested. "I'm going to hate it when you go back to Denver full-time."

"Me, too," Karen agreed. "In fact, I think you should be the one opening a practice here."

"With Rafe as her partner," Lauren said, grinning. "Perfect. Everybody gets what they want."

"Rafe is with a huge firm in New York," Gina pointed out dryly. "I ~~doubt anyone could entice him to move.~~"

"~~I agree,~~" Karen agreed, though without much enthusiasm.

Gina gave a fierce hug to each of her friends. "Thanks for sticking by me tonight. Watching Rafe leave was harder than I'd expected it to be."

"All the more reason to get on the phone and tell him to come back, don't you think?" Lauren asked.

"Leave her alone," Emma advised. "She needs time to think."

"No," Lauren said adamantly. "What she needs is to listen to her heart for the first time in her life."

"Hey, you guys can stop talking about me as if I'm not here," Gina said, waving a protesting hand in front of their faces. "I don't know what I need or what I want decide to stay before the end of the trial. It's what Caitlyn wants. It's what your family wants. It is most definitely what Ford Hamilton wants."

Emma scowled. "Leave Ford out of this. He has nothing to do with any decision I make."

"I don't think he'll agree to be left out," Lauren teased. "Have you guys seen them together?"

"I've heard them," Karen said, grinning. "They argue. Morning, noon, night, it doesn't matter, they argue." She gave an exaggerated shiver. "All that untapped passion just waiting to cut loose."

"I refuse to listen to another word of this," Emma said with a huff. "I'm going home, where I will get a good night's sleep, untroubled by dreams of Ford Hamilton or any other man, for that matter."

"Give me a lift?" Gina asked. "I told Rafe I needed this time to think. I guess I'd better start doing it."

Lauren glanced at Karen. "I guess it's just you and me then. Can we stick around and listen to the music?"

"Smart was Emma," Karen noted. "She hasn't said anything, but I heard she took on two other cases while she was here last week. I think that's very telling, don't you?"

"Whoa," Emma said. "Let's not leap to any conclusions here. Sue Ellen's case is a one-time thing, a tragic situation for someone we know. When it's over, that's that. I'll be back in Denver."

"What about the other cases?" Lauren asked.

"They were quickies," Emma insisted. "Nothing the least bit complicated. I wrote a will for someone and helped another person straighten out a billing error. They're both already over and done with."

"We'll see," Lauren said smugly. "I predict you'll

or even what my heart is saying." She smiled to take the sting out of her words. "I'll keep you posted."

She got her first clue when she walked into her room at the hotel and saw the message light blinking. Sure that Rafe must have called, her heart thumped unsteadily. Filled with an unfamiliar sense of anticipation, she grabbed the phone and asked for the message.

"Deidre called," the desk clerk reported, dimming Gina's excitement. "She says it's urgent. Call her at the restaurant or at home, no matter what time it is."

"Thanks, Lucille," Gina told the woman. Now her heart was beating too hard for another reason entirely. She glanced at the clock, then dialed the restaurant's number. Deidre picked up at once. "Hi, it's Gina. What's going on?"

"Three of our biggest investors were in here earlier tonight demanding to see you or Bobby," she said without preamble. "I didn't know what to do, so I lied. I told them you were away on a family emergency and couldn't be reached and that Bobby was due back soon. They seemed to accept that."

Gina was surprised they'd bought it. "Are you sure they didn't know Bobby had taken off with the money?"

"Apparently not, or maybe they were on a fishing expedition. My hunch was that they'd heard rumors and came by to check them out, but they took my story at face value."

"Did they leave right away or cause trouble?"

"Neither. I invited them to stay for dinner. I made sure they had the best meal of their lives, a bottle of our best wine and great service. It didn't hurt that the place was packed. They left happy men. I still think you might want to call them, though, follow up on their visit, so to speak. I got their business cards."

"Give me the names," Gina said, taking them down. "I'll call first thing in the morning. Thanks again, Deidre. I honestly don't know what I'd do without you."

"Are you coming back soon?" Deidre asked wistfully. "I like running this place and I'm good at most of it, but dealing with this kind of thing gives me hives. I'm a wreck."

"But you did exactly the right thing," Gina said. "That fib you told was pretty close to the truth, and it got the job done."

"You didn't answer my question. Are you coming back soon?"

"Another couple of weeks," Gina said. "I promise."

By then Tony and Francesca should be back. With any luck Gina would have sorted through her own options and be ready to deal with the fallout, whichever way she went.

"Okay, I can hold the fort that long," Deidre said, sounding more optimistic. "By the way, I've managed to bring nearly half the bills up to date. If business stays like this for the rest of the fall, they should all be caught up by the time you get here. That'll just leave the payments to the investors for you to handle. And with the holidays coming and all the parties and catering, you should be in good shape."

"Business is that good?" Gina said, surprised and pleased. "We have catering jobs booked for the holidays?" There had been a trickle of requests for information before she'd left, but she'd expected word of their financial straits to make most people too skittish to book them for critical holiday entertaining.

"Business is great," Deidre said. "We have a big catering job for almost every night between Thanksgiving and New Year's. And Ronnie and I have been able to cut a few costs in the kitchen. Nothing to harm the quality of the food," she said hurriedly. "We're just cutting waste."

"Thank you again," Gina said with heartfelt sincerity, as an idea began to take shape in her head.

If her sous-chef and Deidre were doing such a great job of running Café Tuscany and the catering staff, maybe Gina could end up having it both ways. Maybe she could work out a partnership with them for the restaurant and the catering business, and divide her own time between Winding River and New York. It was definitely something to consider.

That just left Rafe. She would never have believed it a few weeks ago, but deciding what to do about him was a whole lot more complicated—and more important than figuring out how to straighten out the mess that Bobby had left her in. She had a feeling that fate had brought him into her life for a reason, and she'd be a fool to let him get away.

No sooner had she said goodbye to Deidre than the phone rang again. She picked it up, still lost in thought. "Did you forget something?" she asked, assuming it was her manager calling back.

"Only you," Rafe said, his voice low and seductive. "I never should have left you behind."

Gina sighed and settled back against the pillows. Suddenly space didn't seem nearly as important as letting the sound of his voice wash over her. "Is that so?"

"Are you through thinking things over yet?"

She chuckled at the wistful note in his voice. Hearing that filled her with an amazing sense of satisfaction. "You've only been gone a few hours. I'm just getting started. Are you home now?"

"I'm in New York," he said. "Funny thing about that, though."

"What?"

"It doesn't feel half as much like home as that hotel room did, especially the last few nights."

"Oh, Rafe," she whispered. "You shouldn't say things like that."

"Why not? It's true."

"But it just makes it harder."

"Makes what harder?"

"Thinking."

He laughed. "I told you before, stop thinking so hard. This is something you have to decide from the gut."

"What is your gut telling you?" she asked curiously.

"That what I've found with you is too important to let slip away."

His words were oddly reassuring because they so closely echoed her own thoughts. He hadn't yet mentioned love. She had a feeling if he had she would have felt overwhelmed and even more pressured. These words simply hinted that what they had should be explored, tested…clung to until they knew exactly what it meant. She could live with that without panicking.

"Call me tomorrow?" she asked.

"Tomorrow and every day after," he said. "Sweet dreams, Gina."

If only, she thought. Something told her that without Rafe beside her, she'd be lucky to sleep at all, much less dream.

15

Rafe felt an overwhelming sense of relief when Charlie Flynn called to report that he had Bobby Rinaldi under surveillance in the Cayman Islands.

"He's living pretty quietly," Flynn said. "He's certainly not throwing his money around."

"What's your take on the guy?"

"Frankly, I was surprised. I expected a lot of flash and dazzle, a woman on each arm, especially after what you'd said about the way he took in your mother."

"And?"

"He's just an average guy. There are no women, though he hangs out at the hotel bar most evenings. If one comes on to him, he certainly flirts back, but he goes back to his room alone."

Rafe was as startled by that as Flynn. "That doesn't fit the image I had, either."

"What do you want me to do?" the investigator asked.

"Keep an eye on him. If the opportunity presents itself and you can do it without stirring up any suspicion, get to know him. See if you can figure out what his motive was in running out with all that cash."

"Will do," Flynn said. "I'll check in when I have something."

"Just don't lose track of him," Rafe warned.

"As if I would," the investigator said scathingly. "Not for what you're paying me. I don't shut my eyes for a second."

"I'm counting on that."

Rafe hung up, his expression thoughtful. Why would Bobby Rinaldi betray Gina, run off with all that cash and hide out in the Caymans? He'd left a reasonably clear trail, so Rafe doubted he was trying to drop out of sight to avoid paying heavy gambling debts. What else could it be? Was he in trouble with some married lover's husband? With the IRS? Rafe wondered if anyone at the restaurant might have a clue.

Knowing Gina would probably object, he didn't tell her his intentions. Instead, he dropped in at Café Tuscany just before opening the next day. From the instant he entered the soothing, classy foyer, he understood what Lydia had been saying all along about the place. It was a step above most flash-in-the-pan successes. Café Tuscany wasn't a trendy fluke. It was here to stay. Somehow he found that reassuring. It suggested that once she'd sorted through some things, Gina would be back. They could resume their relationship right here in New York, where they both belonged.

A slender, dark-haired woman wearing a simple, stylish black dress came toward him from the kitchen, a questioning expression on her face.

"We're not open for another half hour," she said with a warm smile.

"I know. You must be the famous Deidre that Gina has told me so much about."

Her expression faltered. "And you are?"

"Rafe O'Donnell."

"Ah," she said slowly. "The attorney for the investors."

Rafe tried not to let it matter that she'd heard of him only in his professional role, not as Gina's lover. Maybe that was for the best, since he was here to get answers.

"Some of them," he admitted. "If you have a minute, could we talk?"

She shook her head. "Without a subpoena, I have nothing to say to you."

"It won't take long," he promised, though he could see from her expression that time wasn't the issue. He was pretty sure he knew what was. He added, "It could help Gina."

That seemed to surprise her. "You want to help her?"

"Yes," he said with total sincerity.

She studied him intently, then nodded and led the way to a table. She gestured for him to sit.

"Would you like some coffee? A cappuccino?"

"Nothing, thanks."

She sat opposite him. "What do you want to know?"

"How well did you know Bobby Rinaldi?"

"Not intimately, if that's what you're suggesting," she said with a touch of indignation.

"I'm not suggesting anything improper," he soothed. "I'm just trying to get a picture of the guy. Why would he run off with all that money?"

"A woman," she said at once.

"But he's in the Cayman Islands all alone," Rafe said.

Her eyes widened. "You know where he is?"

"Yes."

"Does Gina know?"

He nodded. "Was Bobby a gambler?"

"No way," she said.

"A big spender?"

"Yes, but he had the money. His take out of here was pretty substantial."

Rafe was relatively certain that Gina had been taking very little out of the business. Why had Bobby gotten so much more? And why hadn't that shown up on the books he'd picked up from Deidre a couple of months back?

"More than Gina's salary?" he asked.

"I think so. I could look at the books. I've been paying bills while Gina's away."

It occurred to Rafe then that the books he'd been given had been for the restaurant's early years, not the current one. Perhaps quite a lot had changed in the months immediately before Bobby had disappeared.

"Let me take a look with you," he said, concluding there was no point in criticizing Deidre for not giving him the current financial records along with the others, even though the subpoena had been for everything.

He followed her into the office. She removed the latest record book from a file cabinet and opened it to the first of the year. Sure enough, Bobby's draw from the company was dramatically more than Gina's and higher than what he'd been taking out in past years. Had Gina known about that? Was it part of some deal they'd made? Maybe he was supposed to be paying the investors with the additional funds, though that would certainly be an unorthodox way of conducting business.

"Who wrote those checks? Gina or Bobby?" he asked Deidre.

"Until this mess, Bobby handled all of the financial details," she revealed. "I don't think Gina ever touched the checkbook, though she could sign checks if she needed to."

That must have been what Bobby had counted on, that she wouldn't even see the size of the checks he'd written to himself. He'd taken four careful years to establish a routine, then taken advantage of Gina after she'd been lulled into a false sense of complacency. Rafe's impression of the man, never very high, sank even lower.

"Thanks, Deidre," Rafe said when he'd jotted down a few notes. "One last thing. What was Bobby's relationship with Gina like?"

"He adored her," she said without hesitation. "In fact, I think he might have been half in love with her, though she wouldn't give him the time of day, not that way. He paraded women through here, but I always thought he did it because he was trying to get Gina to pay attention, not because he cared about any of them."

Deidre's assessment echoed in Rafe's head throughout the day and for the rest of the week. *He did it because he was trying to get Gina to pay attention. Pay attention. Pay attention.*

Dear God, was *that* what this had been about? Was this entire mess an attempt on Bobby Rinaldi's part to get Gina to look at him? It was a screwy idea, but once it occurred to Rafe, he couldn't seem to shake it. Goodness knows, *he* knew the power of her appeal. Why wouldn't Rinaldi, who was reputedly an expert on women? To a charming scoundrel used to getting any female he wanted, the one who proved immune was bound to be the most alluring.

There was only one way to find out if he'd hit on the answer, Rafe concluded. He needed to talk to Rinaldi face-to-face, to confront him with what he suspected and see how he reacted.

He called Charlie Flynn. "I'm coming down there. Make sure Rinaldi sits tight. I can't get away this week and possibly not next week. I'm due in court on a couple of cases, and I can't ask for postponements."

"He won't go anywhere," Flynn promised.

"Thanks." He hung up slowly. What if he was right? Did Gina suspect that Bobby might be in love with her? How would she feel if she knew? Was that the reason she was so hesitant to commit to Rafe, because she returned Bobby's unspoken feelings? Rafe really, really hated that idea, but he couldn't ignore it.

And until he knew a whole lot more than he knew right now, maybe it was best if he kept not only some physical distance between himself and Gina, but some emotional distance, as well. Losing her now wouldn't hurt any less than losing her later, but it might be just a little easier on his pride.

Rafe hadn't called for three weeks, not since the night he'd left town. Gina was beside herself trying to figure out what it meant. One minute she was furious with him, the next resigned, the next hurt.

"I don't get it," she said to Emma. "He was the one who was so anxious for us to see where things would go."

"He's probably just busy. He was away from New York for a long time. I'm sure he was swamped with work when he got back. I know the type. I *am* one," she admitted ruefully. "When I'm caught up in a case, I don't see anything else."

"I suppose," Gina said, but she didn't entirely buy it. And if this was the way a future with Rafe was going to play out, with him getting so caught up in work that he forgot all about her, did she want him in her life, anyway?

"If you want to know what's going on, call him," Emma advised. "You have his number."

"No. I'm the one who said I wanted space. I guess I ought to be grateful that he's giving it to me."

On top of Rafe's odd behavior, there was Bobby's. She hadn't heard a word from him, either. Nor had he sent a dime to pay off the restaurant's debts. She was half tempted to fly down to the Caymans and snatch back every penny he had stolen.

Of course, it was an idle threat. She couldn't go anywhere until Tony got back. He had called the week before and asked if she would mind if he and Francesca extended their stay in Italy.

"Who knows if we'll ever get back here again," he'd said. "We'd like to take advantage of our time here now, that is, if you're sure you can stay on in Wyoming."

"I can stay," Gina said, praying that Deidre would understand the delay. "You and Francesca enjoy yourselves. How's her sister?"

"Much improved, thank goodness. Francesca is very relieved. In a few days her sister might even be well enough to go with us to Florence and Venice."

Gina had sighed. It sounded wonderful. She had loved her time in Italy. "Enjoy every minute of it," she told Tony. "And take lots of pictures."

"You are an angel, *cara mia*. And when I get home, there are things you and I must discuss."

"What things?"

"Not yet. Face-to-face," he insisted. "A few more weeks. No more. I don't want to take advantage of you."

"You could never take advantage of me," she told him. "I owe you way too much. If it's going to be longer than a week or so, though, would you mind if I closed for a few days so I can take a quick trip to New York? Everything's running smoothly at Café Tuscany right now, but I need to look in on Deidre before she starts feeling totally abandoned. Also, it might help me to decide a few things I've been thinking about."

"Go, of course. Anything that will help you to clarify what you really want. Perhaps we are on the same wavelength," he said hopefully.

"Perhaps," she said, though she was not entirely certain what was on his mind. He'd been way too vague for her to interpret his intentions. "I love you guys. I miss you. So do the customers."

"I doubt that, when they have you," Tony scoffed. "But it is nice of you to say."

Ever since that conversation, she had been putting off the trip she had mentioned to Tony. With no word from Rafe and with Deidre still reporting that everything at Café Tuscany was under control, Gina lost the sense of urgency. In fact, the only place she felt truly needed was right here in Winding River. Tony needed her to stay. Karen seemed glad of her company. Her parents were delighted she was nearby, even if they thought it was absurd that she was wasting money on a hotel room when her room at home was empty. Maybe it *was* crazy, especially now that there was no longer any potential danger that she might be dragging them into her problems with Bobby.

In the end, though, purely by chance she happened across a small apartment with big windows, cozy nooks, comfortable furniture and a surprisingly spacious kitchen filled with light. It was tucked behind a house on Main Street, in what had once been a garage. She spotted the For Rent sign while walking to Tony's one morning. The next day she stopped by to see it.

Now she stood in the middle of that kitchen and suddenly felt at peace. Without pausing to consider the ramifications, she pulled out her checkbook and turned to the owner.

"I'll take it," she told Mrs. Garwood.

"For how long? Are you home to stay?" her mother's friend asked. "I know that would please your mother."

Gina's hand faltered over the check. "I don't know," she admitted. "Is that a problem? Could we go month to month for now?"

"Normally I wouldn't agree to that," Mrs. Garwood said, then smiled. "But for your mother, I will take a chance that you'll decide you're back for good."

"Thank you," Gina said and wrote the check for a deposit and a month's rent.

"I'll leave you alone, then," Mrs. Garwood said. "If you need anything, just knock on the back door."

After she had gone, Gina turned slowly. The sun was streaming through the kitchen window. Funny, she thought, recalling Rafe's words a few weeks earlier. This place felt more like home already than the apartment she'd had in New York for years.

"He's right over there," Flynn told Rafe, pointing to an unremarkable-looking man sitting at the poolside bar, his expression glum as he sipped beer.

"That's Bobby Rinaldi?" Rafe asked, not even trying to hide his shock. He'd expected someone more handsome, but maybe Bobby's appeal wasn't obvious to a man.

It had taken Rafe almost a month to fit this trip into his schedule. The holidays were approaching. He wanted this settled so he could spend them with Gina. With any luck at all they could be engaged by New Year's.

"The one and only. Come on. I'll introduce you. We've had quite a few chats lately." Flynn hesitated. "Is he going to recognize your name?"

"Most likely."

"Want me to use an alias?"

Rafe grinned. "No, let's play it straight. What's the worst he can do?"

"Run," Flynn suggested.

"Maybe, but I'm sure you're faster, and between us we're not going to let him out of our sight until we get him back to New York."

"Whatever you say."

Flynn led the way across the deck, which was crowded with vacationers escaping the oncoming winter in the States. Soothed by bright sun and fancy rum drinks, many of them were half-asleep and oblivious to the sudden tension at the bar when Flynn made the introductions.

Once again surprising Rafe, Bobby looked more disappointed than fearful upon hearing his name. His expression lent credence to Rafe's theory that he was down here hoping that Gina would be the one to follow him.

"Expecting someone else?" Rafe inquired lightly. "Gina, perhaps?"

Bobby sighed heavily. "What did you do? Forbid her to come, so that you could be her knight in shining armor?"

"She doesn't know I'm here," Rafe said.

"Why not?"

"I wanted to clarify a few things before I filled her in." He gave Bobby a pointed look. "Or before you did that yourself."

"I'm not going back," Bobby said.

"There's a return ticket in your room that suggests otherwise," Flynn said.

Bobby frowned at him. "You searched my room?"

"Of course," Flynn said. "I wouldn't have been doing my job if I hadn't."

"You lousy, no-good creep," Bobby muttered, but without much venom. He seemed to have lost his enthusiasm for the game.

"Let's stay focused," Rafe suggested. "First question, why did you take that money?"

"Because I wanted it," Bobby said at once. "Why does anyone steal? Because they want something or they need it or just for the thrill of it."

"Really? You didn't do a very good job of covering your tracks. The payments to you were right on the books, but you counted on Gina not seeing them, at least not until after you'd taken off, right? So, I have a theory."

"Do share it," Bobby said sarcastically.

"You're in love with Gina," Rafe speculated, keeping his gaze fixed on Rinaldi's face. Sure enough there was a flicker of surprise in his eyes. He went on. "She wasn't interested in you. Now that the restaurant is doing so well, she doesn't even need you the way she once did. This was a way to get her to pay attention."

"If that was my plan, it certainly was a bust, wasn't it?" Bobby said, not quite admitting to it.

"Because she doesn't love you, except as a friend." Rafe regarded him with a surprising burst of compassion. "She does care about you, though. She was devastated by your betrayal. For weeks she tried to convince herself that you hadn't meant to ruin the business, to ruin her. She wouldn't lift a finger to help me nail you."

Bobby seemed surprised by that. "She wouldn't?"

"Not at first. One of the most amazing things about Gina is her sense of loyalty. As time has passed, she has transferred that loyalty to the people you bilked out of money. Every single one of them will be paid back, no matter what it takes. She's committed to that, but she won't run to you to get the money. Her days of trusting you are over, Rinaldi. If your plan was to get her to need you, it backfired. She's found other people to count on."

"Like you," Bobby said with a sneer.

"I'm one of them, but there are lots more. It seems to me if you really care about her, though, you'll go back, return the money and keep her from having to struggle for months or even years to make it all right."

Bobby stared at him, first with defiance, then eventually in defeat. "What the hell?" he said at last. "I was getting sick of all this sunshine, anyway."

Rafe nodded. "Think of it this way. You'll be giving Gina the best Christmas present you could possibly give her, one she's not likely to forget."

16

Gina could no longer avoid her parents. They had been in the restaurant several times, asking questions, regarding her with undisguised worry. Each and every time, she had been busy enough to avoid responding to the interrogation. But on Thanksgiving Day, she knew that her time had run out.

"For once, you just sit there and let me cook," her mother commanded the minute Gina entered the kitchen. "I can certainly fix a turkey and stuffing. I've been doing it for years."

"I don't mind helping," Gina protested.

"I know that, but you need a break. You're working too hard trying to avoid making some tough decisions. At least that's the way it seems to your father and me. Are we right? Is this about Rafe or New York? Not that we aren't delighted that you're still here, but it's not like you to stay away from your business for so long, not when you spent so much time making it successful."

"A lot's been happening," Gina said defensively. "First with Karen, then with Tony and Francesca. I couldn't abandon them."

"That's very noble, I'm sure, but I know you, my darling girl. Tony came back on Monday. Yet you're still here, still in that little apartment behind Nancy Garwood's house. That tells me that you're hiding from something."

Gina sighed. She had never been able to keep things from her mother, which was one reason she'd been steering clear of the house so much lately.

Gina toyed with a napkin. She folded it into an elaborate swan, then unfolded it and made a simple triangle more in keeping with her mother's table setting. The silence in the room deepened as her mother stirred the pots on the stove and waited for a reply to her question. Gina recognized that she wasn't going to be able to avoid giving an answer.

"You know about the problem with the business," she said. "That's how Rafe and I met. He thought I had something to do with Bobby stealing that money. He distrusted me."

"But you fell for him, anyway," her mother said. "And he for you. So you got past the initial distrust and resentment."

Gina nodded and reached for a carrot stick just to have something to hold.

"Then you're not hiding from Rafe?"

"Actually I am, in a way." She sighed heavily. "It's complicated."

"Because you've fallen in love with him," her mother concluded. "And that scares you."

The carrot stick snapped in half. Gina stared at it in surprise, then looked at her mother with even greater shock. "You can see that?"

Her mother grinned. "Darling, you never were any

good at hiding your emotions. Even your father figured this part out. What we didn't understand was why you didn't just admit it. It's obvious he cares about you, too. Whatever complications there were at the beginning will resolve themselves in time."

"I thought so, too, for a while, but he hasn't been in touch lately. And now there's another wrinkle. It just came up this week when Tony got back."

"What's that?"

"Tony asked me to go into partnership with him." She took a deep breath, knowing that her parents were going to be delighted by the news, though they would never try to influence her decision. "He and Francesca want to spend more time in Italy. He says eventually the business would be mine, if I want to stay here."

Just as she'd expected, her mother was wise enough not to reveal her reaction. Instead, she asked, "How do you feel about that?"

Gina permitted herself a slight grin. "I really, really want to do it. Despite all of the chaos the past few months, I've loved being here. Until I came back I hadn't realized how much I missed you guys and my friends and even Winding River. I really don't want to live in New York anymore."

"Which brings us back to Rafe," her mother guessed.

"Exactly."

"There's only one way to figure out what to do," she told Gina. "You have to go to New York, settle things with Rafe and with Café Tuscany, then make a final decision. You can't make such an important decision in a vacuum, certainly not from here, when everything involved is across the country."

"You're absolutely right," Gina said, reaching the

same conclusion. "That is exactly what I have to do. If I can get a flight, I'll go in the morning."

Unfortunately, because of the holiday, she couldn't get a flight until the middle of the following week. When she called Rafe's office from the airport, they told her he was out of town on business and not expected back for a day or two.

"Is this Lydia?" Gina asked.

"Yes."

"This is Gina Petrillo. When he gets back, will you tell him I'm in New York and that I'd like to see him?"

"You're back? That's fantastic. I know you'll be the first person he wants to see when he gets back. I'll tell him," she said. "I'm glad you're here."

Gina wasn't quite sure what to make of that. Since the next stop on her agenda was Café Tuscany, she put off considering Lydia's words until later and took a cab straight from the airport to the restaurant.

When she walked through the front door, waves of pride and nostalgia washed over her. The restaurant was every bit as elegant and tasteful as she'd remembered. She had accomplished that, she and Bobby.

As she stood there basking in the good memories, Deidre stepped out of the kitchen and caught sight of her. Her eyes lit with delight. "You're back," she said, striding across the room to hug Gina. "I am so glad to see you. We have really missed you around here."

"It doesn't look like it. The place looks terrific."

Deidre waved off the compliment. "The cleaning crew keeps it spotless. Are you here to stay?"

"We need to talk about that," Gina said. "Can you come into the office? Is Ronnie here?"

"He's in the kitchen. Shall I get him?"

"Do that and bring some cappuccino with you," Gina suggested. "I need a jolt of caffeine."

When the two of them were settled into the chairs opposite her desk in the cramped office, she announced, "I've been doing a lot of thinking while I've been away."

Deidre's face fell. "You're going to close it down, aren't you? You're going to stay in Wyoming and close this place down. I knew it when you didn't come back right away. That Tony guy you were always talking about made you an offer too good to refuse."

"Whoa!" Gina said, chuckling at the rush of words. "You're only half-right. I am considering the possibility of staying in Wyoming."

Ronnie Carson, a quiet young man with a good head on his shoulders, as well as tremendous potential as a chef, studied her intently before he spoke. "But you have a plan for this place, don't you? You're not just going to shut the door and walk away."

"No, but whether or not it is feasible depends on the two of you and what you want."

As Deidre and Ronnie exchanged a look, Gina thought she caught a glimpse of something more than colleagues awaiting word on their fate. She had a feeling they had discovered each other while she was away. There was a distinct stirring of romance in the air. Maybe they'd wind up like Tony and Francesca, bound not only by love, but by working together at something they loved.

"Okay, here's the deal," she said. "Since you have managed to not only keep this place afloat under extremely daunting conditions, but to make it thrive, it occurred to me that you might be interested in taking over for me permanently."

"You mean we'd go on running it?" Deidre asked cautiously, her expression brightening ever so slightly.

"And eventually buy it from me," Gina said. "I'm in no rush about this. I don't need the money for what I want to do in Wyoming, at least not right away. We could work out a price and an arrangement that would give you time to get your feet on the ground financially. That could take a while because the first thing we'd need to do is get all of the old investors paid off. But I'd say in four or five years this would be yours, if you want it. Are you interested?"

"Ohmigosh," Deidre whispered, her gaze on Ronnie. "What do you think? Can we do it?"

He met her gaze, eyes shining, his expression serious. "Of course we can. If it's what you want. Is it?"

She reached for his hand. "Yes. Absolutely. And you?"

A half smile tugged at his lips. "It's the answer to a prayer."

Gina suddenly felt completely serene. She was making the right decision. She didn't have a single doubt about it. Not only was she making Ronnie and Deidre deliriously happy, but she was getting what she wanted, as well. Everybody would win.

The only potential blot on her happiness was Rafe's reaction. Maybe she should have consulted him first, but this was her business, her decision. Her relief at finally having made it was astonishing. She felt as if a two-ton weight had been lifted off her shoulders.

Now all she had to do was wrap up her personal affairs and wait for Rafe. It sounded so simple, but in her heart she knew there was going to be nothing simple about telling him that she intended to move a couple of thousand miles away for good.

* * *

Over the next twenty-four hours, Gina put all of her business affairs in order. She contacted each and every vendor to explain about the forthcoming changes and to assure them that their accounts would be settled and that she hoped they would continue to do business with Deidre and Ronnie. Most of them had such high praise for the two that she was certain they were going to succeed.

She also called all of the investors with a similar message, reassuring them that despite recent difficulties their investment was not only safe but would soon be extremely profitable. Satisfied that she was leaving town with her good name intact—at least as solid as it could be under the circumstances—she left her office for what she anticipated to be the last time and went back to her apartment to finish packing.

When the doorbell rang, to her total astonishment she found not just Rafe on her doorstep, but Bobby, as well.

"I tracked down a friend of yours," Rafe said unnecessarily. "He has something he wants to say to you before we go off to talk to the D.A. about the charges he's facing."

Bobby didn't look as if he were in a particularly talkative mood, but Rafe towered over him, and his grim expression never wavered.

"I'm sorry," Bobby said finally. "This was all a huge mistake."

"A mistake!"

He nodded. "I got some crazy idea in my head that you would turn to me if the business were in trouble."

Gina stared at him incredulously. "Why would you do something like that?"

Bobby remained mute, until Rafe scowled at him. "Tell her, Rinaldi. All of it. She deserves to know why you turned her life upside down."

"Because I'm in love with you," Bobby said in a voice that was little more than a whisper. "I have been since we met. But the only time you even looked at me was when we were pulling the business together. I wanted that back again."

She tried to make sense of it, but she couldn't. "You had to know I would blame you, not turn to you."

"Like I said, I wasn't thinking very clearly. I was sitting down in the Caymans waiting for you to come down and give me hell. It would have been better than the indifference I usually felt from you. I dated all those women, paraded them under your nose, and nothing. You didn't care."

"Oh, Bobby," she whispered. She couldn't make herself regret how this was turning out for her, but she was brokenhearted over the damage he had done not only to the business, but to the rest of his life. She looked at Rafe. "What happens now?"

"We have an appointment at the D.A.'s office. A lot depends on how much of the money he still has and pays back."

"It's all there," Bobby assured her. "Every penny."

"Then they should go easy on him," Rafe promised. He glanced at the packing boxes and her luggage. "Running again, Gina?"

"No," she said with certainty. "Not running away. Going home. When you get back I'll explain."

He nodded. "I'll be counting on it."

As he and Bobby went out the door, Bobby turned

back. "I really am sorry. I never meant for you to be left holding the bag. I really didn't."

"I know," she said quietly, and to her surprise, she really did believe that.

Rafe had had a nasty moment when he'd seen the state of Gina's apartment. Even before she'd explained, he had known that she intended to go straight back to Wyoming. What he didn't know was what that meant for the two of them. He had some ideas of his own, decisions he'd made over the past few weeks, but he wasn't so sure they meshed with her plans.

When he returned to her apartment, he found her dressed in some sort of velvety robe that covered her from her shoulders to her feet. Oddly enough, it was the sexiest thing he'd ever seen her wear.

Despite the chaos in the apartment, she had a fire blazing on the gas logs. The lights were turned down low, and she'd opened a bottle of extremely expensive wine.

"Interesting," he said as he looked around. "If I didn't know better, I'd say you were out to seduce me." A smile came and went. "Again."

"What if I am?"

"I'd have to ask why."

"Because I want you to know exactly what I'm feeling, exactly what I want," she said at once.

"Sex?"

She grinned. "That, too."

"What else?"

"You," she said evenly. "I want you to come back to Wyoming with me. I know it's a lot to ask, that your law practice is here, but you were happy there, once you got used to it, anyway, and I think you love me and—"

"Yes," he said, interrupting her.

Her eyes widened. "What?"

He grinned. "If that was a proposal, the answer is yes."

"That easy?"

"You wanted me to be difficult?"

"Well, I did have all these very persuasive arguments I was hoping to use," she said, moving into his arms.

He lowered his head to capture her mouth. Only after she had been thoroughly kissed, did he take a step back. "By all means," he teased, "persuade me, but I've got to tell you, I'm an easy mark where you're concerned. I have been since the beginning."

"Not since the beginning," she argued.

"Definitely the beginning," he insisted. "In fact, I've been considering a partnership of sorts with you for some time now."

"My experience with partnerships hasn't been all that great," she reminded him. "I told Tony I'd come back and work with him. I've known him my whole life. He would never betray me."

"Maybe not, but this thing with you and me would be a very personal partnership," Rafe pointed out. "No comparison."

"Can I trust you not to run out on me?"

"Absolutely."

"What are the terms? I want to know exactly what I'm getting into."

"Love, honor and cherish. Now and forever. The usual."

It sounded like a pretty decent deal. "Just one more thing. I intend to work for Tony. Eventually I'll take over. If the place is swamped, are you going to help cook?"

"Only if the chef rewards me later."

Gina held out her hand. "It's a deal."

But—typical lawyer—Rafe wasn't satisfied until they'd sealed it with a lot more than a handshake.

Epilogue

There had never been a doubt in the world about where their wedding reception was going to be held. Tony and Francesca started planning it the day Gina and Rafe shared the news that they were getting married. Now that the day had arrived, however, Tony had barred Gina from the kitchen.

"I will do this, *cara mia.* You are not to worry."

"But I could help," Gina protested uselessly. "Besides, I'm the bride. Shouldn't I have some say over what the cake looks like, at least?"

Tony regarded her with exaggerated indignation. "Do you not think that my Francesca knows what will please you?"

"Of course, but—"

"Go," Tony ordered. "The wedding is in an hour. You must be beautiful."

"Okay, okay," she said, though she didn't think an hour was going to make much difference. The summer heat had already frizzed her hair, and it would melt her makeup the moment it was applied.

The instant she stepped outside the restaurant, she

was surrounded by the Calamity Janes. "Francesca called you, didn't she?"

"She did," Emma said. "She said you were getting in her way."

"I wasn't in her way. Tony wouldn't even let me near the kitchen."

"This is one meal you are not going to cook yourself," Karen insisted. "Besides, as bridesmaids it is our duty to make sure you're dressed and at the church on time. You don't want to make us look bad, do you?"

Cassie was amazingly quiet as she studied Gina. "Prewedding jitters?" she asked eventually.

Gina gulped and nodded. "How did you know?"

Cassie and Karen exchanged knowing looks. "Been there, done that," they said in unison.

"Trust us, though, you are going to be deliriously happy. Rafe will see to it."

Gina smiled at last. "He already has."

"Well then," Emma said briskly. "There's nothing to worry about, is there? Let's get this show on the road. I have my list right here. If we follow it, we'll stay right on schedule."

Gina chuckled. "Wait till it's your turn," she warned Emma. "We are going to show you no mercy."

"I predict this fall," Lauren said.

"Definitely before Christmas," Karen said.

"Oh—" Emma began.

"Go suck an egg," they all chimed in. "You're not convincing anymore, Emma, so give it up," Lauren added. "You and Ford are next."

Gina looked around at her best friends and felt tears begin to well up in her eyes. She loved these women, and thanks to Bobby's treachery and Rafe's understanding, she had them back in her life. The Calamity Janes were a gift worth treasuring. She'd never lose sight of that again.

"Oh, no, she's about to start blubbering," Cassie noted. "Stop that, right this second. You can't get married with your eyes all red and puffy."

"Rafe won't care," she said with a sniff.

"Maybe not, but you will when you have to look at the wedding pictures in the years to come," Lauren added, giving her a hug. "Trust me on this. If there's one thing I know about it's how a bad picture can turn up years later to bite you in the butt."

They got her to the church and into her gown with five minutes to spare. She spent those minutes with her parents.

"Thank you," she said, hugging them fiercely.

"For what? The wedding? It was our pleasure," her mother said. "We've dreamed of this day for a long time."

"Not just that," Gina told them, holding her father's hand tightly. "For letting me go all those years ago and for welcoming me back now."

"Just give us some grandbabies and you will have paid us back in full," her mother said.

Her father scowled. "Don't rush the girl, Jane. She hasn't even said 'I do' yet."

"That's okay," she told her father. "I think Mother and Rafe are on the same page on that one. For a man who claimed to know nothing about relationships or family, he's adapting to the concept pretty quickly."

"How does that mother of his feel about being a grandma?" her father asked. "I can't imagine she's happy about it. I've never seen a woman so determined to shave twenty years off her age."

Gina grinned at the assessment. It was true. Rafe's mother worked astonishingly hard at being youthful. Grandchildren were going to rattle her.

"She'll adapt," Gina's mother said. "And if she doesn't, I'll get those precious grandbabies all to myself."

There was a knock on the door just then. "I think they're ready for us," Cassie called out. "And Rafe is prowling around the front of the church looking impatient."

Gina opened the door. "Then by all means, let's not keep the man waiting."

Rafe had worn dozens of tuxedos in his time, but he was fairly certain this one was going to choke him to death. He ran his finger under the shirt collar.

"Stop fidgeting," his mother mouthed from the front pew.

The admonition made him grin despite himself. How many times had he heard that as a boy? A million, probably. It was good to know that some things never changed.

At last the music began, and his gaze flew to the back of the church. The procession seemed endless. First Cassie, Lauren, Karen and his own sister as the bridesmaids. Then Emma, looking softer and more feminine than he'd ever seen her, as Gina's maid of honor. Finally Caitlyn as the flower girl, happily scattering rose petals along the aisle as she grinned at Rafe.

There was a pause in the music, and Rafe's breath caught in his throat. Gina appeared on her father's arm, and his throat went dry. How had he ever gotten so lucky?

Her dress was simple, but she looked like a million bucks in it. He grinned at the thought. That was exactly the price tag that had been put on Café Tuscany a few weeks ago, when the paperwork for Gina's deal with Deidre and Ronnie was being drawn up. All three of them had stared at the bankers in disbelief. Gina had insisted that the deal be for less than half of that.

"They've paid the difference a thousand times over," she had told the bankers. "It's because of them that it's worth so much now."

To Rafe's amusement she had gotten her way and the deal had been struck. Now there was nothing left to tie them to New York. They were in Winding River to stay.

"I love you," he whispered when Gina reached his side.

"You'd better," she whispered back, but her eyes were filled with laughter.

When the time came for the vows they had written for themselves, Rafe shocked the crowd with his first words. He could hear the gasps as he began by saying, "From the moment I met you, I knew you were a thief."

The only person who wasn't the least bit startled was Gina. She watched him solemnly with love in her eyes.

"You stole my heart," he said quietly, drawing a relieved sigh from the onlookers and the beginnings of a smile from Gina. "Even when I struggled to get it back, you held on and taught me what it means to share love and friendship. You taught me about loyalty and commitment. Today I give you my heart willingly, because I know you'll keep it safe forever."

There were tears shining in her eyes when he finished. She brushed at them impatiently as she began her own vows. "I know the value of what you are giving me, because I know how difficult it was for you to overcome all of the doubts you had about me at the beginning. It's a funny thing about distrust. It can destroy a relationship or it can make it stronger. I think ours is stronger because of the way it began. I will spend a lifetime proving to you that I deserve your trust and giving you everything that my heart has to share—my family, my friends, my town, and most of all, my love."

When the priest pronounced them man and wife and blessed them, Gina held her face up for his kiss. Rafe covered her mouth with his own, and once again he was back at the fairgrounds on a hot, steamy afternoon, tasting her lips for the very first time, unable to stop, savoring every single second of the kiss.

The congregation erupted into laughter and applause when he finally released her. Gina grinned.

"I guess we're destined to giving them something to talk about," she said.

He winked. "It certainly works for me. How about you?"

"Any time. Any place."

"Forever?"

She stood on tiptoe and kissed him again, another slow, melting kiss that rocked him to his core.

"Definitely forever," she said.

* * * * *

THE CALAMITY JANES

Prologue

The only light on in the kitchen was coming from inside the well-stocked refrigerator. Emma stood on the tiled floor in her stockinged feet, still clad in the designer suit and simple gold jewelry she'd worn to court hours ago, and ate strawberry-cheesecake yogurt from its plastic container.

"Welcome to my glamorous life," she muttered as she spooned the food into her mouth without really tasting it.

It was ten o'clock at night. She'd left her high-priced Cherry Creek home that morning at six-thirty. She'd managed to snag a piece of toast on her way out the door and a tuna on rye at the courthouse at lunchtime. This yogurt was dinner. Unfortunately, it was all too typical of her daily diet, all too typical of her nonstop schedule.

It had been weeks since she'd been able to sit down at the table with her six-year-old daughter for a leisurely meal. Caitlyn was so accustomed to eating with the housekeeper that when she and Emma talked on the phone during the day, she rarely ever asked if her mother was coming home. A part of Emma was relieved not to have to deal with the added pressure of

Caitlyn's disappointment, but another part of her knew that she ought to be appalled by the lack of time she and her daughter shared and—even worse—Caitlyn's resigned acceptance of that lack.

Emma's ex-husband hadn't been as forgiving. Kit Rogers had married her while Emma was still in law school. In one of those inexplicable failed-birth-control flukes, she had gotten pregnant before graduation. For some reason, Kit had assumed that she would become a traditional stay-at-home wife once Caitlyn was born. His own law career was well established, his income well into six figures. Emma hadn't needed to work for financial reasons.

But Emma refused to cooperate. She hadn't excelled in law school only to give it all up. Her determined pursuit of a career with a top-notch, demanding Denver law firm had turned from an annoyance into a full-fledged bone of contention in their marriage.

As her star at the firm had risen, the arguments had increased in intensity. His manipulative efforts to sabotage her career had escalated. When nothing—not even the worst kind of betrayal, so painful that even now she couldn't bear to think about it—had worked, he'd walked out, threatening to sue for custody of Caitlyn. The clash in court, complete with the city's best legal talent on opposing sides, had promised to be the stuff of headlines. Emma had actually begun to relish the challenge.

That should have been a wake-up call about her driven lifestyle and her misplaced priorities, but it hadn't turned out that way. Kit had met someone else almost immediately after their separation and had backed off on his threats. Emma had won without going to court and without having to change. In the end it had been a hollow victory. Now Kit saw even less of Caitlyn than Emma did. Her daughter was resigned to that, too.

In fact, Caitlyn had been forced to accept too darned much, Emma concluded as she angrily tossed the yogurt container into the trash and shut the refrigerator door. There had been too many canceled plans and broken promises.

After switching on the overhead light, she reached for the invitation that had come in that day's mail. Her high school reunion was coming up in a few weeks in Winding River, Wyoming. Caitlyn's private school would be out by then. It would be a chance for Emma to spend some quality time with her daughter, a chance for Caitlyn to see her grandparents, aunts, uncles and cousins—extended family she needed more than ever now that her father was pretty much out of their lives. Caitlyn deserved this trip. They both did. Visits to Wyoming had been too rare thanks to Emma's demanding schedule. It had been two years. The time had just slipped by.

Emma picked up her datebook and thumbed through the pages. Appointments and court appearances jammed every page. She took out a pen—not a pencil that could be erased when second thoughts set in—and circled the weekend of the reunion. She made a note by tomorrow's date to have her secretary cancel everything for that Wednesday through Sunday. Even though the Fourth of July holiday was only a few days later, she couldn't quite bring herself to take an entire week off. Well, five days was better than nothing… and considerably more than the occasional day she snatched for herself.

Five whole days away from her job, away from Denver. The thought boggled her mind. Best of all, she would get to see her dearest friends, the indomitable Calamity Janes—so named for their penchant for trouble and heartache—who could make her laugh and remind her of who she'd been before work had become an obsession. It would be good to get some perspective—some balance—back into her life. If anyone could help her accomplish that, Lauren, Karen, Cassie and Gina could.

It was ironic, really, that five women could be so different and yet have so much in common. Lauren was now a Hollywood superstar, Karen a rancher. Cassie was a struggling single mom, Gina a gourmet chef with her own restaurant in New York. Yet they shared a history, a friendship that had weathered time and separation. The last time they had all been together had been at Emma's law school graduation. Since then, they'd stayed in touch through occasional phone calls, e-mails and hastily jotted notes on Christmas cards.

But even if the contact had been sporadic, the depth of the bond had never suffered, Emma reflected. These women were her best friends and, though she sometimes neglected them, she treasured the friendships. Lauren, twice-divorced herself, had listened endlessly when Emma had gone through her divorce. Cassie had provided a shoulder to lean on as Emma had struggled with the guilt of not having enough time for Caitlyn. Happily married Karen had been steady as a rock, offering nonjudgmental advice whenever Emma had sought it. And ever since the divorce, Gina had sent periodic care packages of gourmet baked goods to cheer both Emma and Caitlyn.

But even as anticipation of seeing them began to stir

inside her, Emma sighed as she thought of the work that would be waiting for her on the following Monday. For once, though, she couldn't let that matter. The truth was that the work could wait. She was not indispensable. She had more money than she had time to spend it. So did the partners at her firm. A few less billable hours would hardly ruin her fast-track career.

Who knew when a chance like this would come along again? The prospect of seeing the Calamity Janes was too good to pass up. The usual dread of listening to her mother grumble that she hadn't been eating right actually brought a smile to Emma's lips for once. And knowing that her father would likely remind her that she was brilliant and beautiful and worth loving...well, that was something she'd been needing to hear ever since her divorce. Even though the breakup had been for the best, even though Kit had proved himself to be a world-class jerk, the divorce had been a blow to Emma's self-esteem. A high achiever from grade school on, she'd never expected to fail at anything.

Pleased with her resolve to take a much-needed break, she could hardly wait to tell Caitlyn. She could already imagine the rare, shy smile that would light up her daughter's face. Unfortunately, she could also envision the child's hesitancy, her reluctance to believe that the trip would actually happen.

"I won't let you down, baby," she vowed as she flipped off the light and headed for her home office, where she had another hour's worth of paperwork to get through before bedtime. "Not this time."

This trip was going to be all about relaxation, laughter, family and friends. Nothing was going to interfere with that, nothing at all.

1

Ford Hamilton stared at the computer screen on which the front page of the weekly *Winding River News* was laid out. There was a big gap where his lead story should be. Because it was the paper's first edition since he'd taken over ownership, he'd wanted something splashy to fill that space, something to make the locals sit up and take notice.

"So, boss, want me to go out and interview the people planning their class reunion about who's coming and what will be happening?" Teddy Taylor asked. Teddy was eighteen and intended to major in photojournalism. He was enthusiastically interning with Ford for the summer and itching for a page-one photo or byline. On a paper just starting out on Ford's shoestring budget he was doing everything. Even an intern's inexpert help was welcome.

Ford sighed. A class reunion was not the sort of local news he envisioned for his front page. He'd been trained in hard news in big cities, where the stories competing for page-one headlines were about politics and corruption and crime. There wasn't much of any of those things in Winding River, Wyoming. It was a sleepy, quiet town where very little happened— which, he reminded himself, was precisely the reason he'd chosen it. He was tired of chasing bad guys all the time, to say nothing of arguing with editors about how a story should be played in the paper. Now he was in charge, and maybe, just maybe, he could put out a paper that would actually make a difference in the community.

Unfortunately, the very things that had drawn him here—the peace and quiet—were thwarting his plans to make a big impression with this first edition. He was just waking up to the true meaning of the term "slow news day." He had a feeling that he'd just gone through what was destined to be a slow news *week,* if not a slow news *year.*

Still, that did not mean he had to resort to filling prime front-page space with puff pieces about a class reunion, even if it was all anyone could talk about around town. He'd list the scheduled events the week before the event, then send a photographer when the time came. A picture spread inside was enough coverage for a non-news event.

That still left an empty hole on page one for this week's edition, and time was rapidly running out. He couldn't count on an accident or even a little cattle rustling happening before his deadline. After twenty minutes spent skimming through a half-dozen press releases for community events, Ford resigned himself to going with the most exciting thing he had—that blasted rinky-dink reunion. Maybe there was an angle that would work, give the story a little substance to justify placing it on the front page.

"Teddy, how about going over and interviewing the sheriff?" he suggested. "Ask him what the plans are for security, especially since I hear that actress is coming in for the weekend. Is the county paying overtime for extra help in case there are any problems with crowd control?"

Teddy's mouth gaped. "Crowd control? In Winding River?"

"Lauren Winters is pretty hot since she won her Academy Award this spring," Ford explained, regretting that his predecessor had announced her attendance. *That* could have been his big story. "If word leaks out that she's going to be here, every tabloid from around the globe will be sending in a photographer. While you're at it, check to see if all of the hotel rooms are booked. The paparazzi get testy if they can't stay close by. If nothing's available, they'll be sleeping in their cars on her front lawn or wherever it is she's staying. Ask Ryan if he's prepared to deal with that."

Teddy's expression brightened. "Are you serious? You'll let me interview the sheriff?"

Ford barely contained a grin at the boy's eagerness, especially since the sheriff was his uncle. Chances were real good that Ryan Taylor would dictate the story just the way he wanted to see it in the paper. Normally Ford wouldn't leave the interview to an unseasoned reporter, but Teddy needed to get his feet wet, and this was as good a story as any.

"Go for it. You have two hours to talk to him, write up the article and get it in. I want this edition on the street on time. The old owner tended to play fast and loose with deadlines and distribution. I'm not going to."

"Got it," Teddy said, and raced out, tape recorder in hand.

Ford sighed again. Had he ever been that young, that energetic? Not that he was exactly dragging at thirty-two, but after just a month he was already adapting to the slower pace of Winding River. He no longer got up at dawn, no longer worked twelve-hour days. He lingered over coffee at Stella's for a chance to chat with the locals.

At first he'd welcomed the change from the lightning-fast speed of things in Atlanta and then Chicago. Slowing down had been one of the reasons he'd sought out a paper to buy and a place to settle and build a life for himself before stress leveled him with a premature heart attack. Eventually he hoped to marry, maybe have a couple of kids. He wanted more than a career. He wanted a life.

He'd spent a couple of years using vacation time to look for a community that was growing, one where a solid newspaper could make a difference, where his editorials and news stories might really have an impact on a way of life. He'd been drawn to Wyoming because of the rugged beauty of the landscape and because of the changes that were happening every single day now that it had been discovered by big name celebrities. Development was bound to follow in their wake, which promised challenges to the environment and to a way of life.

Everything had come together the minute he'd visited Winding River and talked to the paper's prior owner. They'd made the deal on a handshake over the winter, and now, just a few months later, he was in business, publishing his own weekly paper, albeit with very limited resources for the moment.

He knew enough about small towns to recognize that he had to move cautiously. Change was always viewed with suspicion. Ironically that had been one of the reasons Ford had left his hometown in Georgia and settled in Atlanta after college. He'd seen how resistant people back home were to change of any kind.

Unfortunately, he'd realized belatedly that things weren't that much better in a big city, especially when he had to fight his own newspaper bureaucracy before getting some of his tougher pieces in print. Chicago had been more of the same, a constant battle between the pressures of the advertising department and editorial independence. Years ago the separation would have been a given, but these days, with tough economic times for newspapers, the suits were having more of an impact on the journalists.

Ford was still finding his way in Winding River, getting to know the movers and shakers, listening to anyone and everyone who had something to say about the way the town was run or the way it ought to be.

Change was on the horizon. The downtown was testament to that. A chic boutique had moved in just down the block from a western wear store. There were Range Rovers parked alongside pickups hauling horse trailers. High-priced gifts were being sold next door to the feed-and-grain store. And fancy corporate jets sat on the airstrip next to crop dusters.

The previous owner of the paper, Ronald Haggerty, had stayed on long enough to introduce Ford around, give him a slap on the back and a hearty recommendation to the various civic organizations. Then he'd retired and moved to Arizona. Ford was on his own now.

He was already beginning to formulate some opinions that he was eager to get into print, but it was too soon. He needed to wait for the right opening, the right story to show everyone that the *Winding River News* and its new owner intended to participate in every aspect of life in Winding River. A big, splashy, controversial front-page story, that's what he needed.

So far in life, Ford Hamilton had found the odds were usually in his favor. And if his luck held, he'd have that front-page story very soon.

"Am I really going to learn to ride a horse?" Caitlyn asked for the tenth time as she and Emma made the drive from Denver on Wednesday.

"Grandpa said he'd teach you, didn't he?"

Emma nodded, curls bouncing. "I am sooo excited. I never rode a horse before."

"So you've mentioned," Emma said wryly.

"And how many cousins do I have?"

"Five. You met some of them last time we were here."

"But I was just a baby then. I was only four," Caitlyn said. "I forgot."

"Okay, there's Jessie—"

"How old is Jessie?"

"She's six, the same as you."

"Do you think she can ride a horse already?" Caitlyn asked worriedly. "Will she make fun of me?"

"I don't know if she can ride, but Grandpa won't let her make fun of you."

Caitlyn nodded, evidently satisfied. "Who else?"

"There's Davey, and Rob, and Jeb and Pete."

"They're all boys," she said, clearly disappointed. "And they're all littler than me, right?"

"That's right."

"But me and Jessie will be friends, right?"

"I'm sure you will be," Emma reassured her. "You had a wonderful time together the last time you were here for a visit. You had tea parties for your dolls and played games with Grandma and baked cookies."

Caitlyn's eyes shone with excitement. "How soon will we be there?"

"A half hour, maybe less."

"What time is that?"

"Twelve-thirty."

Caitlyn touched a finger to the clock on the dash. "When the big hand is here and the little hand is down here, right?"

"Exactly."

A worried frown puckered her brow again. "I thought Grandma said we'd have lunch at twelve. Will they eat without us?"

"No, baby, I don't think they'll eat without us. I called to let Grandma know we got a late start, remember?"

"'Cause you had to go to the office," Caitlyn said. "Even though we're on vacation."

"That's it till Monday," Emma promised.

"Then how come your phone keeps ringing?"

Emma sighed. It kept ringing because she hadn't cut it off. Getting away from the office was one thing. Deactivating her cell phone was something else entirely. There could be emergencies, questions from her paralegals...all sorts of crises that simply couldn't wait.

"Don't worry," she told her daughter. "It won't ring all that often. I won't let it interfere with our plans."

As if to prove her wrong, the cell phone promptly rang. With an apologetic look at Caitlyn, Emma answered. "Rogers."

"Is this the famous Denver lawyer who only handles the most challenging cases in the universe?"

Emma grinned. "Lauren? Where are you?"

"I'm sitting at a table with your family, waiting for you to get here. We are growing impatient. I, for one, am starved, and they won't let me eat till you show your face. Where *are* you?"

"Just outside of town, about a mile from the ranch now. Tell Mom to put the food on the table and pour the iced tea."

"Already done. I helped."

"Was the family impressed that a glamorous actress was fixing lunch?"

Lauren chuckled. "Not that I noticed. Rob has smeared strained peas all over my designer blouse, but he's only a baby, so I've forgiven him."

"Good thing. I don't think Rob's daddy can afford to pay for a replacement. It probably cost more than he makes in a month."

"Pretty close," Lauren agreed. "I told him *you'd* replace it. You can afford it."

"I guess it's a good thing that I'm about to turn into the driveway, so I can protect my interests," Emma said.

Even as she made the turn, she could hear the squeals announcing that the kids had spotted her car. As they neared the house, she glanced over at Caitlyn and saw her eyes widen as all of her cousins except the baby tumbled out of the house, followed by Emma's younger brothers and their wives, then Lauren—still holding the portable phone—and then her grandparents.

Suddenly shy, Caitlyn held back when her grandmother opened the car door and reached for her. Not permitting even the tiniest hint of the hurt she must have felt, Emma's mother gently touched Caitlyn's cheek.

"I am so glad you've come to visit," she said quietly. "Your grandpa and I have missed you."

"Really?" Caitlyn said, looking surprised.

"You bet. Would you like to come with me to see the surprise he got you? It's down at the barn."

Caitlyn turned to Emma. "Can I, Mommy?"

"I thought everybody was anxious to eat," Emma said, casting a pointed look at Lauren.

"That's okay. I'm sure I won't starve," her friend said with an exaggerated pout.

Emma grinned at her. "Nice acting." She released Caitlyn's hand. "Of course you can go." She glanced at her mother. "What's the big surprise?"

"You'll see," her mother teased. "I'm not giving away a thing."

As the two of them went off hand in hand, trailed by the cousins, Emma turned to her brothers, who enveloped her in bear hugs even as they chided her for staying away too long.

"Leave her alone," her sister-in-law Martha said. "She's here now. That's what counts. And we're going to make the most of every minute of it."

"That we are," Lauren said, stepping forward for her own hug. "You look tired."

"It was a long drive."

"Not that long," Lauren chided, leading her inside where the dining room table had been set for a celebration, complete with her mom's best dishes. "And dark circles like that don't happen overnight. I ought to know. I'm an expert on what lack of sleep can do to a person's face. Lucky for you, I am also an expert on makeup tricks that will disguise it. By the time we go to the reunion dance on Saturday, you'll look like a million bucks. Men will fall at your feet."

"I'm here to see my friends, not to nab a man for myself," Emma scolded. "Besides, with you around, no one will be looking at me."

"Wait till I get through fixing you up," Lauren retorted. "You can't take a chance that you'll bump into the perfect man. You don't want to scare him to death."

"I don't think we need to worry about that. There are very few perfect men in Winding River." She glanced at her brothers and grinned. "Present company excluded, of course. That was one of the reasons we left, remember?"

"I'm an optimist," Lauren declared cheerfully. "A lot can change in ten years. For one thing, acne usually clears up." She poked an elbow into Matt's ribs. "Right?"

Matt frowned and ignored her.

"Absolutely," Martha said to cover her husband's silence. "Not only that, we can even get cappuccino or a latte on Main Street now. Of course, the locals pretty much go to Stella's the same as always. The gourmet stuff is for the tourists."

Emma stared at her in surprise. "We have *tourists* now? What do they come to see?"

"The real west," her brother Wayne reported dryly.

"Of course, while coming to gawk at the genuine article, they can't do it without a few of the frills from back East, but what the heck, it's pumping a few dollars into the economy."

"It's going to destroy us in the end, you mark my words," her brother Matt chimed in, his expression dire. "And that new newspaper editor is going to be leading the charge."

"Ford Hamilton's not such a bad guy," Martha chided her husband. "Give him a chance."

"To do what? Ruin the place with his fancy, big-city ideas?" Matt countered.

"How do you know he has big-city ideas?" Martha demanded. "You won't even talk to him!"

"He's from Chicago, isn't he?" Matt grumbled. "I guarantee you he's going to be the first one to call for opening up the land to all kinds of greedy developers. We'll have subdivisions all the way from here to Laramie if we're not careful."

Emma's mother held up her hand. "Okay, Matt, enough. Let your sister at least get something to eat before you start all this doom-and-gloom stuff over the fate of Winding River. That kind of thing is bad for the digestion."

Nevertheless, over lunch Emma got an earful on the changes in the town in the past few years—none of them good, to hear Matt tell it. She also heard quite a lot about this man, Ford Hamilton, whose first two editions of the paper had been the talk of Winding River.

"Took out the local columns that Ron had been running for years," Matt groused.

"Everybody around here already knew what everybody else was doing," Martha argued. "We didn't need to read about it in the paper." She regarded her husband defiantly. "Besides, I think he's gorgeous. It's about time somebody exciting and available moved into town."

"Why do *you* care? You're married to *me,*" Matt reminded her.

Martha rolled her eyes. "That doesn't mean I'm dead. Besides, a man like Ford Hamilton could be just what it takes to persuade Emma to move back here."

Emma held up a hand. "*Whoa!* Don't even go there. I am *not* looking for a man and I am *not* coming back here. Don't go getting any crazy ideas on that score, Martha—or any of the rest of you, either."

"Well, we can all dream," her mother said. "I, for one, think it would be wonderful if you'd at least give the idea some thought."

"Don't push the girl," her father said. "She just walked in the door."

"Oh, be still. You're just as anxious to have her back here as I am," her mother retorted. "That's what that pony is all about."

Emma stared at them. "What pony?"

"That was the surprise," Caitlyn said, her eyes glowing. "Grandpa got me a pony."

Emma's father grinned at her. "That was supposed to be a secret till after lunch, cupcake."

Caitlyn's face fell. "Oh, yeah. I forgot."

"That's okay, sweetie. *Somebody* needed to tell me," Emma said, giving her hand a squeeze, even as she shot a reproachful look at her father.

"You had one when you were her age," her father pointed out.

"But I *lived* here," she retorted, then let the subject

drop. She was not going to ruin lunch by getting into an argument at the table.

"Let's get back to Ford Hamilton," Martha suggested diplomatically.

"Yes, let's," Lauren agreed. "If Emma's not interested in a gorgeous, available newspaper editor, maybe *I'll* check him out."

"Right," Wayne scoffed. "As if you'd ever come back here to stay."

"You never know," Lauren said so seriously that it drew stares from every adult at the table.

"Lauren?" Emma said, regarding her curiously. This was the first she'd heard of any disenchantment Lauren felt with her glamorous lifestyle.

"Oh, don't mind me," Lauren said, pushing back from the table. "I've got to run. I promised Karen I'd drive over to the ranch this afternoon and help with the horses."

"Now *there's* a picture the tabloids would pay to have," Emma's father teased. "Millie, where's my camera? I could probably make enough from this shot to pay for a couple of new bulls."

"You don't want to do that, Dad," Emma warned. "I'd have to advise Lauren to sue you."

"As if I could ever sue my favorite surrogate dad," Lauren said, pressing a kiss to his cheek that made him blush.

He shook his head. "Who knew that one of Emma's friends would grow up to become one of the most famous beauties in the world? I remember when you wore your hair in pigtails and made mud pies in my backyard."

"Now *that* is a picture the tabloids would love," Wayne said. "And I think I know where one is."

"In the scrapbook," Matt said, grinning for the first

time since Emma had arrived. "Shall I get it? We can split the profits."

"You do and you're a dead man," Emma warned. "I'm in that picture, too. If Lauren doesn't kill you, I will."

She glanced across the table to see tears in her mother's eyes. "Mom? What's wrong?"

"I'm just so happy to have all of you around this table again, squabbling the way you used to. You, too, Lauren. I can't tell you how much I've missed having my whole family under one roof."

Guilt spread through Emma. "I'll get home more often, Mom. I promise."

"You say that now, but once you're back in Denver, you'll be deluged with clients, and the next thing you know another two years will have slipped by."

"I won't let that happen," Emma vowed.

But, of course, it would. She was powerless to stop it. Her career defined her. Being the best and brightest in her class had challenged her to become the best and brightest in the firm. She wanted to be the first lawyer people thought of when there was a high-profile case in Denver. She'd failed at marriage. She was a neglectful, if loving, mom and daughter. But she would be somebody when it came to her profession. Men made sacrifices for their careers all the time, and no one thought any less of them. Why should it be different for a woman? And at least she was setting an example for Caitlyn that a woman could achieve whatever she wanted to in a man's world.

But at what cost? some would ask. Emma even asked herself that from time to time in the dark of night. So far, though, she hadn't come up with a satisfactory answer. She wondered if she ever would.

2

Ford hadn't intended to go anywhere near the Winding River High School class reunion. With no other reporter on staff, he'd assigned Teddy Taylor to cover it and given him a camera to take along. Teddy had been ecstatic.

"Be sure you get a few shots of Lauren Winters," he reminded the teenager. "Everyone's going to want to see the big celebrity deigning to mingle with the small-town folks."

Ford's sarcasm was unmistakable, even to Teddy. The boy had frowned. "I don't think Lauren's like that. Uncle Ryan says she's great. She was the smartest kid in the class. He says she was real serious back then. Nobody expected her to wind up an actress."

"Whatever," Ford said, dismissing the ardent defense. "Just get lots of pictures. You probably know who's important better than I do."

"I hope so. I got a list from Uncle Ryan. He knows everybody. There's a lady named Gina who has one of the hottest restaurants in New York—"

"Gina Petrillo?" Ford asked, startled. "Owns a place called Café Tuscany?"

Teddy glanced at his notes, then nodded. "Yeah, that's it. You've heard of it?"

"I've eaten there," he said. The editors of a New York paper had taken him there when they'd been courting him, trying to steal him away from an investigative team in Chicago. He'd been impressed by the food and the ambience, if not by the New Yorkers' pitch. The owner's name had stuck with him, though he'd only caught a glimpse of her as she rushed from the kitchen to greet favored guests. Discovering that Gina Petrillo came from Winding River was a surprise.

"And there's someone named Emma, who's some kind of courtroom barracuda in Denver now," Teddy had continued. "And Cole Davis, the big computer-programming genius—well, he wasn't in the class, but his girlfriend was. Uncle Ryan says he'll probably be there even though he's a couple of years older. Everybody's turning out because it's such a big deal for the town that Lauren's coming."

Ford had been even more startled by the complete litany of success stories. Even though he'd come from a small town himself, he'd always felt that the odds of success were stacked against him. To find so many high achievers coming out of one small class in Winding River—okay, two classes, if Cole Davis had been a year or two ahead of the others—was intriguing.

The more he'd thought about it, the more convinced he'd become that there was a story there. Who or what had motivated these four people to work so hard? Was it a teacher? A parent? A community-wide commitment to education? Their stories could well provide motivation for the current crop of students.

Because of his fascination with the idea, he'd bought a ticket to the Saturday night dance. He had his tape recorder in his pocket, but for the moment he was content to stand on the fringes of the party and watch the dancing.

It was early yet. There was plenty of time for tracking down the class celebrities. Not that he expected to have any difficulty identifying them. The others would probably be fawning all over them, with the possible exception of the attorney. They might be giving her a wide berth. In his experience, most sensible people were wary of lawyers.

"Young man, why aren't you dancing?" Geraldine Hawkins demanded.

Ford glanced down into twinkling blue eyes framed by gray bangs. The veteran English teacher was sixty-five and barely five feet tall. Yet, according to Ron Haggerty, she could intimidate a six-five, two-hundred-forty-pound linebacker. She'd been one of the first people Ford had met, the introduction preceded by an admonition not to underestimate her. Mrs. Hawkins, despite her diminutive size, was a well-respected powerhouse in town. A decade ago, she had been mayor twice, but now she claimed she no longer had time for that "nonsense."

She stood before him now with increasing impatience. "Well, young man?"

"Two left feet," Ford told her.

"I don't believe that for a minute." She gestured across the room to five women sitting at a table with one man. One of those women was unmistakably the gorgeous Lauren Winters. Another he recognized as Gina Petrillo. "Now go on over there and ask someone to dance. Nobody should be a wallflower at their own class reunion, especially not when there's a handsome, available man in the room."

Ford grinned at her. "I'd rather dance with you, Mrs. Hawkins. How about it? Care to take a spin around the floor with me?"

Color flamed in her cheeks, but she demurely held out her hand. "Why, I don't mind if I do. Just stay off my toes, young man. I have corns."

He laughed at that. "I'll do my best, but I'm not making any promises."

He swept her into his arms and waltzed her gracefully around the floor. When the music ended, she scolded, "Young man, you fibbed to me. You know perfectly well how to dance."

"You inspired me," he insisted.

"Nonsense. Now go ask someone your own age to dance."

"Anyone in particular?"

She glanced over at the same group of women. One of them was clutching a cell phone to her ear and nodding, her expression intense. She was beautiful in an uptight, regal way, Ford mused.

"I'd recommend Emma," Mrs. Hawkins said. "The one on the phone. She needs a distraction. Whoever invented cell phones ought to be shot, but since it's too late for that, we can only try to get them away from the people who are addicted to them."

"Emma?" Ford repeated, recalling his conversation with Teddy. "She's an attorney?"

"A fine one, from what I've heard. Works too hard,

though. I've heard that, as well. Just look at her. Here she is at a dance with all of her old friends and she's on the phone. I guarantee you that it's a business call."

Even as they stared at her, Emma reluctantly handed the phone to Lauren, who dialed, spoke to someone, then hung up, her expression triumphant. When Emma reached for the phone, Lauren held it away from her.

"Good for Lauren," Mrs. Hawkins said approvingly. "Now it's up to you. Ask her to dance. If ever there was a young woman in need of some fun, it's our Emma."

Ford sensed that the teacher was not going to give up until he was back out on the dance floor, preferably with the workaholic attorney. Since he'd intended to seek Emma out anyway, he nodded. "You win. But if I step all over her toes and she sues me, I'm holding you responsible."

"I'm not concerned," the English teacher said with a blithe expression.

Ford crossed the high school gym. By the time he reached the table, Emma was sitting all alone, her expression glum.

"I've been commanded to dance with you," Ford told her.

She gazed up at him, her expression startled. "Commanded? Now there's a gracious invitation, if ever I heard one." She might be an uptight workaholic, but Emma was even more attractive up close. For a brief moment Ford was grateful the English teacher had sent him on this mission of mercy. He suspected though, that Emma was going to do her very best to see that he got over that benevolent feeling.

"Mrs. Hawkins," he said, nodding in the teacher's direction.

To his surprise, a smile spread across Emma's face, softening the harsh lines of her mouth and putting a sparkle into her eyes. "She does have a way of getting what she wants, doesn't she? She actually managed to nudge me into reading Shakespeare. I hated it, but she never once let up. Eventually I began to like it."

"She must not have had to nudge too hard," Ford said. "From what I hear, you were a terrific student. I'm Ford Hamilton, by the way."

Her expression cooled considerably. "Ah," she said, "the new owner of the paper. I've heard about you."

"Nothing too damning, I hope."

"So far no, but then you've only been here a few weeks. I'm sure you haven't done your worst yet." She stood up. "Thanks for asking me to dance, but I have some old friends I need to see."

She brushed past him and headed straight for the hallway. Ford stared after her, wondering what he'd said to offend her. Or was it nothing more than the fact that he owned the paper?

"Ms. Rogers?" he called after her.

She hesitated but didn't turn around. Refusing to talk to her back, he walked over and stepped in front of her.

"When you have a few minutes, I'd like to speak with you," he said.

Her expression remained cool. "About?"

"What or who motivated you when you were at Winding River High. I'm hoping to talk to all of the major success stories from your class. I think there might be some lessons in what drove you to succeed."

Her gaze narrowed. "What's your measure of success, Mr. Hamilton? Fame? Money?"

"Both, I suppose."

"Then we have nothing to talk about. You see, the people I view as successful from our class are the ones who are doing what they love to do, who are happy with their lives. For instance, my friend Karen. She's not famous, and she probably has very little savings. But she's working a ranch she loves with a man she adores. That's success, Mr. Hamilton, not what *I* do."

Before he could respond, there was a scuffle of some kind across the gym. A man who looked as if he was probably drunk was tugging on the arm of a woman, while another man looked as if he might intervene. Only after a subtle nod from the woman did the second man back away with a shrug. Finally he turned and left the room.

Beside Ford, Emma tensed. He glanced down and saw genuine worry on her face. "You know them?"

"Of course. Everyone in Winding River knows everyone else. Sue Ellen was in my class. Donny was a year older. They were high school sweethearts."

"They don't look so happy now," Ford observed. "Would they qualify as one of your success stories?"

"I really couldn't say. I haven't kept up," Emma replied frostily. "Look, Mr. Hamilton, I wish you luck with the paper. I really do—Winding River needs a good newspaper. But I'm not interested in being interviewed."

"Not even for the sake of inspiring a student?"

"Not even for that," she said firmly. "Now you really will have to excuse me."

"Has the media given you a tough time, Ms. Rogers?" he asked, halting her in her tracks. "Is that why you won't take five minutes out of your busy schedule to talk to a reporter from your hometown paper?"

Eyes flashing, she faced him. "Why I don't care to talk to you is my business. The bottom line is that I won't. Good night, Mr. Hamilton."

This time when she walked away, Ford let her go. He'd run across her type before. She wouldn't be above using the media if it served her purposes, but the rest of the time she treated each and every journalist with disdain. He hadn't expected to run across that kind of attitude in Winding River, but, of course, Emma Rogers lived in Denver now. Whatever bee she had in her bonnet about reporters came from a bad experience there. He'd bet his tape recorder on that.

He should let it pass. What did it matter if she didn't want to talk to him? He had other prospects for his story. But the competitive part of him that hated being beat out of any potential scoop rebelled. First thing in the morning, he'd go on the Internet and do a search of the archives of the Denver papers. If Emma Rogers was as high profile as everyone said, there were bound to be mentions. They would give him some insight into what made the woman tick.

Once he knew that…well, it remained to be seen what he would do with the information.

"Don't tell me what I saw!" Donny Carter shouted, weaving in place in front of his wife. "You were flirting with Russell. The man's hands were all over you."

The sound of Donny's voice carried across the dance floor to where Emma sat with her friends. This was Donny's second outburst of the evening, and their former classmate was threatening to get out of hand. He was clearly drunker now…and angrier.

"I see Donny's still getting sloshed at the slightest provocation," Emma said to her friends. "I thought his beer-drinking days would be over by now."

"They're not," Karen said tersely.

"And he's still taking out his bad temper on Sue Ellen," Cassie added. "They've been at it all weekend. Not that the Carters' battles are anything new. My mother says their neighbors are constantly calling the sheriff over there to break up fights. And Sue Ellen's been to the hospital twice in the past few months."

Emma felt her stomach clench. Donny and Sue Ellen had always had a volatile romance. She'd hoped that would change with maturity, but obviously it hadn't. If anything, it was even worse than she'd suspected when she'd witnessed the earlier incident. She'd recognized all the signs of an abusive relationship, but she'd been praying it was mostly verbal. Cassie's information suggested otherwise.

"Why doesn't she leave him?" Lauren asked, viewing the scene with indignation. "She shouldn't have to take that kind of treatment from her own husband."

"She says she loves him, that it's her fault for upsetting him," Karen said, her worried gaze on the arguing couple. "I guarantee you, if you were to walk over there right now, she'd be apologizing all over the place for saying hello to Russell—which by the way, is all she did. I was standing right there with her earlier. But you'd never persuade her husband of the truth. Donny is jealous and possessive when he's sober. Drunk, he's even worse. He's downright mean."

A few minutes later, as the argument escalated

again, Emma saw the sheriff intervene, settling Donny down by escorting him outside for a chat. Donny went along with Ryan Taylor docilely enough. As they exited, Emma noticed that Ford Hamilton was observing the scene with interest.

"I hope he doesn't intend to report that little drama in next week's paper," she murmured, half to herself.

"I don't think Ford would do that," Karen said.

"He's a journalist, isn't he? It's his job to muckrake whenever the opportunity arises," Emma replied, leaving little doubt of the contempt in which she held Ford Hamilton's profession.

"Maybe in the city, but not here," Cassie said. "Mom likes Ford. She met him when he came into the hair salon one day when she was there and asked if Sara Ruth cut men's hair."

Despite herself, Emma bit back a grin. The Twist and Curl had been strictly a women's domain for two generations. "Oh, my. How did that go over?"

"Actually, after the initial shock, he charmed everyone in the room," Cassie reported. "Mom's been thinking of inviting him over for Sunday dinner. He's a bachelor. She's worried he might be lonely."

"A little young for your mom, though, isn't he?"

"Very funny," Cassie said. "She's just being neighborly."

Emma turned another speculative look on the journalist. Maybe she'd judged him too harshly earlier, but she knew the type. There was no mistaking the arrogance in his stance. What she'd at first dismissed as idle curiosity was clearly the far more dangerous nosiness of a professional snoop.

Over the years Emma had had more than her share

of run-ins with reporters. She didn't have much use for them as a breed. Most of them managed to get their facts straight, but in her view they had the sensitivity and discretion of a runaway bulldozer. That alone would have been enough for her to give the press a wide berth, but there had been one incident that had come close to destroying her career with a little help from Kit. Hell would freeze over before she gave another reporter any assistance on a story, even if the story itself was as well-intentioned as the one Ford had described to her earlier.

"Didn't I see him asking you to dance earlier?" Lauren asked, regarding her curiously. "Did he say something to upset you?"

"Not really. He was just acting on Mrs. Hawkins's orders." Emma wondered if she might have warmed more to the classically handsome newspaperman if she'd thought he'd been drawn to her by appreciation of her own charms, but decided no, she wasn't that vain. Still, it irked her ever so slightly that it was Mrs. Hawkins's prodding that had sent him her way.

"Mrs. Hawkins was matchmaking?" Cassie said, chuckling. "Imagine that. I seem to recall she spent most of my sophomore year trying to keep Cole and me separated. And we weren't even dating at that point."

"Maybe she just has good instincts about who belongs with whom," Lauren said, casting a speculative gaze at Emma. "I can see you with a journalist."

"Me? *Never,*" Emma said fiercely. "They're always poking their noses in where they don't belong. Just look at the way he's been watching Sue Ellen and Donny, taking mental notes. If the opportunity arises, he'll report this without giving a second thought to the consequences."

"Which are?" Lauren asked.

"If Donny and Sue Ellen have a serious problem, putting it in the paper will only escalate the tension," Emma predicted.

"Or maybe getting it out into the open will force them to face what they're doing to each other," Karen said, looking thoughtful. "Everybody tiptoes around it, because Sue Ellen clearly doesn't want to acknowledge that Donny hits her. It's just one of those unspoken truths that everyone knows."

"And you think publicly humiliating her will make the situation better?" Emma demanded. "I say she needs to be able to cling to whatever dignity she can."

The others sighed.

"I doubt we're going to solve Sue Ellen's problems for her," Cassie said. "She has to want to get out of the relationship."

"Let's just hope she doesn't wait too long," Emma murmured. She glanced in Sue Ellen's direction, but when their classmate realized she was the subject of Emma's scrutiny, she fled, her cheeks flaming.

"Okay, enough of this," Karen said. "I'm going to look for my husband. I want to dance."

Gina and Cassie drifted away as well, leaving Emma alone with Lauren.

"You're really concerned about Sue Ellen, aren't you?" Lauren asked.

Emma nodded. "I've seen too many women like her in my pro bono work. They're scared to go and they're terrified to stay. Either way, their lives are hell. A few make it out. Too many stay and wind up severely beaten or dead." She shuddered. "It's the most depressing kind of case I handle. I don't do it often, because it takes a terrible toll on me emotionally. I keep thinking, 'there but for the grace of God go I.'"

Lauren stared at her in shock. "Kit?"

Emma nodded reluctantly. She never spoke about what the last days of her marriage had been like, but she couldn't bring herself to skirt the truth with Lauren. "He never laid a hand on me, but the psychological abuse was almost as bad."

"You never said a word about this," Lauren said, her gaze filled with concern. "What did he do?"

"He did everything he could to convince me I would never make it as an attorney," Emma said, chilled by the memory. "He wanted me dependent on him, emotionally and financially. I was lucky—I'm stubborn and strong-willed. He couldn't intimidate me. I believed I could succeed without him. After all, I had made it into one of the best colleges in the country and had finished law school at the top of my class. I refused to let Kit diminish those accomplishments."

"Yet even now that he's out of your life, you're still proving yourself to him, aren't you?" Lauren said, regarding her thoughtfully. "That's why you work so hard."

Emma opened her mouth to disagree vehemently, but the denial died on her lips. "You could be right," she admitted slowly. "I never considered that before."

"Maybe you should think about it now," Lauren advised, "so you'll be able to give yourself permission to slow down. You don't want to wake up one day and realize you've missed every single important event in Caitlyn's life all because you were trying to prove something to a man like Kit Rogers."

"Caitlyn's only six," Emma said defensively. "She hasn't had a lot of important events."

"She's had birthdays, hasn't she? And Christmases? And school vacations? How many of those have you spent with her?" Lauren asked.

"I've never missed a birthday or Christmas," Emma retorted.

"Good. But I know for a fact that this is the first trip the two of you have taken in two years. Part of the joy of being a mother is seeing things through your child's eyes. You're missing that." Her expression turned wistful. "If I had what you have, I wouldn't waste a second."

Lauren's words struck a nerve, which was probably why Emma felt inclined to snap at her. She resisted the urge, confining herself to a pointed question. "When did you get to be an expert on motherhood?"

"Wishful thinking," Lauren said lightly.

"I've never heard you talk about kids before."

"Maybe I just never heard my biological clock ticking quite so loudly before." Lauren forced a smile. "Enough of this. I'm going out right this second to find myself the handsomest man in the room to dance with, even if he's married to somebody else."

"Just don't forget to give him back," Emma teased. "I don't want to have to rescue you from a vengeful wife."

Lauren waved off the suggestion as she began weaving through the couples on the dance floor. Only after Lauren had gone did Emma realize that her friend had taken Emma's cell phone with her.

"You look a little lost," Ford Hamilton noted, pulling out the chair next to her. "Missing your phone?"

She was startled by his intuition. "As a matter of fact, yes."

"Do you conduct a lot of business on a Saturday night?"

"When necessary." She frowned at him. "I still don't want to be interviewed, Mr. Hamilton."

"I got the message. You don't object to dancing with a journalist, though, do you? I promise I won't take notes if you miss a step or two."

Emma hadn't been on a dance floor in…well, too long. Listening to the oldies being played by the band reminded her that once she had loved to dance. She'd been good at it, too. If she could forget for a minute who and what he was, it could be fun.

"Let's wait for a fast dance," she said, eyeing him with amusement. "Then we'll see if you can keep up."

"No contest," he retorted. "Anything you can do—"

Emma laughed. "Don't finish that thought. I might view it as a challenge."

"It was meant to be." His gaze clashed with hers.

To Emma's astonishment, she felt a little tingle of anticipation in the pit of her stomach. Her pulse did an unexpected dip and sway that left her feeling giddy. Fascinating. Lately the only time she felt any stirring of excitement was in a courtroom. Discovering that Ford Hamilton could have the same effect was more than mildly intriguing.

One dance, she promised herself. No more. Just for the sheer exhilaration of it. And if she felt a bit off-kilter, a bit breathless at the conclusion, she could blame it on the unfamiliar exertion. It certainly wouldn't have anything at all to do with the man who was regarding her with such an amused glint in his blue eyes.

The beat of the music slowed, as the band slid from one tune to another, but then the pace quickened. Emma recognized an old Chubby Checker hit.

"They're playing our song, Mr. Hamilton," she said, reaching for his hand and drawing him onto the floor.

He was a tall, lanky man, and the twist was definitely not his dance. He was a good sport about it, though, laughing when they drew a cheering, clapping crowd of her friends.

At the end of the song, Emma was ready to claim victory, but Ford wasn't quite so quick to release her. As the band began a slow song, he drew her into his arms. She went with less reluctance than she'd intended.

For a beat or two, Emma held herself stiffly, but then the music, the scent of Ford's aftershave, the gentle pressure of his hand against her back, had her relaxing into the rhythm. Her cheek fit perfectly against his shoulder. It was rare that she'd been with a man who had several inches in height on her own five-ten. She caught herself right before she sighed with the pure pleasure of it.

This time, when the song ended, he released her, then took a step back. He seemed suddenly wary, as if the dance had been more than he'd bargained for, as well.

"Thanks for the dance," he said. "Maybe I'll see you around town."

His dismissal irritated her, but she managed to keep her voice and her expression cool. "I doubt that. I'll be leaving on Sunday."

"On your next visit, then," he said. "Or will that be a long time coming?"

She didn't like the implied criticism. "I get home when I can."

"Every couple of years is what I hear."

"Been asking a lot of probing questions tonight, Mr. Hamilton?" she inquired, disconcerted by the thought. A part of her had hoped she'd been wrong about him being like all the other reporters.

"A few. You obviously lead a busy life."

"I do."

"Too bad it's not fulfilling," he said, then gave her a jaunty wave as he started away.

This time she was the one calling him back. "Why would you say something like that?" she demanded indignantly. "Who have you been talking to?"

"Deductive reasoning," he said. "Besides, you admitted as much earlier."

"When?"

"When I said I wanted to interview the town's success stories," he answered. "You gave me your interpretation of success, then all but said you couldn't claim to have that kind of achievement."

Emma hadn't realized her words had been so telling, or that Ford Hamilton was sensitive enough to pick up on what she'd left unspoken.

"Well?" he prodded. "Are you denying it?"

She forced a grim smile. "No comment."

He grinned. "I'll take that as a no."

"And if you quote me on it, I'll call you a liar," she retorted.

"Oh, this isn't for publication," he assured her. "It's

just between us. I like to tuck away useful information about the people I meet."

Something about the way he said it—the way he looked at her when he said it—suggested she might have been better off giving him the interview he'd wanted hours ago. This conversation had red flags all over it.

3

Emma had expected to be on her way back to Denver first thing Sunday morning, but somehow Cassie and the others had persuaded her to stay over for a class picnic.

"We're playing baseball. We need you," Cassie had insisted.

It had been sometime after midnight, and Emma's resistance had been low. After her conversation with Ford Hamilton about the lack of fulfillment in her life and Lauren's suggestion that she was trying to prove something to her ex-husband, she hadn't been looking forward to going back to Denver, anyway. It hadn't taken a lot of persuasion to convince her to spend one more night in Winding River. The promise that she could manage her team had been the clincher.

The women were doing surprisingly well against the men, largely thanks to Lauren. She distracted the men so badly that they'd had only two hits in six innings. They were even less successful at fielding the hits made by the women. As a result, the women were winning two to nothing. Emma didn't trust such a slim lead. She wanted more runs.

She glanced around in search of her star player. Emma finally spotted Lauren sitting in the shade, Ford Hamilton stretched out beside her, obviously hanging on her every word. Something that felt suspiciously like jealousy streaked through Emma at the sight of Lauren staring raptly at the charismatic journalist in his faded, formfitting jeans, sneakers and T-shirt.

Irritated by her reaction, Emma turned away, wiped the beads of sweat from her brow, glanced down at her lineup and realized that Lauren was next up to bat. How was Emma supposed to manage her team to a victory when her star player was more interested in a good-looking guy than she was in winning?

"Lauren, if it's not too much trouble, could you take a couple of warm-up swings?" she called out testily. "It's almost your turn to bat."

Lauren merely waved an acknowledgment, then turned back to Ford. He said something that made her laugh just as she stood up and strolled back toward the bench, hips already swaying in the suggestive way that had the men on the field all but panting. Cassie's little bloop of a hit, which should have been an easy out, landed untouched in short center field, and she reached first base before a single male reacted. Emma grinned, her mood improving.

"Everything okay?" Lauren asked, regarding her curiously.

"Of course. Why do you ask?"

"Something in your voice a minute ago. You sounded almost jealous that I was chatting with Ford, but that couldn't be, could it?" She seemed to find the possibility highly amusing.

"Don't be ridiculous. I hardly know the man. If you're interested in him, he's all yours—though I'm surprised that you of all people would give the time of day to a journalist," she said, figuring Lauren knew better than most people how annoyingly intrusive the press could be.

"So? I hear reporters can be decent human beings. The *Winding River News* isn't some sleazy tabloid. Besides, Ford seems like a nice guy."

Emma lost patience. "Do we have to have a discussion of Ford Hamilton right this minute? You're up to bat. And the pitcher's beginning to look irritated."

Actually the pitcher's tongue was all but hanging out as he ogled Lauren's short shorts and snug tank top.

"Don't mind John. He'll wait," Lauren said. "This is important."

"No," Emma said firmly. "It's not. Winning this game is the only thing that's important."

Lauren shook her head. "Sweetie, you are in serious need of an adjustment in your priorities, but I suppose I can't fix everything in a single weekend."

When Emma started to speak, Lauren patted her hand. "Never mind. I'm going." She picked up a bat, slung it over her shoulder and headed for the batter's box, where she promptly wiggled her hips outrageously. Four pitches later she had drawn a walk. John grinned as he watched her sashay to first base.

"Amazing," Ford said, sitting down on the bench next to Emma. "I think your team definitely has an unfair advantage."

"We wouldn't if men weren't so predictable," Emma

retorted. "What are you doing here, anyway? Still stalking your prey?"

"I prefer to think of it as interviewing my sources," he countered. "It's going to be a great story. Too bad you won't be part of it."

"Be careful about libel, Mr. Hamilton. It can be a nasty business."

"I hardly think there can be anything libelous in reporting how several Winding High grads achieved success."

"I suppose that depends on how conscientious you are when you write your article."

"Do you have a lot of experience with libel cases?" he asked, studying her curiously.

"No. It's not my area of expertise, but that doesn't mean I don't understand the law."

"I'll keep that in mind. Of course, that is a subject I wrote my thesis on when I got my graduate degree, so I have a working knowledge of the law as well. Perhaps we can compare notes sometime."

Refusing to admit that she was startled by his degree or his area of study, she frowned at him. "I wouldn't count on it. Just be sure you keep your facts straight about my friends, and you and I won't have a problem. Now, if you don't mind, I have a game to play."

A smile tugged at his lips. "Why doesn't it surprise me that they chose you to manage the team? Do you take everything you do so seriously?"

"Pretty much," she said, then added defensively, "I don't consider that a character flaw."

"Not a flaw," he agreed. "Just boring." He glanced toward the ballfield where Lauren and Cassie were hamming it up in the outfield. "Now, take your friend Lauren. *She* obviously knows how to enjoy herself."

The observation rankled, possibly because it implied that he approved of Lauren more than he approved of Emma. She found it extremely exasperating that it mattered to her whom he preferred.

"Don't let her fool you," she said tightly. "She's a very smart woman."

"Did I say she wasn't? You don't have to hide your brains to have fun."

The remark hit a little too close to what Lauren had said to her. Emma was getting tired of everyone suggesting that she was leading a dull, predictable life.

"I enjoy myself, Mr. Hamilton. Maybe it's just that you don't amuse me."

His grin spread. "Then I'll have to work on that. Good luck with the game," he added, then stood up and sauntered off.

Emma stared after him, once again feeling more off-kilter than she had in years. It was definitely a good thing she was going back to Denver first thing tomorrow. She wasn't sure she wanted to discover how effective Ford Hamilton could be once he set his mind to charming her.

Emma Rogers was pretty much an aggravating pain in the butt, Ford concluded as he went off to find friendlier company. Even so, he couldn't deny that she intrigued him—not as a woman, he quickly assured himself, but as a *person*. There was a distinction, though he was having difficulty pinning that down at the moment.

At any rate, even while he sat with the men as they

took their turn at bat, his gaze kept straying to Emma, noting the intensity of her expression as she watched her players perform in the field. Suddenly an image of her in his bed, just as intent on their lovemaking, swept through his mind. Heat climbed up his neck at the improbable but thoroughly erotic fantasy.

"What's going on, buddy? You look a little flushed," Ryan Taylor said, amusement threading through his voice.

Ford forced his attention away from Emma and glanced at the sheriff. "It's hot out here."

"Maybe so, but I'll bet it's not half as hot as wherever your head was. Thinking about our Emma, were you?"

"Don't be ridiculous. I hardly know the woman. And what I do know doesn't recommend her. She's an annoying, stuffy know-it-all."

Ryan's grin spread. "Some men would find that challenging."

"Not me."

"Too bad. She could use a man who's not afraid of her intellect, maybe even one who's perceptive enough to see through to her vulnerability."

"Emma, vulnerable? I don't think so."

"Like I said, it takes a certain amount of perception to see past that tough facade. I guess I misjudged you. I thought you might be used to digging below the surface to see what a person is really like."

The comment hit its mark. "Well, it hardly matters whether I am or I'm not. She's definitely not inclined to let me get close enough to find out. Besides, she's heading back to Denver any day now. In fact, based on what she said at the dance last night, I thought she'd be on the road first thing this morning."

"Were you disappointed to find her still here today?"

Ford scowled. "It didn't matter to me one way or the other."

Ryan chuckled. "Yeah, I can see that." His expression suddenly sobered. He paused, as if he were choosing his words with care. "By the way," he began finally, "Teddy says he got a picture of that little scene with Sue Ellen and Donny last night. You don't intend to use it, do you?"

"No," Ford said without hesitation. "Domestic disputes don't warrant coverage."

"Glad to hear it," Ryan said, looking relieved. "Sue Ellen doesn't need to have her troubles plastered all over the newspaper. She has a tough enough life as it is."

"If that's the case, why haven't you arrested Donny?"

"She won't press charges," Ryan said with evident frustration. "My hands are tied, unless I catch him in the act of hurting her. Believe me, I'm just itching to slap the man with assault charges. He needs help, and he sure as hell won't get it as long as she keeps making excuses for him. It makes me sick to see how he humiliates her over and over again. Sue Ellen was one of the most outgoing kids in our class. She participated in every activity. She always had a smile on her face. Now she barely sets foot out of the house, and I can't tell you the last time I saw her smile."

"I noticed they didn't come today," Ford said.

Ryan's expression turned grim. "Probably because she has bruises she's trying to hide and he's out on the sofa with a hangover."

Ford shuddered at the sheriff's matter-of-fact description. "Even around here, there must be places she could go for help."

"She won't leave. I've tried. Hell, half the town has tried at one time or another, but Sue Ellen believes with everything in her that Donny loves her and that he'll change. Personally, I don't see it happening. Their marriage is a tragedy waiting to happen. The one blessing in all of this is that they've never had kids, so there are no innocent victims suffering because she refuses to get out."

A shadow fell over them. Ford looked up, surprised to see Emma standing there.

"Are you talking about Sue Ellen?" she asked Ryan, carefully avoiding Ford's gaze.

Ryan nodded. "Any ideas on how to get her out of there?"

"None," she said.

Ford was startled by her helpless, frustrated expression. For the first time, he saw a hint of that vulnerability Ryan had been talking about.

"Maybe you could talk to her," Ryan suggested. "She always admired you, Emma, and you are an attorney. You could give her some hard truths about the odds of Donny ever changing."

Emma shook her head. "I'm sure she's been told the statistics a hundred times, and just doesn't want to believe them. She wants to believe that he's the exception, that if she's loyal enough and patient enough, he'll stop hurting her."

"That doesn't mean you shouldn't try to get through to her," Ryan coaxed. "Do it as a favor to me."

"Okay, I will. I'll do it for you. I'll call her," Emma

promised. "I just hope the fact that she's even talking to me doesn't set Donny off. It could, you know."

"I think it's a chance worth taking," Ryan told her. "Thankfully I don't run across a lot of domestic violence around here, so I'm no expert, but I think the tensions are escalating dangerously."

Emma sighed. "I hope you're wrong about that."

"You really care about Sue Ellen Carter, don't you?" Ford said, letting his surprise show.

Emma finally looked at him. "Of course. She's an old friend," she said matter-of-factly. "In Winding River, friends stick together."

"And in Denver?" he taunted. "What do friends do there?"

The question seemed to disconcert her. "The same thing, I suppose."

Her reply was more telling than she realized. In that instant, Ford realized that despite all of the close friends in evidence at the reunion, Emma Rogers was quite possibly one of the loneliest people he'd ever met. And to his very sincere regret, in some gallant, knight-in-shining-armor fantasy, he wanted to change that.

The news that Cassie's mother had breast cancer threw Emma's already shattered timetable into chaos. There was no way she could abandon her childhood friend right now. Thanks to faxes and the availability of overnight couriers, she could stay on the job and remain right here in Winding River for a few more days until they knew how the surgery was going to go.

Making those arrangements and lending support to Cassie pushed all thoughts of Sue Ellen temporarily out of Emma's mind. It was several days later when she remembered her promise to Ryan and set aside time to call Sue Ellen. Maybe it was for the best that she'd waited, Emma told herself as she dialed Sue Ellen's number. Donny would surely be back at work, which would make it easier for them to talk without him influencing what Sue Ellen said or fueling her reluctance to talk at all.

The phone rang and rang without even an answering machine picking up. Since everyone in town had told her that Sue Ellen rarely left the house anymore, Emma left Caitlyn with her grandfather for another riding lesson and drove into town.

Sue Ellen and Donny were living in a small apartment in a converted garage just a few blocks from where Cassie had grown up. It wasn't the best part of town. There had been little effort at upkeep and even less at landscaping. No doubt whatever money Donny earned went for booze, Emma thought, more sadly than cynically.

Emma knocked on the Carters' door, waited, then knocked again. She was almost certain that she heard a faint stirring inside, but no one answered the knock.

"Sue Ellen, are you there? It's Emma Rogers. I'd love to visit with you, if you have a few minutes."

The rustling sound came closer to the door, but it remained tightly shut.

"I'm...I'm not feeling well," Sue Ellen whispered, her voice hoarse. "It's not a good time."

"I'm not worried about catching a few germs," Emma said, deliberately pretending to go along with the excuse but at the same time refusing to leave.

"Please, Emma, not now." Sue Ellen sounded near tears.

Concluding that dancing around the obvious was accomplishing nothing, Emma asked bluntly, "Has Donny hurt you again?"

The question was greeted by a sharp intake of breath, then a sob.

"It's okay, Sue Ellen. I just want to help."

"You can't. Nobody can."

"That's not true. Won't you at least let me try?"

"I can't. It will only make it worse if Donny finds out. Please go away," she begged. "That's the best thing you can do for me, Emma."

Emma took a card for an abuse hotline from her purse, scribbled her own cell phone number on the back, and slid it under the door. "If you change your mind, call me or call that hotline. There is help, Sue Ellen. All you have to do is ask for it."

Only the sound of wrenching sobs answered her.

"Call," Emma pleaded one last time, then reluctantly turned and walked away.

She drove to Main Street, then parked in front of Stella's. She needed to eat something completely and thoroughly decadent, some confection to remind her that life wasn't entirely bleak. Bumping into a few of her friends wouldn't hurt either.

Unfortunately, the only familiar face besides Stella's was Ford Hamilton's. Right this second, she would take whatever company she could get, if only because it would keep her from having to think about Sue Ellen.

Ford eyed her warily when she slid into the booth opposite him. Wariness quickly shifted to concern. "Everything okay? You look a little pale."

"I don't want to talk about it," she said grimly, then

glanced up at Stella. "I want the biggest hot-fudge sundae you can make, extra hot fudge and extra nuts."

"Now I know something's wrong," Ford said.

"Oh, why?"

"Because you strike me as the type who normally splurges on carrot sticks."

"Well, now you know I'm not," she said testily. "And if you're just going to take digs at me, I'll sit someplace else."

He held up a placating hand. "Stay. I'll be good."

She wasn't buying the promise, but she stayed where she was because she was suddenly too exhausted to move.

"Want to talk about it?" he asked.

"No."

"Want to talk about something else?"

"Not especially."

A smile tugged at his lips. "Then you're with me just because you prefer anything to your own company?"

"Pretty much."

"Okay. I can relate to that." He picked up the New York paper he'd been reading. "Want some of this? Hard news? Features? Sports?"

"Business," she said without enthusiasm.

"Checking on your investment portfolio?"

"Nope, checking to see if one of my clients made any headlines this morning."

Ford's eyes lit up. "Big case?"

"In some circles." Despite herself, she began to grin at his obvious yearning to question her about it. "Go ahead. Ask."

"What company?"

She mentioned the name of the software manufacturer.

Ford whistled. "That *is* big. I've been reading about it. Patent infringement, right?"

"That's the charge. A former employee is suing them, claiming that they stole his idea then fired him."

"And you're claiming it was their property since he developed the idea while working for them," he speculated.

"Exactly. And it's not a claim. It's the truth."

"Still, it must be fascinating."

Emma shrugged. Normally this case—all of her cases—brought on an adrenaline rush, but after her failed meeting with Sue Ellen, none of them seemed all that important.

Ford regarded her intently. "You've been to see your friend this morning, haven't you? Sue Ellen?"

Once again, Emma was surprised by his perceptiveness. "How did you guess?"

"It wasn't that difficult. Even after a couple of encounters, I can tell you're the kind of woman who gets excited by work, yet I ask about the biggest case you're handling and you shrug it off. That had to mean that something else is weighing on your mind."

"Sue Ellen, Cassie's mom—she was just diagnosed with breast cancer," she explained when he regarded her blankly. "Then there's my daughter's unhappiness at the prospect of going back to Denver."

"So you're not having a good day."

"Not especially." She met his disconcertingly blue gaze. "Why did you end up in Winding River?"

"Do you really care about that?"

If it meant avoiding a conversation about Sue Ellen,

she would listen to him talk endlessly about life before Winding River. "Let's just say I'm curious. I heard you were a hotshot reporter in a big city before you came here. Did you get fired?"

"Naturally you would think that, wouldn't you?" he said with a weary expression. "I'm sure there has to be a story behind your distrust of the media. One of these days I'll get it out of you. As for me, the truth is that I did some investigative reporting in Atlanta and then in Chicago, and I was damned good at it."

"That must have been exciting compared to covering a class reunion."

"True, but it wasn't as satisfying as I'd expected it to be. Oh, I liked exposing the bad guys well enough, but there's a lot of bureaucracy on a large newspaper, a lot of economic pressure. I got tired of fighting it. I quit."

"And here you're in control," she guessed, understanding the need to be in charge. For the first time since they'd met, she could relate to him.

"In charge and in a position to make a difference. If I do this right, I might be able to influence the future of this town."

"In what direction?"

He grinned. "Hard to say. I'm still getting to know it. I'm not going to start out recommending that we bulldoze the trees and encourage development."

"Glad to hear it."

"Which is not to say that I might not recommend that very thing at some point in the future."

Emma tried to imagine Winding River as something other than the small, peaceful town it had always been. The image bothered her more than she'd expected. "I hope you don't. Winding River is...I don't know...special. It shouldn't be tampered with too much."

"So it's too small for you to be happy here, but you want to know it's unchanged for those rare occasions when you feel like coming home?" he challenged.

"Exactly," she said without remorse. "Some things should never change."

"Then maybe you need to stick around so you can have a say in what happens."

She shook her head. "No, my life is in Denver now."

"What life?" he asked.

She scowled at the deliberate challenge. "My career, my daughter."

"Interesting that you put your work first," he noted. "But let's stick to your daughter for the moment. Don't you think she'll be happy wherever you are? Besides, didn't you just tell me she didn't want to go back?"

The reminder grated. "She has friends there. School. She loves it."

"She just likes it here better. Why is that?" he prodded.

"Her grandfather just bribed her with a horse."

Ford laughed. "That would do it for most kids, but are you sure that's all of it?"

"What else could it be?"

"I'm hazarding a guess, but could it have something to do with the fact that she sees more of her mom here than she does at home?"

"You haven't interviewed my daughter, have you?" she asked, only half in jest.

"So that *is* it?"

"Probably part of it," she conceded.

Ford gathered up his newspaper and slid out of the

booth. "I'm the last person on earth qualified to give parenting advice, but it seems to me there's a message there that's worth taking to heart. I'll leave you to think about it."

Emma sighed as he left her alone with her still-troubled thoughts. Now, though, she was focused on her own problems instead of Sue Ellen's. Funny thing about that. A few days ago she wouldn't have said she had any problems. Now, thanks to a pushy reporter who was more intuitive than she'd imagined, she realized that she'd just spent the past few years sweeping them under her very expensive rug.

4

"Where's Caitlyn?" Emma asked, walking into her mother's kitchen and snagging an apple. After that hot-fudge sundae, she hadn't expected to be hungry for days, but she'd taken a brisk walk up and down Main Street before driving back out to the ranch.

"Where do you think?" her mother asked with a chuckle. "In the barn with her grandfather. She's helping with the chores, though my impression is that she's more hindrance than help."

"Maybe I ought to go out and rescue Dad."

"Don't you dare. He's having the time of his life. He swears it's like having you back again. Don't you remember how you used to shadow his every move when you were Caitlyn's age?"

Emma felt the tug of a smile. "I did, didn't I? No wonder he was so shocked when I announced I was going to be a lawyer. He must have been certain I was going to take over the ranch."

Her mother's expression turned nostalgic. "Of all the kids, you were the one who showed the most interest in it. Now it looks as if Matt's going to take over by default."

Emma was startled by the observation. "Why do you say it like that? He's doing a good job, isn't he?"

"Of course. Matt's a hard worker, but his heart's not in it, not the way it should be."

"I thought he wanted this," Emma said.

Her mother shook her head. "No, there just wasn't anything else he wanted more. It didn't help that he and Martha married so young. Maybe if he'd gone to college…" She shrugged, her voice trailing off.

"You're really worried about Matt, aren't you?" Emma asked.

"I am. I'm afraid your brother is adrift. That's why he's so unhappy. You heard him at lunch the other day. He grumbles about everything. He sounds like an old man."

"Who's an old man?" Emma's father demanded, coming in at the end of the conversation. "Not me."

Her mother stood on tiptoe to kiss his weathered cheek. "Never you. You won't ever get old."

Caitlyn tugged excitedly on Emma's arm. "Mom, guess what? Grandpa taught me to muck out the stalls."

"Really?" Emma said, barely containing her amusement. "And you liked that?"

"It's kind of yucky, but it's real, real important, isn't it, Grandpa?"

"Very important," he agreed, winking at Emma. "You bought it when you were her age, too. Don't disillusion her."

A puzzled frown knit Caitlyn's brow. "What's disillusion?"

Emma brushed her hair away from her face. "Nothing you need to worry about, my love. How did your riding lesson go?"

An incandescent smile lit Caitlyn's eyes. "It was sooo fun. I'm getting good, aren't I, Grandpa?"

"You're terrific, baby doll."

Emma's eyes misted at the endearment. It was what he had once called her. As if he understood what she was feeling, her father clasped her hand in his large callused hand and squeezed.

Thinking of her conversation with her mother, Emma whispered, "I'm sorry, Dad."

He seemed startled. "For what? You have nothing to apologize to me for."

"I know you'd hoped that I'd stay here and work with you."

"That was *my* dream, not yours. You're entitled to the life you want. All that matters is that you're happy."

Of course, that was the problem, Emma realized. In the past few days she'd been forced to face the fact that she didn't even know what real happiness meant anymore. Worse, she couldn't seem to remember when it had ceased to matter. Maybe she and her brother Matt were in the same sinking boat.

Ford was putting the finishing touches on the layout of photos from the class reunion when Ryan strolled in. The sheriff peered over his shoulder.

"Teddy did a good job, didn't he?" he said, sounding surprised.

"The boy's definitely got a way with a camera," Ford agreed.

"Having you as a mentor is real good for him," Ryan

said. "I'm grateful. Ever since his dad left, he's been desperate for a role model."

"An uncle who's the sheriff isn't a bad one," Ford pointed out. "He idolizes you."

"In some ways, not in others," Ryan said. "I always thought he was wasting his time and my sister's money by shooting five rolls of film at every family gathering. It took someone like you to channel what he loves into a money-making proposition. Now all he talks about is being a photojournalist. He can't wait to get to college this fall. Before, he was going just because his mother and I pushed him to."

"He is motivated," Ford agreed. "He'll make the most of it." He studied the sheriff speculatively. "What brings you by? I'm sure it wasn't to get an advance peek at this week's headlines."

"Nothing specific," Ryan said. "I had a few minutes to kill before I head over to the town council meeting. You going?"

"Of course. Anything exciting on the agenda?"

"I hear there's a zoning request to subdivide the old Callaway ranch into a housing development."

Though his attitude was nonchalant, something in Ryan's voice alerted Ford that he wasn't happy about the plan. "Is there a problem with that?"

"The plan calls for low-cost, subsidized housing. I'm afraid we're going to be attracting nothing but trouble."

"There's not a need for it around here?"

"No. Housing costs are modest as it is. I've checked. Locally there aren't any families in dire need of low-cost housing. It would be a draw for folks from the bigger cities. I've got nothing against that on principle, but a whole development all at once will end up putting a strain on the school and on all the other services, law enforcement included. There will be an economic impact on the community, no doubt about it. Winding River's just beginning to get back on its feet. Tourism is starting to flourish. We've had a few people with big bucks move into the county. Last year a few small businesses opened. I don't want to see anything come along to change that direction."

What Ryan was saying made a lot of sense. Development *per se* wasn't necessarily bad, but the wrong kind could sabotage all efforts to improve the town.

"Is this a done deal?" Ford asked.

"Not by a long shot."

Ford grinned at him. "Then let's go do our part to inject a little common sense into the discussion and put a stop to it. You talk, and I'll give you coverage in this week's paper. I can still get it in before tomorrow's deadline, along with an editorial in opposition to the development."

The sheriff slapped him on the back. "I had a feeling I could count on you."

As they walked toward the school, where council meetings were held in the auditorium, Ryan cast a sideways look at him. "Heard you and Emma had quite a little chat over at Stella's today. Looked real cozy."

"Who's your source?" Ford asked.

"Now a newspaperman ought to know better than to ask a question like that," Ryan taunted. "Were they right?"

"Emma and I talked. I don't know how cozy we were. Having a conversation with that woman is like dealing with a porcupine. You never know when she's going to take offense and come after you with a sharp barb."

"You look to me like a man whose hide is tough enough to take a few pointed remarks and to give back as good as you get."

"There is a certain amount of intellectual stimulation involved, but it can take a toll. I must admit, though, she's a more complicated female than I first imagined."

"Complicated, huh?" Ryan grinned. "Watch yourself, pal. Complicated women have a way of getting under a man's skin and staying there."

"Emma Rogers is not getting under my skin," Ford insisted, but even as the words left his mouth, he knew he was lying through his teeth.

"The last man who said that wound up married to her."

Ford regarded him with surprise. "You knew her husband?"

"We'd met. My sister knew him better."

"Teddy's mom?"

"No, my oldest sister, Adele," Ryan explained. "She dated Kit Rogers for a while at college. That's how he and Emma met. Kit was here visiting over the holidays one year—we were all at the same party. Then he got one look at Emma, and that was it for him and Adele. They broke up that same night. Can't say I was sorry. For that matter, neither was Adele. She told me he had 'control issues,' which I took to mean that he was a possessive son of a gun."

Ford digested that news with a sense of astonishment. "I can't imagine any man controlling Emma."

"Not for long, that's for sure," Ryan said. "Emma

hasn't said, but I suspect that's what broke up their marriage. She might have tolerated it for a while, but she's too strong willed to be anybody's doormat." He slanted a look at Ford. "A word to the wise."

"You don't have to tell me that," Ford said. "If I were interested, which I'm not, I'd know better than to think there was a single submissive bone in that woman's very attractive body."

Ryan hooted. "All right!"

"What?"

"You noticed that Emma has a fabulous body. I was beginning to worry about you."

"I noticed," Ford said, then added firmly, "not that I have any intention of doing anything about it...even if she'd let me..." He met Ryan's gaze. "Which she won't. She's none too crazy about my profession, in case you hadn't noticed."

"And that's enough to scare you off?" Ryan asked indignantly. "You're not even going to try to get her to see past that?"

"Absolutely not."

"Then maybe I'll give her another shot," Ryan said, his expression innocent. "We were pretty tight back in high school."

Ford scowled at him. "Whatever."

"You wouldn't care?"

"It's not up to me."

"But you wouldn't feel even the tiniest little twinge if I asked her out?" Ryan persisted.

A twinge? He'd probably want to slug the man, sheriff or not. He refused to admit it, though. "Nope."

"Liar," Ryan accused.

Ford sighed heavily. "You got that right."

* * *

"Emma, sweetie, wake up!"

Emma heard her mother's voice, and for a moment thought she must have been caught up in a dream. Then she felt her mother's hand on her shoulder, gently shaking her.

"Emma!"

For the first time in months she had actually been in a deep, restful sleep. She came to slowly. "What is it, Mom? Caitlyn's not sick, is she? Is it Dad?"

"No, no, it's Lauren. She's on the phone. She needs to talk to you now. She says it's urgent."

Emma tugged on her robe and raced down the hall, heart pounding. Lauren would never call in the middle of the night unless it truly was urgent. Was she sick? Were the tabloids about to break some story that could destroy her career? Had there been an accident? Or was it one of the other Calamity Janes? She had spoken to most of them during the day. They'd all seemed fine.

Clutching her robe around her, she picked up the phone. "Lauren, what's wrong?"

"Oh, Emma, it's so horrible," Lauren said, her voice choked. This wasn't the sexy huskiness she used on screen, but real emotion. "There was another fight between Donny and Sue Ellen. I had the windows open, and I could hear it all the way over here at the hotel. Donny chased her out of their house, screaming and cursing. I called the sheriff, but before he got over here, I heard a shot."

"Oh, my God," Emma whispered. "Please tell me Donny didn't shoot Sue Ellen."

"No, she shot him. He's dead, Emma."

Emma's heart sank. "Where is she?"

"Ryan just took her down to the jail. He told me there wasn't any point in my coming along, that he couldn't let me see her. Can you go over there? Please. She needs an attorney, a really good one. I doubt she has any money, but I'll pay for it."

"I'm on my way," Emma said at once. "And don't worry about the money. This one's on the house."

Emma yanked on her clothes, explained the situation to her mother and raced to the jail. She was only moderately surprised to find Ford Hamilton there ahead of her. He was arguing with Ryan, demanding to see the sheriff's report on the shooting.

"Settle down," Ryan told him. "This isn't Chicago. We take our time and get things right. We don't jump to conclusions. You'll see the report when I have all the facts."

"I wasn't suggesting—" Ford began.

"Whatever," Ryan said, waving off what was obviously the beginning of an insincere apology. "It's going to take a while to talk to Sue Ellen and to the neighbors about what they saw and heard. In the meantime, why don't you go get yourself a cup of coffee?"

Ford frowned. "At this hour? Where?"

"Stella will be in now," Ryan told him. "Whenever there's a crisis, she hears about it and opens early."

Emma's gaze slid past the journalist, searching the room until she spotted Sue Ellen over by the window, still in her bathrobe, her bruised and battered face streaked with dried tears and blood. Her expression, reflected in the glass, was blank.

"Let me talk to Mrs. Carter," Ford said to Ryan. "Just a couple of questions."

"No way," Emma said so fiercely that both men's heads snapped around to face her.

"Emma," Ryan said, his smile not quite reaching his eyes. He looked exhausted and sad. "I didn't expect you to show up here."

"Lauren called. She told me what happened."

"I'm glad," he said, casting a worried look at the woman huddled in a chair across the room. "Sue Ellen's going to need all the legal help she can get."

Ford scowled at them. "If you two are finished, do you suppose we could get back to business?" Ford asked. "I'd like to speak to Mrs. Carter, so I can get a couple of paragraphs into this week's edition. Then I'll get out of your hair."

"And I told you to forget about it," Emma said. "She's not talking to anybody, you or the sheriff, until I've had a chance to talk to her. How did you get here so fast, anyway? Do you have a police scanner in your bedroom?"

"I've been up all night," he said, looking her straight in the eye. "Not that it's any of your business, but Ryan was with me at the paper. I was getting it ready to go to the printer this morning. The call came in about an hour ago."

"Lucky for you, wasn't it?" she said with biting sarcasm.

His gaze never wavered. "Are you going to represent her?"

"For the moment. We'll have to see what Sue Ellen wants."

"She's going to need the best," Ryan said. "As much as I hate to say it, it's an open-and-shut case."

Though she had a lot of respect for Ryan—partly

because he'd let her play on his ball team years ago despite the ribbing he'd taken from his buddies—she wasn't impressed with his lack of enlightenment on this particular issue. "We'll see," she said neutrally.

She noticed that Ford's piercing blue eyes narrowed just a little. What little mellowing she'd done where he was concerned vanished. He was just like all the other journalists she'd run across, after all. He was obviously more interested in a juicy story than in getting to the truth. There wasn't a trace of compassion on his face.

"You're going to try to get her off on a cold-blooded murder charge?" he demanded.

"It's too soon to answer a question like that. Surely you know that she hasn't even been arraigned on a specific charge yet. There were mitigating circumstances. You saw that for yourself. In fact, you're just one of a great many people who witnessed the way Donny was treating her at the reunion dance a couple of weeks ago. I'll be sure to include you on my witness list," she said. Then she added with biting sarcasm, "After all, surely a journalist can be counted on to tell the truth, right?"

"What I saw or heard that night has nothing to do with this. Nothing entitles her to shoot him," Ford said emphatically.

"Okay, okay," Ryan said, intervening. "Let's all cool down. We're getting ahead of ourselves. Emma, go on over and talk to Sue Ellen. I'll take Ford here out for a cup of coffee and explain a few facts of life to him."

Emma scowled at the reporter. "Just be sure Mr. Hamilton understands that what you're saying is off the record, Ryan. In fact, you might want to get his understanding of that in writing."

This time Ford scowled at the sarcasm. "I know what off the record means."

Emma gave him a frosty smile. "Glad to hear it," she said as she walked away to talk to Sue Ellen. She could feel the man's gaze on her as she crossed the room and sat down. The effect was vaguely disconcerting, especially in light of her recent conclusion that her first impression of him had been the accurate one. The sensitivity he'd displayed that morning when she'd been feeling a bit down had obviously been an aberration.

Then all thoughts of Ford fled as she sat across from Sue Ellen and watched her old classmate dissolve into tears.

"I'm sorry," Sue Ellen whispered brokenly. "I'm so sorry."

"For what? Not for killing a man who repeatedly beat you, I hope."

Sue Ellen gasped. "Donny was my husband."

"He was an abuser," Emma corrected. "You were a victim, sweetie. I'm not saying that shooting him was a good thing, but it was understandable. Now tell me what happened tonight. I can't defend you if you hold anything back."

"You're going to represent me?"

"If that's what you want."

"But why?"

"Because you need me. Now, start at the beginning and tell me everything."

Sue Ellen nodded. "He...Donny found that card you had left for me," Sue Ellen told her, choking back another sob. She clenched her hands together and steadied her voice. "It was in my purse. I thought he'd never find it, but he was looking for money. He'd run out of beer and wanted to go out and buy some more. He dumped everything on the floor, and when he didn't even find any loose change, he began to rip open all the compartments inside the purse."

Emma shuddered, suddenly feeling responsible for everything that had happened. She had known what Donny might do if he learned that she'd interfered, but she had gone over there anyway. She'd wanted to be the avenging angel who dragged Sue Ellen out of there. Instead, she had just made matters worse, triggering tonight's attack and ultimately the tragedy that would scar Sue Ellen forever, even if Emma got her acquitted.

"What did he do then?" she asked Sue Ellen.

"He asked me what it meant, who had given it to me."

"Did you tell him?"

She shook her head. "I didn't want him to come after you. He would have, too. He threatened my mom once, and all *she* did was take me to the doctor after he'd told me not to go."

"So, there's a record of your injuries on file with your doctor?" Emma asked.

Sue Ellen nodded. "But I told him I was attacked coming out of the bank, that someone had tried to steal my purse."

Emma doubted that the doctor had bought it, not with everyone in town aware of Donny's mistreatment of Sue Ellen.

"That's okay. It'll still help," she reassured her client. "I'd like to get your doctor in here tonight to see you. Is that okay?"

"It doesn't matter," Sue Ellen said despondently. "Nothing matters."

"Of course it matters," Emma said fiercely. "We're going to win this. You were defending yourself against a man who had brutalized you time and again."

"But I haven't even told you how it happened, how the gun went off."

"And I want to hear that, but it's the history of abuse that will really matter to a jury. That's the heart of your defense. Remember that, Sue Ellen. I heard you went to the hospital a couple of times, too. Is that right?"

"Those were accidents," Sue Ellen insisted.

Emma sighed, though she wasn't all that amazed that Sue Ellen was still lying to the world, if not herself, about what had happened. "Let's concentrate on tonight then. Finish telling me what he did. Did you argue about the card he found?"

The details weren't surprising. Donny had been infuriated by the hotline number that Emma had left. He had begun brandishing a gun, but he was drunk. He had fallen and the gun had gone off.

"Where did the bullet go?"

"It broke the light in the ceiling fan."

Emma made a note to ask Ryan if the bullet that hit the fan light had been recovered. "And then what?"

"Donny was groggy from falling down. I thought I could get the gun away from him and he would just fall asleep like always, but he didn't. He chased me outside. I tried to go back in and lock him out, but he was too fast. He caught me and slapped me. Then he knocked me down and kept on hitting and hitting. He had the gun in his hand. I kept trying to knock it away, but he wouldn't let go." Tears welled up in her eyes again. "And then the gun just went off. For a minute,

I waited to feel the pain, but there was nothing. And then there was all this blood."

She wrapped her arms around herself and began rocking back and forth, her stare vacant. "So much blood," she whispered. "So much blood."

Emma hunkered down in front of Sue Ellen and clasped her hands tightly. "It's going to be okay, Sue Ellen. I swear to you that it will be okay."

Sue Ellen regarded her with a defeated expression. "I can't pay you. Maybe you should just let the court appoint somebody."

"No. Unless you don't want me, you and I are in this together from here on out."

"But you live in Denver."

"I can be here whenever I have to be," Emma reassured her. "You're not going through this alone. I'm a member of the Wyoming bar, thank goodness, and I'm going to provide a first-rate defense for you, Sue Ellen."

Suddenly she recalled the way Ryan had looked at the baseball game when he'd first talked about Sue Ellen's plight and begged Emma to intercede, and again tonight when Emma had shown up at the jail. Despite what he'd said earlier about it being an open-and-shut case, Emma had a feeling that when push came to shove, the sheriff would be in Sue Ellen's corner as well.

5

Ford hated crusading feminists. There wasn't a doubt in his mind after the scene at the jail that that was exactly what Emma Rogers was. She had reaffirmed his first impression from the night of the reunion dance when he'd found her sleek, cool appearance all too reminiscent of some women he'd run across in Atlanta and Chicago. Barracudas in the courtroom. No personal lives to speak of. Ice in their veins.

Of course, he had caught a glimmer of heat just now when Emma had turned on him to keep him away from her client. It had been an interesting little hint of passion, reminding him of the sparks that had sizzled between them when they'd danced. Too bad tonight's evidence of that passion was so misguided.

Sue Ellen Carter was guilty as sin, no matter what had driven her to the fatal deed. Since it was too late for major coverage of the killing in this week's paper, he intended to lay out all of the facts proving the crime on next week's front page. He wouldn't have to convict her in an editorial—the truth would do that very nicely. There wouldn't be a word in the article that Emma could argue was inaccurate.

Not that he expected her to praise the piece he was already beginning to compose in his head. Their earlier conversation about libel came back to haunt him, reminding him to report only the facts that weren't in dispute.

"Any idea why Emma's taking this case?" he asked Ryan when they were in a booth at Stella's, coffee cups in front of them.

A surprising number of locals had, indeed, turned out despite the early hour, drawn by the desire for information on the tragedy that had occurred overnight. Sorrow seemed to cast a pall over the place. Conversations were quieter than usual, silences longer.

"Loyalty," Ryan said succinctly. "That's the kind of person she is."

"But I thought she specialized in corporate law."

"The way I hear it, that's what pays the bills. She takes on cases like this *pro bono.*"

"Why this particular kind of case? I got the feeling this is about more than her friendship with Sue Ellen. It's not as if Emma Rogers and Sue Ellen Carter have maintained close ties all these years, is it? She said as much to me at the reunion."

Ryan shrugged. "I doubt it, but I have no idea. What difference does it make? Sue Ellen needs the best lawyer there is, and by all reports that's Emma. We certainly don't have anyone in town who's up to this."

"Representing Sue Ellen is going to be damned inconvenient with Emma living in Denver, though."

"Apparently she doesn't think so." Ryan's gaze narrowed suspiciously. "You did agree that all of this is off the record, didn't you? I'll be real unhappy if any comments I make about Emma wind up in the paper."

Ford nodded. "Not a problem. This is just background."

"The tension back there between you and Emma... you're not going to let it get in the way of giving Sue Ellen a fair shake, are you?" Ryan asked, his expression even darker.

"Reporters and lawyers are natural enemies when it comes to something like this, at least until the dust settles and everyone knows whose side everyone else is on."

"Do you have a side? I thought journalists were supposed to be impartial."

"I am. I just want all the facts so readers can make up their own minds. Of course, you said it yourself back there, this is an open-and-shut case. And that comment was not off the record."

Ryan's scowl deepened. "Then I suppose you'd better add this to go along with it. It would be an open-and-shut case if Emma Rogers hadn't agreed to handle it."

Ford jotted down the new quote. "Duly noted." He studied the bleak expression on the sheriff's face. "Why do I get the feeling that this whole mess is personal where you're concerned?"

"Like Emma said, Sue Ellen is a friend."

"And that's all? What about Donny? Wasn't he one of your classmates, too?"

Ryan stiffened visibly. "What are you implying?"

Ford held up a placating hand. "I'm not implying anything. I'm asking straight out if there's something between you and Sue Ellen. I noticed you were quick to jump to her defense at the dance, and you sound mighty protective right now. I don't hear a lot of regret for the fact that her husband is dead."

"Of course I regret it, though to be perfectly honest, my reason for regretting it has more to do with what this will do to Sue Ellen than any sorrow over Donny. He was a pitiful excuse for a man." Ryan frowned at Ford. "And *that* is definitely off the record."

Ford studied him curiously. "How do you see her? As a suspect or as a victim?"

"A victim," Ryan said without hesitation.

"I still get the feeling that your concern for her runs deeper than it might for some other victim," Ford said, watching Ryan's face for a reaction. There was an unmistakable tightening of the sheriff's jaw before he spoke.

"She was a married woman," Ryan said finally. "And she loved her husband."

"That wouldn't necessarily stop another man from caring about her," Ford pointed out.

"No more than I care about any other citizen in Winding River who's the victim of a crime. As for my actions at the dance, they were meant to keep the peace. I didn't want Donny starting a brawl and ruining the night for everyone else."

"If you say so."

"I do. Now leave it be and tell me how you intend to get back in Emma's good graces."

Ford accepted the change of topic, even though the new one put him on the defensive. "Being in Emma's good graces doesn't concern me one way or another," he said flatly.

Ryan gave him a wry, disbelieving look. "Yeah, right."

"It doesn't."

"Your denials aren't getting any better despite all the practice you've had making them today."

Ford sighed. "Look, there was never a chance of anything happening between me and Emma Rogers. She's an uppity, uptight lawyer from Denver. I'm just a small-town journalist."

"Aw, shucks," Ryan mocked. "I guess Chicago and Atlanta must not have left any marks on you after all. You still struggling to figure out which spoon to use to stir your coffee?"

Ford laughed despite himself. "Okay, wise guy, maybe we do have a few things in common. I don't know her well enough to say. The odds are good that I never will."

"And that's the way you want it?"

"That's the way it has to be, now especially."

"Because she'll be handling Sue Ellen's case?"

"Exactly."

"I could fill in a few details," Ryan offered. "Save you some time getting to know her."

Despite everything he'd just said, Ford craved more information. He still wanted to know what made Emma tick. She was as fascinating as she was aggravating.

"I imagine what you see is what you get," he said, waiting to see if Ryan denied it.

"I suppose that depends on what you see. For instance, I doubt you know that she was a helluva short-stop."

"She played baseball? That game I saw wasn't some sort of fluke?"

"She played when we were kids," Ryan confirmed. "On my team, as a matter of fact. I took a lot of teasing over that, until she started throwing people out and hitting everything that was pitched to her. Then everybody wanted her on their team, but Emma was as loyal as they come. She stayed with me."

"Did the two of you date?"

"No way. She never looked twice at any guy in town. She had her goals all carved out for herself very early on. And they didn't include getting married and sticking around Winding River."

"She was a snob?"

"No, just driven. She had ambition, and she was determined to achieve her dreams. She didn't intend to let anything hold her back."

Driven. Ambitious. Determined. All were words Ford would have agreed applied to Emma. But somehow they added up differently when Ryan used them. He turned them into compliments. It was obvious he admired and respected her. No, more than that, he genuinely liked her.

Fascinating, Ford thought again. Maybe there was more to Emma Rogers than he'd wanted to believe. Thanks to this shooting tonight and her determination to represent Sue Ellen, he was going to have more of an opportunity to observe her. Maybe he'd invite her out to dinner, spend a little time with her, all in the interest of getting his story about Sue Ellen Carter, of course.

Of course.

At the pleadings of her friends and, most of all, persuaded by the glazed look in Sue Ellen's eyes, Emma knew she had no choice but to go all the way through this as Sue Ellen's attorney. Whatever hope she'd held that she could turn the case over to someone else after the arraignment vanished when she looked around for a likely candidate.

Seventy-year-old Seth Wilkins, who'd been the only practicing attorney in Winding River for the past forty-five years, thought Sue Ellen ought to plead guilty to manslaughter and accept a reduced sentence.

Emma was having none of that, not after she'd heard Sue Ellen's story and talked to all of her neighbors. They had confirmed the frequency of the fights with Donny, the times the police had been called. There was a record of those 9-1-1 calls, which would add to her case, even if Sue Ellen had failed to press charges even once.

"Mommy, are we gonna stay with Grandma?" Caitlyn asked eagerly when another week came and went and they hadn't left.

"For a while," Emma told her. She had flown to Denver with the rest of the Calamity Janes to be with Cassie during her mom's surgery, then taken the time to stop by her office to talk with her secretary and her associates and arrange for them to take over the most pressing appointments, at least for the next few days. Because of her workaholic tendencies in the past, all the partners had agreed that she deserved the time off.

She studied Caitlyn's hopeful expression. "Would you like that? Are you having fun here?"

Caitlyn nodded, then threw her arms around Emma's neck. "I *love* it here," she said enthusiastically. "There's horses and cows and kids my age. And Pete's birthday is coming, and Uncle Matt says there's gonna be cake and ice cream and everything. And Grandpa's promised me that I'll be able to ride my pony all by myself really, really soon."

Emma grinned. "Well, we definitely wouldn't want to miss any of that, would we?"

"No way," Caitlyn said. "And then Jessie's birthday is a month from now. And then pretty soon after that school starts. Jessie says the teacher for second grade is really, really nice. We could be in the same class. Wouldn't that be the best?"

"Whoa, baby. I didn't say we were going to stay forever, just until I can wrap up some of the business I have here. After that we'll just come back and forth when I need to be in court."

Caitlyn's face fell. "But, Mommy, I want to live here. I really, really want to." Her lower lip trembled, and tears spilled down her cheeks. "I hate Denver. I don't ever want to go back. Not ever!"

With that she turned and ran into the house, letting the screen door slam and leaving Emma staring after her. This was a turn of events she definitely hadn't counted on. With every day that passed, Caitlyn was clearly going to become more and more attached to the family and friends she had here. Tearing her away was going to break her heart.

"What's wrong with Caitlyn?" her mother asked, stepping onto the porch. "She just ran through the house sobbing. And now she's clinging to your father's neck as if she'll never let go."

"She's gotten the idea that we're going to stay here forever. When I told her that we weren't, she got upset."

"Then maybe you should consider doing what she wants," her mother said.

Emma was appalled by the suggestion for any number of reasons. "Give in to a six-year-old? She doesn't know what's best for her."

"Oh, really?" Her mother sat down beside her, her expression somber. "Maybe she does, Emma. Maybe even a six-year-old can see that here she has family, that she has room to run and play, that her mother gets home at a decent hour and has time to spend with her. Maybe she's aware that her mother's not really happy in Denver, either, that she's been using her work as a way to hide out from her feelings."

Emma bristled at the criticism. "I work hard to make a good life for us."

"To make money, you mean."

"Are you suggesting that money's not important?"

"Of course not, but there are things that are more important. I've just named a few of them. Can you honestly tell me that you're happy?"

Emma sighed. "Mom, I'm doing the best I can."

"Are you really?" Millie challenged. "Best for whom? You?"

"Both of us," she insisted.

"Obviously Caitlyn doesn't see it that way."

"She's six, dammit."

Her mother frowned at the language. "You know better," she chided gently.

"Sorry."

"I doubt that." Millie kissed Emma's cheek. "Just think about what I've said. You've evaded my question about whether you're truly happy. Think about that. Think about what your daughter's said. Just because she's a little girl doesn't mean you can dismiss what she wants so easily."

"I'll think about it, Mom. I promise. Right now,

though, I'm going to saddle up a horse and go for a ride."

"Good. There was a time when that soothed you, put things back into perspective. Maybe it will again."

"Maybe," Emma agreed, though she didn't hold out much hope for it.

With the sun beating down on her shoulders, she rode up into the foothills of the Snowy Range, letting the horse set the leisurely pace. Whenever troubling thoughts began to creep in, she shoved them aside. Keeping her mind blank was harder than she'd expected, especially when her mother had just given her so much to consider.

On the ride home she let the horse gallop full out, relishing the way the wind whipped her hair and stung her face. She felt exhilarated, if not any less conflicted by the time she got back to the corral.

Finding Ford sitting on the front porch waiting for her destroyed what little equanimity she had managed to achieve. She was still seething over his initial report on the shooting, which had all but condemned Sue Ellen on the front page. Fortunately, thanks to the tightness of the deadline, it had been little more than a four-inch blurb with a comparatively small headline. His report on the town's success stories had been much longer but it hadn't offset Emma's reaction to that small item about the shooting. He'd been calling ever since for a follow-up interview for this week's edition. She hadn't returned his calls. No matter how fair he'd been to Lauren and the others, she didn't fully trust him.

"What are you doing here?" she demanded, pausing at the bottom of the steps, her hand on the railing.

"Waiting for you. I've left several messages. You haven't called me back."

"What do you suppose that means? Could it possibly be that I don't want to talk to you?"

"Sarcasm doesn't become you."

"If you have a question, now that you're here, just spit it out."

"I want to talk to Sue Ellen."

"Not a chance. Anything you want to know, you'll have to ask me."

"Will you answer me?"

"That depends."

"On?"

"Whether I like the question."

"In other words, you have all the cards."

She grinned. "Pretty much."

"Are you sure that you're operating in your client's best interests? Or are you letting some vendetta you have against the media interfere with getting her story out in a way that might help her?"

"You want to help Sue Ellen? Now why do I have a tough time buying that?"

"Because you have a suspicious nature?"

"No, because you've already made it plain in print and in conversation that you've got an ax to grind against her."

"I reported the bare facts in last week's paper. As for any conversation that you and I have had, it was in the heat of the moment."

"Then you don't consider Sue Ellen to be guilty of a cold-blooded murder?" she asked, quoting him precisely.

"I never said that."

"You did," she corrected. "At the jail on the night she was arrested. That's not exactly the kind of open-minded reporter I want her to talk to."

"If you won't let me talk to her, have dinner with me. You can give me her side of things."

Emma hesitated. He was right about one thing. She did need to build sympathy for Sue Ellen's cause, if only to plant a subliminal message in the minds of potential jurors. And, sadly, the *Winding River News* was the only game in town, though many locals took the Cheyenne newspaper as their daily paper. Emma resolved to try to reach someone there first thing in the morning. In the meantime, putting her spin on things for Ford made sense.

"Okay," she said at last. "I'll have dinner with you."

"Tonight?"

"That's as good a time as any."

He grinned. "Your enthusiasm overwhelms me."

She bristled. "It's not a date, it's an interview. If you can't keep that fact straight, why should I trust you with any others?"

"An interview, not a date," he said solemnly. "Got it." He gestured toward his car. "Coming?"

"I'll meet you in town. That way you won't have to drive me all the way back out here."

"Ah, that's the date thing again, isn't it?" he asked.

"Pretty much," she said. "I wouldn't want you to get confused just when things are starting to go so well."

"Oh, I'm sure I can keep it straight for a couple of hours…maybe even all evening long."

"A couple of hours should be enough. I don't want to tax you," she said acidly.

He left that unchallenged. "Where should I meet you for this non-date dinner?"

"Tony's," she said at once. Maybe Gina would be there. She could offer additional insights into the kind of person Sue Ellen had been when they were growing up.

"The Italian place on Main Street," he said. "Great lasagna."

"Better pizza," she countered.

"Are we going to argue over that, too?"

She gave him a faint smile. "More than likely. I'll see you there. Give me an extra couple of minutes to check in on Caitlyn and let my parents know I'm going out."

"I'll get you a glass of wine."

"Forget the wine. It might loosen my tongue."

"That's the whole idea," he said with an unrepentant grin.

"Make it coffee."

"Whatever you say, Counselor," he said with a jaunty salute.

If only, Emma thought as she watched him drive away.

When Ford spotted Gina Petrillo coming out of the kitchen at Tony's, he understood why Emma had picked this particular restaurant. She'd wanted backup. Was that because she was afraid of what she might say about Sue Ellen and Donny Carter? Or because she felt—and feared—the same sizzling awareness that had aroused him? Did it even matter? The bottom line was that they were going to be well chaperoned.

Gina greeted him with a smile. "I'm filling in for

Tony, and the waitress is on a break. Are you here for dinner?"

"Of course. Tony must really rate, if he can lure you into substituting," he said.

"He got me into the restaurant business," she told him. "So, are you here alone or are you expecting someone?"

"Actually, your friend Emma will be joining me," he said. "How about that booth over there? It looks fairly private."

Gina studied him with a penetrating look. "You intending to whisper sweet nothings into Emma's ear?"

"Nope. This is an interview, not a date," he said, dutifully reciting the ground rules.

Gina grinned. "Your choice of words or Emma's?"

Before Ford could answer, she said, "Emma's, I imagine. I really need to have a talk with her. What can I bring you to drink?"

"Red wine for me, coffee for her."

"Two red wines," she corrected.

"As long as I don't end up wearing that second glass," he said, chuckling at her audacity.

"Blame it on me. She'd never toss it at a friend, especially once I explain to her that wasting a perfectly good wine is a sin."

Gina had delivered the two glasses of wine and retreated to the kitchen by the time Emma arrived. She scowled at him.

"I thought I made myself clear about the wine," she said.

"You did," he agreed. "To me, anyway."

"What does that mean?"

The Calamity Janes 339

He nodded toward the kitchen. "Your friend had other ideas."

"Gina?"

"She's subbing for Tony tonight." He studied the guilty flush on her face. "Which you were hoping for, right?"

She didn't answer. He took that for a yes.

"In that case, drink your wine. I promise if you get wild, I'll drive you home and never print a word about it."

"As if I'd believe that."

He frowned at her. "Is it me you distrust, or all reporters?"

"All media," she said succinctly.

"There must be a story there."

"If there is, you'll never hear it from me," she said, then lifted her glass in a mocking toast. "Not even if I drank the whole bottle."

6

Dinner turned out to be surprisingly pleasant. Maybe it was the warm glow Emma was feeling from the wine. Maybe it had something to do with the way Ford seemed to hang on her every word without taking notes. He'd sworn to her that he'd let her know when the conversation shifted from casual chitchat to a formal interview. Not that she wasn't very circumspect all the same, but she had begun to relax just a little.

It had been a long time since she'd had dinner with a handsome, intelligent man who wasn't a business colleague. As long as Ford talked about sports and theater and books, she could almost convince herself that this evening wasn't work related either. Despite her earlier edict, it almost felt like a date—or at least the way she remembered a date feeling. There was even an edgy anticipation that seemed to underscore everything.

As soon as she acknowledged that, she frowned at the glass of wine in her hand. Was it her second or her third? She rarely drank. She should have stopped after one, lest her thinking turn fuzzy and her defense mechanisms weaken. She felt as if they already had, so clearly she must have gone over her limit.

"I need to get home," she said, standing up on legs that wobbled. Obviously alcohol and exhaustion were a lousy combination.

"Oh, no, you don't," Ford said, nudging her back into her chair with surprisingly little effort. "Not until you have some coffee and we do this interview."

She shook her head to clear it. They'd been talking for hours. Surely…she regarded him with confusion. "We haven't done it?"

"Did you see me taking notes?"

"No, but it wouldn't be the first time a sneaky reporter fooled me into thinking he wasn't going to report what I said," she said with feeling.

"Well, I'm not sneaky, and I'm not going to report anything unless you tell me it's on the record."

He sounded sincere, but Emma had vowed never to let herself be taken advantage of again by the media. Until tonight she had restricted her recent media contacts to quick, prepared sound bites that couldn't be misinterpreted. She no longer agreed to in-depth interviews.

"I can't do this now," she said again. She shook her head in a futile attempt to clear it, then said with amazement, "I believe I may have had too much wine."

Ford grinned. "Entirely possible. You've almost finished that first glass."

She stared from him to the glass. "The first? I was sure it had to be my third."

"Afraid not. You don't drink a lot, do you?"

"No."

"Is that a control thing?"

She frowned at the question, fairly sure he had meant it to be insulting. "Meaning?"

"Are you afraid of losing control?"

"Pretty much," she agreed without hesitation. Her

reputation as a control freak was widespread and undeniable. Pretending otherwise would be a waste of time.

"Do you ever let loose?"

"Never."

His look heated as he captured her gaze and held it. "Not even in bed?" he asked in a low, husky voice.

Emma had risked another sip of wine, but the question made her choke on it. "Excuse me?"

"I was just wondering—"

"I know what you were wondering. Isn't that a little inappropriate as an interview question?"

"Sorry," he said without any evidence of real remorse. "I lost my head there for a minute and asked a date question."

She propped her chin on her hand and stared at him with fascination. Maybe this was a good chance to shine a little illumination on the whole dating thing. She'd been out of practice for quite a while. "You actually ask that sort of thing on a date? Times certainly have changed from when I was dating."

Ford seemed to take her question seriously. "Well, not recently, to be perfectly honest, but yes, the subject of sex has come up a time or two."

"On a first date?"

He grinned. "Depends on the date. You've certainly planted the idea firmly in my head tonight."

Emma had a feeling the heat she felt climbing into her cheeks had nothing to do with the wine. Now that she'd opened the door to the topic, she was regretting it.

"I haven't embarrassed you, have I?" Ford asked, his expression innocent. "I figured being a big-city lawyer and all, you would be familiar with the topic."

"It doesn't come up a lot in corporate law."

"Or in your personal life, either, I'll bet," he said in an undertone.

"I know about sex," she said emphatically just as Gina stopped at the table.

"Whoa!" Gina said, backing off a step with exaggerated horror. "Obviously I'm interrupting."

"No, you're not," Emma said, grateful for the intrusion. She was very much afraid that the conversation had veered into a quagmire from which she might never extricate herself. "Can you drive me home?"

Gina glanced at Ford. "What about your date?"

"He is not my date. This was supposed to be an interview, but he never got around to asking any questions, so he loses," she said triumphantly.

"Another time," Ford said, his eyes twinkling and his lips curving into a smile.

Emma gazed into those mesmerizing eyes and lost her train of thought. Lordy, he was handsome when he smiled. Too bad he had such a major character flaw: his career.

"I'll remember to make sure you lay off the wine next time," he added. "I like my women to remember everything about an evening we spend together."

She frowned at that. "I am not one of your women, and I can remember everything that happened tonight."

"We'll see about that in the morning. I'll call you." He glanced at Gina. "Need any help?"

Gina was staring at Emma with a perplexed expression. "No, but how did she get this way?"

"Exhaustion and that glass of wine you insisted on."

"One glass?"

"One," he confirmed. "But she was pretty much this way after the first couple of sips."

Gina shook her head. "Amazing."

Emma scowled at her. "Kindly do not talk about me as if I weren't here."

Gina rolled her eyes. "Okay, sweetie, on your feet. Let's get you home."

Emma brushed aside Gina's outstretched hand, cast one last haughty look at Ford and walked out of Tony's alone. She'd lied when she'd told Ford she would remember everything about this evening. She had a pretty good hunch that in a few more minutes she wouldn't even remember her own name. Oddly enough, though, she couldn't seem to make herself regret it. In fact, she felt as if she'd been through some sort of rite of passage back into the social world of grown-up women. Next time, though, she vowed to steer clear of the wine so she could actually enjoy it. Also next time, it might be best if the male company she chose weren't in a position to derail a client's case.

"You should have seen her," Gina was saying when Emma walked into Stella's the next morning in serious need of coffee and a bottleful of aspirin. She'd hitched a ride into town with her mother so she could pick up the car she'd left outside Tony's the night before.

"She was seriously looped, and on barely a glass of wine," Gina concluded.

"Emma?" Lauren stared from Gina to Emma, clearly incredulous.

"Oh, stop it. I wasn't drunk. I was just a little shaky. I don't usually drink."

"Keep it that way," Gina advised. "You are not a woman who holds her liquor well."

"I didn't do anything outrageous, did I?"

"Other than talking to Ford about sex?" Lauren teased. "Gina told me about that."

"I didn't," Emma said, but Gina's gaze didn't waver. "I did, didn't I?"

"Oh, yeah," Gina confirmed. "I think I came along before things got too hot and heavy. I'm pretty sure you were just assuring him that you were familiar with the concept."

"Why would I do that?"

"Because he asked, or maybe he implied that you didn't know anything about the subject. Ford seems to bring out your competitive streak. Looked to me like you might be about to leap across the table and offer him proof of your experience."

Emma groaned and held her head. "Get me coffee before I die."

Lauren chuckled. "Ah, here comes the man in question now. Maybe he can fill in the blanks."

Ford approached the table, nodded at Gina and Lauren, then fixed his gaze on Emma. "Room here for one more?"

"Sure," Gina and Lauren said in a chorus, just as Emma said, "No."

He slid in next to her anyway. When his thigh grazed hers, she swallowed hard and kept her gaze firmly on the menu. She would not let him see that he had the power to disconcert her in the slightest. She was fairly certain it was not possible to die of terminal embarrassment.

Breakfast seemed to take an eternity. With every second that passed, Emma grew more and more aware of the hard, solid thigh next to her own. All that muscle, all that heat…sweet heaven, what was happening to her? Why had her hormones, which had been dutifully silent for months and months, chosen now to act up? And with Ford Hamilton, of all people.

"Well, as enthralling as it's been to watch the two of you," Lauren said, "I have to go. Karen's expecting me."

Emma ignored the gibe and focused on the rest of Lauren's statement. "You've been spending a lot of time at the ranch. What's that about?"

"Do you even have to ask?" Lauren said, though she avoided Emma's gaze. "Karen needs all the help she can get. Since she refuses to take any money from me to hire extra help, then I intend to pitch in as much as I can."

"And your career?" Gina asked, studying her worriedly.

"You're a fine one to talk," Lauren countered. "I don't see you rushing back to New York."

Emma held up a hand before the two of them could start a contest over which one was working hardest to avoid some problem. "Hey, enough," she said. "I'm sure Karen appreciates having Lauren around, and I'm sure Tony is grateful that Gina's here. And I'm glad you're both around."

Both women stared at her. "Emma as peacemaker? That's a first," Gina said. "That's usually Karen's role."

"Well, she's not here at the moment," Emma said. "I am. And I have negotiated my share of settlements. I don't always have to win in court."

"You just don't like to lose," Gina teased as she slid out of the booth. "Let's go, Lauren. I have a feeling these two have things to discuss."

Emma slanted a look at Ford, who was observing the entire exchange with obvious interest. "I should go, too," she said, but he didn't budge. Short of climbing over him, she was stuck right where she was.

"Not just yet," he countered mildly. "I haven't finished my breakfast. Stick around. Have another cup of coffee."

"Yeah, Emma, have another cup," Gina encouraged. "Those cobwebs in your head can probably use another dose of caffeine. I'll send Cassie over."

"Thanks," Emma muttered.

When Gina and Lauren had gone and Cassie had poured more coffee without comment, Emma scowled at Ford. "Why not sit on the other side? You'll have more room."

"I'm perfectly comfortable right here. How about you?"

She knew that to admit to anything other than total comfort and serenity would be far too telling. "I'm fine," she said, barely resisting the urge to grind her teeth in frustration.

Ford finished his eggs in silence. Emma watched him with mounting tension. How could any man look so perfectly relaxed while instilling such turmoil? Finally, when she could stand it no longer, she scowled at him.

"I thought you had questions you wanted to ask me. If not, I have things to do."

He grinned at her impatience. "Maybe I was just trying to lull you into a false sense of complacency."

"Well, it's not working. I'm getting annoyed, and when I get annoyed, I am not the least bit inclined to be cooperative."

His grin widened. "Yes, I can see that. Okay, then." He drew his tape recorder out of his pocket and put it on the table between them, then met her gaze. "Ready?"

Emma stiffened but nodded. "Any time you are."

He clicked on the recorder, said the date and her name. "You're the defense attorney for Sue Ellen Carter, is that right?"

"Yes."

"And she is pleading not guilty in the death of her husband, is that correct?"

"Absolutely."

"She did shoot him, though? You do admit that much, correct?"

Emma weighed her response. The facts of the case weren't really in dispute. Though the gun had actually been in Donny's hand when police arrived, Sue Ellen hadn't denied that it had gone off while they had struggled over it. The prosecutor had been wise enough not to try for a first-degree murder charge for the same reasons. He'd accepted Sue Ellen's statement that there had been a struggle and agreed to the lesser charge of manslaughter. But a charge with any jail time at all was unacceptable to Emma.

"Ms. Rogers?" Ford prodded.

She chose her words with deliberate care. "The gun went off during a violent struggle during which my client was in fear for her life."

"You're claiming self-defense?"

"Absolutely," she said without any hesitation. "And based on the pattern of abuse, I think it will become clear that she had every reason to be afraid."

"Had your client's husband ever been charged with domestic violence?"

"No."

"Had he ever been arrested?"

"No." She saw what Ford was trying to do and

scowled at him. "But the police had been called on numerous occasions, not only by my client but by the neighbors as well. Those calls are on record."

"If she was so terrified, why didn't she leave?"

Emma lost patience. "Mr. Hamilton, do you know anything at all about domestic violence?"

"It's Ford, and I've read a few articles."

"Okay, *Ford*. The articles you've read must not have been very thorough, or else they were outdated. There is a whole litany of reasons why women don't leave their abusers. Once you grasp that, then perhaps we'll have something more to talk about." She reached over and switched off the tape recorder. "Until then, we're through."

He frowned at her. "Why should I read, when you're the expert? Explain it to me."

"It isn't my job to educate you. You're a reporter. It's your job to explore all of the facts, to seek out the experts."

"I thought I was talking to one."

"I'm an attorney, not a psychologist. I don't testify when we go to court. I bring in professionals who can explain all of this to a jury."

"But you're obviously well versed in this. Why not tell me?"

"Because I don't have time to spoon-feed the information to you. I have a client to defend and a caseload back in Denver that needs my attention."

"Have you got a list of expert witnesses you intend to call?"

"Not yet."

"Okay, I'll ask you again. Let me talk to Sue Ellen."

"No."

"Why not?"

"Because I don't want her to trust you and say something perfectly innocent that you'll twist in print."

"Dammit, Emma, I do not twist things," he snapped, clearly losing patience with her continued distrust. "What the hell happened to you? Did some reporter take something you said out of context?"

"If only it were that simple," she retorted, swallowing back the bile that rose at the memory of how badly she'd been deceived and betrayed. Never again. The last time she'd trusted a reporter, it had almost cost her her career. It had been the end of her marriage.

"Tell me," Ford pleaded.

"No," she said flatly. "I have to get over to the jail."

For a moment, he hesitated, and she thought he might not let her out of the booth. Then he sighed and stood up to let her by.

"We'll talk again," he said mildly.

"Only when you're more fully prepared," she said, then turned away.

"Emma."

Slowly she faced him.

"I'm not the enemy here. In fact, I could turn out to be your best ally."

If he were honorable, *if* she could persuade him that Sue Ellen had only done what she'd had to do, yes, he could be an ally. But those were big *ifs*. Emma had learned a long time ago to hold out for sure things. Anything less was too risky.

Ford considered going straight to the jail, but he knew in his gut that Emma would be furious if he turned up there not five minutes after she'd told him that was where she was headed. He wasn't going to get that interview with Sue Ellen by alienating the woman's attorney. He was going to have to be patient. Sooner or later, Emma would see the value of having Sue Ellen's side on the record and would relent.

Besides, he had a paper to put out. He had enough information now to write this week's article about the shooting of Donny Carter. He intended to be very careful, to stick strictly to the facts and leave out all the lurid details about the ongoing violence of his marriage to Sue Ellen. Everything he'd heard about that to this point was hearsay anyway. Until Sue Ellen could give him a first-person account, he was going to report only what court documents said and Emma's confirmation of the basic facts of the case.

When he got to his office, Teddy was waiting for him with a half-dozen pictures of the couple at the dance. It was evident that there was a heated argument going on. Ford studied the telling photos, then sighed. He'd told Ryan even before the shooting that he wouldn't use them. He intended to keep his word, even though the situation and the stakes had changed.

"Put them in the files," he told the teenager.

"But—"

"I promised your uncle I wouldn't print them."

"Why? Besides, that was before Sue Ellen killed Donny. Maybe it wasn't news then, but it is now."

Ford couldn't argue that point, but he knew of at least two people who wouldn't care: Emma and Ryan. He didn't want to anger either one of them, and using those pictures would be like waving a red flag under the nose of a bull. They would be furious if he printed the potentially prejudicial pictures.

"We have them if we need them," he said flatly. "But I'm not using them now."

He'd expected Teddy to be disappointed, but what he saw on the teen's face, instead, was guilt. "What?" Ford demanded.

"The paper in Cheyenne called about an hour ago. They'd heard I took pictures. I sent one over," he admitted.

Ford was aghast. "Why the hell would you do that?" he demanded heatedly.

The color drained out of the boy's face. "I thought that's what you'd want," he said, his voice quivering.

"Dammit, Teddy, what gave you the right to sell even one picture to another paper? You're working for me."

"I didn't sell it. The editor said it was more like sharing between newsmen. I thought that was the way it's done."

"Sometimes it is," Ford conceded, fighting his anger. "But the decision isn't made by an intern. It's made by the editor. Last time I checked that was me."

"I'm sorry."

"Do you have any idea what you've done? Now if we don't use those pictures and the Cheyenne paper does, it'll look as if we're sitting on a critical piece of evidence. Not only will it make this paper look bad journalistically, but there's a good chance the prosecutor will be all over us, demanding the photos and the negatives. Up until now, only a few people even knew we had them."

"I didn't know," Teddy whispered, his voice shaking. "I was just trying to help. The editor said he was on a deadline. I tried to reach you."

"Did you ever consider walking down the block to check in Stella's?"

Looking miserable, Teddy shook his head.

"What's his name?" Ford asked, aware that calling the man to plead with him not to use the photo would be a waste of time. Still, he had to try.

Teddy handed over the name and phone number. "You're not going to fire me, are you?"

Seeing the genuine panic and contrition on the boy's face, he sighed. "No, as badly as you screwed up, I am not going to fire you. But there's a lesson here, okay?"

"Don't do anything without asking you," Teddy said at once.

"For starters," Ford agreed. "And remember that a photograph is a powerful thing. Most of the time that's exactly what you want on the front page. Sometimes— and this is one of them—deciding whether or not to use something that powerful has to be weighed very carefully. The last thing we want to do is to prejudice the case against Sue Ellen."

Teddy looked even more miserable. "It could hurt Sue Ellen's case?"

"It could," Ford confirmed, glancing at the look of pure hatred and contempt on her face as Donny raged at her. While it might be evidence of Donny's behavior, it was also overwhelming evidence of a motive for murder.

"Uncle Ryan's going to kill me," Teddy said despondently.

Ford thought of his own perception that Ryan had a soft spot for Sue Ellen. He nodded. "He might at that."

7

Emma had barely walked into the house when her sister-in-law emerged from the kitchen, a defeated expression on her face.

"I've had it," Martha announced. "That brother of yours is driving me flat-out crazy."

"Matt?" Emma asked incredulously. Then the memory of her conversation with her mother came flooding back. "Does this have something to do with his mood lately?"

"It has everything to do with his mood. The man can't find anything positive to say about anything. I'm tired of it. The kids are tired of it. If it doesn't change, I swear to you that I am taking them and moving to..." She threw up her hands. "I don't know, Florida, maybe. Someplace that's warm all year round. I'm sick of being frozen—both physically and emotionally."

Emma was too drained by her meetings with Ford and Sue Ellen to go through yet another emotional meltdown, but she didn't seem to have any choice. Leaving might be an idle threat, but Martha's frustration was very real.

"Is Matt here now?" she asked.

"No, he just stormed out the back door because I had the audacity to ask if he wanted to go to Laramie for dinner and a movie tonight with me and the kids. Apparently I don't understand that he has to get up at the crack of dawn, that he can't be gallivanting all over the place to see some fool movie, et cetera, et cetera, much less waste money on a fast-food hamburger, when we have a freezer filled with better beef."

Emma winced. "That's quite a tirade. Maybe he's having a bad day."

"*Every* day is a bad day," Martha said wearily. "If I point out what beautiful, sunny weather we're having, he says if we don't get rain we're going to be in the middle of a drought. It's depressing."

"I can imagine," Emma soothed. "Come have a cup of tea with me. Let's talk about this."

"Tea? I thought you were a dedicated coffee drinker," Martha said, trailing her into the kitchen.

Emma grimaced. "I was until I went through six cups at breakfast trying to get over a hangover."

Martha's eyes widened. "You had a hangover? I've never seen you drink."

"It was one glass of wine."

"But—"

"Don't even ask," Emma said, as she found some herbal tea in her mother's cabinet and put the kettle on to boil.

Martha took cups from another cupboard and set them on the table, then sat down, her expression subdued. She and Matt had been in love as far back as Emma could remember. First grade, maybe, when they'd been seated next to each other alphabetically.

By junior high they were inseparable. By high school they were a couple. They had married two months after graduation, despite pleas from both sets of parents to wait until after college.

Matt had been a promising student who had earned a scholarship to the University of Wyoming, but Martha had been pregnant by the end of summer, and Matt had dropped his college plans to go to work for his father. They had been in Winding River ever since. At twenty-five, they already had three children. Until this visit, Emma had assumed they were happy.

She poured the tea, then sat opposite her normally exuberant sister-in-law. "Okay, what's going on with you and Matt? What's behind this mood of his?"

"He's miserable," Martha said, echoing what Emma's mother had said earlier in her visit. "He just won't admit it. Instead, he takes it out on everybody else."

"Mom seems to think he's unhappy working here at the ranch. Is that your impression, too?"

Martha nodded. "I have begged him to quit and go to college, the way he planned to seven years ago. We could move to Cheyenne for four years. I could work. We could manage, but he won't hear of it."

"Why?"

"Pride. Stubbornness. Fear. Who knows? He won't talk about it. He bites my head off every single time I bring it up."

Emma resisted the temptation to ask just how often Martha brought it up. Had she been nagging him? Like all males, Matt was resistant to what he viewed as "pestering." But instead of suggesting that might be the problem, Emma focused on her sister-in-law. "What about you, Martha? Do you regret not going to college?"

Martha shook her head. "No, I have everything I ever dreamed of. I love Matt and our kids and our life. I couldn't ask for anything more."

"Maybe that's what's holding him back," Emma speculated thoughtfully. She was a bit uneasy being cast in the role of marital arbitrator, but this was clearly an emergency, and she did know the parties involved as well as anyone. If she could help, she had to try.

"How?" Martha asked.

"Maybe he knows you're happy and thinks there must be something wrong with him if he's discontented," Emma speculated. "Add to that the prospect of making you *unhappy* by changing the status quo, and he's in a real quandary."

"But it would only be for four years," Martha said. "And if he would be happier getting his degree and doing something else, then that's what I want for him, for *us*. Things certainly aren't working the way they are now."

"Have you told him that?"

"Over and over."

"Want me to talk to him?"

Martha's expression brightened. "Would you? He admires you so much. If you said it was the right thing to do, maybe he'd believe it."

Emma squeezed her sister-in-law's hand. "I'll do my best. Hang in there, sweetie. Matt loves you. That's the one sure thing in all of this. Don't lose sight of it."

"I'm trying not to," Martha said, then glanced at her watch. "I've got to run. My mom has the kids, and I told her I'd be back for them right after their naps. They have so much energy then, they're too much for her."

Emma grinned. "I can imagine. Caitlyn has more stamina than I can handle sometimes, and there's just one of her."

"Where is Caitlyn? I haven't seen her today since I got here."

"Probably with Dad in the barn. She wants to do everything he does."

"Maybe she'll grow up to be the rancher and take the pressure off Matt," Martha said wistfully. "I have a feeling part of his problem is not wanting to let your father down."

"You could be right," Emma admitted. Matt had always been sensitive. No doubt he had seen how badly hurt her father had been by her decision to leave. Even though her father had refused to make her feel guilty, Matt had probably picked up on the unspoken disappointment. Add to that Wayne's decision not to stay on the ranch, and no doubt Matt felt doubly responsible to take over and not let their father down. "Don't worry. We'll get this straightened out."

As soon as Martha had gone, Emma went in search of her brother, but she found Caitlyn instead. Emma's daughter was sitting astride her pony in the corral, listening intently to her grandfather's instructions. Her gaze never wavered as Emma approached.

The pony began to canter, and to Emma's amazement, Caitlyn maintained perfect control of the animal. She looked as poised as if she'd been riding for years. She reined in the pony right in front of Emma, a beaming smile on her face.

"Did you see?" she asked excitedly. "Did you see me ride?"

"You were wonderful," Emma said as her father scooped Caitlyn out of the saddle.

"Better than wonderful," he told his granddaughter. "Better even than your mom was at your age."

"Really?" Caitlyn breathed, wonder in her eyes. "Am I, Mom?"

"You are," Emma confirmed. "You're a natural, no question about it."

Caitlyn threw her arms around her grandfather's neck and hugged him tightly. "I hope we can stay here forever and ever," she said fervently.

Emma met her father's troubled gaze over Caitlyn's head.

"Sorry," he mouthed silently.

Emma stood on tiptoe and kissed his cheek. "I love you."

He lowered Caitlyn to the ground. "Go into the house and see if your grandmother's back from her trip into town. She might have those cookies she promised you from the bakery."

As Caitlyn scampered away, he looked at Emma. "Any chance of you staying?"

"Not permanently," she said, knowing that she was disappointing him all over again. "My job's in Denver, Dad. You know that."

"Seems to me like you have a job here right now."

"One case," she insisted. "That's not a career."

"Seth will be retiring one of these days. The town will need a good attorney. In fact, I think the only reason he hasn't retired already is out of loyalty to the town."

Emma thought of the challenging cases on her plate in Denver. Drawing up wills, handling misdemeanors and traffic violations couldn't compare. "I can't do it," she said. "The people I work for need me."

"Do they really?" her father said lightly. "Any more than somebody like Sue Ellen?"

There was no comparison and Emma knew it. But, thankfully, a case like Sue Ellen's would come along once in a blue moon around here. The rest of the time, she would be practicing the kind of law that any new law school graduate could handle. She'd be bored to tears. And it would be tantamount to an admission that she couldn't cut it as a big-city lawyer, something her ex-husband had taunted her with on a regular basis.

"It wouldn't be the same," she said, even as she fought considering the possibility that her clients in Denver could get along just fine with some other attorney in their corner. She was good, maybe even exceptional, but so were a dozen others, possibly even more, in Denver alone.

"No," he agreed. "It wouldn't be the same, but it could be better."

"Oh, Dad, I wish I could, but I can't."

He nodded. "You know best, I'm sure," he said stiffly.

"Not about everything certainly," she said, "but about this, yes, I do. Denver is where I need to be."

But despite her fervent argument on that score, right this second she was having a hard time remembering one single reason why.

Ford was really pleased with the front-page story he'd written about the death of Donny Carter and the arraignment of his wife on manslaughter charges. With a vision of Emma front and center in his brain, he felt he'd walked a careful tightrope in his description of the crime and the woman who'd committed it.

The article was impartial and fair, just the way good journalism should be. He quoted neighbors and the sheriff, then added several quotations from his interview with Emma. And, as a result of the debate he'd had with Emma, he'd spent most of the afternoon on the phone tracking down experts on abuse for additional insight.

Because he'd gone the extra mile, he was startled when he walked into the diner for lunch a few hours after the paper hit the stands and every single person in the place looked away, either down at their food or toward a booth in the back.

Then he saw the front page of the Cheyenne paper, which was stacked in a rack by the door, with that damning photo splashed across four columns. He already knew that the photo credit had gone to the *Winding River News*. Nothing he'd said to the editor in Cheyenne had dissuaded the man from using it or giving the credit to Ford's paper.

Looking from that damning front page to the patrons at Stella's, he wanted to shout an explanation, to defend himself and the paper, but a part of him believed that the Cheyenne paper had done nothing wrong. If he hadn't given his word to Ryan, he might have reached a similar decision himself, despite all the arguments he'd recited to Teddy the day before. That picture told a story. The incident had happened and the photographer had witnessed it. It was less suspect, less open to misinterpretation, than any of the words he'd written.

"You going or staying?" Cassie asked, regarding him with a defiant expression.

Ford had never walked away from a fight in his life. He intended to spend the rest of his life in this community. They needed to know he stood behind his actions, even if in this case it had been Teddy who'd sent that picture to Cheyenne.

"Staying," he said succinctly.

"Well, steer clear of Emma. She's in the back, and she's not too happy with you at the moment. I don't want her any more upset than she is already."

"Emma's here?" He searched the diner and spotted her at a booth. No wonder everyone had been looking in that direction when he'd first walked in.

He'd taken a step toward her when Cassie put a restraining hand on his arm. "Didn't you hear me?" she demanded.

"I heard you, but Emma doesn't scare me."

"I'm not worried about *you*. I'm worried about *her*."

He gazed down into concerned eyes. "It will be okay. We need to talk about this."

Cassie sighed and stepped out of his path. "Don't blame me if she poisons your coffee."

"Not law-and-order Emma," he chided.

"No, probably not, more's the pity. I'll bring the coffee. The decision about what to do with it will be up to her."

As he started to make his way toward the back, he heard a collective intake of breath. Clearly everyone in the place was waiting for an explosion the minute he reached Emma. He fixed his gaze on her and kept on walking, ignoring the fact that she was regarding him as if he were little better than pond scum.

When he reached her booth, he didn't ask permission. He just slid in opposite her.

"You've got guts, I'll give you that," she said, though it didn't much sound like a compliment.

"If you have a problem with me, why not spell it out to my face?"

She tossed the paper across the table. "*This* is the problem. Why would you give them a picture like that, especially after you promised Ryan you wouldn't use it? If you think I'm furious, wait till you cross paths with him. He's bouncing off the walls over at the jail. Ryan's always been the most mild-mannered guy around, but he's developed a whole new vocabulary to describe what you've done."

Ford wasn't going to explain Teddy's role in what had happened. "Once the shooting took place, that picture became a legitimate news photo. Don't I get any credit for not running it here?"

"No," she said flatly. "Not when you gave it to a paper with an even bigger circulation."

"How about a little credit for the story I wrote in today's edition of the *Winding River News?*"

"I haven't seen it. I doubt anyone else has, either. This is all anybody's talking about."

"And by tomorrow they will have forgotten about it," he insisted.

"You can't really believe that. A picture is worth a thousand words, and you know it. I can't understand why you did something so prejudicial. How will I ever get an unbiased jury?"

"Do you honestly think you'll be able to get one anyway?" he demanded. "Everyone around here knows Sue Ellen. They also know just how bad her marriage to Donny was. If anything, it will be the prosecution that has difficulty finding unbiased jurors."

"They don't know Sue Ellen's history in Cheyenne or the rest of the state that subscribes to this paper, or at least they didn't until this appeared on the front page so they could look at it while they drank their morning coffee."

Ford knew she was right. Teddy had captured not just a frozen moment in a marriage but its entire history in that photo. "I'm sorry. I take full responsibility for it."

"How gallant of you. That and a buck will get me a cup of espresso in that fancy new tourist restaurant up the block. Maybe you should consider having yours up there."

"I prefer it in here. Stella's is the heart and soul of Winding River. This is where I find out what people are thinking and talking about."

"Well, today all they're talking about is how you betrayed one of their own." She regarded him with regret. "I can't believe I had almost started to trust you."

Ford lost patience. "Stay here," he muttered grimly. He stalked over to pick up a copy of his latest edition and slapped it on the table in front of her. "Read this and see if you still want to condemn me."

Her gaze flew to the headline, which was temperate by anyone's standards: Local Woman Charged In Husband's Death. She began to read.

Emma had an amazingly revealing face. Ford could tell when something annoyed her, when it angered her, even when she was moderately pleased. In the end, though, she looked up at him, her expression studiously blank. "So?"

"Is there a single fact in there that's in dispute?"

"No. Your facts are exactly right."

"And I found not one, but three experts on domestic violence."

"Bully for you," she taunted.

"And you're still not satisfied, are you?" he said, surprisingly hurt by that.

"No, because they're just dry, perfunctory quotes about abuse statistics. A good reporter looks beyond the facts, don't you think? A good journalist uses sound judgment and compassion."

"I spoke to those experts to get some balance into the article, just the way you wanted me to," he said. "Even they agreed that what Sue Ellen did was probably an extreme reaction to the situation."

"Of course it was extreme," she exploded impatiently. "So was the provocation. People don't just go around shooting their spouses *unless* they've been driven to extremes. She was beaten, Ford. Every week, if not every day, during her marriage. Imagine that. Picture the humiliation. Put yourself in her shoes and imagine the fear she felt every time her husband stepped through the front door of their home."

She rose to her feet, spine straight, then leaned down to level a look that seared him. "A decent *person* thinks about the horrible life Sue Ellen lived day in and day out, before they condemn her without a trial."

"I didn't condemn her," he protested. "And how can I understand what she went through when you won't let me talk to her?"

"That's your excuse, that I won't give you access to my client? After this and what you did with that photo, can you blame me?"

She was gone before Ford could think of an adequate response. She was gone before he could grasp the fact that the unfamiliar feeling stealing over him was shame. Maybe he didn't deserve all the disdain she was heaping on him, but on some level, she was right. Maybe he didn't get it. Maybe a man who hadn't lived with abuse never could.

Just as that thought occurred to him, so did another. If it was difficult for a man to understand something he'd never experienced, why not a woman? Was Emma's understanding and compassion for Sue Ellen born out of her own experience? Dear God in heaven, what if it was?

Before he could grapple with that, he looked up and spotted Ryan stalking toward him with a dire expression.

The sheriff stood beside the table, hands jammed into his pockets, scowling down at Ford. "What the devil were you thinking, Hamilton? I thought you and I had an understanding."

"We did," Ford agreed, debating whether to give him an explanation.

"Then why in hell did you betray me?"

Just then Teddy popped up in the next booth, his face pale. Obviously he'd overheard the entire conversation Ford had had with Emma. He apparently didn't intend to let his boss take all of the heat with Ryan as well.

"It was my fault, Uncle Ryan. I gave the picture to the Cheyenne paper. Ford didn't have anything to do with it. Once they had it, he tried to stop them from using it, but it was too late."

Ryan's gaze shot from his nephew to Ford. "Is that the way it happened?"

Ford nodded. "He didn't realize what he was doing."

The wind seemed to go out of Ryan then. He frowned at Teddy, but he didn't condemn him. Instead, he sat down across from Ford and raked a hand through his hair.

"Sorry. I shouldn't have jumped all over you like that."

"Not a problem. You're not the first."

A faint smile tugged at Ryan's lips. "Emma? Yes, I imagine she was in fine form. The woman does have a temper."

"Tell me about it," Ford said. He eyed Ryan curiously. "Any idea how I can get back in her good graces?"

"So she'll let you get to Sue Ellen?"

"That's one reason," Ford admitted.

"And the other?"

Ford frowned. "I wish to hell I knew. She's prickly and tough as nails, but she gets to me."

Ryan grinned. "Nice to know you're not immune to a challenge."

"Not a challenge," Ford insisted. He thought of his earlier suspicion that Emma might have had personal experience with abuse. "A puzzle...I guess that's it. She's got more contradictions than any female I've ever met. The journalist in me wants to make sense of them."

"So this is just a professional fascination?" Ryan said, regarding him with amusement.

"Of course."

"That's why the two of you were discussing sex at Tony's the other night? It came up in a professional conversation?"

"Does everybody in this town know about that?" Ford grumbled.

"More than likely," Ryan said. "Welcome to living in a small town. So, were you or were you not talking about sex?"

"Yes, but it was a casual thing. I just threw the topic on the table to rattle her." He grinned. "Worked like a charm. If she hadn't been married, divorced and had a child, I would have said it was the first time she'd ever heard the word."

"Maybe it was just the first time she'd heard it brought up by a relative stranger in the middle of a business dinner. Frankly, I'm surprised she didn't douse you with a glass of ice water."

"She probably would have, if she hadn't been just the slightest bit tipsy. I think her reflexes were a little slow."

"Good thing, because Emma always had damned fine aim."

"I'll remember that if the situation ever arises again."

Ryan's expression suddenly sobered. "Maybe it *shouldn't* come up again."

Ford looked at him quizzically. "I thought you were all for something happening between me and Emma."

"I was," Ryan admitted. "But it sounds to me as if you're treating her like some sort of intellectual puzzle you want to unravel. Seems to me she might mistake your interest for something more. I don't want Emma getting hurt. She's been through enough."

"You mean with that ex-husband of hers?"

"Yep. I don't know the details, but the divorce was a nasty one, according to her brothers. She had to all but hog-tie them to keep them from beating the man to a pulp. Given how she feels about you already, I don't think you want to tempt fate by riling her any more. She might not be so eager to tell them to lay off *you*."

"I'm sure you told me that to warn me off," Ford said.

"Of course."

Once again his suspicions came to mind. "Too bad, because all you've really done is whet my appetite for the story behind the divorce."

"Leave it alone," Ryan advised. "Emma won't talk about it. Neither will Wayne or Matt."

"If it was messy, there are probably public records," Ford said slowly. Maybe even newspaper reports, which might explain why Emma was so wary of reporters. He never had gotten around to checking that out.

"You're going to put her life under that kind of a microscope?" Ryan demanded indignantly.

"It's one way to get answers," he said defensively.

"A better way would be to ask her whatever you want to know. She might take your head off, but at least it would be the honest way to go about it."

Ryan was right, Ford conceded reluctantly. Snooping around in Emma's past would have to be a last resort. But in order to get the story from the horse's mouth, so to speak, he was going to have to find some way to convince her to start talking to him again. He weighed his charm against her fury and concluded it was going to be a real challenge.

He could hardly wait.

8

Emma was still stewing over her run-in with Ford Hamilton as she sat in the swing on the front porch at the ranch, idly pushing herself back and forth. A glass of her mother's fresh lemonade and the sound of Caitlyn's giggles as she rode the lawn mower around the house with her grandfather slowly began to have an effect, settling Emma down, washing away her anger over that awful photo in the Cheyenne paper and Ford's role in giving it to them.

It just proved that she'd been right all along about all journalists—they simply couldn't be trusted. The competitive drive for a scoop would win out over ethics every time, no matter how well-intentioned and honorable they claimed to be.

The fact that Ford hadn't run the picture in the *Winding River News* meant nothing. Actually he'd seen to it that it was published in a far more damaging place, a statewide newspaper that had a greater reach and more apparent credibility than a small local weekly would have.

His decision was unfortunate, really, and untimely.

She had been starting to like Ford, starting to believe he might be different from his colleagues of the fourth estate. The story he'd done about her classmates and their success had been fair and factual. Of course, there was the tiniest possibility that the shift in her opinion might have been entirely self-serving. She'd been fighting an attraction to the man ever since the moment they'd met.

Too bad. Her suddenly awakened hormones were just going to have to wait until a more suitable prospect came along—one with higher ethical standards at the very least.

Emma gave the swing an idle push, stirring a slight breeze as it went back and forth on creaking chains. How many afternoons had she spent out here, a book in one hand, her mom's lemonade in the other? As a girl, she'd been a Nancy Drew addict, reading every book in the series she could find in the attic and in the town library. By her teens, she'd become a John Grisham and Scott Turow fan. And for her sixteenth birthday, her brothers had given her a collection of Perry Mason tapes. By then, the die had been cast. She'd known she was destined to be a lawyer. Only her father hadn't seen it coming, or hadn't wanted to admit it.

Thinking of how clear-cut her goals had seemed back then, Emma sighed. Only now was she beginning to realize how many lives had been affected by her drive and determination…how many people had been disappointed. If she had known, would it have changed anything? She didn't think so. Maybe it would have kept her from marrying a man incapable of letting his wife work, but then she hadn't known how fiercely possessive Kit was until after the wedding.

Moreover, she wouldn't have had Caitlyn. How could she possibly regret anything that had given her such a beautiful daughter?

She glanced up just in time to see Caitlyn steering the lawn mower straight for Millie's flower bed. A gasp from just inside the screen door suggested Caitlyn's grandmother had seen the same thing.

"I'm going to kill your father," Millie said, stepping onto the porch.

At the last second, Emma's father took control of the machine and steered away from the flowers, casting an apologetic look toward the porch. Emma chuckled when her mother raised her fist and shook it at him.

"I swear that man has no sense at all when it comes to Caitlyn," she told Emma, her amusement plain despite her annoyance. "If she tried to follow him onto the roof, he'd help her up."

"Probably," Emma agreed.

"He's spoiling her."

"I know, Mom, but it's okay. It's only for a short time. Let them have their fun."

Her mother sighed heavily. "It's going to break his heart when you leave again."

"Mom, please."

"I know. I'm sorry. I don't mean to pressure you."

"Yes, you do." Emma glanced at her mother, hoping that she could distract her by getting into the problems faced by another of her children. "By the way, I had a talk with Martha. She's worried sick about Matt. I promised I'd talk to him."

Her mother looked relieved. "That's wonderful. Any idea what you're going to say?"

"Mostly I'm going to listen."

"Will you tell him to go to college, the way Martha wants?"

"It's not what *she* wants. She thinks it's what *Matt* wants but refuses to admit."

Her mother seemed taken aback by her daughter-in-law's grasp of the underlying situation. "She's probably right," Millie conceded. "Sometimes I forget that she's an adult now, and how much she's matured. A part of me still sees her as the schoolgirl who had a crush on my son."

"Will you and Dad be able to manage if Matt decides to go back to school?"

"We always have."

"But will Matt have your wholehearted blessing?"

"Of course," her mother said fiercely. "How could we do otherwise? We backed you and Wayne. We want Matt to be happy. That's all we've ever wanted for any of you."

"Maybe Dad should be the one talking to him, then," Emma suggested. "He could convince Matt not to feel guilty for wanting a different life."

"I wish it were that simple," her mother said.

"Why isn't it?"

"I'm no psychologist, but I think I know my children. As much as I hate to say it, I think Matt's enjoying being a martyr. And I think there might be a part of him that's afraid of going back to school after all this time. He was a good student in high school, but that was a while ago. You know how Matt hated to fail at anything."

Emma was shocked by Millie's assessment, but she knew her mother would never have said such a thing if she didn't believe it. Her insights were usually right on target, too.

"Then it's about time somebody put a stop to that," she said adamantly. "I'll talk to him first thing tomorrow. I won't have Matt being a martyr and wasting his life. I'll remind him that studying skills come back. All it takes is a little determination. And if money's an issue, I'll help him with his tuition until they get on their feet."

"He won't take your money."

"Oh, yes, he will," Emma said with grim determination. "It won't be an offer he can refuse."

Her mother reached over and squeezed her hand. "It's little wonder you're such a fine attorney, Emma. You do everything with such passion. I only wish…" She cut herself off. "Well, never mind about that."

Suddenly her eyes lit up. "Well, well, who have we here?"

Emma's gaze followed her mother's. An unfamiliar car was coming up the driveway at a breakneck pace. Emma tensed, surmising who it was, even though she didn't recognize the car. Ford had parked around back when he'd been here the last time, which was one reason he'd taken her by surprise. She hadn't realized anyone was visiting, or she might have slipped in the kitchen door. It might have been better if she had. There was no escaping now, though, not with her mother sitting right beside her.

When Ford emerged, her mother's smile spread. If she was aware of the tension between the journalist and Emma, it certainly didn't show on her face.

"Ford, how nice to see you," she called out, even though Ford's gaze was locked on Emma.

"Do you agree?" he asked Emma.

"Frankly, no."

"Emma," her mother scolded. "Ford is a guest."

"I didn't invite him. Did you?"

"That's not the point. Don't be rude." She stood up and patted her place in the swing. "Have a seat, Ford. I'll bring you some lemonade—I just made it. It's the perfect thing for a warm evening."

"Thank you, ma'am," he said, still watching Emma warily.

Her mother tapped her on the shoulder. "Be nice," she admonished before going inside.

The second they were alone, Emma scowled at him and demanded ungraciously, "What are you doing here?"

Ford ignored the lack of welcome, just as he had at the diner, but he wisely settled into a rocker next to the swing rather than taking the seat her mother had vacated. "I thought we needed to talk."

"About?"

"I'm not the bad guy here," he said carefully.

"No? Couldn't prove it by me."

He held out his cell phone.

"What's that for?"

"Call Ryan."

"Why?"

"Just do it. Ask him how that picture really wound up in the Cheyenne paper."

Emma studied Ford's expression. "You didn't give it to them?"

"No."

"It was your picture. The photo credit said as much."

"It was Teddy's picture," he corrected mildly.

Emma regarded him in stunned silence, thinking of Ryan's eager nephew. It made an awful kind of sense. Teddy was so anxious to become a big-time journalist. But would he have done such a thing on his own?

"*Teddy* actually gave it to them?" she asked cautiously. "He works for you. He must have had your permission."

"He didn't. The paper called. He couldn't find me, so he sent it on over. He thought he was doing the right thing. He knows otherwise now. If you don't believe me, call Ryan. Teddy told him the truth."

"Why not you? You could have told me."

"Because the buck stops with me. I might not have given the picture to the Cheyenne paper, but my employee did."

"So you were willing to take responsibility, rather than put Teddy into a tough spot with his uncle or me."

"That about sums it up. But Teddy overheard you yelling at me. Then Ryan came storming in and lit into me. It was too much for his nephew. Teddy confessed the whole story."

"I see."

"Still mad at me?" he asked, regarding her with a hopeful expression.

"Yes," she said at once. "Just not *as* mad."

He grinned. "You do know how to cling to a grudge, don't you?"

"It's not a grudge," she said with exasperation. "This isn't some whim, Ford. My client's future is on the line. That doesn't seem to matter to you."

"Of course it matters. That's why I want her side of the story."

Emma considered the request yet again, then shook her head. "I can't risk it."

Ford sighed. "I'm not going to give up or go away."

For some reason, Emma found that oddly reassuring.

His gaze locked with hers. "And it's not all about Sue Ellen, either."

Her breath caught in her throat. "Meaning?"

"There's something between us."

"Innate animosity?" she suggested.

"If only," he said wryly. "No, I'm afraid it's more than that. It's damned inconvenient, but it's a fact. It's pointless to try to ignore it."

"So what are you suggesting?"

"That we start over, try to keep Sue Ellen's case from becoming a roadblock to the two of us becoming better acquainted."

Emma considered the suggestion, debated the merits of getting any more deeply involved with a man she instinctively distrusted. In the end, she admitted that she might not have been entirely fair to him. And there were her hormones to consider.

"I suppose I can do that," she said finally.

He cast a speculative look in her direction. "Do you think the results will be any better?"

Emma sighed. "Probably not."

He grinned. "I'm pretty much thinking the same thing."

"Then why bother?" she asked.

He leaned forward and touched his lips to hers. That was it. Just his mouth on hers, light as air, hotter than fire. Emma saw stars.

"Oh, my," she murmured, when he eventually pulled away.

"Still need an explanation?"

She shook her head. "No, I think you've presented sufficient evidence to make your case."

"Good." He stood up. "Tell your mom I couldn't stick around for the lemonade."

Startled, Emma stared. "Why not?"

"Because there's an old rule of show business—always leave them wanting more."

He winked and took off down the steps, leaving Emma staring after him. She lifted a hand and touched her still-burning lips.

Oh, my, indeed.

Ford allowed Ryan to talk him into joining a Sunday afternoon baseball game in the park. He had no idea why the sheriff was so eager for his participation, but he was fairly sure it wasn't because he desperately needed another outfielder, which was all Ford was qualified to be. He certainly wasn't a powerhouse at the plate or capable of playing any critical defensive infield position.

When he arrived at the park, he took one look at the opposing team and had his answer. Emma was sitting on the bench, legal pad in hand, brow furrowed as she barked out orders to her team of women. She was wearing shorts, a baggy T-shirt and well-worn sneakers that he had a hunch she'd found in the back of her closet. It definitely wasn't the attire of a dress-for-success hotshot attorney. The longer she stuck around Winding River, the more her standards seemed to be relaxing—when it came to clothes, anyway.

Her gaze narrowed when she spotted him standing over her. "What are *you* doing here?"

"Ryan invited me."

She shot a suspicious look at the sheriff, who was studiously avoiding her gaze. "Oh, really?"

"He didn't tell me who was playing," Ford said.

"Would that have made a difference?"

"In the interest of keeping that newfound peace between us, it might have."

"You certainly don't think your team is going to win, do you?"

"Of course I do," he said. Then, just to see the quick rise of indignant color in her cheeks, he added, "We are guys."

"You were here the last time we played, correct? You do remember the score?"

"Sure, but you're forgetting two things. One, Lauren went back to California yesterday. Two—"

Emma interrupted. "Wait. How do you know that?"

"Big news," he said succinctly. "It was the talk at Stella's this morning. Everyone was speculating how long it would be before she found an excuse to come back again."

"What's the prediction?"

"A week. Two at most. Everyone's concluded that Lauren would like to move back here permanently but just hasn't talked herself into it yet. What's your take on that? Think she could give up the glamour?"

"As a matter of fact, I've been thinking pretty much the same thing about Lauren," Emma said, her expression thoughtful. "Okay, what's the other thing I'm supposedly forgetting?"

"*I'm* playing this time."

She hooted at that. "And you're some sort of superstar baseball player?"

"Could be," he lied. He was a Little League dropout, but she certainly didn't need to know that. He had a hunch his primary useful skill today was going to be rattling the manager of the opposing team.

Emma frowned at him. "We'll see."

Ford leaned down and planted a hard kiss on her lips, then retreated. "We certainly will," he said, and strolled out to the mound where Ryan was having a conference with the other men. He could feel Emma's gaze on him the whole time.

"Glad you could join us," Ryan said to Ford, amusement threading through his voice. "I thought for a while there you were going to join the *other* side."

"I doubt she'd have me," Ford said.

"That's not the way it looked to me," Ryan needled. "How about it, guys? Think Emma would take on Ford?"

The question drew a few ribald responses, along with a grin from Ryan.

"Yeah, that's what I thought too," the sheriff said. "But since you've chosen to be with us, how about playing center field?"

"Why center field?"

"You'll be directly in the line of sight of anyone up at bat," Ryan said deviously. "I expect you to make the most of that when Emma's up. She's their strongest hitter."

"I thought she was just managing," Ford said.

"Not today. Some of her key players—"

"Lauren," the other men said in a chorus.

"Right, Lauren. She's not here. Emma's filling in. I don't want her on base. Not even a walk. That means I need to pitch strikes and Ford needs to rattle her composure. How about it, pal? Think you're up to it?"

Ford grinned. "It will be my pleasure."

It wasn't long before he had the opportunity to test his skill. Emma had placed herself in the lineup batting cleanup. Her lead-off batter was on base. The next two batters had struck out.

Ryan glanced over his shoulder at Ford. "Ready?"

Ford acknowledged the question with a salute, then focused all of his attention on Emma. She had a loose and easy stance at the plate that was belied by the intensity of her gaze, which never once shifted from Ryan. Ford concluded that drastic measures were called for. He stripped his T-shirt off over his head. Her attention caught, Emma blinked, mouth gaping. Ryan's perfect pitch sailed right past her.

"Strike one!"

Emma whirled on Stella, who was umpiring the game. "You call that a strike?"

Stella held her ground. "I do."

"I wasn't ready."

Stella gestured toward the outline of the batter's box. "You were standing there, weren't you? Can I help it if your attention wandered?"

Emma muttered something that had the diner owner grinning, but she eventually returned her attention to the field and stepped back into the batter's box.

Ford turned his back to the plate and bent down to tie his shoe. He figured it was the ultimate test of whether those women who'd voted him as having the best butt at the Chicago paper were right.

"Strike two!" Stella said.

If Ford wasn't entirely mistaken, she was chuckling when she called it out. Turning slowly around, he saw that Emma, however, wasn't the slightest bit amused. She looked as if she might argue the call, then shook her head and scowled in Ford's direction. That look said that she knew what he was up to and didn't like it. No, he corrected, what she disliked most was the fact that it was working. Baseball might not be his strong suit, but strategy was quite another matter.

Emma's gaze locked on Ryan. Just as he wound up to pitch, Ford touched his fingers to his lips and blew a kiss in Emma's direction. She swung the bat and missed the ball by a mile.

"Strike three! You're out," Stella said, laughing openly now.

Ford began jogging in to the bench only to find Emma firmly planted in his path, eyes blazing.

"What do you think you're doing?"

He managed what he hoped was an innocent expression. "I have no idea what you mean."

"Of course you do! You're deliberately trying to distract me."

"You mean the same way Lauren was distracting the men the last time you played?"

"Exactly," she said, then blushed. "Never mind. Just stop it."

"Sorry, darlin', I can't do that. Ryan gave me an assignment."

"What assignment? You're playing center field."

"But I have a much more important defensive role for the team than chasing after the one or two fly balls your players are likely to hit."

Her gaze narrowed. "Which is?"

He winked at her. "I think you already know the answer to that."

"I'm your assignment," she said slowly. "Me specifically."

"That's right."

"Why?"

"Because he wants to win, of course."

"But why concentrate on me?"

"Because you're good, I imagine."

"Well, of course I am," she said impatiently. "I meant why would he use *you* to get to me?"

Ford chuckled at that. "It seems to be working."

She frowned, apparently realized that her gaze seemed to be locked on his bare chest, then snapped impatiently, "Oh, put your shirt on."

"Seeing me bare-chested doesn't bother you, does it?"

"I have seen bare-chested men before," she assured him.

"Not me."

"I can't imagine why you think that would make any difference. You, Ryan, Randy, it's all the same to me. A chest is a chest."

Ford grinned. "Randy's not wearing his shirt."

"He's not?" Her startled gaze shot to the man jogging in from left field.

"The only bare chest you noticed was mine. I rest my case."

"Oh, go suck an egg," she muttered, stalking past him and heading for her position at short stop.

Ford knew that she resorted to that particular expression only when she was most at a loss. He'd heard her use it when her friends were hitting just a little too close to some truth she didn't want to acknowledge.

"Good job," Ryan said, patting him on the back. "Just one thing? Without turning this game into something X-rated, what the devil are you going to try to get her attention next time she's up at bat?"

9

After the baseball game, the entire crowd descended on Stella's, where Emma found herself the target of a whole lot of good-natured ribbing. For the most part, she took it in stride, but every now and again, when Ford caught her eye, she felt her cheeks burning.

She had let the man get to her, not just during one at-bat, but during three. She hadn't been able to tear her gaze away from him. All that exposed skin and sinewy muscle had heated her body worse than the blazing sun.

And he knew it, too, damn him. He had enjoyed every single second of knowing that he had that much power over her. She could have denied it, but the air practically crackled with electricity when she got within a few feet of him. It would pretty much have destroyed her credibility if she'd brazenly tried to lie about it.

"Something on your mind?" Ford asked, slipping into the booth beside her when Cassie vacated the spot.

"Not a thing," Emma fibbed blithely.

"Sorry you lost."

"Don't even try to pretend you're sorry," she retorted. "I saw you gloating with the men on the way over here. You're their hero."

He regarded her with a totally fake innocent expression. "Me?"

"Yes, you. And why not? You neutralized my team's best player."

He grinned. "That would be you?"

"Of course."

"Neutralized, huh?"

"Oh, don't be so blasted proud of yourself," Emma snapped. "It was a sneaky, low-down tactic."

"One with which you ought to be especially familiar," he responded.

Emma ignored the reference to her use of Lauren's particular talents in the last game she'd managed. Better to stay on the offensive. "I should have expected it of you," she said. "Do you have a single ethical bone in your body?"

Ford held up his hand. "Let's not go back to that. I thought we had established that my ethics are firmly in place."

"I don't seem to recall that. Journalist? Ethical? Hmm, it doesn't compute for me."

"Okay, Emma, that's it," Ford said, clearly losing patience with her attitude. "If you're going to keep saying things like that, I deserve to know what's behind it. I want you to tell me exactly what happened to make you so suspicious of journalists. Obviously something did. Were you quoted out of context? Did somebody report something you'd said off the record? What the hell happened?"

"Forget it," she said, facing him stubbornly. "I'm not talking about it."

"Yes, you are," he said just as firmly. "You owe me that much."

She stared at him incredulously. "I *owe* you that much? I don't *owe* you anything."

"Sure you do. You're doing exactly what you once accused me of doing. You're condemning me without a trial. Worse, you're doing it based not on something I did, but on what someone else did. I'll take any knocks you want to deliver when I screw up, but I'm getting tired of paying for what somebody else did to you."

There was barely contained anger behind his words, and something else, she realized with a sense of shock. There was real hurt. She'd had no idea she could hurt Ford Hamilton. Even though they had both acknowledged the attraction simmering between them, she'd been convinced it didn't go any deeper than that. She hadn't realized she had any power at all to touch him with her accusations and her distrust.

Actually what she'd really been convinced of was that he didn't have any emotions at all. Her mistake.

"I'm sorry," she said slowly. "You're right. I shouldn't be blaming you for something you had no part in."

"But obviously whatever this was affected you deeply. I need to understand it," Ford insisted.

"Why?" she asked, genuinely perplexed about why it seemed to matter to him so much.

"You need to ask that?"

She nodded. "Apparently I do. Spell it out for me, so there's no miscommunication."

"Because you're starting to matter to me, Emma. If I've got an uphill battle to fight, I need to know all the obstacles."

She stared at him as if he were speaking a foreign language. "I matter to you? What does that mean?"

He shook his head, his expression pitying. "You honestly don't know, do you?"

"I know you're attracted to me," she acknowledged after a brief, though charged, silence.

"And?" he prodded.

"That's it. There's an attraction."

He sighed heavily. "Okay, I suppose that's as good a place as any to start." His gaze locked with hers. "But it's just the start, Emma. I think there's going to be a whole lot more before we're done." He touched her cheek. "If you'll let it happen."

Emma trembled at his touch. Could she let anything happen? She honestly didn't know. There were a million and one reasons not to. How many were real and how many were roadblocks she had deliberately put in their path to prevent any risk of heartache? She had no idea. Her ex-husband had hurt her in so many ways, and her ability to trust had been damaged as a consequence. More than that, he'd called into question her judgment when it came to men.

"Will you let something happen between us?" Ford asked quietly.

"I shouldn't," she replied, desperately wishing it could be otherwise. Ford was the first man to make her want a relationship, the first to rekindle her desire.

A smile tugged at his lips. "Neither should I. We're like oil and water, but that doesn't seem to stop me from wanting you. Will you let this progress to its natural conclusion, Emma?"

"What conclusion?"

"We won't know until we get there."

"I can't make any promises."

"But you're not saying no?"

His persistence exasperated her, even as it set off a

tiny thrill deep inside. "You're determined to pin this down, aren't you?"

"Like you said earlier, I don't want any misunderstandings down the road."

"Okay, then, I'll try not to shut any doors."

"Will you open one by telling me what happened to you that made you so skittish about journalists?"

She thought back to that terrible time in her life, to how much she had almost lost, to the unbearable sense of betrayal that had almost destroyed not just her career, but everything she valued. Only the backing of some very important people at her law firm had pulled her through, both professionally and emotionally.

"I can't talk about it," she said, feeling the surprising sting of tears. She thought she had shed all the tears she had a long time ago. "Not yet."

Ford seemed to accept that. "One day, then. When you're ready."

"I might never be ready," she warned him.

"You will be," he countered. "You just have to realize that you can trust me."

She searched his gaze, wishing she could believe in him, that she could make the leap of faith. "Can I?"

"Yes," he said firmly. "You can."

Looking into his eyes, feeling his strength and compassion, she wanted to believe that. Maybe he was right. Maybe one of these days she would.

It had been weeks now, and Emma was just as much of an enigma to Ford as she had been when he first met her. It would have been annoying, if he hadn't seen just how deeply troubled she was by whatever had happened in her past. There had been real torment in her eyes when he had pushed for answers. That was the only reason he had backed off and agreed to wait.

Now he sat in front of his computer and stared at the blank screen. The temptation to jump onto the Internet and see what he could find by digging around in the Denver newspaper archives was tremendous, but a nagging voice in his head kept reminding him that he had told her she could trust him. If she found out that he'd been checking out her past to fill in the blanks she refused to discuss, she might never forgive him. And Ryan had made his feelings on that subject known as well. Ford didn't want to disappoint either of them.

He sighed, turned off the computer and headed for the door. If he was going to be so blasted honorable, he needed to get away from temptation.

Or else track down the biggest temptation of all, Emma herself.

He found her at the ranch, sitting on the front porch once again, staring into space, looking as if she were at peace with herself, a glass of lemonade close at hand, an open book lying on the seat beside her. He realized that every time he'd found her there, the restless energy he'd associated with Emma from the beginning was nowhere in evidence. Since it was one of the things that had attracted him, he couldn't decide if its absence was good or bad.

"Busy?" he asked from the bottom of the steps.

The question seemed to startle her. "What?"

"I asked if you were busy. I was joking, but maybe I shouldn't have been. Where were you, solving the riddle of the universe?"

"Nothing so important," she admitted. "Just trying

to decide whether I can get back to Denver this evening or if I should wait till Monday."

"If it's up for a vote, I say Monday."

Her lips twitched. "Is that so? Any particular reason?"

"I have big plans for us this weekend—starting right now, in fact."

"Oh, really? What plans? Grilling me for another story?"

He held up his hands. "My grilling days are over, for the time being, anyway."

"What then?"

"A date," he said, keeping his voice deliberately casual. "Dinner and a movie, maybe. Caitlyn can come along."

Her eyebrows rose at that. "You want my daughter on our date?"

"I thought *you* might."

"Why?"

"Protection."

"She's six."

He grinned. "Exactly. I'll have to keep my hands to myself."

"True," she said thoughtfully. "How would you feel about driving somewhere to a mall?"

It was his turn to be startled. "A mall?"

"Don't say it as if it's an alien concept. I'm sure you've been to malls before."

"I have, just not on a date. Not since high school, anyway."

"Then this should make you nostalgic."

"Okay, a mall it is. Mind telling me why?"

"I need some clothes that are less—"

"Uptight?" he suggested.

She frowned at that. "I'll have you know I was voted one of the best-dressed women in Denver last year."

"Really?" he said with blatant skepticism.

"The article said I had class and style." She regarded him with genuine puzzlement.

"You really think my clothes are uptight?"

"The power suits certainly are."

"When have you seen me in a power suit?"

"At Sue Ellen's arraignment. The rest of the time, you just *look* as if you're wearing a power suit. It makes my blood run cold." He emphasized his comment with an exaggerated shudder.

"Then I'm surprised you want to spend any time with me at all," she said stiffly.

"That's okay. Mentally I just strip you out of them."

Emma choked on her sip of lemonade.

"I have a really vivid imagination," he added, thoroughly enjoying her reaction.

"Apparently." She studied him with evident curiosity. "If I had other clothes, do you think it would put a stop to these thoughts of yours?"

"Do I get to pick them?"

"Probably not."

"Then my hunch is you're going to choose a new wardrobe that I'll have to work just as hard to strip away—mentally, that is."

"Mentally. Of course."

"Unless you'd like me to act on it," he suggested hopefully.

"I think we'll just wait and see on that," she said. "So, are we on for the mall or not?"

"We're on."

She beamed at him. "Good. I'll get Caitlyn." She stepped off the porch. "This could take a while. Make yourself comfortable. Can I bring you a glass of lemonade?"

"No need. I'll just finish yours." He tipped up the glass, sipped, then made a face. "It's tart. Haven't you ever heard of sugar?"

"Tart suits me," she responded, then sashayed off in search of her daughter.

"It would," Ford muttered, setting the glass aside.

He heard a sound, turned and found Millie Clayton, a fresh glass of lemonade in hand.

"I think you'll like this better," she said, grinning at him. "Of course, where my daughter's concerned, you seem to be satisfied with her just the way she is. Am I right?"

"You are."

She regarded him with obvious pleasure. "Smart man. I don't think Emma's likely to change for any man. Her husband tried."

"Did he succeed?"

"Only in discovering that he was sadly mistaken to think he could change one single thing about her."

Even though she had given him the perfect opening, Ford resisted the urge to probe more deeply. Information—unless, of course, it just happened to fall into his lap—needed to come from Emma herself. He caught Mrs. Clayton studying him.

"I thought you'd have a million questions," she said.

"I do."

"Why aren't you asking them?"

"Because Emma's the one who has to answer them. I don't want her to think I'm prying."

Mrs. Clayton's smile spread. "Something tells me you'll do, young man."

"Do?"

"For Emma."

"Then you approve of me seeing her?"

"It's not *my* decision," she said righteously, then grinned, "but yes, I approve. And if you can get her to stay here, I'll love you forever."

Emma, here for good? Ford was taken aback. "Is that even a possibility?"

"Not to hear *her* tell it," she admitted candidly.

"Then what can I do?"

"Use your imagination," Millie said, getting up as she spotted Emma heading their way with Caitlyn in tow. "From what I heard earlier, it's highly developed."

For the first time in his adult life, Ford felt himself blushing. "I'm sorry," he stammered.

"Don't be. Use it to your advantage." She patted his shoulder. "That's my advice."

He regarded her with amazement. "You're quite a woman, you know that?"

"Well, of course, I am. Why do you think Emma turned out so well?" Millie turned toward Caitlyn. "Have you been playing in the hayloft again?"

"Uh-huh. I've got straw everywhere." She regarded Ford shyly. "Hi."

"Hi. Are you going to the mall with your mom and me?"

"If she can ever get me clean," she said with a resigned expression.

"I can do that," Millie said, casting a pointed look at Ford. "You and Emma enjoy yourselves. This won't take a minute."

"I think you're being overly optimistic," Emma retorted.

"I'm a grandmother. I know a few tricks." She winked at Ford.

After Millie and Caitlyn had gone inside, Emma studied Ford. "What was that all about?"

"What?" he asked blandly.

"What was my mother saying to you before I got back here?"

"Just sharing a little advice."

"About?"

"Life."

"That's a broad topic. Care to narrow it down?"

"I don't think so. I don't want to give away any of her tricks."

Emma frowned. "Don't you start conspiring with my mother," she warned.

"What would we have to conspire about?" he asked, all innocence.

"Me, for starters."

Ford reached for her hand and tugged her closer. "Give me a little credit. When it comes to you, I think I can handle things on my own."

"We'll see," she murmured just before his lips claimed hers.

She still bore the tart taste of lemons, which he found to be surprisingly improved thanks to an undercurrent of heat and passion. He lingered and savored, drawing a sigh for his efforts.

"How am I doing?" he asked after several minutes.

"Amazingly well," she admitted, and reached for him, turning what had been a simple experiment into something bold and dangerous.

A subtle cough and a giggle from inside the door suggested the return of her mother and Caitlyn. Ford drew away but kept his gaze locked with Emma's.

"I think we've been busted."

"It wouldn't be the first time," she said, grinning. "My mother always did have radar when I was just about to get lucky out here."

"Emma Clayton Rogers!" her mother protested, coming outside.

Emma winked at Ford. "She knows it's true."

"I am shocked, nonetheless," her mother said. "Get lucky, indeed."

She turned from her daughter to Ford, and he saw Millie's indignation fade, to be replaced by amusement.

"Watch your step, young man," she scolded, eyes twinkling.

"Yes, ma'am. Emma, I think we'd better get out of here before she decides to ground you."

Caitlyn watched the adults with increasing bemusement. "Grandma, are you gonna ground Mommy?" The prospect seemed to fascinate her.

"You never know. I might," Millie threatened.

Caitlyn tucked her hand in Emma's. "Don't worry, Mommy, I'll come to see you."

"Me, too," Ford declared seriously.

"Which would pretty much defeat the purpose," Emma's mother said. "Now, go. I have things to do around here, and I can't get them done with all of you underfoot."

Caitlyn scampered off the porch at once, followed more slowly by Emma. Ford paused and kissed Millie Clayton's cheek. "Remind me to tell your husband how fortunate he is."

She chuckled. "Oh, he knows. I remind him all the time."

10

Listening to the exchange between Ford and her mother, watching the two of them grinning at each other like co-conspirators, rattled Emma worse than the few stolen kisses she had shared with the man. She knew exactly what her mother's agenda was: to get Emma and Caitlyn back to Winding River permanently. Apparently she was willing to enlist an unsuspecting Ford Hamilton in her plan, hoping that his methods of persuasion would be more successful than her own.

Emma stewed about that all during the trip to the mall, all during the movie and all during their outing for Mexican food before heading back to Winding River. Despite Ford's speculative glances, he didn't try to ferret out the reason for her silence.

In the car on the way home, though, she saw him glance into the rearview mirror as if to assure himself that Caitlyn had finally fallen asleep in the back seat. Then he turned briefly to Emma.

"Okay, spill it."

"Spill what?"

"Something's been on your mind all day. Tell me."

Emma started to deny it, then sighed. They needed to get this out in the open. "It's you and my mother."

He shot her an incredulous look. "Excuse me?"

"I want to know what you were up to back at the house."

"Up to?" he echoed as if the phrase had no meaning he could divine.

"Don't you dare play dumb with me, Ford Hamilton. I saw you. I heard you."

"Well, if you *saw* us and *heard* us, why don't you tell *me* what we were up to, because I'm clueless."

"A journalist admitting he's clueless," Emma said scathingly. "That has to be a first. I figured if you didn't know the facts, you'd just go right ahead and make something up."

A scowl settled over his features, and for a minute Emma thought she had gone too far. She had promised to stop taking potshots at him. Her vow was only a few days old, and she was already breaking it.

Finally Ford turned to her. "Do you honestly believe that? Have I ever given you any reason to think I would do such a thing?"

Emma struggled to put fairness above her own history. "No," she conceded reluctantly.

"Okay, then, why don't you tell me about what you think your mother and I have done, and leave out the uncalled-for slams against my character?"

She accepted the rebuke as her just deserts. "I'm sorry," she said. "But it looked to me as if you were conspiring."

Ford chuckled.

"I'm serious, dammit."

His expression sobered, but she suspected there was

still a twinkle in his eye. In the dim light of the car she couldn't see it.

"Don't you think that's a little overly dramatic?" he asked. "What were we supposedly conspiring about?"

"Me."

"Keep talking."

"She wants you to influence me into staying here, doesn't she?"

"As if I could," he said with another deep-throated chuckle. "Emma, is there a person on earth who could make you do something you don't want to do?"

"No," she said flatly.

"Well, then, what are you so worried about?"

"You could try," she said.

"But I wouldn't succeed, right?" He glanced at her. "Or is that the real problem? Are you afraid I might convince you that Winding River is where you belong?"

"You could never convince me of that."

"Well, then, there shouldn't be a problem."

Somehow she didn't find his response as reassuring as she should have. "As long as you understand that," she said.

He regarded her solemnly. "I do."

The words made her shudder. Apparently he noted her reaction, because he grinned.

"Those two little words don't scare you, do they? *I do?*"

"It depends on the context, doesn't it?" she said carefully.

"Exactly. You and I are a long way from standing in a church, repeating vows to each other, wouldn't you say? We haven't even made it through a single date without sparring over something or other."

"Absolutely."

"Good, then we're on the same wavelength."

"Good," she agreed, but for some reason the thought brought little comfort. If anything, she found it annoying. It was no wonder she had so much trouble with relationships. Clearly she was totally perverse, declaring one thing, wanting another, and unable to reconcile the two. She'd better stick to the one thing she was really good at—being a lawyer.

For once, though, the idea brought scant comfort.

Ford couldn't quite figure out Emma's mood. She had been quiet at the mall, letting Caitlyn's exuberance fill in all the conversational gaps. The child had charmed him, suggesting what Emma must have been like as a girl. Once she'd gotten over her shyness, Caitlyn had talked a blue streak. In some ways he already knew her better than he did her mother.

As for Emma, he concluded he might never figure her out. He had thought she might be relieved to have everything out in the open, to have his agreement that they were very much on the same wavelength when it came to their relationship...or lack thereof. Instead, she'd gone quiet on him again, maybe even a little more despondent.

Pushing for answers didn't seem likely to get much clarification. He had a feeling Emma didn't understand her mood—or the reason behind it—any better than he did. Since he was familiar with conflicting emotions, he decided it was best to let the subject alone, to let her mull it over and sort through it on her own. She would let him know when she'd reached a conclusion about whatever it was that was troubling her now.

They rode on in silence, the night closing in around them. Even from the car the splash of stars in the black-as-velvet sky was visible. Normally Ford found peace in these surroundings, especially on a night like this when the sky was clear and the temperature had dropped to a more hospitable seventy degrees. Tonight, though, he was finding Emma's edginess contagious. When she finally spoke, he jumped.

"Ford?"

"Uh-huh."

"Can I ask you something?"

He braced himself. "Sure."

"Are people in town condemning Sue Ellen for what happened?"

He stared at her. "You're asking me? Why?"

"Because you probably hear things they wouldn't say to me. I just want to know what I'm likely to be up against when we go to court. What's the popular sentiment? And how are you going to cover it in the paper?"

It grated on him to admit that most of the people he'd spoken to had been unswervingly on Sue Ellen's side. Though he'd listened to the remarks without comment, he'd wanted badly to explain that a man was dead because of what had happened that night. How could that be an acceptable solution, no matter what the provocation? He just couldn't see Sue Ellen being eligible for sainthood, the way some of her neighbors seemed to think she should be.

"I think most people understand what Sue Ellen did. They've known her for years. They want to believe what happened was an accident. Many of them believe that Donny got what he deserved in any case," Ford conceded grimly.

"You don't agree?"

"Did he deserve to die?" Ford demanded, tossing the question back at her. "Does anybody have the right to take another person's life?"

"He was threatening her with a gun," Emma said sharply. "What would you have had her do? Maybe try to reason with him? Let *him* shoot *her?*"

"No, of course not, but there had to be a better way." He believed with everything in him that resorting to violence was never an answer.

"You tell me what that would have been," she said impatiently. "Name one thing she could have done."

"She could have left," he said, though even as he spoke the words, he knew he was oversimplifying. Emma wasn't likely to hesitate to tell him exactly that, either.

"She tried," Emma reminded him. "Donny came after her. The struggle went out into the street, remember? Then she tried to get inside so she could lock him out. He followed her."

"I'm not talking about that night. I'm talking about weeks earlier—or months earlier. Maybe even years earlier." To him, it was so clear-cut: If someone was hurting you, physically or emotionally, you got away. You didn't stay and take it.

"Just like that?" Emma asked mockingly. "Assuming she was brave enough to make the break, where would she have gone that he couldn't have found her? Who would have taken her in, knowing that Donny would be on the warpath? And he would have been—

make no mistake about that. After all, it was that violent possessiveness that was behind every beating."

"I'm sure there are plenty of people who were willing to protect her," Ford insisted, though his certainty of that was wavering.

"A few," Emma corrected. "Most wouldn't get involved if it meant putting their own families at risk, and who could blame them? Many of Sue Ellen's friends our age have children at home. How could they knowingly endanger them, even to protect Sue Ellen?"

Ford tried a different tack. "She could have gone to Ryan for protection."

"She could have," Emma conceded slowly.

Surprised by the concession, he asked, "Okay, then, at last we agree about something. Why didn't she go to Ryan?"

Emma's expression was thoughtful as she considered the question. "I think there's a whole other dynamic at work there," she began at last. "Ryan may be the sheriff, but he's also an unmarried man who has very strong feelings for Sue Ellen. He has ever since high school, but she was always Donny's girl. I suspect she understood Ryan's feelings and feared that she would be endangering him if she got him involved. After all, Donny's biggest problem, aside from alcohol, was his jealousy. Ryan was the target of it as often as not. On some level Donny knew that Ryan cared about Sue Ellen, even though Ryan was very careful never to let it show. There was bad blood between them as a result. It had been that way for years."

Ford had guessed as much, both from what Ryan had said and what he hadn't said. He was surprised Ryan had remained as calm as he had when he'd intervened between Sue Ellen and Donny the night of the dance. He was equally surprised, under the circumstances, that Donny had left with Ryan peacefully.

"Still," he said, "if Sue Ellen had filed charges even once, Ryan could have arrested Donny."

"Let me ask you something. When you were a kid, did you ever have a best friend who was a screwup?"

Ford thought back to Cory Sullivan. Cory had gotten into more mischief than any other kid in their small Georgia town. It hadn't been long before innocent mischief turned into something more serious—vandalism, for starters, then shoplifting. He'd pleaded with Cory to stop before he ruined his life.

"Well?" Emma prodded.

"One," he admitted.

"Did he get in a lot of trouble?"

"Oh, yeah."

"Did you ever turn him in? Stop being friends with him?"

He saw where she was going with this. "No, but it's not the same. The only person Cory was endangering was himself."

"Are you sure no one else ever got hurt thanks to his actions?"

Ford swallowed hard. There had been one person. Cory had beaten up old man Jensen because the grocer had tried to stop him from stealing cigarettes and beer from his store.

"Just once that I know of."

Her gaze locked on his. "Could you have prevented it by turning him in before it came to that?"

"Possibly."

"So who was guiltier—you or your friend?"

"Cory, of course. He committed the crime."

Her smile didn't quite reach her eyes. "And Donny committed this one. Not Sue Ellen. He beat her over and over and over. Would it have been better if she'd had him arrested? Of course. But she loved him. She wanted to believe he would change, just as you wanted to believe your friend would change."

"Are you saying she was right to stay and take it?"

"Absolutely not," she said fiercely. "I'm just saying that it's understandable, that it happens all too often, either because the victim is scared or has such low self-esteem that she blames herself for what's happening, or because she keeps clinging to a false hope that things will get better—if only she's nicer, better, less confrontational, whatever. With Sue Ellen it was that unwavering faith that her love could make Donny change. I'm sure they had good patches. That only convinced her she was right, that underneath he was a good man."

"Was he? Do you remember him from high school?" Ford asked. "Were the signs there then that he would be an abuser?"

"Honestly, yes. He was always jealous and possessive. And his own father had a reputation as a mean drunk. Donny was all but preordained to be violent."

"Did any of Sue Ellen's friends try to warn her?"

Emma's expression turned sad. "I don't think any of us recognized what those signs meant, not back then. My perception is based on hindsight and what I've learned about domestic violence more recently."

Ford glanced at her, but she evaded his look. "Emma?"

"What?" she asked, still not looking at him.

"Why is this case so personal to you?" he asked,

almost dreading the answer. Once again, he feared he knew what it might be—that her husband had been abusive, and that she had stuck it out longer than she should have.

"Because Sue Ellen is a friend," she said tersely.

"And that's the only reason?"

She turned then and met his gaze. She even managed to hold hers steady. "What other reason could there be?"

Ford debated with himself before responding with the question that was really on his mind. It was exceptionally personal and he wasn't sure he had any right to ask it yet, but he had a feeling it was critical to understanding Emma. Finally he chose a circumspect approach that might elicit the truth…if Emma was willing to share it.

"Tell me about your marriage," he suggested mildly, thinking of her mother's comment that Emma's husband had thought he could change her. In what way had Kit Rogers found her deficient? And how had he handled it?

Even though he considered his question to be innocuous, alarm flared in Emma's eyes.

"I don't know what you want to know," she said, looking uneasy.

Staying determinedly on neutral turf, he focused on the beginning of the relationship, not the end, and asked, "How did you meet?" Though he'd heard the story from Ryan, he wanted Emma's take on it.

"Right here in town, ironically, though we were both in the same law school. Kit was dating Ryan's sister, Adele. We met at a party during a school break."

"That must have been awkward."

She nodded. "It could have been, but Adele and I talked. She said she wasn't upset about it, so Kit and I started to see each other."

"How long did you know each other before you married?"

"A year."

"Then you got married when you got out of law school?"

"No, when he got out. I still had another year."

"And Caitlyn, when did she come along?"

"Right after I graduated. Kit was already doing very well. He'd had a couple of high-profile cases that had gone really well—his career was on a fast track."

"Did you consider staying home, instead of going to work?"

She frowned at the question, probably without any idea of how much she was giving away by that simple reaction. "No," she said, her voice suddenly tight.

Ford was feeling his way now, trying to step lightly through what was clearly a minefield. "How did your husband feel about that?"

"He wasn't happy," she admitted candidly. "Look, I really don't like to talk about this. I don't see what it has to do with anything, anyway."

He smiled. "It's called getting to know each other, Emma. I ask you a few questions. You answer. Then you ask me questions and I answer."

"Okay, then, you've had your turn. Let's switch," she said a little too eagerly.

Ford knew better than to pursue his own line of questioning, but he was satisfied that he was on the right track. Emma more than understood Sue Ellen's plight. In one way or another, she had lived it. The thought made him shudder. Please, God, he prayed, let it have been emotional abuse over the work issue, not physical abuse. But even as he mentally uttered the prayer, he had to wonder if the scars were likely to be any less deep.

When she woke up the next day, Emma was still shaken by her conversation with Ford the night before. He had come far too close to discovering the truth about her marriage. Even as wary as she was, she had found herself answering questions she normally called a halt to much sooner. In the end, though, she hadn't wanted him to know just how rough a time she'd had during the months before she and Kit had finally called it quits. If Ford knew, he might pity her, and that was the last response she wanted from him.

To get her mind off her own problems, she left the house early in the morning and went in search of her brother. When she didn't find him in the barn or stables, she saddled one of the horses and rode out looking for him. It almost didn't even matter whether she found him. The physical exertion of riding combined with the rugged landscape worked like a balm to help her forget just how disconcerting Ford could be and how much she was coming to count on his presence in her life.

She was riding over the rough terrain of the foothills when she spotted Matt and several of the other men with the herd of cattle. Her brother saw her, waved and rode over.

"What brings you out here?"

"Clearing the cobwebs," she said. "Besides, Matt, you and I haven't had much of a chance to talk since

I've been home. Even when you come by to see Dad, you don't stick around."

He bristled at once. "Meaning?"

"That you're my brother, and I think you're avoiding me. I want to know what's up with you."

He scowled at her. "Why does anything have to be up with me?" He took off his hat and slapped it against his thigh. "Dammit, Em, I don't have time for this."

Emma scowled right back at him. "'This?' What does that mean? I'm not cross-examining you. I'm asking how you're doing. Is that a problem?"

Matt sighed. "Sorry," he mumbled defensively. "I'm a little touchy lately."

"No kidding," she said, keeping her tone determinedly light. "Why is that?"

"Because Martha and Mom are nagging at me every time I turn around."

"About?"

"Whether I'm happy, what I want to do with my life, et cetera, et cetera. I'm getting sick of it. I don't understand why they can't just let things alone. I'm working here for Dad. End of story."

"Is it?" Emma asked mildly. "Is it the end of the story?"

"Not you, too?" he said, regarding her with disappointment. "Who put you up to this? Mom or Martha?"

"Nobody put me up to anything," she chided. "Sisters can figure out all on their own when something's not right. I've never seen you so short-tempered and moody before." Suddenly she had a thought that nobody else seemed to have considered, or else had refused to verbalize. "You're not involved with another woman, are you, Matt?"

"Good grief, no," he said.

He was staring at her so incredulously that Emma was instantly relieved.

"Have you lost your mind?" he demanded. "When would I have *time,* for one thing? For another, I love my wife, even if she is a damned nag."

Emma grinned. "Glad to hear it. Now let's get to the bottom of what's really wrong. Martha thinks you're not happy working the ranch."

"Martha has a big mouth."

"Mom agrees."

He frowned but resisted any temptation to criticize their mother.

"Are you unhappy?" Emma asked.

"This is what I do," he said.

She regarded him with exaggerated patience. "That's not what I asked. Are you happy being a rancher?"

"Okay, if you want the unvarnished truth, the answer is no. Are you satisfied? The bottom line is, I hate this but Dad needs me here, and that's that."

"That is not that," Emma retorted. "Tell him. Do you know what you'd rather do? Do you want to go to college?"

"Emma, that's a pipe dream. I have a wife. I have kids. And I have a job working for a man I can't abandon as easily as some other people did."

She winced at that. "Dad got over my leaving. He accepted Wayne's choice."

"Wanna bet? One of these days ask him about the blueprints he has stashed in his desk."

"Blueprints?"

"For your house and for Wayne's. He picked out the rise just beyond the main house for you. Wayne's would have been about five hundred yards from mine, overlooking the creek."

Tears stung Emma's eyes. She'd had no idea. "I didn't know," she whispered.

"Of course you didn't, because you were hell-bent on getting away and doing what you damned well pleased. I watched Dad die inside every time you left to go back to school, but even then he held out hope that someday you'd be back. Even when you got married, I think he thought you and Kit would settle here after you'd graduated. Not until the day you went to work for that law firm in Denver did he finally give up and accept the truth that you were never coming home."

"I did what I had to do," Emma said in her own defense.

"Yeah, and it's made you real happy, hasn't it? I see the haunted look in your eyes, sis. You're on a merry-go-round and you're miserable, but you just haven't figured out how to get off."

Emma had ridden out here today to help Matt face a few hard truths about his life, but he'd turned the tables on her. Now she was the one suddenly consumed with painful regrets.

"Perhaps you're right," she said softly.

"Well, when you get your own life straightened out, maybe then I'll let you have a crack at mine," Matt said, then turned and rode away.

It was just as well. Emma was pretty much speechless anyway.

11

"Mommy, is Ford going to be my new daddy?" Caitlyn asked as she spooned cornflakes into her mouth on Sunday morning.

"No, absolutely not," Emma snapped. After her disconcerting conversation with Matt, this was absolutely the last thing Emma needed today. She swallowed hard when she realized that Caitlyn's eyes were brimming with tears. "I'm sorry, baby. I didn't mean to yell."

"I like him," Caitlyn said with a sniff. "I want him to be my new dad. Besides, if you married him, we could live here."

Emma didn't have the patience or the words to explain all of the flaws in her daughter's logic. What worried her most, though, was how eager Caitlyn was to claim Ford as a father. The two of them had only spent one day together, yet Caitlyn was already making up fantasies about him. That suggested she was desperate for a replacement for the man who paid no attention to her back in Denver.

"Baby, you don't really know Ford all that well," Emma explained. "Before somebody can be your daddy, we both have to get to know him and make sure he's the right person."

"I *know* he is," Caitlyn said, regarding her seriously.

"What makes you so sure?" Maybe her six-year-old daughter had insights that would help her see Ford in a new light. How pathetic was that?

"Because he was really, really nice to me," Caitlyn began predictably. "And he's cute, and he understood that it was really, really important for me to have ice cream even though we'd already had pizza."

"Yeah, I can see why that would be a clincher," Emma said wryly. "But there are more important things to consider."

"What things?"

"Grown-up things."

"But I get a say, don't I?"

"When the time comes, of course you get to express an opinion," Emma assured her. "Yours is just not the most important opinion."

"Who gets that?"

"Me."

"Maybe I should pick," Caitlyn said, a frown puckering her brow. "You didn't do such a good job last time."

It was all Emma could do not to burst into tears. For her daughter to say something so matter-of-factly condemning her own father—and her mother's judgment—spoke volumes about what she'd been through, about what the adults in her life had put her through. Emma had always prayed that Caitlyn had been oblivious to most of it. Obviously she'd been wrong.

She reached for her daughter's hand and pressed kisses to her fingers. "I'm so sorry, sweetie. But there's one thing we should never, ever forget, no matter how mad or sad your dad makes us."

Caitlyn regarded her doubtfully. "What?"

"If it weren't for him, I wouldn't have you," Emma said softly. "And you are the very best thing that has ever happened to me. So every single day I thank God that your dad and I made you."

Caitlyn seemed intrigued by the concept. "You mean like you'd make a doll? Did you put me together?"

Emma laughed. "No, it didn't work like that. Someday I'll explain."

"I want to know now. I saw Pepper have her kittens in the barn yesterday. Was it like that?"

Emma had forgotten how many lessons there were to be learned on a ranch at a very early age. "Something like that."

"I was inside you?"

Emma was beginning to regret opening up this particular topic. "Yes."

"And Daddy put me there?"

"Yes."

"How? By kissing you?"

"That was part of it."

Caitlyn's eyes widened. "Does that mean you and Ford are gonna have a baby?"

"Good heavens, no."

"But he kissed you when he brought you home."

Emma was clinging to her sanity by a thread. "It wasn't the same kind of kiss," she explained patiently. "Now finish your cereal. I think your grandfather is waiting for you down at the barn. He wants you to help him groom your pony this morning."

"I'm done," Caitlyn said, suddenly eager, the disconcerting topic of making babies forgotten. She jumped down from her chair. "Bye, Mommy. Did Grandpa tell you I could have one of the kittens for my very own?"

"No, he neglected to mention that," Emma said, already resigned to the inevitable. Maybe the prospect of taking home a kitten would make the break easier for Caitlyn when they went back to Denver tomorrow.

Caitlyn regarded her worriedly. "It's okay, isn't it?"

"It's okay."

Her daughter raced back and threw her arms around Emma's neck. "I love you, Mommy."

"I love you, too," Emma whispered, but Caitlyn was already gone, the screen door slamming behind her.

A sound had Emma turning around to find her mother lurking in the doorway to the dining room.

"Out of the mouths of babes," her mother said.

"I think she's six, going on sixteen. What on earth is she going to be asking me when she's a teenager for real?" Emma asked.

"The same things, only she'll want to know because *she's* interested in some boy. Now it's because she thinks *you* are." Her mother studied her with a penetrating gaze. "Are you?"

"I like Ford, Mom," she said cautiously, hoping to dispel the hopeful look in her mother's eyes. "As a friend."

"He seems like an awfully nice man."

Emma regarded Millie with exasperation. "You would say that. He's a pawn in your scheme, isn't he? I saw the two of you the other night with your heads together. He wouldn't tell me what you were talking about, but I know you. Don't use Ford, Mom. It's not fair to him."

"I would never use anyone," her mother retorted with indignation, then shrugged. "But if there's an attraction there, I am not above fanning it."

"Stay out of it," Emma advised. "No good will come of encouraging him."

"Because you're too stubborn to see what's in front of your face, I imagine."

Emma sighed. "I am not having this conversation again. I'm going into town. Should I get Caitlyn and take her along?"

"Absolutely not. She's fine with your father. If she starts getting in his way, she can help me bake cookies until it's time to go to church. She seemed surprised when I took some out of the oven the other day. She said she thought cookies came from the store."

"Some do," Emma said tightly. "Caitlyn is not deprived just because I don't bake cookies with her."

"Did I say she was?"

"More or less," Emma said. Her defensiveness was firmly in place, and it wasn't even eight in the morning yet. "I'll see you later."

She left before she could get into a full-blown argument with her mother. One thing for certain, she couldn't stay here much longer without all of the unspoken criticism of her lifestyle bubbling to the surface. She had to leave before there was a rift in the family that could never be mended.

"You look as if you've lost your best friend," Ford said when he spotted Emma sitting in a booth at Stella's, an untouched cup of coffee cooling in front of her. "Can I help?"

"Not unless you can think of a way to convince my

mother that I am not ruining my daughter's life because I don't have time to teach her to bake cookies."

He could see how such an accusation might get Emma's dander up. She was the kind of woman who needed to believe that she was excelling at whatever she tackled, motherhood included. Obviously she wouldn't like her shortcomings pointed out to her.

"Tensions running high at the ranch this morning?" he asked, keeping his tone light.

"You could say that. I've always sensed that they disapproved of the way I was raising Caitlyn, but now that I've been here a while, it's all beginning to come out. Before, my visits were so brief there wasn't time to get into anything serious. Now the potshots are starting to fly."

"It's only because they care about you and Caitlyn," he said.

Emma regarded him with obvious impatience. "I *know* that. That doesn't make it any easier to take. To top it off, my daughter seems to think she should get to choose the next man in my life, because I didn't do so well the last time."

Ford bit back a grin. "Does she have any particular candidate in mind?"

Emma frowned at him. "As if I'd tell you."

He couldn't help it. He smiled. "Dare I hope that she picked me?"

"Don't be so smug. You were convenient. Besides, it was the pizza and ice cream combination that did it. And that was a one-time-only concession on my part. If you try it again, I'll shoot you down."

"She didn't get sick, did she?"

"No, but that's not the point. That's a little too much

indulgence for a six-year-old. Next thing I know, you'll be plying her with hot dogs and cotton candy and ice-cream sundaes. She'll want to move in with you."

"A treat now and then can't hurt her."

"*Now* and *then* being the key words. Keep them in mind."

"Are you really upset because Caitlyn had a good time the other night, or is the real problem that *you* did?" Ford challenged her.

He could tell from her startled reaction that his perception was right on the mark. "You did have a good time, didn't you, despite worrying about what your mother and I were up to?"

"Okay, yes, it was nice to spend a relaxing day out with nothing more important on my mind than choosing shorts and T-shirts for Caitlyn." She regarded him curiously. "How about you? Were you bored to tears? Men usually hate shopping."

"I was in it for the company." His gaze locked with hers. "You could never bore me, Emma."

She looked shaken by his claim. "Don't say things like that."

"Why not, if it's true?"

"It can't be true."

Ford chuckled. "You don't want me to think of you as an intellectually stimulating, exciting, attractive woman?"

She seemed surprisingly puzzled by the description. "That's how you see me?"

"Of course," he said at once, then studied her. "Emma, how do you see yourself?"

"Oh, I suppose I'm smart enough, but the rest...I don't know."

"Trust me, you are exciting and attractive. When did you begin to doubt that? Was it your husband? What did he do to you, Emma?" He could barely keep the anger out of his voice. The man had obviously been a first-class jerk.

She gave him a faint smile. "Leaping to my defense, Ford?"

"Just speaking the truth. If he did anything to convince you that you were somehow unworthy or less than who you are, he was an idiot."

"Thank you for saying that."

"You still haven't answered me. What did he do?"

"I don't want to get into a discussion of my ex-husband."

"I think you need to," he said. "I think you need to talk about it. Have you ever told anyone what your marriage was like?"

"My friends know, more or less."

"My guess is less. Did you keep it to yourself because you felt humiliated in some way? Failing at marriage isn't that uncommon in this day and age. It doesn't make you any less of a woman." He looked directly into her eyes. "Unless, of course, you're a perfectionist."

That faint smile came and went again. "You got me," she said lightly.

"Well, it takes two to make a marriage work. Whatever happened in yours, your ex-husband deserves his share of the blame. In fact, one of these days, when you trust me enough to tell me what really happened, I have a feeling you're going to realize that in this case, he deserves most of the blame."

She gave him a rueful look. "Funny thing about that. Intellectually I know you're right. Everything played out exactly the way it had to." She tapped her chest. "In here, though, I'm having a hard time buying it."

"Stick with me," Ford said lightly. "I'll work on convincing you."

Something told him it was going to be worth the effort, that Emma Rogers would be a helluva woman once she believed in herself again. Right now, she valued herself only when it came to her skills as a lawyer. To give her a boost in the new direction, he leaned down and pressed a hard kiss to her lips.

"Gotta run," he said, once he was satisfied that he'd stirred enough heat to get her attention. "I promised the pastor at the Methodist church that I'd come to hear his sermon this morning. I believe he's talking about second chances."

Apparently he'd rendered her speechless, because she simply watched him go, but the blush on her cheeks and the glimmer of hope in her eyes spoke volumes.

"Well, now, that was absolutely fascinating," Cassie said, fanning herself as she slid into the booth opposite Emma. "I do believe I'm breathless just from watching."

Emma scowled at her. "Leave it alone."

"Why? The man doesn't scare you, does he?"

"Of course not."

Cassie grinned. "Liar. You're scared spitless. You're actually starting to feel something for Ford Hamilton, and that would be darned inconvenient, wouldn't it?"

"Inconvenient doesn't begin to cover it," Emma muttered. "I don't trust him. I can't."

"Ford?" Cassie said incredulously. "Why on earth not?"

"He's a journalist."

"So?"

"He's in a position to do considerable damage to my client. He already has, by letting that picture Teddy took make its way into the Cheyenne paper."

"By the time this case goes to trial, people will have forgotten all about that picture," Cassie predicted.

"You can bet the prosecutor won't have forgotten. I'm betting he's already gotten a warrant for the original," Emma told her friend.

"That would have happened anyway. Too many people knew Teddy took pictures that night and that there was a fight. Don't you think a halfway decent prosecutor would have found out sooner or later and come after the film?"

"I suppose." Actually, Emma acknowledged to herself, Cassie was right, though the prosecutor might have had less luck getting his hands on anything incriminating if none of the photos had been printed. She could have made a case that Ford had no obligation to turn over anything that hadn't been in the paper. It might have worked.

"You're not going to let that picture stand between you and Ford, are you?"

Emma sighed. "Not really. I did go out with him. We took Caitlyn to the mall over in Laramie and went to a movie."

Cassie beamed. "That's terrific. Give him a chance. I don't think Ford is the kind of man who'll let you down."

"Should I point out that you don't know him any better than I do? You just got back in town yourself."

"Right. But since I've been working at Stella's, I've heard things. Ford's already earned a lot of respect around here. He's been moving cautiously, trying not to rattle too many cages until he knows more about the town. Ryan likes him. So does Stella. They're both good judges of character."

"True," Emma said. "But I'm not looking for a relationship, especially in Winding River. I need to get back to Denver, anyway. Sue Ellen's case won't go to trial for a few weeks yet. There are things I could be doing at home."

"You'll be breaking Caitlyn's heart if you take her back there now."

"I know, but it's for the best. She has to understand that staying here isn't permanent. The longer we stick around now, the harder it will be on her when we go back for good."

Cassie nodded. "I suppose you're right. But I'm going to miss you, Emma. When will you go?"

"Tomorrow, I think. I have a case going to trial in Denver next week. This will give me a few days to catch up and prepare for that."

"When will you be back here?"

"That's hard to say. I'll have to make a few more trips to interview prospective witnesses for Sue Ellen."

"Will you see Ford when you're in town?"

"It would probably be better if I didn't, especially as we get closer to trial. I don't want to give him the opportunity to try to pump me for information."

"Ford wouldn't do that," Cassie protested.

"So you say. I can't take any chances."

"Do you think Ryan would take any chances where Sue Ellen's future is concerned?"

"No, of course not."

"He spends time with Ford."

Emma regarded her wryly. "I don't think it's quite

the same thing. I doubt Ford has the same expectations where Ryan's concerned."

Cassie grinned. "Are you saying that Ford might use sex to pry information out of you?"

Emma felt her cheeks burn. "Absolutely not."

"Well, then, there shouldn't be a problem," Cassie said. "You're tough. You'll tell him what you want him to know and nothing else."

"I think it might be easier if I didn't tell him anything at all, if I just steered clear of him."

"Seems like a waste of a perfectly good man, if you ask me. You're throwing away your best chance at a relationship."

"If I wanted a man in my life, I would have one," Emma insisted, though the reality was that she hadn't accepted a single invitation to go out on a date until Ford came along. "I certainly don't want one in Winding River, and I don't want him to be Ford."

"Well, I think you're wrong on both counts," Cassie said. "And time is going to prove me right."

Emma was more afraid of that than she dared to admit.

Cassie's words were still ringing in her ears when Emma arrived at the jail to bring Sue Ellen up to speed on her plans. She found Ryan in her client's cell, with the door slightly open.

"Security's a little lax around here, isn't it?" she teased.

Ryan jumped up guiltily. "I was just giving Sue Ellen a pep talk. She's beginning to get discouraged. She thinks everyone in town blames her for what happened."

"That's not true," Emma said fiercely, thinking of what Ford had told her when she'd asked him what he'd been hearing. "No one is blaming you, least of all anyone who knows the facts."

"That's what I said," Ryan added, his gaze warm as it rested on Sue Ellen's face. He tucked a finger under her chin. "Keep this pretty chin up, darlin'. Emma's going to have you out of here in no time."

"And then what?" Sue Ellen asked, sounding weary. "I don't have anywhere to go."

"You have a sister in Montana. You can stay with her for a while," Ryan observed.

"I'll need to work," Sue Ellen said, her expression still bleak. "What can I do? I haven't had a job in years."

"One bridge at a time," Ryan told her firmly. "When the time comes, you'll have plenty of options."

Emma had the distinct impression that a life with the sheriff was going to be one of Sue Ellen's options. That worried her a little. She was pretty sure Ryan didn't have a clue what he was letting himself in for. More than Sue Ellen's body had been bruised during her marriage. It was going to be a long while before her soul healed sufficiently to allow another man to get close.

Emma glanced at him. "You going to be around when I'm through talking to Sue Ellen?"

"I can be," he said.

"Good. I won't be long."

When Ryan had left them alone, Sue Ellen's gaze followed him. "He's a nice man, isn't he?"

"He always was. Ryan's the best."

"I wish…" Her voice trailed off.

"What do you wish, sweetie?"

Sue Ellen shrugged, her expression desolate. "It's too late now."

"It's never too late," Emma insisted. "Ryan is right. You'll have plenty of time for making better choices when you're out of here. You'll be able to start over."

"How can I?" she whispered, tears spilling down her cheeks. "How can I ever be happy again?"

"Because you deserve to be happy," Emma said fiercely.

Sue Ellen shook her head. "No, I don't. How can I? Donny's dead, and it's because of me."

"No, it's because of *him*. He was going to shoot you, Sue Ellen. You know that. You were just protecting yourself."

"He wouldn't have shot me. Donny loved me."

"No, dammit, he didn't. If he'd loved you, he could never have treated you the way he did. Never." She took Sue Ellen's hands and held them tightly. "I want you to believe that. What Donny felt for you was the opposite of love. He needed to control you, to possess you. That is not love."

Sue Ellen continued to weep quietly. As Ryan had done moments before, Emma tucked a finger under her chin and made Sue Ellen face her. "I want to have a counselor come in to talk to you. You need help to understand that what Donny did to you was wrong. You're a wonderful person, Sue Ellen. I see it. Ryan sees it. So do most of the people in Winding River. It's time *you* see it, as well. Will you talk to someone?"

For an instant there was a rare flicker of hope in Sue Ellen's eyes. She nodded.

"Good. I'll make the arrangements," Emma promised. "In the meantime, I'm going to give you my number in Denver. If you need me, morning or night, just call. Ryan will facilitate it. I'll be back in a couple of weeks or sooner, if anything comes up."

Sue Ellen clung to her hand. "But you will be back?"

"Absolutely. We're in this together, and I won't let you down. I promise."

"I don't know why you're doing this for me, Emma, but I'm grateful."

"I'm doing it because you're a good person." Emma patted her hand, then left the cell. She stood for a minute outside the door. "I won't rest until you believe that."

"Thank you," Sue Ellen whispered, curling once again into a fetal position on the cot that was the only furniture in the cell.

Emma felt sick inside at the thought of leaving her there, but until the trial, there was nothing she could do for Sue Ellen. She went to Ryan's office and knocked, then walked in.

"Keep an eye on her, will you?" she said. "I'm worried about how depressed she is."

He nodded grimly. "I know. I'm spending as much time with her as I can."

"She's agreed to let me send in a psychologist. I'll make the arrangements before I leave tomorrow."

"You're going back to Denver? I thought…"

"I can't stay here indefinitely, Ryan. I'll be back as often as I can be."

"What about Ford?"

She frowned at him. "Ford is not an issue."

"Oh, really?" he said, grinning. "You could have fooled me."

"I'd rather talk about your feelings for Sue Ellen," she countered.

His grin faded. "I never denied caring about her," he said, instantly on the defensive.

"I know that. I just want you to understand what you're in for. It's going to take a long time before she can trust another man. She may never be able to."

Ryan sighed. "In my gut, I guess I know that. I have to try, though. I've spent my whole life caring about her. I can't stop now."

Emma smiled at him. "I was hoping you'd say that. Despite everything that's happened, Sue Ellen's a lucky woman. You're one of those rare good guys, Ryan."

"I just hope that one of these days she'll see it that way," he said, his expression sad.

"If anybody can help her get there, you can," she said with conviction. "Just be patient."

"I've waited all these years. A few more won't matter."

She walked over and pressed a kiss to his cheek. "You're a wonderful man, Ryan Taylor."

He caught her hand when she would have walked away.

"What?"

"So is Ford."

Emma sighed. "I know that."

"Then give him a chance."

"Why is it that all my friends and my family think they get a vote in this?"

"Because we love you."

"So you say," she said. "Right now I could do with a little less love and a little more faith that I know what's best for me."

He grinned. "Sorry, no can do. You're just going to have to put up with us nudging you."

"That is not the way to get me to spend more time here," she pointed out.

"Because you're stubborn."

"Probably," she conceded.

"Just one thing, Emma darlin'. I've known you for most of your life. I know how much pride you have, so a word of caution—don't cut off your nose to spite your face."

Much as she hated to admit it, that was probably good advice.

12

"Emma's leaving for Denver in the morning," Ryan announced casually when he stopped by the paper to see Ford after church on Sunday afternoon.

Ford's gaze shot up. "She didn't say anything to me about that. When did she decide to go?"

"When was the last time you saw her?" Ryan asked.

"This morning."

"Then I imagine that's when she decided."

Judging from the smirk on Ryan's face, Ford was definitely missing something. "Meaning?"

"Our Emma is running scared."

"Of me?" Ford asked incredulously, then sighed. "I imagine that's not as ridiculous as it sounds. I think of her as being tough as nails, but she's not when it comes to the 'R' word, is she?"

"'R' as in relationship?" Ryan asked.

"Yes."

"No, when it comes to that, I think she's completely out of her element," Ryan said. "How about you? Do you think about a relationship when you're with Emma?"

Truthfully, what Ford thought about was sex, but, yes, the happily-ever-after thought had crossed his mind...and then fled. He did know, however, that he wasn't anxious for her to leave town.

Rather than admit that to the protective sheriff, he asked, "Why do you think she's so gun-shy when it comes to men? Are you sure you don't know any more about her marriage than what you've told me?"

Ryan's expression suggested he was well aware that the change of topic had been deliberate. Still, he seemed to consider the question thoughtfully before answering.

"I don't know anything more about her marriage, but I think her skittishness goes back even longer than that. Remember I told you that Emma didn't date a lot back when I knew her? She was too goal oriented. I don't know what she did in college, but I imagine that didn't change. Then she married, had a child and divorced, all in pretty short order. That may be the sum total of her experience with men. Since then I have the distinct impression that she's been totally absorbed by her career, probably by choice."

He studied Ford with interest. "So, what are you going to do about her decision to go?"

"Why should I do anything?"

Ryan shook his head. "You're pitiful, both of you. She's clearly in denial. What about you, Ford? Are you going to start denying that you're interested, or are you just going to evade my questions altogether?"

Ford considered it for the sake of his pride, but knew it would be futile. "No. No evasions. I'm definitely interested." It was a deceptively lukewarm description of the way she managed to tie him in knots.

"Well, then, what are you going to do?"

"I honestly don't know. Any suggestions?"

"Go after her."

"And do what? Stop her from leaving?"

Ryan laughed. "I don't think the entire United States Marines could do that. She's hell-bent on running. I meant go after her in Denver. Stick around for a few days. Show her you're willing to compromise."

"Compromise about what?"

"The future. The living arrangements. Whatever needs to be compromised on to make it work."

Ford shuddered at the suggestion. "Now you're the one who's talking crazy. I'm not going to live in Denver. I've paid my dues in big cities. I like it here. And I have a paper to run, in case you've forgotten."

"Does that matter more than being with Emma?"

"It's not a competition. Why do I have to choose?" he demanded. "Is it up to me to choose just because she won't?"

"Do you want her or not?"

"I want her," Ford admitted, then met Ryan's gaze evenly. "Maybe just not enough."

"Will you ever know for sure if you stick around here and let her get away?"

"Okay, you have a point," Ford conceded. "I'll try to catch her before she goes. At least, I can take another reading on the situation."

Ryan regarded him with evident exasperation. "And do what? Talk the subject to death? Emma needs action, something dramatic to catch her attention, something that will tell her you're putting her first."

"And chasing her to Denver will say that?"

"It'll be a start," Ryan insisted. "What you do after you get there will do the rest."

Ford had a vision of going to Denver, getting Emma to give their relationship a chance, then discovering that it would all be on her terms and only if he was the one who relocated. "I don't know," he said, expressing his reservations aloud. "I came here to uncomplicate my life, not to get into a situation that can't be resolved without somebody having to give up too much."

Ryan shrugged. "Your choice. But take it from a man who's waited a very long time to grab a shot at what he wants, when the right woman comes along, you shouldn't waste a minute. You never know what fate has in store just around the corner."

It was the closest Ryan had come to making a direct admission of his feelings for Sue Ellen—at least Ford assumed she was the woman he meant. Since he was eager for a change of subject anyway, he decided to pursue it. "You're talking about you and Sue Ellen?"

"Yeah, isn't that a kick in the pants?" Ryan said, his expression rueful. "I have to wait more than ten years till her husband is dead before I get a real chance with her and, because of how he died, it may be too late."

Ford was startled by Ryan's defeatist attitude. "Do you really believe that? I thought you had faith in Emma's ability to get her off."

"I do, but that's the least of it. The fact is that Sue Ellen's got a lot of baggage to deal with. There's no telling if she'll ever get past it." His eyes lit with a sad smile. "You should have known her back when we were kids. She was so lovely, so fragile and yet full of life. Donny literally beat that out of her, but once in a while when I look into her eyes I see a glimmer of the woman she used to be. That's why I keep hanging in there. I want to help her find the old Sue Ellen again."

"Careful," Ford warned. "Be sure you're not mistaking the knight-in-shining-armor syndrome for something else."

"I'm not. I loved her long before she needed rescuing."

Ford thought once again about what a fine man Ryan was. "She's lucky to have you."

"That remains to be seen. Meantime, you concentrate on Emma. The man who catches her will be one lucky son of a gun."

Ford thought about that all the way out to the Clayton ranch. He'd barely set foot on the porch when Caitlyn came barreling through the front door and skidded to a stop in front of him.

"I was hoping you were gonna come see me," she said. "It took a long time."

Ford grinned. "I've had a few things to do."

"I know. Mommy said you publish a newspaper. I don't know what that is, but it sounds real important."

"I don't know about important, but it takes a lot of time."

Caitlyn gave him a shy smile. "Now that you're here, wanna see my pony? Remember, I told you all about him?"

"I remember."

Emma stepped outside and Ford's gaze immediately went to her. She was studying him warily.

"I don't think Ford has time to pay a visit to your pony, Caitlyn."

Since he was pretty sure he heard a challenge in there, he rose to it. "Sure I do," he said, taking the child's hand. He returned Emma's look with a dare of his own. "Want to come along?"

"Sure," she said with no hint of reluctance. She followed them down the steps and toward the barn.

Caitlyn released Ford's hand and danced along ahead of them. "You could ride my pony sometime," she offered. "But she might be too little for you." Her solemn gaze assessed him from head to toe. "You've got really, really long legs. She's just right for me, though. Grandpa says when I'm bigger, he'll buy me any kind of horse I want. I got one all picked out."

"You do?" Emma said, regarding her with surprise.

"Grandpa took me with him to this other ranch after church this morning, so we could look at all the horses. They had the prettiest horse I ever saw. It was all golden, like a magical horse in a storybook. I can't have that horse, because it'll be a long time before I'm growed up," she explained matter-of-factly. "But Grandpa says he'll find me one just like it."

"Grandpa spoils you."

"I know," Caitlyn said happily. "He loves me."

"He does indeed," Emma said, sounding oddly resigned.

When Caitlyn had run on ahead, Ford looked at Emma. "Is that a problem?"

"Only because it means it's going to upset him when we leave."

"I hear you're going tomorrow. Is that true?"

She nodded. "Is that what brought you out here? The rumors of my imminent departure?"

"Yes, as a matter of fact. You didn't mention it when I saw you earlier."

"I told you on Friday night that I'd probably leave Monday. I need to get back. I have a trial next week."

"Big case?"

"Not especially. In fact, if I'd had my way, it would never have gone to trial, but the client refused to plea-bargain, so here we are, about to waste a lot of taxpayer dollars on a case we're likely to lose."

Ryan was surprised at her apparent resignation to defeat. "I thought you were supremely confident about your skills as a lawyer?"

"I am, but I'll be the first to admit that my heart's not in this one. If you print that, I'll deny it, though. I'll be walking a tightrope in the courtroom, trying to give my client a fair shake without using some technicality to get him off."

He regarded her with surprise. "You want to lose?"

"I want justice," she corrected. "Unfortunately, there's no predicting juries. The law may be the law, but they're the human factor, and there's no telling whether the facts and the evidence will resonate with them the way I expect them to."

"Still, I imagine you're extremely persuasive when you want to be."

She glanced at him sideways. "Why would you believe that? I haven't been able to persuade you to steer clear of me."

"That's because I've got my own issues with being overly confident. I think I can change your mind."

She chuckled. "I should probably have set out to be less of a challenge. You would have lost interest by now."

His gaze locked with hers. "Somehow I doubt that. We both know there are a whole lot of reasons why this shouldn't or can't work, yet I don't seem to be able to make myself stay away. I figure we'll just have to play it out."

"You sound resigned."

"Do I?" He grinned. "Trust me, that's not how I feel. I can hardly wait."

When he leaned forward to touch his lips to hers, he felt the shudder that swept through her. He found that reassuring. It was also what convinced him that Ryan was right. Risky or not, he had to follow her to Denver at the first opportunity.

But first he'd give her just a little time to start to miss him.

Emma could hardly wait to get away from Winding River in the morning. Ford kept catching her by surprise, rattling her with those innocent kisses that stole her breath.

The fact that he hadn't prodded her for more details about the case she was handling had also been reassuring. She had been less than circumspect in admitting that she wanted to lose. In print, those words would have been damning and could have cost her the confidence of all of her clients, if not gotten her disbarred. His failure to ask more probing questions had reassured her that, this time at least, he wouldn't betray her confidence.

Beside her in the car, Caitlyn was pouting. She'd barely said a single word since Emma had told her the night before that they were going home.

Outside the car, her parents were looking on with disappointment written all over their faces.

"We'll be back soon," she promised.

"I don't see—" her mother began, but Emma's father cut her off.

"Leave it alone. Emma knows what she has to do. She has obligations in Denver," he said. He leaned through the car window and kissed Caitlyn's forehead. "Be good for your mommy."

"I want to stay with you," Caitlyn whispered as huge tears rolled down her cheeks.

"Not this time, baby. You'll be back soon, though. You heard Mommy promise." His gaze met Emma's. "We love you both."

Tears welled up in her eyes now. "I know, Dad. I love you."

As he stepped away from the car, she put it into gear, backed up, then headed down the driveway, giving one last wave to her parents, who were standing arm in arm, their expressions doleful.

"I don't know why we have to go," Caitlyn said with a sniff.

"Because Mommy has to go back to work."

"I hate Denver," Caitlyn said vehemently. "And I hate you."

Guilt bubbled up inside Emma, but she couldn't let her daughter's words deter her from doing what she had to do.

She sighed and reached over to squeeze Caitlyn's hand.

"I know, but I love you. And I always will, no matter what."

Caitlyn fell into a fitful sleep after that and didn't awaken again until they were almost home.

"Can I have Kelly and Laura Beth over?" she asked the minute they'd walked in the door, instinctively knowing that this was the time to play on Emma's guilt. "I want to tell them all about my pony and Grandpa's ranch and the kitten I get to bring home next time we come."

The last thing Emma wanted was to have three little girls squealing while she tried to concentrate, but she also knew it would make it easier for Caitlyn to accept being back in Denver.

"You call them," she said, regretting the fact that she'd given the housekeeper several weeks off while they'd been away. Emma had called her that morning, but the woman wouldn't be back until tomorrow. "I'll speak to their moms."

"Can they spend the night?"

"Sure," she said, resigned to the inevitable. "We can order pizza."

Caitlyn beamed at her. She ran to grab the portable phone, then raced back, skidded to a stop and regarded Emma solemnly. "I don't really hate you, Mommy. I just said that 'cause I was mad."

"I know, baby. Now give your friends a call before it gets too late."

Emma spoke to the girls' mothers, assuring them that it would be fine for their daughters to spend the night. "Caitlyn's looking forward to it."

"And you?" Laura Beth's mother asked, chuckling. "You're a brave woman to do this on your first day back from a trip."

"Not brave, pragmatic," Emma told Darla. "They'll keep Caitlyn occupied and happy while I go over the mountain of paperwork that's stacked up while we've been away."

"The girls could come over here," Darla said.

"You're an angel for suggesting it, but another time.

Caitlyn was unhappy about leaving her grandparents. I think it'll be good for her to see she can have just as much fun right here."

"What time should I pick Laura Beth up in the morning?"

"I'll drop her off about nine. I want to run by the office first thing anyway."

"Then leave Caitlyn with me," Darla suggested. "Kids are like puppies. When they're in pairs, they're much easier to deal with. They entertain each other. I love my daughter, but it's been a long summer, and it's just the end of July. Another whole month to go before school starts."

"Are you sure you don't mind?"

"Of course not. See you soon. You can tell me all about your reunion."

Emma tried unsuccessfully to hide a groan.

"I heard that," Darla said. "Don't panic. I'll take the condensed version and then get out of your hair. Any gorgeous men there?"

Emma immediately thought of Ford. "One, as a matter of fact."

"Aha," Darla gloated. "Maybe this will take longer than I thought."

Emma was chuckling when she hung up. Darla was a perpetual optimist, a romantic at heart, who believed in silver linings and happily-ever-after. They weren't good friends. In fact, they were little more than acquaintances, but they'd seen a lot of each other since their daughters had become fast friends in kindergarten. If Emma told her about Ford and how disconcerting she found him to be, Darla would be encouraging her to start picking out wedding invitations, especially since he was the first man Emma had ever mentioned to her.

It didn't help that Darla and Laura Beth arrived just as the phone rang.

"Ford?" Emma said when she heard his voice. "I wasn't expecting you to call."

Darla gave her a thumbs-up.

"I just wanted to be sure you got back okay. Any problems?"

"Nope. Clear sailing."

"Are you back in your routine already?"

"No, actually Caitlyn is having guests. Two of her classmates are coming over for a slumber party."

"Do I detect an attempt at bribery?"

"You've got it," Emma said, not especially surprised that he'd read the situation so accurately.

Kelly arrived just then, and the squeals escalated. Darla's attempts to hush the girls were pretty much ignored.

"It sounds as if you have your hands full," Ford commented. "I'll let you go. I just wanted you to know I was thinking about you."

"Thanks for calling."

"No problem."

She was about to hang up, when he said, "Emma?"

"Yes?"

"Don't be surprised if I'm the one showing up on your doorstep one of these days."

"What?"

"Sweet dreams," he said, and hung up before she could demand an explanation.

Sweet dreams, indeed! He'd just given her one more thing to worry about.

"Was that him?" Darla asked, watching her closely.

"Yes."

"You're barely home and he's already checking in. You must have made quite an impression. What does he do?"

"He owns the newspaper in Winding River."

"Sounds promising. You can't get much more respectable than that."

"I suppose that depends on your point of view," Emma said wryly. "Journalists are not my favorite people."

"I don't know why. You're a master at using the media to help your clients. You have all of those TV reporters eating out of your hand. You've mastered the art of sound bites. My Jimmy says he's never seen anything like it, and he's been a TV news director for five years now," she said, referring to her husband, who worked for a local network affiliate. Before that he'd worked for a newspaper in town as one of its brightest political columnists.

"But I maintain a cautious distance even then," Emma said. "I certainly never dated reporters."

"Well, maybe you should make an exception. I *married* one and he's definitely a keeper," Darla said, grinning. "So, what's his name? Ford, right? If he's caught your attention, he must be something. Give him a chance. I know you had a lousy time with your divorce. I read about some of it when it was in the papers, and Jimmy heard a lot of the rumors, but not all men are like that. I caught myself a prize, and there are more like my Jimmy in the sea. I believe the right one will come along for you."

Though Emma didn't handle them herself, an awful

lot of divorces were handled by other attorneys she knew. Seeing the sheer volume of them and the bitterness they stirred had made her even more jaded than she'd been by the end of her own. "How did you know Jimmy was such a prize?" she asked, genuinely curious.

"I saw it in his eyes, the first time I looked into them. He has an old soul, you know what I mean? There was all this gentleness and kindness and wisdom." Darla grinned. "It didn't hurt that he was gorgeous, either."

"You knew right away that he was the one?"

"On the first date," Darla confirmed.

"I thought I knew on my first date with Kit. I was wrong. What's to say that my judgment has improved?"

"So that's it? You don't trust your own judgment? I can remedy that. Get this Ford down here to Denver and I'll check him out. My track record as a matchmaker is unparalleled. Ask my friends."

"I'm not sure I want him anywhere near Denver."

"That's fear talking," Darla said confidently. "I saw the look on your face when you realized it was him on the phone. You want him here." Her grin turned wicked. "In fact, you just plain want him. You can deny it to me, if you like, but don't deny it to yourself." She patted Emma's hand. "I'll get out of your hair. If the girls get too rambunctious, you have permission to threaten my Laura Beth with permanent grounding and no TV. That usually gets her attention."

"I'll keep it in mind," Emma said. "See you in the morning."

"Right-o."

"And thanks for the advice."

"Don't thank me—take it! I know what I'm talking about."

Emma sighed as she watched Darla leave. It must be nice to be so confident about your own intuition about men. She didn't trust hers at all.

But Darla had been right about one thing, and Emma wasn't afraid to admit it: She really, really wanted Ford Hamilton. She just wasn't sure she was brave enough to do anything about it.

Emma haunted Ford's dreams like a sexy ghost. He hadn't been this hot and bothered by a female in a very long time. And he'd never let a woman who professed to be unattainable get under his skin this way. He usually preferred to cut his losses and stick with women who were as eager to see him as he was to see them. Maybe it was just because his options in Winding River were so limited. The town wasn't exactly crawling with single women his age.

But, if he was being totally honest, he knew it was more than that. Emma would have drawn him if he'd met her during singles night at a bar crammed with available women. She was intelligent and attractive and mysterious. All in all, a worthy challenge. And as Ryan had so rightly pointed out, there was that surprising hint of vulnerability just below the surface.

He knew Emma had been taken aback by his mentioning that he might turn up in Denver. He'd heard her unmistakable gasp, but he'd deliberately hung up before she could demand an explanation or try to talk him out of making an impromptu visit. He intended to let the notion simmer a few days until she got used to it. Then he'd make good on it.

But the waiting was killing him. He'd made it through one week, but he couldn't see lasting through two. In fact, by the time he got this week's edition of the paper on the stands, he'd lost the battle. The urge that had him climbing into his car and heading south was, no doubt, a foolish one. That didn't keep him from whistling cheerfully the closer he got to Denver. It was going to be downright fascinating to tackle Emma— so to speak—on her home turf.

13

Emma was actually relieved to be back in Denver, heading to work. Sue Ellen's case alone, especially in these preliminary stages, wasn't enough to keep her mind fully engaged, not when she was used to a non-stop barrage of challenges. Her colleagues had stepped in for her while she was away, but she was eager to jump back into the fray. She took on two new cases her first week back and handled pretrial motions for two others that were scheduled for trial later in the fall.

This was the life she understood, the life she'd been born to lead. She had goals here, respect and an important job to do, even though the trial she'd primarily come back to handle was one she was very likely to lose and she would even be relieved to do so.

Most of all, this was giving her a much-needed break from Ford Hamilton. His promise—no, she viewed it as a threat, actually—to visit her soon had left her completely rattled when he'd made it the week before. As time had passed and he hadn't shown up or called again, she began to hope that he'd had second thoughts.

It was unlikely, though. It didn't seem to be in Ford's

nature to give up. How could she possibly be so wildly attracted to a man who was as pigheaded and insensitive as he was?

Except, she was forced to admit, he *wasn't* insensitive. She had seen more and more evidence of that as he'd interacted on a few occasions with Caitlyn and her family. In fact, he'd won over just about everyone in Winding River with his easygoing charm. From a tight-knit town not known for welcoming strangers, his acceptance was a testament to Ford's determination to fit in. A part of Emma could actually envision their acceptance as a couple.

As for their disagreement over Sue Ellen's case, if Emma was totally honest with herself, she would be forced to concede that Ford wasn't just being difficult. He was coming from a perspective that was based on deeply held values about the ultimate sanctity of life, no matter what the circumstances. Though he had listened to her and talked to a few experts, she knew she hadn't been able to convince him that Sue Ellen had simply been struggling over that gun to defend herself. Ford couldn't see that years of escalating abuse had convinced the desperate woman that this time her life had been truly endangered. Even Emma had to admit it was a thorny issue with compelling arguments to be made on both sides.

For the moment, though, that case was on the back burner. Later this morning Emma had another case to fight for a major client of the firm, a drunk-driving case that never should have made it to court. As Emma had hinted to Ford without sharing any of the details, her client should have pleaded guilty—which he was—and taken his punishment, including the loss of his driver's license because of repeated offenses. Instead, he had insisted on a jury trial.

She would have given anything to turn the case over to someone else, but the man wanted her and no one else. His long-standing ties to the firm meant he got what he wanted, though why he felt so strongly about that was beyond her. She had made no secret of her contempt for his behavior. Maybe he'd assumed that she would be an even stronger advocate, because she would force herself to hide her distaste in order to represent him fairly.

And she would do her best, but the truth was, she wouldn't be one bit sorry if there was a conviction that involved alcohol-abuse treatment and maybe even jail time. She had repeatedly told him as much, but he hadn't been dissuaded from pleading not guilty or from keeping her as his attorney.

Once they were in court, the case went predictably, with all of the evidence stacked firmly against her client. If the jury had known that he had arrived with a strong scent of alcohol on his breath, deliberations would have taken about three seconds, but thankfully she had been saved that humiliation.

Emma was delivering her final argument when she caught sight of Ford in the back row of the courtroom. It threw her off-stride in front of a jury for the first time ever. She paused for a sip of water, remembered where she'd been and continued finally, but the disconcerted feeling remained.

When the jury had been sent off for the night, with deliberations to begin in the morning, Emma delivered a terse lecture to her client that his wife had better be behind the wheel when he went home and that he'd better arrive stone-cold sober in the morning.

After he'd gone off, looking chastened, she took a very long time putting papers into her briefcase. Every nerve in her body went on full alert when Ford approached, proving that she'd been wrong when she'd convinced herself that with time she could get him out of her system.

"You were good," he said. "Too bad it was a losing cause."

"Let's hope so," she said, grateful that no one else was around to hear her.

"I'm surprised you argued that passionately on behalf of someone you want convicted."

"Convicting's not my job," she replied. "Every defendant deserves the best representation he can get."

"How can you rationalize that, when you know a client's guilty?"

There was the moral compass that she found both admirable and, unfortunately, at times too rigid. "I never use questionable tactics, I never try to win a bad case on a technicality and I believe with every fiber of my being that justice will triumph."

He shook his head. "I'm glad I'm not you."

She forced a smile. "There are days I wish I weren't me, too. This happens to be one of them." She finally dared to meet his gaze, then couldn't look away. "Why are you here?"

His gaze never wavered. "You're a smart woman. I think you know the answer to that."

She knew, and her insides melted at that knowledge. "It's a bad idea. It was a bad idea in Winding River. It's still a bad idea."

"It's inevitable," he corrected. "I've been thinking a lot about this since you left, Emma. I think we need to get it over with and then figure out where we go from there."

She frowned at him. "Now there's a romantic proposal. Is this a technique that usually helps you get the girl?"

"It's honest." His gaze locked with hers. "I don't want there to be any misunderstandings between us. I'm attracted to you. I think you're attracted to me. It's there whether we like it or not. Sex is a powerful thing. It loses its power once it's been acknowledged and dealt with."

She regarded him with amusement. Could he possibly be that naïve, or was this just an incredibly clever tactic? Was he hoping to weaken her resolve by addicting her to incredible sex? "You think so?"

He returned her gaze solemnly. "It's a theory."

"Ever tested it?"

"Nope. How about you?"

"No, but I'm highly suspicious. Also, I'm not exactly sure how I feel about going to bed with someone just on the chance that I'll never want to do it again. That is what you're hoping to prove, isn't it?" She wanted to be absolutely clear about his intentions before she risked the rest.

"Not 'never,'" he insisted. "I just want to get the urgency factor out of the equation."

"An interesting approach."

"Shall we give it a try?"

Because he was right, because—despite everything that divided them—she wanted him in a way she'd wanted no one in a very long time, she nodded. She would try anything that might put an end to this inexplicable yearning that stirred in her whenever they

were together. And this was one instance when actions seemed more appropriate than words. Talking it
to death would resolve nothing.

She took out a piece of paper and wrote on it, then
handed it to him.

He never even glanced at the paper, just kept his
disconcerting gaze right on her face, on her mouth.
"What's this?" he asked.

"My address."

He grinned then. "I'm a journalist, darlin'. I've had
this for days."

She brushed past him, then called over her shoulder,
"Then I'm sure you also have the directions."

He did. In fact, he beat her there by ten minutes.

Emma had had second thoughts, third thoughts,
maybe even fourth thoughts, on the drive home.
When she found Ford waiting in her driveway, lounging against the side of his car, his lanky body looking
sexy as hell in jeans, cowboy boots and a dress shirt
with the sleeves rolled up, all of those thoughts fled.
She swallowed hard, walked past him, fumbled with
her key, then finally managed to get the door open.

She headed straight for the kitchen in search of a
bottle of wine. For once in her life, she was in desperate need of a little artificial courage. She was doing
battle with the corkscrew when she heard him step
into the room.

"Emma."

The soft command made her pause. Her gaze
shifted, met his. "What?"

He reached out and put his hand over hers. The
touch was warm, reassuring.

"Slow down," he said softly. "We're not in a race to the finish line."

"Oh? I thought you had something to prove."

"I do," he said, amusement tugging at his lips. "Just not in the next five minutes. Where's Caitlyn?"

"She has a swimming lesson this afternoon. After that, the housekeeper will take her out for dinner." She glanced at the clock. "Which gives us approximately two hours."

Ford winced, then retrieved the bottle of wine and finished opening it. He poured them each a glass. He handed one to her, then touched his to it. "Then I suggest we postpone this experiment of mine."

Emma felt an immediate letdown, followed by a quick flash of annoyance. "You want to postpone this? Why? It was your brilliant idea."

"Because you're a nervous wreck, and the timetable's a little too tight for my comfort. When you and I finally get together, I want us to have all the time in the world, not a two-hour deadline that could be cut even shorter by the unexpected arrival of a six-year-old."

She sighed at the explanation. He was right. Thank heavens one of them was using his head. How exasperating that it was Ford. "Okay, now what?"

He arched an eyebrow conspiratorially. "Now we have a glass of wine—" he grinned "—maybe a little less for you, and talk. Maybe you can give me a tour of your house so I can imagine you here when I'm back at the hotel in my lonely bed."

"You're staying at a hotel?"

He nodded. "I think it's best."

She actually hadn't considered the arrangements he might have made in order to come here. The fact that he hadn't counted on staying right in her house with her made her feel better. He might have been confident about tonight, but he hadn't taken her acquiescence for granted.

"For how long?" she asked.

"A day or two, until I have to get back to pull next week's edition of the paper together."

She struggled with a surprising surge of disappointment. Somehow in the past few minutes she had warmed to the idea of having him around, seeing how he fit into her life.

He set his glass of wine on the counter, and then beckoned to her. "Come here."

Eyeing him warily, she stepped closer. He took her glass of wine and set it beside his own, then leaned down to cover her mouth with his. His lips were cool and tasted of wine, but in mere seconds they heated as the kiss went on and on. When he finally pulled away, Emma was shaken.

"I thought you said there wasn't enough time," she whispered.

"There isn't, not for anything more than this," he said, then tasted her again.

Maybe because she was away from Winding River and on her own turf, she relaxed and let herself feel all of the sensations that his kisses stirred in her. She swayed into him, wanting more, needing to feel the heat from his body surrounding her. Her fingers slid up the column of his neck, then buried themselves in his hair as she clung to him.

The kiss was...magic. Light as a fantasy one minute, it turned to something dark and mysterious and dangerous the next. Because it was all she was likely to have for now, she savored every second, every nuance. When his tongue traced the seam of her mouth, she jolted, then parted her lips on a sigh. The invasion that followed was bold, primal and hot as a flash fire.

When Ford moaned and drew back, she felt shaky and bereft.

"No," she whispered. "More."

"Darlin', any more and we're likely to find ourselves in a whole lot of trouble." He picked up her wine and held it out. "Have a sip."

Dutifully Emma took a sip, but his kisses had been far more intoxicating, far more satisfying. Her gaze met his. "It's a poor substitute," she murmured.

He grinned. "Glad to hear it."

Emboldened by the heat still simmering between them, she said, "Since your plan has gone so wildly awry, want to hear mine?"

"Sure. I'm not afraid to let a female take charge."

"Caitlyn will be in bed by nine. The housekeeper is back and she lives in."

"Sounds crowded."

"Your hotel room won't be," she said with an unwavering gaze.

He seemed surprised. "Then you haven't had second thoughts?"

"I can barely think at all," she conceded. "If there's a way to make this off-kilter feeling go away, I want to try it."

"Is this the best time to make a decision, then?"

She studied him with a narrowed gaze. "You aren't the one having second thoughts, are you?"

"After those kisses, are you kidding me? Not a chance."

"Well, then?"

"Okay, the hotel it is, on one condition."

"Which is?"

"You let me buy you dinner first. I want to take you someplace elegant. I want to see you all decked out in something slinky and sexy and sophisticated."

Emma was too impatient for that. "How about a compromise?"

"Name it."

"Room service and my prettiest negligee?"

Ford looked as if he might be having difficulty breathing. "We have to wait till nine, huh?"

She found his impatience reassuring. "I could leave a note. I can call Caitlyn from the hotel to tell her goodnight. Unfortunately she is all too used to me having to work late."

Ford shook his head. "But for once you're here before she is. I don't want to spoil that for her. We'll leave right after she goes to bed."

"You're going to stick around?"

His gaze narrowed. "Don't you want me to?"

"I'm not sure how I feel about her knowing you're here. She already likes you. I don't want her to get the wrong idea. I don't want her to count on you. Her father's let her down so much—I don't want to add to her disappointment in that arena."

He looked as if he might argue, then nodded. "You're probably right. Once you and I figure out where we're headed, then I can spend more time with Caitlyn."

Emma studied him with surprise. "You almost sound as if you're looking forward to that."

"Why wouldn't I? She's a great kid and she has excellent taste in men. She already likes me." He planted a hard kiss on Emma's lips. "I'll be back at nine on the dot, but I'll wait outside in case she's not in bed on time."

"I can drive over or take a cab," she offered as an alternative.

He seemed amused by her last grasp at control over the situation. He shook his head and brushed a curl back from her cheek. "I don't think so. When I have a date, I pick the woman up."

With one more kiss, he was gone.

Emma made it through Caitlyn's bedtime ritual with a knot in her stomach the size of Wyoming. The edgy anticipation she had been feeling for the past few weeks around Ford was now a commanding, consuming presence. The story of Cinderella and the handsome prince took on a whole new meaning as she read it to Caitlyn.

"Mommy, I thought you were tired of that story. You said we read it too much," Caitlyn murmured sleepily. "How come you picked it tonight?"

"Because I know you love it," she said, leaning down to brush a kiss across her daughter's forehead. "Sleep tight, angel. I love you."

"Love you, Mommy." Caitlyn sighed and snuggled under the covers.

Emma stood in the doorway staring at her for a moment, thinking about how lucky she was and how often she took her precious little girl for granted. That was one more thing she needed to work on as she tried to get some balance back into her life.

And speaking of balance, she thought with a renewed surge of energy, Ford was likely to be waiting outside for her by now. She was just about to run down the stairs when the doorbell rang. Surprised, she hurried to answer it before it woke Caitlyn. She opened it to find a police officer and a sheepish-looking Ford on the doorstep. Mrs. Harrison arrived from the kitchen at the same time.

"What's going on?" Emma asked.

"There was a strange man loitering in the driveway. I didn't want to come upstairs and mention it in front of Caitlyn, so I called the police," the housekeeper said, scowling at Ford. "Young man, you ought to be ashamed of yourself."

Emma had to try very hard not to laugh. "I'm afraid there's been a mistake," she told the policeman. "Mr. Hamilton is a friend of mine."

"You know him?" Mrs. Harrison asked, her cheeks flushed with embarrassment. "Then why on earth was he lurking in the bushes?"

"I suggested he wait for me outside until I had put Caitlyn to bed. Mr. Hamilton is one of her favorite people. I was afraid seeing him might make her too excited to sleep."

"Oh, dear, I'm so sorry," Mrs. Harrison apologized.

"Not a problem," Ford said. "It's good to know you're so protective of Emma and Caitlyn."

"That's right," the policeman said. "Better to be safe than sorry. If everything's okay here, I'll be on my way."

"Thank you, Officer," Emma said.

"I'll go on up to my room now," the housekeeper said after casting one more apologetic look at Ford.

"Keep an ear open for Caitlyn, will you?" Emma requested. "Mr. Hamilton and I are going out for a while."

"Of course," the housekeeper said, giving Ford a more careful survey. "You two enjoy your evening."

As soon as they were alone, Emma grinned at Ford. "Never a dull moment when you're around me, huh?"

"Since you rode to my rescue, I have a feeling this will make a good story down the line. We can tell the grandkids all about the time Grandma almost had Grandpa arrested."

Emma's heart lurched at the teasing remark. "Let's not mention the word *grandkids* just yet. I'm still grappling with our plans for tonight."

"Want to cancel?"

And go through this panic all over again another night? Not a chance. "No way," she said. "Just let me grab a few things."

It took her less than ten minutes to gather what she needed. Ford eyed the small bag with surprise. "That's it? You going to court naked in the morning?"

"I'll be back here long before then. Is that a problem?"

He regarded her with disappointment. "You're going to crawl out of a warm bed to come home in the middle of the night?"

"Yes." Even though she was likely to leave the house before Caitlyn got up in the morning, it was a point of honor with her not to be out all night.

"Let me guess—because of Caitlyn," he said.

Emma nodded.

He held out his hand and took the bag. "Then I guess we'd better make the most of the time we have."

Emma released the breath she'd been holding.

"We'll take my car," Ford announced when Emma had written a note with the hotel phone number and left it on the refrigerator door for the housekeeper.

"Are you sure? How will I get back? You shouldn't have to get out of a warm bed, just because I have to."

"Yes, I should. We've already been over this. The decision is made. I'll bring you back," he promised.

When she was about to argue, he touched a finger to her lips. "It's a date, Emma. That's how it works. You got to set the rules for the interview. I get to set them for our first official date. Besides, I don't want to have to wait an extra five seconds for you to get there, much less ten minutes while you dawdle along behind me talking yourself out of coming like you did earlier this evening getting here."

"I did not dawdle coming home earlier."

"Didn't you?" he challenged.

"Okay, maybe a little."

"There you go," he said. "Was that so hard? You can be scared, darlin'. The honest truth is I'm a little uneasy about all of this myself."

"You? Why?"

"You're a formidable woman." He grinned. "What if I'm not exciting enough for you?"

Emma laughed. "Oh, I don't think we need to worry about that. I'm on the way to your hotel room, aren't I? Trust me, it's not something I'm likely to do on a whim."

Ford's expression sobered at once. He reached for her hand and held it as he drove. "Me, neither. I don't know what any of this means, but I know it's definitely not a whim."

Emma had a feeling that discovering exactly what was going on between them was going to take a whole lot longer than one night in a hotel room, but maybe Ford was right. Maybe it was a good place to start.

* * *

The negligee never made it out of her bag. Nor did they so much as glance at the room service menu. In fact, by the time they reached the room that Ford had reserved at a fancy downtown hotel, the only thing on Emma's mind was discovering if the feelings he stirred in her meant anything at all.

It didn't help that the first thing she saw when they entered the room was a king-size bed, topped with a luxurious comforter that had already been folded down for the evening. There were mints on the pillows. Though the room was spacious, the bed dominated it. She couldn't have ignored it if she'd tried.

Unable to tear her gaze away, she wandered straight to it and sat gingerly on the edge, then bounced.

"Nice mattress."

Ford grinned. "I'm glad you approve." He sat down next to her, captured her chin in his hand and turned her head until he could kiss her.

Ironically, that kiss seemed to settle her nerves, but only for a fleeting second. Then all hell broke loose inside her as he deepened it, claiming her in a way no man ever had. Her senses were scrambling by the time he released her. She gazed around, feeling dazed, and was stunned to discover that she was still sitting on the edge of the bed, fully clothed. She felt as if that kiss alone had taken her straight to some sort of precipice and tossed her over.

"Hungry?" Ford asked.

Mutely she shook her head.

"Want to change?"

Again she shook her head. "This is what I want," she said, reaching for him.

Ford accepted the challenge. He made love the way he did everything—slowly, intently, methodically. He studied Emma as if she were the most unique, precious female he'd ever encountered, his gaze on her heated, his touches inflaming, his exploration of her body daring.

Another siege of gentle kisses gave way to all-consuming kisses that stole her breath. When her mouth felt tender and swollen, he seemed to know. He moved on to her neck, then brushed aside her blouse to reach the curve of her shoulder. The sensation of his lips against her skin was amazing. The liquid fire created as his tongue tasted her made her quake deep inside.

But that was all a warm-up for the attention he paid to her breasts. His gaze solemn and intent, he removed her blouse completely, then slowly reached around her to unclasp her bra. As if it were some sort of erotic ritual, he carefully slid the straps over her shoulders, then freed her breasts from the confines of the lace, all without touching her with anything except his eloquent, heated gaze.

Only then, when her heart was pounding in anticipation, did he actually touch her. With a single finger he stroked down each gentle slope until he reached the pebble-hard bud. Emma felt as if she'd been holding her breath forever by the time he took the sensitive peaks deep into his mouth. She moaned softly and arched toward the source of the incredible sensation. Ford took his time satisfying her, taunting her with a delicate flick of his tongue, then, finally, a more powerful suckling that shot fiery heat straight through her.

He studied her with a lazy, hooded gaze. Then,

seemingly satisfied, he eased her skirt over her hips and tossed it aside until all she was wearing were her panties, a garter belt and hose. The heat in his eyes as he realized what she was wearing was enough to sear her.

He took his own sweet time acting on it. She was restless and overheated by the time he began a whole new exploration with his hands. Light, gliding caresses became ever more deliberate and clever. His hands were amazingly wicked, the brush of his lips provocative, the stroke of his tongue even more so.

In short, the man was driving her mad. Her shuddering gasps apparently weren't enough for him. Nor did he seem satisfied that her body was arching frantically toward his. Sighs of pleasure, desperate moans, nothing seemed to be enough for him. He wanted more from her, demanded it, coaxed her until she reached some new, impossible level of need.

Only then did he allow her to unbutton his shirt and shove it frantically aside so she could touch the hard planes of his chest. Only then did he permit the slide of his zipper, the release of his throbbing arousal.

She couldn't wait for more. "Now," she pleaded. "Ford, hurry. Inside me. I want…come with me, please."

She must have communicated the urgency, because he kicked aside his pants and entered her with a hard thrust that made her gasp at the sheer wonder of it. Her fingers dug into his tight, hard bottom as she held him in place, wanting to exult for just a moment in the sensation of being filled so completely.

Then he began to move with a rhythm that teased and tormented, just as his touches had earlier. Slow, fast, then slow again, until she thought she would scream. When the magnificent release washed over her in wave after wave, she did scream, the sound muffled only because he captured it with another devastating kiss before he joined her with a shattering climax of his own.

When the shudders eased, she fell back against the pillows, exhausted and tremulous. She had never experienced that exquisite, careful attention to her pleasure before, never flown quite that high…or returned to earth quite so reluctantly.

Because now that it was over, she knew that despite this amazing moment in time they had shared, two things hadn't changed.

First, Ford was still a journalist. And she was still terrified to put her faith in his integrity. As long as Sue Ellen's fate hung in the balance, that would always stand between them.

Second, and just as troubling, she wanted him even more now than she had before they'd made love.

14

Ford was still recovering from the most shattering release of his entire life when he realized that Emma was scrambling out of his bed as if she'd just remembered a life-or-death appointment. Unfortunately he had a hunch something else entirely was motivating her hurried departure. He reached for her hand and held on tight. She stilled at once, but he could sense the tension swirling through her as she sat on the edge of the bed, her rigid back to him.

"So, what's the deal, Emma? Where are you going?" he asked, deliberately keeping his tone calm.

"I need to get home," she said without meeting his gaze.

Determined to keep up the pretense that her behavior was nothing out of the ordinary, he glanced at the clock. "It's early yet. Just call Mrs. Harrison to check on Caitlyn, then we can order that dinner I promised you."

She was already shaking her head before the words were out of his mouth. "I'm not hungry."

"Then stay while I eat. I'd like the company."

"I don't think so. You don't need to get up. I'll call a cab."

Clearly something was going on that Ford didn't grasp. Something in the past couple of hours had made her panic. He recalled what Ryan had said just before Emma had left Winding River, that she was running scared. If she'd been frightened of what was happening between them then, it was little wonder she was panicky now. He couldn't let her run this time. She might never stop.

"Emma, what's this all about? Why are you running away?" he asked, deliberately choosing words that would annoy her.

"I'm not running away," she claimed, her cheeks flushed with indignation at the accusation.

"You could have fooled me."

"Just because I have responsibilities does not mean I'm running away."

"We talked about our plans for the evening. We were going to share dinner, make love and then I was going to take you home later. Aside from the sequence of events, what's changed?" He tucked a finger under her chin and forced her to face him. "Did I miss something here? Wasn't this as good for you as it was for me? If not, you need to tell me."

"Typical male ego," she said sarcastically. "All you're worried about is your performance in bed."

"No," Ford said patiently. "What I'm trying to do is get to the bottom of your sudden change of heart."

Sparks flashed in her eyes. "There's something wrong with me because I want to go home?"

"No, not because you want to go home. Because you want to do it right this second. And there's nothing wrong with that, either. I just think I deserve an explanation. Obviously something has shaken you. Come on, Emma. Talk to me. If this isn't about the sex, what is it about? Is it about the two of us?"

"Oh, for heaven's sake," she said, regarding him impatiently. "You're not going to be satisfied until I spell it out for you, are you?"

"No."

"Okay, then it is about the sex," she said with heart-stopping candor.

Even though he was convinced it wasn't that simple, Ford felt the breath go out of him. He'd just had the most incredible sexual experience of his life and she had a complaint? How could they have been on such different wavelengths? He'd watched her eyes, seen the wonder when she reached her climax. He'd felt her trembling beneath him, felt the way her body responded to every caress.

"Okay, lay it on me," he said, bracing himself for the worst.

"It was good," she said with obvious reluctance. "In fact, it was very, very good."

Now he was totally confused. "And that's bad?"

"It's awful," she admitted. "This was supposed to put an end to the attraction, right? Wasn't that what we both expected?"

"Hoped for, maybe, but expected? No, that is not what I expected," he told her, relieved that his initial grasp of the problem, at least as she saw it, was pretty much on target.

"Well, I did. I wanted it to be over after this, because you can't matter to me."

"I can't?" he said cautiously. Wasn't it usually the

man who was commitment shy? Just his luck to find a woman who was terrified of happily-ever-after just when he was beginning to think about it.

"Absolutely not."

"But, somehow, after this, I do matter?"

She nodded, looking so genuinely miserable that he couldn't bring himself to laugh.

"Darlin', you're going to have to explain that one to me."

"Nothing's changed. You're still a journalist, and I cannot, I *will not* get involved with a newspaperman. This…" She waved her hand around to include the rumpled sheets, his hand, which rested possessively on her thigh. "It's wrong. We couldn't be more wrong for each other."

"I think that horse may already be out of the barn. We're involved, and saying we can't be won't change anything."

"Of course it will. I don't have to see you again— not like this anyway. I'd hoped I wouldn't even want to, but that was a mistake." She sighed. "A huge mistake."

Despite her words, Ford was taking heart from the sentiment behind them. "No, you don't have to sleep with me ever again, but I would certainly be disappointed if you didn't. And, to be perfectly honest, I think you would be, too. We're good together, Emma. Better than good. We're incredible."

"In bed, maybe."

"In bed, definitely," he corrected. "And in other ways as well."

Her chin tilted up. "Well, it's not going to happen, not the sex, not anything, and that's that," she said flatly. "I will not have you in my life, Ford. I must have been out of my mind to let it go this far. I should have been honest from the minute we met and told you straight out that there was no future for us."

"Because of what I do for a living?" he asked carefully, needing to be absolutely sure he was getting the correct message here.

"Yes."

Ford had done his best, he had clung to his patience by a thread because she was so evidently rattled, but this was the last straw. He was getting damned tired of being blamed for something some other journalist had apparently done to destroy her trust in everyone associated with the media. For her to continue to hold it against him, even after all these weeks when she'd seen the kind of man he was, was infuriating. No, it was more than that. It was insulting.

"Okay," he began slowly. "If it's what you really want, what you're determined to do, I'll let you go, not just tonight but for good…on one condition."

"What?" she asked, eyeing him suspiciously.

"Tell me why you have it in for journalists. I think I deserve to understand that much at least, especially since you claim that's the only reason we can't be together."

"They're not trustworthy," she said, uttering the blanket condemnation with a perfectly straight face. "I can't be with someone who isn't trustworthy."

"You can go into court and defend a man who's guilty as sin of repeated drunk-driving offenses without making any moral judgments, and yet all journalists are untrustworthy, including one you know as well as you know me?" he asked with barely concealed irony.

"One thing has nothing to do with the other," she insisted.

He shook his head. "You're going to have to do better than that. I'm not letting you off the hook this time. I want specifics."

To his astonishment, he realized there were tears leaking from her eyes and spilling down her cheeks. "Emma?"

"I don't want to talk about it."

His annoyance faded in the face of her very real anguish. "I think you need to. Please tell me. I've asked you before and you've put me off, but I have to know. Did someone misquote you?"

She shook her head. "If only it had been something that simple."

"What then?"

When she lifted her gaze to meet his, there was a brief flash of anger in her eyes, but mostly she just looked sad. "I never even talked to him, not even once, but nobody would believe that," she whispered with a hitch in her voice.

"Him?"

"A reporter for one of the Denver papers."

"What happened?"

She sighed then, but she finally began to talk. "There was a story about a case I was handling. Very high profile. Very tricky defense."

"Okay," he said quietly, then waited for the rest.

"They all thought I had spilled confidential information about a client to a reporter." She looked as stricken as if it had happened just yesterday. "My partners were ready to fire me. After all, there it was in black and white, information only I could have known, enough to put my client behind bars. Maybe that's where he belonged, but that wasn't the point. I would never, *never* do something so unethical."

Ford held his breath through the soft confession. She glanced at him and he saw the terrible price she had paid for what had happened, for having her integrity called into question by the people she worked with, people she respected.

"I believe that," he said. "I know you're not capable of doing anything like that."

She met his gaze. "Do you really?"

"Of course. Did you clear your name?"

"Eventually."

"How?"

"I proved that someone else had leaked the information, that the reporter knew the information wasn't coming from me but linked my name to it anyway for a price."

Ford was stunned. "Who would do such a terrible thing?"

For the longest time, he thought she might not answer. Her lower lip quivered, but finally she drew in a deep, shuddering breath and faced him with a look of resolve on her face. "My husband."

He felt as if the wind had just been knocked out of him, which, of course, was nothing compared to the way Emma must have felt when she made the discovery. "What? How? Why the hell would he do something like that?"

"To get me fired," she said wearily. "He wanted me to stop practicing law. He'd begged, pleaded, cajoled, ordered. It was a control thing with him. He couldn't stand it that I was thought of as his equal, that I brought home as much money as he did. He belittled me every chance he got."

"And you stood for that?" he asked, incredulous

and yet somehow not surprised. It was why she felt so strongly about Sue Ellen's reasons for staying so long with Donny.

"For far too long," she admitted. "I'm not proud of it, but he was the father of my child. I wanted to believe that once he saw how good I was, he'd be proud of me."

"But he wasn't," Ford guessed.

"Not even close. Since nothing else had worked, he decided to discredit me, to get me disbarred. He went to an acquaintance at one of the papers, a man known for not being particularly scrupulous about where he got his information. Kit fed him the information about my client on the condition that I be the one quoted. Naturally the story was too juicy for the man to resist. Apparently he had no qualms at all about using the information and linking my name to it—only in the most carefully chosen words, of course."

"The man told this to the authorities? He admitted that Kit had manipulated the whole thing?"

"Never," she said with disdain. "He was so blasted self-righteous. He claimed he was protecting his sources, that he'd never actually said I was the one who gave him the information, but it was all there for anyone with half a brain to reach the conclusion that I was the one who'd leaked the story."

"Then how do you know your husband was involved?"

"I hired an investigator. He discovered that there was a rather timely deposit in the reporter's bank account that he couldn't deny. It matched a withdrawal that Kit had made from our account. When I confronted Kit, he didn't deny it. He said he'd done it because he loved me."

"Dear God," Ford whispered. "I'm sorry. But surely

you know that not all journalists are like that. The business has its sleazy reporters, but most are honest, hardworking people who care about getting the facts right and exposing corruption, not becoming corrupt themselves."

"Intellectually, I suppose I can accept that," Emma said, then touched a hand to her stomach. "But in here, I lump the whole lot of you together with that slime who conspired with my ex-husband."

"I suppose that's understandable," Ford said slowly. "But I'm going to change your mind, Emma. I promise you that. I'm going to do whatever it takes to prove to you that I'm not one of the bad guys."

Unfortunately, he had no idea how he was going to pull that transformation off. Her distrust was deep-rooted and, now that he knew the reason why, he could also see that it was understandable. Proving to her that the reporter who'd harmed her had been the exception, not the rule, wasn't going to be as simple as reminding her that it was never wise to stereotype. It was going to take time and patience. And with Sue Ellen's case the only thing bringing Emma back and forth to Winding River on a frequent basis, he was going to have to work quickly or he would lose her.

He glanced at her profile, let his gaze travel the curve of her spine, the swell of her breast. He felt himself grow hard, felt his heart begin to pound, and reached a conclusion. Losing Emma was not an option.

Emma couldn't believe she had told the whole horrible story to Ford. Few people knew the depths to which Kit had sunk in his attempts to control her life. It was part of the agreement she'd made with him at the time of the divorce. She had promised to say nothing, as long as he didn't contest the divorce and cleared her name with her law firm. Because his career was so all-important to him, he had agreed. She hadn't given him any choice.

She would have used the same leverage to keep him from claiming custody of Caitlyn, but it hadn't been necessary. The doting new woman in his life had gotten pregnant before the ink was dry on the divorce papers. He'd been able to focus all of his obsessive attention on the second Mrs. Rogers. She was more than willing to stay at home and be kept in style.

When Emma thought back to those days, she couldn't believe she had survived them. She had been as close to despair as it was possible to get and still pull out of it without counseling or prescription drugs. Sheer determination and a commitment to her own career and to Caitlyn had kept her going.

Even so, she had paid a price. She didn't trust easily, and certainly not journalists. Rarely did she even trust men in general. No, that wasn't entirely true. What she didn't trust was her own judgment when it came to men. Ford had somehow slipped past her defenses and gotten closer than any man had in years.

For a week after the night in his hotel room, she had difficulty falling asleep. The memories of his touches, of his tenderness, made her restless. The yearning she had hoped to end that night had only intensified. The prospect of going back to Winding River, of seeing him again, both terrified and excited her.

She wasn't sure what she'd expected when she'd told him the story of Kit's betrayal. In truth, she hadn't given a thought to how he might take it. She had simply responded to the confusion that her hurry to leave his bed had stirred in him. Once the words had begun, they had tumbled out in a rush, leaving her oddly relieved when they were out in the open. Only the Calamity Janes had heard even part of the messy story of her divorce, and she hadn't given them as much of it as she'd given Ford. She'd managed to keep her family in the dark about most of it, as well. Matt and Wayne would have beaten Kit to a pulp if they'd known the rest.

Ford had said very little, but he had enticed her back to bed, where he had simply held her until her tears had dried. Then he had taken her home, kissed her so thoroughly it had made her knees weak and promised to call the minute he got back to Wyoming.

He had called the next day and again the next night. In fact, he had been phoning regularly, but she hadn't taken any of the calls. She knew he had hoped that her resolve would waver, but it wouldn't, so what was the point? She had made her decision. Prolonging the contact wouldn't be wise for either of them.

But she couldn't put off going back to Winding River forever. A trial date had been set for Sue Ellen and in the intervening weeks Emma had a dozen different witnesses she needed to depose. She was flipping through her calendar, trying to make a decision about the timing of her trip, when her secretary buzzed.

"It's Lauren Winters on line two," she said.

"Thanks, Liza." Emma grinned as she answered the call. "I thought you were on location for your next movie."

"I am, but there's this incredible new technology. It's called the cell phone. It even works from the wilds of Vancouver."

"Okay, very amusing. It's just that you're usually so

absorbed with work at the start of filming, we never hear from you. What's up?"

"Just checking in. I hear you've been away from Winding River for a few weeks now. Hiding out, are you?"

Emma bristled at the accusation. "Why would you say something like that?"

"I know you, sweetie. Ford Hamilton has you running scared. I picked up on that the minute you skedaddled out of town."

"Don't be ridiculous. I came back because I had a case going to trial here."

"If you say so," Lauren said skeptically. "So, has Ford been to Denver?"

"Yes, as a matter of fact."

"Thought so. How did that go?"

"He was here for one night. I told him it wouldn't work and he went back. End of story."

"He took no for an answer?" Lauren sounded disappointed.

"Actually I didn't give him much choice."

"He hasn't called once?" Lauren asked.

"He's called," Emma admitted. "I haven't taken the calls."

"Why on earth not?"

"Because it's pointless."

"Why is it pointless?"

"He's there. I'm here. He's a journalist. I don't trust journalists. The list of reasons goes on and on."

"You could be there in Winding River with him," Lauren suggested. "As for the whole journalist thing, that has never made any sense to me. I know it has something to do with something Kit did right before the divorce, but you surely can't blame Ford for that."

"Trust me, I have good reasons for the way I feel."

"I'm sure you do, but isn't it misdirected? Ford never did you any harm. He's been straight with you from the beginning, hasn't he?"

"Pretty much," Emma conceded.

"Then be fair. You wouldn't expect a jury to convict him of a crime he personally didn't commit. How can *you?*"

Emma sighed. "It's not that simple."

"Yes, sweetie, it is. Go home. Give the man a chance. I have it on good authority that the man is highly respected."

"What authority?"

"Cassie, Karen—even Gina—have chimed in with their approval. He's winning us over."

"Well, bully for him," Emma grumbled.

"If you won't give him a chance for your own sake, do it for mine."

"Why do you care whether I give Ford a chance?"

"Because if you do, you could end up in Winding River. That would make it that much easier to get all the Calamity Janes together whenever I get back there."

"And how often are you planning to get back? Face it, Lauren, your life's as jam-packed with work as mine, and yours takes you all over the world."

"Yes, well, I've been thinking about that."

Emma went still. "Oh?"

"Once I finish this movie, I may go back to Winding River for good."

"You mean as a home base between movies?"

"I mean permanently, period."

Emma couldn't hide her shock. "What? When did you decide this?"

"I've been thinking about it for a long time. Everything that happened at the reunion and since then has convinced me that I really want to be close to the people who matter to me."

"You're giving up movies?"

"Yes," Lauren said without hesitation. "Or maybe I'll do an occasional one when a fabulous script comes my way. I have to see how I feel. Right now I just know I want my life to be different."

Emma was stunned. "What aren't you telling me? You're not sick, are you?"

"No, just lonely. I wasn't cut out for this life. It's not real."

There was no mistaking the sad, wistful note in Lauren's voice. "Then by all means, come home," Emma said readily. "In fact, if you can get away this weekend, fly home. I'll drive up. We can talk this all out. You can even try to knock some sense into my head where Ford's concerned."

Lauren chuckled. "Now there's an incentive. I'll be there."

"I'm not promising you'll have any luck," Emma warned.

"Sweetie, I've persuaded millions of moviegoers that I can act. Surely I can persuade you to give a handsome, decent man a chance."

Maybe she could, maybe she couldn't, but as Emma hung up, she realized that a part of her wanted Lauren's attempts to succeed.

Emma had been right. Making love with her had been a very bad idea. Because now that he had, Ford knew he could never give her up.

There were a million and one reasons why he should write the whole thing off as a moment of craziness, but he couldn't. He wasn't even deterred by the fact that she was refusing to take his calls. He considered that to be a hopeful sign, actually. She wouldn't be avoiding him if she wasn't afraid that he could get to her.

Not that he had any real choice. Without even realizing it was happening, without even guessing it was possible, he'd gone and fallen in love with her. She was the most intelligent woman he'd ever met, and the most passionate, not just in bed, but about the very same ideas that mattered to him. As often as not, they were on opposite sides, but he could live with that. He wondered, though, if she could.

And that was at the very core of their relationship. He felt certain they could overcome the small stuff. Even her career in Denver was manageable. He didn't have a problem with her staying on there if need be, commuting himself if necessary, but he had a hunch even she might be almost willing to admit that she was ready to move back to Winding River full-time.

He'd picked up on the brittle tension in her that very first night at the class reunion. He'd watched that slowly ease away as she fell into a more comfortable rhythm surrounded by her family and her friends. She had laughed more readily by the time she left. She had watched her daughter without that worried furrow creasing her brow.

Back in Denver the brittleness and the furrowed brow had both returned within days. He'd been appalled by their presence when he'd gone to visit Emma. Even though she'd been back in what she considered her natural milieu, she'd been frighteningly uptight.

Not all of that could be blamed on her uneasiness about their relationship.

He wondered if she was aware of the transformations and their implications. He also wondered how long it was going to be before she stopped running scared, before she admitted that she wasn't truly happy with her life in Denver and came back to Winding River.

That thought was still very much on his mind when he glanced up from his cup of coffee and saw Cassie regarding him speculatively.

"Everything okay?" he asked.

"I should be asking you that," she said. She glanced around, satisfied herself that the few customers at Stella's were okay, then slid into the booth opposite him. "Have you heard from Emma?"

"No."

"Have you tried to reach her?"

"Repeatedly," he admitted. "She's not taking my calls."

Cassie grinned. "Good. In fact, that's great."

"I thought so myself. Mind explaining why *you* think it's good news."

"Sure. It's proof that she considers you to be a risk. Emma's not scared of much, but apparently she's terrified of you. That's the way the rest of us had it pegged from the beginning, but she was in such deep denial that we weren't sure. Now I am."

Her logic was complicated, but Ford was pretty sure he was following her. "How do I break the impasse?"

"You don't. You wait. She'll be back. In fact, Lauren called last night and said she'd managed to lure Emma back here for this weekend. Emma thinks she's coming to save Lauren from making some drastic career decision." Cassie waved that off. "I don't understand all the particulars of that, but the bottom line is that you'll get your chance to see her in person. Emma's not capable of being rude to a person's face."

Ford grinned. "So she won't slam the door on me?"

"No way."

"Any idea when she's getting in?"

"I'd guess midday Friday, but check with her mom. I'm sure she'll know." Her grin spread. "And if I know Mrs. Clayton, she'll be more than happy to let you be the welcoming committee. In fact, I imagine she'll insist on it."

Ford pictured Emma's stunned expression when she discovered he was the one assigned to greet her. It was that image that got him through the rest of the week.

15

Emma had her bags packed and was about to carry them downstairs when the doorbell chimed.

"I'll get it," Caitlyn shouted happily from the front hall. She was so eager to get on the road to see her pony and her grandparents that she had been waiting impatiently at the bottom of the steps for the past half hour pleading with Emma to hurry.

"Uncle Matt!" Caitlyn squealed in a voice that carried up the stairs.

Startled, Emma peered over the railing. Sure enough, there was her brother, unshaven, his hair rumpled, a suitcase in his hand. She hurried down the steps to give him a hug, then took a more thorough survey of his disheveled state. She immediately put her own departure on hold. Something was obviously wrong, and she needed to deal with it before she went anywhere.

"You look like hell," she observed.

Matt managed a feeble smile. "You sure do know how to give a pep talk, sis."

"How come you came to see us, Uncle Matt? We were coming to see you," Caitlyn said, clinging to his hand.

Emma interceded. "Let's go into the kitchen and fix your uncle some coffee and some breakfast," she said, then gave him a pointed look as she added, "I'm sure he'll answer all of our questions then."

Caitlyn's face fell. "But, Mama, we got to go. Grandpa's gonna be waiting."

"Why don't you go and call Grandpa and tell him we're going to be running a little late?" Emma suggested. It would give her a few minutes to try to get to the bottom of her brother's unexpected arrival, and maybe talking to her grandfather would keep Caitlyn's disappointment at bay.

When Caitlyn had raced off to make the call, Matt regarded Emma wearily. "Do we have to get into this now? All I want is a little sleep. I drove most of the night. I'm beat."

"I can see that," she said. "That means your resistance will be weaker and I'll be able to get a few straight answers out of you."

"That's an unfair tactical advantage."

She grinned at him. "I know, but if you really didn't want to talk, you would have avoided me like the plague and gone to a motel." She took his hand, at least partly so he wouldn't bolt, and led him into the kitchen. "Sit. I'll make the coffee. Want some eggs?"

"Sure, why not?" he said, sounding resigned.

"Did you and Martha have another fight?" she asked casually as she scooped coffee into the coffeemaker and turned it on.

"You could say that."

"About?"

"Actually, she and Mom and Dad ganged up on me. They called it an intervention, whatever the hell that is."

Emma tried to picture the scene and failed. Since it was obviously a sore point, she resisted the temptation to grin. "About?"

"My future, what else?"

"What was the bottom line?"

"They kicked me out."

Emma hadn't been expecting that. The measure was far more drastic than she would have imagined. Obviously they felt Matt was so deeply entrenched in his self-imposed martyrdom that he would continue to ignore anything less. Maybe her own failure to get through to him had been the turning point, convincing them that he would have to be pushed into doing something to change his life.

She nodded. "Okay, then, what are your plans?"

He gave her a long-suffering look. "They kicked me out last night. Do you honestly think I've had time to make plans beyond coming here?"

With the coffee brewing, she sat down and gave his work-roughened hand a squeeze. "Whether you want to admit it or not, Matt, I think you've been dreaming about this moment for years," she told him quietly.

He frowned at that. "A dream is not a plan."

"It's the beginning of one. What's yours? If you could do or be anything in the world, what would you choose?"

The question seemed to completely befuddle him. For the longest time, he simply sat there, gazing off into the distance as if trying to envision a different future from the path he'd been on.

"I think I've got a good head for business," he finally said slowly. Then he added sheepishly, "Dad says the ranch has never been running better, and I've made a little money investing."

The news about the ranch wasn't unexpected, but Emma was surprised about the investing. "Really? How much?"

"Enough to pay tuition for college, actually. I haven't said much to Martha about it, because the whole subject of investing in stocks gives her hives. She thinks ranching is unpredictable enough."

"If you have the money for tuition, why on earth have you been waiting to do this?" Emma asked.

"You know why."

"Because of Dad," she guessed.

"My mistake," he said wryly. "Turns out he's pretty eager to throw me out."

"You know that's not true. You just said he's told you that the ranch has never been better off, and that the credit for that goes to you. All he wants is for you to be happy doing something you really want to do." She met Matt's gaze evenly and saw a faint spark of hope in his eyes, something she realized had been missing for far too long. Her baby brother was long overdue for a chance at the life he wanted.

"It's not too late to enroll for the fall semester at the University of Colorado in Boulder. You could stay here," she said impulsively. Even as the words left her mouth, she began to warm to the idea. It had been lonely around here. She had realized just how lonely when she'd been back in Winding River with family underfoot every time she turned around. And since Ford had been to visit, her life had seemed emptier than ever.

"Bring Martha and the kids," she added. "There's

plenty of room, and Caitlyn would love having you around."

"I can't impose on you like that."

"You can't *not* do it," she said. "Besides, when is it an imposition for a brother to visit his sister?"

"For four years?" he said. "That's a helluva long visit."

She grinned. "If you hate living with me, you'll be motivated to finish in less."

He regarded her doubtfully. "Emma, are you sure? This is a big step for both of us. You haven't even had time to think about it."

"Of course I'm sure. And if you're not happy here or the commute for classes starts to be a drag, in a few months you can find something closer to school."

"I have money for tuition, not rent."

"Then Martha will find a job," she said, knowing that her sister-in-law would jump at the chance to do something to help her husband find happiness. "She's offered to do that. And I'll help out. One of the perks of being a successful lawyer is that I have buckets of money and no time to spend it. I'd be happy to invest a little of it in you, especially if you graduate from college and become some sort of hotshot investment broker and triple my savings for me."

"That might be a little overly ambitious," he warned. "The market can be tricky."

"Then you'll keep me from making any foolish choices." She met his gaze. "Stay, Matt, please. Do this for yourself. Do it for Martha and the kids."

"Do you really think I can?"

He so clearly needed reassurance that Emma resisted the temptation to chastize him for being so hesitant. "I know you can. So does everyone else in the family. You're the only doubter."

He drew in a deep breath and met her gaze. "If I can get a degree at my age, then I can surely cook myself a couple of eggs. You and Caitlyn go on and hit the road. I know she's anxious to get to Winding River. I imagine all you've heard about the last few weeks is that pony of hers. She's on the phone to Dad half a dozen times a week to check on it."

"I know. I've seen the phone bills," Emma said. "Shall I tell Mom and Dad what you've decided?"

He shook his head. "I'll call. I'll let them know you're on your way and that I'm moving to Colorado." His gaze locked on hers. "They might not be so disappointed, if they thought you were coming back to Winding River to stay."

"I said I'd share my house with you, not give it to you," she chided. "I'll be back in a few days. In fact, I'll help Martha get things packed up and bring her with me. You concentrate on getting enrolled in school before you chicken out."

She bent down and gave him a kiss. "You're going to be great at this," she assured him.

"I hope you're right."

"I'm always right."

He chuckled. "So you think."

She started out of the kitchen.

"Hey, sis."

"What?" she asked, turning back.

"Now that I've mustered up the courage to make a dramatic change in my life, maybe it's time for you to do the same. I have it on excellent authority that a certain newspaperman cares a lot about you. Mom and

Dad and my wife aren't the only ones who can mastermind an intervention," he reminded her.

"Don't press your luck, little brother. I could still put you out on the street."

"I'd like to see you try." He leaned back in his chair, his hands linked behind his head in a relaxed pose. "This place is beginning to look mighty comfortable."

Emma was chuckling as she left the kitchen, but as soon as she reached the front hall, her laughter died. She had the strangest feeling that Matt had been only partially teasing. Her family had already proved in her brother's case that they weren't above using extraordinary tactics to accomplish the impossible. She and Ford were certainly that. It might be just the challenge they were looking for, coming off this latest success with Matt.

Too bad, she thought grimly. She was highly motivated, and Ford Hamilton was definitely not in her future…even if she couldn't seem to get him out of her head.

Emma didn't like the jolt to her heart when she pulled up in front of her parents' house a few hours later and spotted Ford lounging in a rocker on the porch. It didn't help that a smile spread across Caitlyn's face and she all but broke her neck leaping from the car to race up and throw herself at him.

"I've been missing you and missing you," she said enthusiastically as he scooped her up.

"I've missed you, too, munchkin."

"Talking on the phone's not nearly as good as seeing you," Caitlyn said.

Ford's gaze sought Emma's. "No, it's not, but it's better than nothing," he said quietly.

Emma felt as if she'd been punched in the stomach. She'd had no idea Ford had been in touch with her daughter. Nor was she sure how she felt about it. Maybe she'd know once she found out why he'd been calling her.

"Caitlyn, why don't you go and look for your grandfather? I'm sure he's down at the barn."

"Actually he and your mom have gone to Laramie for dinner and a movie," Ford announced.

That was yet another shock. "But Matt called. They knew I was on my way," she said, feeling increasingly disconcerted and not one bit happy about it.

"That's why I'm here."

"They asked you to be here when I arrived?" she asked skeptically.

"Yep. In fact, your mother thought it was a splendid solution."

"Solution to what? I have a key. I could have let myself in."

"Yes, but you might have felt neglected. Now that I'm here, there's no chance of that. I'm taking the two of you out for dinner. Gina's cooking at Tony's. She's promised to make the munchkin's favorite pizza. Extra cheese and pepperoni."

Caitlyn planted a loud, smacking kiss on his cheek. "You're the best."

Emma wasn't as easily persuaded of that as her daughter was. In fact, she didn't like this sneaky scheme of Ford's one bit. It had his fingerprints all over it. Her parents would not have thought of it on their own. In the past she had never arrived home to find them gone. In fact, they were most often all too eager to greet her. They usually assembled the entire family as if welcoming the return of the prodigal daughter. Of course, the family was one short with Matt in Denver, but that was beside the point.

"Caitlyn, take your bag inside. I need to speak to Ford before we go into town."

"But—"

"Go."

As soon as Caitlyn had gone, Emma whirled on Ford. "What did you do? Bribe them to stay away?"

"Why would I do something like that?" he asked reasonably.

"Because you wouldn't want them around when I tell you what a low-down, sneaky, conniving man you are."

"No, I wouldn't want that," he agreed. "It wouldn't speak well of you to say such things when you know they're not true. I've been up-front with you about where I see the two of us heading."

"That is not what I meant."

He grinned unrepentantly. "I know."

"And I want to know why you've been talking to my daughter behind my back."

"It wasn't behind your back. I called. She answered. We talked. You certainly weren't eager to take my calls."

"For good reason."

"In your opinion."

"Ford—"

He cut her off. "I hope you're hungry. I told Gina to make the pizza a large one."

"I'm not going to dinner with you."

"Oh?" he said, clearly only mildly disappointed. "What will you tell Caitlyn? She's really looking forward to this."

Emma sighed. He had her over a barrel and he knew it. "Okay, you win, but I don't have to like it."

"No," he agreed, then leaned down to give her a totally unsatisfying peck on the cheek. "But I'll do my best to see that you do."

Ford was downright pleased with himself at how smoothly it had all gone. Emma had fallen right in with his plans. Okay, not without a protest, but he'd anticipated that. He'd known she wouldn't deny Caitlyn an outing she had her heart set on.

Contrary to what he'd claimed, he wasn't above admitting to himself that it was sneaky and low-down, but it had worked. Once in a while extreme measures were called for, even if they were destined to haunt him. Emma was likely to consider it one more black mark against his character. It would probably make her happy that this one she could lay squarely at his feet without being accused that she was unfairly projecting the bad behavior of others onto him.

He also knew she had been floored by the discovery that he and Caitlyn had been in touch. He figured he was going to pay for that later, as well. In fact, he was counting on her having quite a lot to say to him, which would necessitate another, more private meeting. Even as annoyed as she obviously was, she wasn't likely to blast him publicly or in front of her daughter. She might not care about his reputation, but she was very concerned with her own.

It was late afternoon, well before the usual dinner

hour, when they arrived at Tony's. The restaurant was all but deserted, but Gina was waiting for them. Ford had called to give her a heads-up when they left the ranch. She was proving to be a surprisingly eager ally.

"The pizza just went in the oven," she announced. "Peggy's off till five, so I'll be your waitress, too."

"You most certainly will not," Emma scolded. "You'll sit and join us." She shot a triumphant look at Ford, very pleased with her own sneakiness.

"How's the pizza going to get from the kitchen to the table?" Gina asked.

"Since this little outing was his idea, Ford will handle it," Emma said.

"Of course I will," he said, regarding Emma with amusement. "I'm always eager to impress the most beautiful women in town with my good manners."

Gina chuckled. "You're good," she said.

"I know. Now, sit, ladies. I will be back with your drinks in just a minute. You don't mind, do you, Gina?"

"Heavens, no. I'm always grateful to have a few minutes off my feet. I'll take a glass of wine."

"Me, too," Emma said.

He regarded her with surprise. "Really? I thought you'd want to have all your wits about you."

"No need," she said airily. "I have Gina to protect me."

"At least you're being honest about it," he said, then smiled at Caitlyn. "What about you, darlin'? A soda?"

She nodded eagerly. "A really, really big one."

"A small one," Emma corrected. "You can have more, after you finish that."

Ford returned to the table with the drinks and the steaming hot pizza. He left it to Gina to keep the conversation light, while he sat back happily and watched Emma visibly unwind. In fact, if he didn't know better, he'd almost believe she was as happy to be there with him as she was to be with her old friend.

As soon as they'd finished eating, Gina grinned at Caitlyn. "I have a sudden yen to go to the toy store before it closes. Want to come with me?"

Caitlyn's eyes widened. "Really?"

"You bet. We can see if Barbie has anything new. I think your mom and Ford have things to talk about, anyway."

"We do not," Emma said, clearly flustered. "I'll come with you."

Ford reached over and put his hand atop hers. She jolted visibly, then met his gaze and sighed. "Go ahead, Caitlyn. But don't try to talk Gina into buying out the store."

"Little chance of that," Gina said with a rueful expression. "One toy's my limit."

When they were gone, Ford said quietly, "Thank you."

"For what?"

"Not running away."

She scowled. "I'm getting sick and tired of people accusing me of running away from things."

"Then stop doing it," he suggested mildly.

"Oh, go suck an egg."

"Have you ever noticed that whenever the truth hits a little too close to home, you resort to that particular phrase?" he asked.

"I do not."

He chuckled at her fierce expression. "I work with words. I pay attention to how others use them. Believe me, you use that phrase whenever you're rattled. Shall I ask Gina? I'm sure she could confirm it."

"Maybe you should spend more time worrying about why I use it so often with you," she grumbled. "Could it be because you annoy me?"

"Could be," he agreed cheerfully.

"That is not a good thing," she pointed out.

"Sure it is. You wouldn't be annoyed if you didn't care about me. You'd just dismiss whatever I said or ignore it."

"Now there's a good idea," she said a little too eagerly, and stood up. "I think I'll catch up with Gina and Caitlyn."

He saw no need to try to block her. Instead, he merely noted, "You're wobbling."

"I am not," she said, though she sat down heavily.

"You really ought to lay off the wine."

She held her head. "I know," she said. "Why did you let me drink that?"

"Let you? Could I have stopped you?"

"No," she conceded. "But you wanted me tipsy, didn't you?"

"It did occur to me that you might be slightly more amenable if your head wasn't absolutely clear."

"Amenable to what?" she asked suspiciously.

"Going out dancing with me after we take Caitlin back to the ranch."

"No way."

"Tomorrow night, then."

"Forget it."

He sighed. "Maybe I should have recommended a second glass of wine. Oh, well, as long as I at least have you with me now, let's talk about our relationship."

"We don't have one," she said flatly.

"Sure we do. It might be on shaky ground right now, but we definitely have a relationship. I'm willing to work to make it a better one. How about you?"

"No."

"I thought you were more broad-minded than that."

"Well, I'm not. And while we're on the subject of things that annoy me, you are not to call my daughter anymore. She obviously looks forward to talking to you."

"And that's bad because?"

"Because she shouldn't start to count on you. Eventually you'll move on to some other woman, and you'll lose interest in trying to get to me through Caitlyn."

"Is that what you think I'm doing?"

"Isn't it?"

"No. I talk to her because she's a bright little girl and I enjoy talking to her. The fact that she's your daughter is just a bonus."

"Sure, every thirty-year-old single man wants to spend his spare time chatting with a six-year-old."

"I can't speak for all single men, but I happen to like kids. They're not as jaded as some adults I could mention."

She frowned at him, then struggled to her feet once more. "I need to go over to the jail to talk to Sue Ellen."

"Bad idea."

"Why?"

"Given your shaky condition, Ryan's going to have some questions."

"And I'll see to it that the answers don't reflect well on you."

"He won't believe you. He likes me."

"But he's liked me longer."

Ford couldn't help it, he chuckled. "If I hadn't heard you argue before a jury myself, I would never have believed all the hype about your debating skills."

She frowned. "Why?"

"Because I've heard similar exchanges on a playground."

"Oh, go—"

"I know, suck an egg," he said, laughing.

"I could start to hate you," she muttered.

"Really? That's the most promising thing you've said today."

She looked completely bewildered. "Why?"

"Hate, love, two sides of the same coin," he explained. "I think we're making progress." He stood up and held out his hand. "Come on. I'll walk you over to the jail."

"Why?"

"So I can bail you out if Ryan gets any ideas about arresting you for public drunkenness."

"I am not drunk."

"Could have fooled me."

She opened her mouth, then snapped it shut again. She stood up with careful grace, gave him a haughty look, then strolled to the door. Ford took his time following. There was no point in pushing his luck. He was pretty sure he'd riled her sufficiently for one day.

Of course, he intended to keep right on doing it until she realized that she could do her worst and he wasn't going to go away. It might be a shaky first step, but it was nonetheless a first step toward building the trust she believed was so impossible between the two of them. One of these days she was going to have to concede that she could be or do whatever she pleased and his feelings wouldn't change. Call it a relationship or whatever made her comfortable, he was in this for the long haul.

16

Emma's visit with Sue Ellen hadn't gone any better than her meal with Ford. Sue Ellen was growing increasingly depressed. Not only didn't she believe Emma could win her case, she clearly didn't care one way or the other about it. She believed she deserved to spend the rest of her life in jail. Emma left her cell feeling more discouraged about a case and a client than she'd ever felt before. She felt doubly awful because Sue Ellen was a friend, as well as a client.

"See what I mean?" Ryan asked when Emma went into his office after the visit. "She's scaring me."

"I'll get the psychologist back in to see her," Emma said, relieved that Ford hadn't stuck around during the visit. She'd had about as much of his disconcerting company as she could handle for one day.

"I thought of that," Ryan said. "She turned me down flat. She said she didn't like the woman."

"Then we'll find another one."

He shook his head, looking almost as miserable and discouraged as Sue Ellen had. "I don't think that's the answer. I'm guessing she'll find fault with a new one, too. In fact, I'm certain she'll disapprove of anyone who thinks she deserves another chance at life. She's as much as told me I'm crazy to give a damn what happens to her. The last few times I've tried to talk to her, she's just curled up on the cot and ignored me. She won't even look me in the eye anymore."

"Has she been this way ever since I left town?" Emma asked.

His expression turned thoughtful. "No, now that I think about it, I'm pretty sure it started last week. Up until then, she was sad, but not utterly despondent. In fact, she seemed more hopeful than she had in years. I spent a couple of evenings in her cell playing cards with her and she even laughed a few times."

"Any idea what triggered the change? Did something happen? Did she have a visitor?"

"People have been coming and going ever since she was arrested. As far as I know, all of them have been well-wishers who wanted her to know they were standing behind her," Ryan said, then hesitated. "Let me check the sign-in sheet. Maybe it will give us a clue."

He brought the book in from the front desk, flipped back two weeks and began to run his finger down the column of signatures. "Sweet heaven," he murmured after a minute, looking stricken. "Here, take a look."

Emma went to peer over his shoulder. There, halfway down the page, was the signature of Kate Carter. "You let Donny's mother in to see her?" she asked incredulously.

"Not me. Look at the time. It happened on the night shift. I had a town council meeting that night—I wasn't around. What the hell was Frankie thinking?"

"Don't blame him entirely," Emma said, knowing

the procedures for visits. "Apparently Sue Ellen agreed to the visit."

"True, but why would she do that?" Ryan asked. "She had to know that Kate wouldn't have anything good to say to her."

"Maybe she was hoping for forgiveness, or at least understanding," Emma suggested.

"From Kate?" Ryan said incredulously. "She spent her entire life being beaten by her father and then her husband. She was bound to think that's just the way marriage works, that Sue Ellen should have sucked it up and taken it." He muttered a curse. "I'd heard Kate was saying a lot of stuff around town. I should have warned Frankie to keep her out, no matter what Sue Ellen said."

"What stuff?" Emma asked worriedly. The last thing she needed was to have Donny's mother poisoning the minds of potential jurors. Public sentiment had been firmly on Sue Ellen's side up until now. She didn't need a shift just as the trial date neared.

"Just what you'd expect, that Sue Ellen murdered her precious son, that she was going to have to pay for it. There was a lot of hellfire and damnation thrown in for good measure."

"If she said the same thing to Sue Ellen, it's little wonder she's so depressed," Emma said. "I'm getting that psychologist in here whether she likes it or not."

She reached for the phone, but Ryan stilled her hand. "Call a minister, instead."

Emma considered the suggestion, then nodded. "Good idea. Reverend Foster is kind and compassionate."

"More important, so is the God he believes in,"

Ryan said quietly. He fixed his gaze on Emma. "What if this doesn't work? It won't be good for her to go into court acting guilty, will it?"

"Don't even think about that," Emma scolded. "This is going to work. It has to."

Ford was sitting in his office, savoring his progress with Emma earlier that evening, when a woman came staggering in, her face flushed, her pupils dilated. If she wasn't drunk, she was well on her way.

"You the editor of the paper?" she demanded.

He lowered the front legs of his chair carefully to the floor. "I am. Who are you?"

"Kate Carter. It's my son who was killed by that she-devil over at the jail."

His stomach rolled over. "I see."

"I want you to print a story about what a fine man my son was. Anybody will tell you that," she said, weaving on her feet. "Donny Carter was a fine man."

"As his mother, I'm sure you feel that way," he said cautiously. "Why don't you have a seat and tell me about him."

Kate Carter sank heavily onto the chair he pulled out, then glanced around. "You got anything to drink in here?"

He shook his head. "Sorry."

"If I talk to you, how much will you pay me?"

"I don't pay for interviews."

She seemed taken aback by that. "I heard them big tabloids pay millions for stories."

"I don't," he said flatly. "Not even five dollars, much less millions. But if you want to talk about your son, I'll listen."

"And print what I say? Word for word?"

"Anything I print will be accurate," he assured her. "But it will be balanced."

"I don't know what that means."

"It means other people might express other opinions in the same article."

She considered that for a long time, then eventually nodded. "Get out your pen," she ordered.

"I'd rather use a tape recorder, so there won't be any question of accuracy later."

"Whatever," she said, then leaned forward to talk directly into the microphone as if she didn't trust it to pick up her words.

Ford began his questioning carefully. It was obvious that Kate Carter had an agenda—getting her former daughter-in-law convicted. It was going to be tricky getting her to present any sort of unbiased view about what had happened in her son's household to bring about the shooting. So far, though, this was the best chance he'd had to get an inside view of that marriage, even if it was bound to be shaded in Donny's favor.

"Did you spend a lot of time with your son and his wife?" he asked.

"I had my own husband at home to tend to," Kate Carter said with a self-righteous expression. "I couldn't be gallivanting off to visit them every time I turned around, but I was there often enough to know what was what."

"When you were there, did you ever hear Donny and Sue Ellen argue?"

"Never," she declared. "He was a sweet boy. He doted on her. Had ever since high school. He never said a cross word to her."

"That's not what the neighbors have said," Ford pointed out. "They said there were loud arguments almost every night."

"They were lying," she said flatly.

"Why would they do that?"

"Who knows why people do what they do?"

"What about your own marriage, Mrs. Carter? Did you and your husband get along?"

She seemed taken aback by the question. "My husband's been dead for six months now, God rest his soul. Besides, what does that have to do with anything?"

"I just wondered what sort of example might have been set for Donny?"

"My husband had a temper, if that's what you mean. Some men do. It's natural."

"He ever hit you?"

Her gaze narrowed. "Not unless I deserved it."

Ford resisted the temptation to tell her that no husband had a right to hit his wife, nor did the wife ever deserve it. "So, Donny grew up thinking this was acceptable? You never told him it wasn't?"

She frowned at the question. "Are you trying to trick me?"

"Trick you how?"

"Make me say my husband and I set a bad example for our boy."

"Is that possible?"

"No, it's not possible. Donny was a good husband. A good provider. Sue Ellen should have been grateful."

"And if he hit her occasionally, that was just part of the package?" Ford suggested dryly.

"Exactly," she said, then caught herself. "He never hit her. If you write that I said that, I'll call you a liar."

"Your words are on the tape."

She grabbed the recorder and hurled it across the room. The tape sprang free and unraveled as it fell to the floor. "You find those words on there now."

"I will," he said quietly. It would be easier than she imagined to recover the tape. "I believe the interview is over, Mrs. Carter. If I'm going to use you as a source, I have to know you're being honest with me."

To his dismay, tears welled up in her eyes and spilled down her cheeks. "Don't you make my boy look bad," she whispered. "He was a good son."

Ford took pity on her. Clearly she believed that. And maybe he had been. That didn't mean he'd been a good husband.

"I'm sorry for your loss," he said quietly.

"Nobody understands that it *was* a loss," she whispered. "For me, it was a loss. When his father came after me, that boy tried to protect me, even when he was an itty-bitty little thing. More than once he was the one who wound up taking a beating. Can't you see, the least I can do is protect his memory."

"I'm sorry," Ford said again.

After she'd gone, he sighed. Kate Carter wasn't isolating her remarks to him. He knew better than that. She was going to tell anyone who'd listen exactly what she'd told him. She was going to try to convince people that Donny deserved their pity, maybe even their respect. It might play well before a jury, too.

Emma needed to know about this. She also needed to know that some of those words were going to wind up in print, which made it more critical than ever that she let her client talk to the media.

He envisioned her reaction to that, then heaved another sigh. The dinner she'd finally agreed to have with him tomorrow night was no doubt going to leave them both with indigestion.

Emma glared at Ford. "You interviewed Kate Carter?" she asked, her voice climbing until it carried throughout Stella's. Silence fell from one end of the diner to the other as everyone turned to hang on every word of their exchange.

"She came to me," he responded quietly. "I thought you should know."

"Are you going to print what she said?"

"Some of it."

"Well, if that isn't the most irresponsible, one-sided excuse for journalism I've ever heard," Emma said.

"It doesn't have to be one-sided," he reminded her. "Let me talk to Sue Ellen."

She saw what he was trying to do. Once more he was trying to manipulate her. "I've already told you that there's not a chance in hell I'll let you do that," Emma said. Especially now. With Sue Ellen's state of mind so unpredictable, she couldn't allow it. Sue Ellen was entirely likely to say that she deserved to be convicted for her crime.

"Even if it means that Kate Carter's side of the story is the only one people will read about?" He reached across the table and covered her hand. "I'll be fair, Emma. You know that. But I can't do it without your help. You know that, too."

Emma sighed, not liking any of the options available to her. If she let Kate's words go unchallenged, it would be bad for Sue Ellen. If she allowed Sue Ellen to speak up for herself, there was a chance she would condemn her own actions out of her deep-rooted sense of guilt.

"I'll think about it," she promised eventually.

"You've been thinking about it for weeks now," Ford pointed out. "The trial date is just around the corner. There's not a lot of time left."

"Dammit, don't pressure me. I hate being pressured."

Ford held up his hands. "Fine. You think it over and let me know what you decide. I'm running my story in next week's paper, with or without Sue Ellen's side of things."

Emma felt as if the walls of the diner were closing in on her. "I've got to get out of here."

"We haven't even ordered dinner yet."

"I'm not hungry."

"Okay, then, what would you rather do?" he asked, tossing a couple of bills on the table to pay for their iced tea.

"You stay. I'll go for a walk."

"I'm coming with you." He stood up and followed her outside.

Once they were on the sidewalk, Emma leaned against the building and closed her eyes. "I'm sorry. I know I caused a scene in there."

"I don't give a damn about that," he said. He touched her cheek, then gently brushed a stray curl away from her face. "Are you okay?"

She shook her head. "Can I be honest with you about something?"

"Of course."

"Off the record?"

He smiled. "We're on a date, darlin'. Everything that happens tonight is off the record."

She nodded, and because she was feeling so completely lost and alone, she decided to trust him. "I'm scared."

"Of?"

"Losing this case. I don't think I've ever had one with the stakes so high. Oh, I've had cases with more money on the line, but never one where my client could spend the rest of her life in jail if I mess up."

"You're a good lawyer. You're not going to mess up."

"What if I'm wrong about how strong Sue Ellen's case is? Or how well she's likely to perform on the witness stand? What if she breaks under the pressure? What if I should have told her to accept a plea bargain?"

"Do you believe that she would have been better off if she had?"

"No," she said honestly. "She doesn't deserve to spend one single minute in prison for this."

"Then you're giving her the best legal advice you can, right? No client can expect more." His gaze met hers. "Why the doubts, Emma?"

She sighed heavily. "A whole lot of things, I suppose. Sue Ellen's discouraged. Kate got in there the other night and began badgering her about being guilty, so now she doesn't even want to fight. Ryan's scared for her. Then you tell me that Kate's gotten your ear and you intend to print what she said."

"But you haven't really changed your mind about what happened that night, have you? You still believe that Sue Ellen merely defended herself."

"With all my heart," she said firmly.

"Then I don't see that you have any choice. You have to handle things exactly as you are."

She studied his face, tried to read exactly what he was thinking, but his expression was neutral. "You disagree with me, though, don't you?"

"It's not about what I think."

"Isn't it? If I can't convince you, how I can I convince a jury?"

Ford sighed and raked his hand through his hair. "Emma, I only know part of the story, at least first-hand. You know all of it."

"We're back to the interview again."

He nodded. "It's the only way. Do you intend to put Sue Ellen on the stand?"

"Yes, of course. I'll have to."

"Do you doubt for a second that the prosecutor will be harder on her than I could ever be?"

"No," she admitted.

In fact, one of the things that terrified her was that Sue Ellen would crack under the pressure of cross-examination. Worse, Emma feared that Sue Ellen would retreat into a passive, accepting behavior that allowed the prosecutor's verbal assaults to go uncontested. Emma's objections would only protect her so much.

And no matter how well Emma tried to prepare Sue Ellen for being questioned, Emma couldn't guarantee that Sue Ellen would fight on her own behalf. There had been too many years of battering, too many years of thinking that she deserved to be mistreated. The pattern might be too ingrained to change before the trial. If the prosecutor started to badger her, she might simply consider it her due.

"Talking to me could help prepare her for court," Ford said.

But allowing Sue Ellen to be interviewed would require a huge leap of faith on Emma's part. She wasn't sure she was ready to take such a leap just yet. She looked into Ford's eyes and saw only the thoughtfulness and compassion she had come to expect from him.

"There would have to be ground rules," she said slowly, coming to a decision she prayed she wouldn't regret.

"Whatever you say."

"I'd need to see what you intend to print."

He shook his head. "I can't do that. You're going to have to trust me."

"But—"

"That's the way it has to be, Emma. I don't send stories out for approval. No respectable journalist does. If there is any question at all in my mind about accuracy, I will go over it with you, but that's the best I can promise."

It wasn't so much the accuracy that worried her, it was the slant he might put on the piece. And once it was in print, if it was devastating to Sue Ellen's case, it would be too late to fix things.

He tucked a finger under her chin and met her gaze. "I am not out to get Sue Ellen," he assured her. "I only want to get to the truth. The whole truth."

Emma felt her heart lodge in her throat. She was fairly certain—no, she *knew*—that Ford wouldn't deliberately try to sabotage her case. Because he cared about her, because he had something to prove to her, he was probably the most sympathetic journalist she could ever find. He would be fair to Sue Ellen, at least as fair as he knew how to be.

"I'll make the arrangements," she said finally, knowing that there was a lot more on the line than Sue Ellen's future. Their fate—hers and Ford's—was hanging in the balance as well.

Glancing into his eyes, she could see that he understood that as clearly as she did. He leaned down and pressed a kiss to her cheek.

"I won't let you down," he said solemnly.

For all their sakes, Emma prayed he was right.

17

Ford knew exactly what was at stake in the interview Emma had promised to arrange. Her face had been a mirror of her emotions. She was terrified that she was making a mistake, yet she had weighed the odds, struggled with her own biases and, in the end, decided to trust him. He didn't take that trust lightly, because he knew what it had cost her. If he failed her—or even if she only perceived that he had—it would destroy them.

A part of him chafed at being put to such a test, but another part understood it. Her ex-husband and the reporter who'd conspired with him had given her good cause to be wary of journalists.

His interview with Sue Ellen had been scheduled for two o'clock. In the meantime, he spent his morning writing out questions, reading through the stack of books he'd accumulated on battered-wife syndrome.

When he was as prepared as he could possibly be, he went on the Internet to do a few last searches for information. And while he was there, he called up the archives of the Denver papers in search of the story that had almost destroyed Emma's life.

It wasn't that difficult to find amid the list of references to her name. Only one had a screaming headline about a breach of ethics. He read that and the story that had preceded it, the actual news story that suggested Emma had leaked confidential information.

The reporter had been clever, Ford would give him that. His wording had been precise, relying on innuendo rather than explicit statements that could later be pointed to as libelous. As she had told him, anyone reading it casually would get the distinct impression that Emma was the source for the inside information about her client. Only a more thorough scrutiny would prove that the reporter had never actually said that.

Indignant on her behalf, he called the paper and asked for the city editor, listed on the masthead as Clay Jennings. When the man came on the line, Ford explained who he was.

"I'm wondering if a reporter named Guy Northrup still works for you," he said.

There was a hesitation, then the editor said, "No, he left about three years ago."

"Was he fired?"

"No, he resigned," Jennings said.

"In the wake of the Emma Rogers debacle, I imagine."

The man didn't even try to hide his surprise. "You know about that?"

"Yes."

"What's your interest in it?" he asked. "Guy's not looking for a job with you, is he? I thought he'd pretty much given up on getting a job in the newspaper business. We certainly haven't given him any references."

"Not a chance," Ford said. "I just wanted to see if the man got what was coming to him."

"Last I heard, he was selling fertilizer at one of those mega-home stores. Seemed to me like it was a job right up his alley," Jennings said wryly. "By the way, isn't Ms. Rogers handling a case up your way now?"

"As a matter of fact, she is."

"Keep an eye on her. She's damned good at what she does."

Ford found himself grinning at the admiration in the man's voice. "I know that. Glad to hear you recognize it down there."

He hung up, feeling better for some reason he couldn't precisely explain. He wasn't even sure why he had made the call other than to be sure that there had been no lasting damage to Emma's reputation and that the man who'd harmed her had paid by losing his job. As for Kit Rogers, he was pretty sure that losing Emma would have been punishment enough for him. He was probably still reeling from the discovery that she had been strong enough to walk away.

Ford didn't intend to make the same mistake.

Emma was more nervous than she would have been if she were the one being interviewed. The minute the words had left her mouth the night before, she'd wanted to retract the offer. How could she put Sue Ellen's fate in Ford's hands?

How could she not?

As a result of the internal struggle, she hadn't slept a wink all night. Instead, she had played through different scenarios, trying to figure out ways she could leap into the middle of the interview if things started to go awry. An image of Ford's indignant expression if she did just that was the only thing that gave her any reason to smile.

When she could stand her own company no longer, she went into town and headed straight for Stella's. Lauren had flown in again the night before and had promised to meet Emma to lend her some much needed moral support.

When she walked into the diner, she found not only Lauren, but Karen, Gina and Cassie, as well.

"I see you've rallied the troops," she said to Lauren, managing a weak smile as she sat down.

"Only because you sounded as if you needed us. *We* all know you made the right decision," Lauren said with absolute confidence.

"Oh, really? And how do you know that?"

"Wisdom," Karen said, grinning. "We *are* getting older and wiser, you know."

"It doesn't have anything to do with us. We have faith in your judgment," Cassie corrected.

"And confidence in Ford," Gina added.

"You sound so sure," Emma said wistfully.

"Everything is going to work out, not just for Sue Ellen, but for you and Ford," Cassie insisted. "I've never seen two people better suited for each other."

"Or who make more sparks fly," Gina added with a grin.

"I can't even think about that," Emma responded. "There's too much riding on this interview."

"Well, I recommend hot-fudge sundaes all around," Lauren said. "Nobody can be depressed when they're eating all those gooey calories."

"I thought you were back on carrot sticks and yogurt," Gina said, regarding her curiously.

"Yeah, well, things change. If I want hot fudge, I can have it."

"Of course, you can," Karen soothed, then beckoned for Stella and placed the order.

They were still indulging when Ford strolled in and came straight to the table in the back. He nodded at the others, but his gaze locked on Emma's.

"Moral support?" he inquired lightly.

"Yes," she said unrepentantly.

He sighed. "You don't need it, you know."

"We've been telling her that," Gina said, reaching for another chair and pulling it over. "Join us."

Emma scowled, but she scooted over to make room for him. He sat down, then gazed at the empty sundae dishes. "It must have been a heavy conversation if it required hot fudge."

"It was," Emma said tightly.

"I need to get back to the ranch," Karen said suddenly.

"I'm coming with you," Lauren added.

Gina and Cassie stood up as well.

"Where are you going?" Emma demanded.

"Things to do," Gina declared.

"Cole's waiting for me," Cassie explained with a shrug.

"He wasn't waiting five minutes ago," Emma complained.

"Nope. It's later now." Cassie grinned, then gave her a kiss. "You're in safe hands."

"I wish I believed that," Emma said.

Ford watched the hurried departures without comment. Emma frowned.

"You certainly do know how to disrupt a party," she grumbled.

"Is that what it was? The atmosphere didn't seem very festive."

"How could it be under the circumstances?"

"Emma, if you still have a problem with me interviewing Sue Ellen, we can call it off."

"You know I can't do that," she protested. "I need people to see her side of things."

"There are other reporters," he pointed out. "I can hire a freelancer to do this interview if it will make you less uneasy."

She shook her head at once. She might not be sure she was doing the right thing, but she did know that she was better off with Ford asking the questions than a total stranger.

"It has to be you."

"Not if it's going to ruin our chances of being together," he said. "You mean a lot to me, more than I ever expected anyone to mean. I want us to have a future."

When she was about to argue the point, he held up a silencing hand. "Look, I know what's on the line here. If I fail you, if I get this story wrong or misquote Sue Ellen, whether it's right or wrong, you're going to use it as an excuse to end things between us. I know that." His gaze locked on hers. "I also know that if I don't do this, you'll never know in your heart if you can trust me and we won't stand a chance then, either. Talk about a rock and a hard place…but that's okay. I have no intention of giving you any excuse to break things off."

She swallowed hard. He had pegged it exactly right, and even she could see how unfair she was being.

"I'm sorry it has to be this way."

"So am I. Let me ask you something. Are you aware that Guy Northrup resigned in the wake of what he did to you?"

She regarded him with surprise. "How do you know that?"

"I checked into it. I suppose I wanted to be sure he had paid for what he'd done."

"Paid? You call that paying?"

"He lost his job."

"He resigned. He wasn't fired."

"But I got the sense that he would have been, if he hadn't quit. And the city editor down there reports that he's working at some home improvement store, that he can't get a job for a legitimate paper. Doesn't that reassure you at all that responsible journalists weed out the bad apples?"

"I'm relieved to know that he hasn't merely moved on to wreak havoc on someone else's life," she conceded. "But what he did was a crime for which he'll never pay." She regarded Ford sadly. "Where's the justice in that?"

Judging from his silence, he didn't have an adequate answer to her question.

Emma stood up. "Let's get this over with."

Ford stood beside her, but when she would have started from the restaurant, he held her back. "I won't let you down, Emma. You might not like every word I write, but I swear to you it will be evenhanded and fair and accurate."

His words weren't nearly as reassuring as he clearly intended them to be, but she knew they were the best she could hope for. "I know you'll try. If I didn't believe that with all my heart, we wouldn't be doing this."

At the jail, Ryan met them and escorted them into

his office. His gaze locked with Ford's. "I'm counting on you," he said grimly.

Emma's gaze was on Ford's face, and she saw the anguish in his expression. In that instant, she knew just how deeply he cared not only for her, but for his friend, and how deeply he was hoping not to let them down while still being true to his own ethics and values. They were putting him in a potentially impossible situation, but all three of them knew that there was no other way. She also knew that Ford would do what he felt was honorable and right, no matter the cost to him—or them—personally.

"I'll get Sue Ellen," Ryan said.

It was several minutes before he returned. Sue Ellen had been allowed to wear a dress for the interview, and she had taken time to brush her hair. She wore no makeup, though, and her expression was haggard. Her gaze darted from Emma to Ford and back again.

"Sue Ellen, you know Mr. Hamilton," Emma said quietly. "He wants to ask you a few questions."

Sue Ellen twisted her hands in her lap, but she nodded. Ryan put a reassuring hand on her shoulder and gave it a squeeze. For just a second she seemed to lean into his touch, but her gaze never left Ford's face.

"I'll do my best to answer them," she whispered.

Emma had spent an hour the night before and another hour this morning briefing Sue Ellen. Emma had advised her client to go into as much detail about what living with Donny was like as she felt comfortable doing. She was going to have to get used to telling the sordid story anyway, because the prosecutor would be eager to punch holes in it.

Emma sat back silently as Ford asked his questions,

his tone gentler than she'd expected, his expression faltering as the grim picture emerged. She watched his hands bunch into fists, heard his barely contained gasps, saw the color drain from his face at Sue Ellen's matter-of-fact description of her life with the man who'd vowed to love, honor and cherish her.

"Was your husband always like this? From the very beginning?"

Sue Ellen nodded, silent tears streaking down her cheeks.

"Why didn't you leave?"

"I loved him," she said simply. "Besides, where would I have gone?"

"Surely there were family members or friends who could have helped," Ford said.

Sue Ellen swallowed hard. "I was too ashamed. Besides, Donny said no one would believe me anyway."

"But there must have been bruises, cuts, broken bones? A doctor would have known."

"I only went to the doctor once. I told him I'd been injured in an accident."

"Show him your arm," Emma instructed gently.

Sue Ellen held out her right arm where the bone had clearly been broken at one time and not set properly.

"He broke your arm?" Ford said, his face pale.

"Yes."

"Did you get treatment?"

She shook her head. "Donny put a splint on it. He said it would be fine."

Ford muttered a harsh expletive under his breath. "Had he ever threatened you with a gun before that night when he died?"

"All the time," she said in a whisper. "He had at

least three in the house that I know of. One night…"
Her voice broke.

Emma reached for her hand even as Ryan rubbed
her shoulders. "It's okay. Tell him."

"One night he held it to my head and made me have
sex."

Ryan turned away, but not before Emma saw the
fury in his eyes, the heartache on his face.

"He raped you?" Ford asked.

Sue Ellen started to shake her head. "He was my
husband," she began, but this time Emma cut her off.

"He raped you," she said fiercely. "I don't care if he
was your husband, that's what it was."

Sue Ellen broke down then. Covering her face with
her hands, she wept. Ryan was at her side at once,
kneeling beside her, whispering encouragement. Sue
Ellen's gaze locked with his as if he were her lifeline.
Emma couldn't help wondering what was going to happen when Ryan had to testify about the shooting in
court. Would Sue Ellen feel betrayed yet again? Or
would she understand that Ryan was just doing his job?

Emma sighed. Would she be any more forgiving
when Ford did his?

"I think that's enough," she said quietly.

Ford nodded.

And without another word to any of them, he got
up and walked away. Emma had seen how shaken he
was. She prayed that would somehow come across in
whatever he chose to print.

Over the next couple of days she watched as Ford
visibly waged a war with himself and the values he
held so dear. He was so alone. He sat by himself in
Stella's, refusing all offers of company, including Em-

ma's. The isolation was so uncharacteristic that Emma
began to worry. If Ford wouldn't turn to her, *couldn't*
turn to her, surely there was someone he could talk to.
She went to Ryan.

"I think you need to spend a little time with Ford.
He won't talk to me. I'm pretty sure he thinks it would
be wrong under the circumstances, but he's obviously
upset. He needs a friend."

"Would I really be any better?" Ryan asked. "He
knows where I stand on this."

"Try, please," she pleaded.

Ryan patted her hand. "You're in love with him,
aren't you?"

"No, I..." Her voice trailed off.

"Emma," Ryan chided. "Be honest with me. You
and I go back too far for you to lie to my face and get
away with it."

She swallowed hard and forced herself to say aloud
what she hadn't even permitted herself to think. "Yes,"
she said softly. "I love him. I don't know how it happened, or why, of all the people in the world, he had to
be the one, but he is. I'm just so afraid that we won't
survive this."

"Want some advice from an old friend?"

She grinned. "As if you're an expert."

"Maybe not an expert, but I've waited a very long
time for the woman I love to take a second look at me.
In all this time, my love for Sue Ellen has never wavered, not once. That should tell you something."

"That you're a masochist?" Emma asked, only
partly in jest.

Ryan frowned at her. "You know better," he chided.
"It proves just how powerful love is. It doesn't bend
or break so easily. It's something that just is, some-

thing so strong that nothing can destroy it unless you permit it to."

"Ryan, you're a romantic," she said with some surprise.

He shrugged. "What can I say? I had a good example. You know any couple in town more solid than my parents? They were childhood sweethearts, and I still catch them making out when they think I'm not around. They've taken some tough knocks over the years—my dad losing his job, my mom's miscarriages, my sister's pregnancy with Teddy—but they've survived because they both believe with everything in them that they're better together than they would be apart. That's the way I feel about Sue Ellen. I just pray when this is all over, she'll let herself feel the same way about me."

"She counts on you," Emma said. "I can see it in her eyes and in the way she turns to you. There's a whole lot of respect there."

"Respect, yes," Ryan confirmed. "But how does a woman who's gone through what she's gone through ever believe in love?"

Emma thought about the faint flicker of hope she'd seen in Sue Ellen's gaze when she was with Ryan. "Give her time. She'll get there," she said with conviction.

And if Sue Ellen with her tragic past could make such a tremendous leap of faith, then how could Emma not be just as strong when it came to Ford?

She gave Ryan a hug. "Thank you."

"It's going to be good to have you home again," Ryan said.

Startled, Emma simply stared. "Home again?"

"When you and Ford get together," he said.

"But…" The protest died on her lips, when she realized that a part of her was ready for just such a move. It had been happening slowly but surely for weeks now.

With school about to start, now would be the perfect time to make the decision final. Caitlyn would be ecstatic. Matt and Martha would have her place in Denver to themselves to get their marriage back on track. And she and Ford would have time to explore their feelings without distance separating them.

Ryan was grinning at her stunned silence. "You're going to do it, aren't you? You're going to move home?"

She nodded slowly, her own smile spreading as she accepted the decision she'd been avoiding for far too long. "Yes, I am."

"I knew it," he gloated.

"Oh, go suck an egg."

He wrapped her in a fierce hug and spun her around. "Now that I know you're staying," he said, "I think I'll go tell Ford the good news."

"Shouldn't I be the one to tell him?"

"He's not talking to you right now," Ryan reminded her. "And I think this news will definitely cheer him up."

"Just don't make too much of it. I'm not moving back because of him."

"Yeah, right."

"I'm not," she protested, then sighed at Ryan's knowing expression. "Not entirely, anyway."

He chuckled. "Like I said, this is definitely going to improve his mood."

A good thing, Emma supposed, because her own mood was turning decidedly sour as she contemplated all the gloating that was going to go on among her friends and family.

18

Ford had been struggling to find the right words for days now. He stared at a blank computer screen, then listened to his tape of the interview with Sue Ellen. Each time he heard the stark portrayal of her married life, it sickened him. He'd known all of the statistics about domestic violence, had even read other articles in other papers about tragedies, but this was someone he knew. It made it real and far more devastating than he'd ever imagined when he'd made his sanctimonious declarations about what Sue Ellen had been driven to do.

To his astonishment, more than once as they'd talked Sue Ellen had actually defended that creep of a husband. As she had told her story, Ford had begun to see the psychological damage that years of abuse had wrought. He wondered if Ryan had any idea how difficult it would be for Sue Ellen ever to have a normal relationship, to believe in the possibility of a loving marriage?

He had to write the story. For hours on end Ford debated where to begin. How could he describe Sue Ellen's marriage as bravely as she had? There had been no self-pity in her words, and he was not entirely sure that was a good sign. If ever anyone had a right to feel sorry for herself, it was Sue Ellen. But how could he, the outsider, allow pity to creep into the article, when she had none to spare for herself?

Had that been Emma's dilemma? Had she feared that Sue Ellen's refusal to cut herself the slightest break would somehow make her less sympathetic to both Ford and, ultimately, a jury? In the few days since the interview he'd understood Emma's torment over permitting this interview more clearly than ever before.

He wanted desperately to do justice to all sides of the story, but even he—as hard-nosed as he'd been for weeks now—felt his sympathy shifting toward Sue Ellen.

He wrote a sentence, then a paragraph, then deleted it all with a muttered curse. He was tempted to throw the damned computer across the office. Instead, he stood up, kicked a trash can halfway across the room and began to pace.

"I recommend a drink," Ryan said, coming through the door just in time to catch the display of temper and dodge the flying trash can.

"If I thought it would solve anything, I'd drink an entire bottle of Scotch," Ford said with feeling.

"Let's start with just one drink. I'm buying. We'll go to the Heartbreak, listen to a little music and chill."

Ford regarded his friend gravely. "You can do that after what you heard the other day? Didn't you want to punch someone?"

"Who? Donny's dead. Besides, it's not like it was the first time I'd heard it," Ryan said tightly. "Every time, it makes me want to break things. Do you know how many calls I responded to at their house? How many times I was forced to walk away because Sue Ellen wouldn't press charges? For a long time what I most wanted to break was Donny Carter's face—and maybe his father's—for teaching him by example that it was okay to treat a woman that way. I tried to make him get help, but he thought it was just a way to get him out of the picture, so I could take Sue Ellen away from him. It was so blasted frustrating that I wanted to hit him myself."

"But you resisted the urge," Ford concluded. "How?"

"By doing exactly what I'm recommending to you, going to the Heartbreak and having a drink. Just one. More, and all that celebrated self-control of mine would have gone out the window and I'd be the one in jail now." He sighed, his expression soul-deep weary. "Maybe that would have been better."

"You can't believe that," Ford chided. He turned off the computer. "Let's go, though if I'm going to get this story done tonight, I'd better stick to soda."

Ryan gave him a slap on the back as they left the building. "I have some news that might put you in a better frame of mind," he said, mustering a faint smile.

"Oh?"

"Not till I get that drink, and trust me, mine won't be soda."

When Ryan finally had his beer and Ford was sipping on a cola, he studied the sheriff's somber expression. "I thought you said you had good news."

"For you," Ryan said. "And all of Winding River, for that matter."

"Oh?"

"Emma's staying."

Ford felt his pulse take a leap. "She's staying?" he said cautiously. "How long?"

"For good."

"When did this happen?"

"We were talking earlier. I tossed out the suggestion, she protested automatically, then caught herself. She finally realized that it's what she's wanted all along. She just didn't have the nerve to take that last leap."

"And you talked her into it," Ford said, feeling vaguely disgruntled that it had been Ryan, not he, who'd accomplished the impossible.

"I just got her to say it out loud. You, my man, laid all the groundwork. Not that she admitted it, but it's plain to me that she's crazy about you. And Caitlyn's happy here. Her family is here. All in all, I think it was a foregone conclusion from the minute Emma came home for the reunion, especially with her friends moving back here one by one." He studied Ryan. "You don't look especially ecstatic about the news."

"Believe me, I am," Ford said. "I wasn't looking forward to having to chase her to Denver again. And I really wasn't happy about the prospect of commuting on a regular basis. Still…" He sighed.

"You think this article about Sue Ellen could still ruin your chances," Ryan guessed.

Ford nodded. "It's a real possibility."

Ryan shook his head. "I'll tell you what I told her. Love can survive anything if two people want it to. Otherwise even the tiniest obstacles can become insurmountable."

"This isn't just some little bump in the road. She's testing me. And I might not like it, but I understand where she's coming from."

"Okay, she's testing you. So what? Are you an objective reporter?" Ryan challenged.

"Of course."

"And an honorable one?"

"I like to think so."

"Then you've got nothing to worry about."

"Even though I'm more sympathetic than I was, I can't give Sue Ellen a free pass," Ford said.

"No one expects that," Ryan insisted.

"Are you sure? I think Emma's hoping for exactly that."

"Well, hell, when it comes right down to it, so am I," Ryan said. "But we both know you'll do what's right, even if we disagree with some of what you print. Unless you give Kate free rein and cut out Sue Ellen's side of things, I'm not going to beat you up over it, and Emma won't hate you."

Ford sighed. "I wish I were as confident of that as you seem to be." But then he was the only one who knew just how badly Emma had been burned by another reporter and by a man she had once loved.

Because he'd been deliberately avoiding her, not until she saw the story in the paper would Emma know how Ford was going to resolve his own internal conflicts. She hadn't tried to contact him, hadn't wanted to risk the accusation that she was trying to use their personal relationship to influence him. Beyond telling her not to worry, Ryan had said nothing after the night she'd sent him to talk to Ford.

As a result of all this discretion and silence, she had lived in torment the past few days waiting for the paper to hit the stands. Now that it had, she was almost afraid to read it. It lay on the table in front of her, the headline and front page story facedown.

"Go on," Cassie said, pouring her a cup of coffee. "Read it."

Her gaze flew up. "You've read it?"

"Every word."

"And?"

"I think you're going to be pleased. Ford did a fantastic job," Cassie reassured her. "I don't think anyone could read it and not understand the hell that Sue Ellen went through every single day of her life. Even Kate's comments help Sue Ellen's case, though I doubt that was what Kate intended when she went to see Ford."

Emma drew in a deep breath and picked up the paper. Heart in her throat, she began to read.

The article was stark, its recitation of facts grim, its accompanying editorial far more compassionate than even Emma had dared hope.

The love that had been building inside her for weeks deepened as it was joined by respect and an understanding of what it had taken for Ford to admit that he'd been wrong, that he'd judged too harshly without taking a moment to walk in Sue Ellen's shoes. He was generous in his sympathy for Kate's loss of a son, who'd tried as a child to protect her but in the end had learned his father's worst traits.

There were tears in her eyes by the time she had finished the last word. It was ironic that she was in the same booth at the diner where she had first seen that damning photograph in the Cheyenne paper all those weeks ago. Her feelings for Ford now were the polar opposite of what she had felt that day. Animosity and distrust had slowly given way to something she had never expected to feel for any man again, much less a journalist. Though she had denied it to Ryan, she knew that Ford had been a big part of her reasons for wanting to relocate to Winding River permanently. She was finally ready to give this fragile love of theirs a chance to flourish.

Without looking up, she knew the precise moment when Ford walked through the door, because Stella dropped the plate she'd been carrying and rushed over to hug him. Every other patron stopped him to congratulate him as he made his way to where Emma sat.

Finally he stood beside the table, his expression more vulnerable than she'd ever seen it.

"May I join you?" he asked.

Unable to speak past the lump in her throat, she merely nodded. His gaze fell on the open paper.

"You've read it?"

"Every word."

"And?"

"What you wrote was wonderful," she said, meeting his gaze. "I hope I can be that eloquent in court."

"You'll be even better," he said. He looked away, clearly uneasy, then finally faced her. "When this case is over, you and I need to talk."

She thought she knew what was on his mind, thought she knew exactly why he wanted to wait, but she couldn't, not one second longer. She called on every last nerve that had ever gotten her through a tough court case.

"Why not now?" she asked. "I have a couple of things on my mind."

He regarded her warily. "Such as?"

"I've decided that I'd like to relocate my practice to

Winding River. Caitlyn's happy here. I'm happy here.
What do you think?"

"Ryan mentioned that you'd been thinking about
that." He sounded somewhat miffed.

"Actually, I hadn't been," she said. "Not consciously,
anyway. If anything, I'd been fighting the idea. Then
the other day, Ryan said something and everything
clicked into place. I just have one question—how would
you feel about it?"

A smile tugged at the corners of his mouth. "Sounds
like a good plan to me. To tell you the truth, I wasn't
all that crazy about commuting to Denver."

That he'd even been considering such a thing reassured her that she was making the right decision.
"Then you wouldn't mind having me around to butt
heads with?"

The smile spread to a full-fledged grin. "I wouldn't
mind having you around for a whole lot of reasons,
butting heads included."

"Care to name any of those other reasons?"

"There's the sex for one thing," he said, chuckling
at her startled reaction.

Then Emma couldn't help it, she laughed too.
"There is that. Anything else?"

"I've gotten pretty attached to Caitlyn and the rest
of your family," he said.

"I've noticed that. You and my mom have become
especially tight lately."

"We have a lot in common."

"Only one thing I can think of," Emma said. "Getting me to move back here."

He grinned. "Like I said, a lot in common. And I'm

pretty sure she and all the rest of them have expectations," he added.

"Expectations?" she repeated, ignoring the sudden leap of her heart.

"You know, where you and I are concerned."

"And you wouldn't want to disappoint them?"

He shook his head. "No, but the person I really don't want to disappoint, the person I never want to disappoint, is you."

Emma thought of the article and knew that she would never doubt his integrity or honor again. She had known for some time that she didn't doubt his love. "You couldn't if you tried."

His grin was rueful. "Would you be saying that if that story hadn't done exactly what you'd hoped for?"

"As long as it was honest, as long as the facts were accurate and nothing was misrepresented, yes."

"Can you really be sure of that?" he asked, his gaze intense as he studied her. "I'm always going to be a journalist, Emma. I'm always going to call things the way I see them. If you're going to be practicing law here, there will be other cases and other stories. I won't slant things to suit you."

"I wouldn't expect you to."

His gaze held hers. "Are you sure? Really sure?"

Because the answer was obviously so important to him, she took the time to think it over. Deep down, she knew that he might write things that would rankle, things that might not be favorable to a client of hers, but she also knew that he would never do it with malice. He would never in a million years do to her what Kit and his pal had done, because deep down Ford was the most decent man she'd ever known. He'd proved it with this story about Sue Ellen and in myriad other ways.

"I'm sure," she said quietly. "Absolutely sure."

He nodded slowly, but that serious expression in his eyes never wavered. "This may not be the most romantic time or place for this, but since we seem to have an audience, I'll do it anyway. It might improve my odds of getting the right response."

"Audience?" she said, and looked up to see all of the Calamity Janes lurking nearby, nodding encouragement. Her gaze shifted back to Ford.

He reached for her hand and pressed a kiss to her knuckles. "Marry me, Emma."

It was her turn to ask if *he* was sure.

"Oh, I'm sure," he said with heartfelt conviction. "I think I fell in love with you the second you told me what an idiot I was."

"Way back then?"

"Yes, way back then. Not too many people can be so blasted sexy when they're busy insulting a person."

"Not many people can take it so well." She studied him intently. "You really think we can survive all the disagreements that are bound to come up?"

"Do you think there will ever be one more important or more heartfelt than this last one?" he asked.

"I hope not, but you never know."

"Darlin', I think we can survive just about anything. We just have to make sure we never stop believing in the power of love."

She thought about Ryan and Sue Ellen, thought about her childhood friend's faith in the endurance of love. His had been sorely tested, and yet it had survived. She believed with all her heart that Ryan would one day get his wish and have the chance to prove to Sue Ellen that she was worthy of being loved by a kind, gentle man.

"I can do that," she said softly.

"No," Ford corrected. "*We* can do that. From now on, we're a team."

She laughed. "I'm going to remind you of that when you sit down at the computer to write an editorial."

"Only if I get to remind you right before you make an argument to the jury."

Emma held up her hands. "Okay, okay, we only take the teamwork so far."

Suddenly Lauren, Cassie, Gina and Karen were beside the table.

"Well?" Lauren demanded impatiently. "Did she say yes?"

Ford grinned up at her. "To what?"

"If you didn't ask her to marry you, then you're not the man I thought you were," Lauren said.

"He asked," Emma said, then waited a beat to let the anticipation build.

"Tell us, dammit," Gina said. "I'm getting gray hair waiting for you."

"As if," Emma said. "Okay, I said yes."

"Well, thank heaven," Gina declared. "I was beginning to worry about your good sense."

As if they'd all shared the exact same thought, four pairs of eyes turned to Lauren.

"Your turn," Emma said. "You're the only holdout. Karen's finally with Grady, Cassie's marriage to Cole is on solid ground at last and Gina's with Rafe."

"Oh, I don't think you need to worry about her," Karen teased.

"Meaning?" Emma asked.

Lauren scowled at Karen. "Meaning that she has a big mouth," she grumbled. "Besides, this is Emma's big moment. Let her have it."

"I'm willing to share," Emma countered.

"Well, I'm not," Lauren said. "When I have any news at all, you'll be the first to know, but I'm not sharing the spotlight."

"Typical actress," Gina teased. "She wants to be sure she's the one with all the lines."

"Hey, everybody, remember me?" Ford asked plaintively.

Lauren squeezed into the booth beside him and planted a big kiss on his cheek. "The prospective groom. How could we forget you?"

"Hey, keep your hands off my guy," Emma grumbled.

Lauren uttered an exaggerated sigh and confided to Ford, "She was always jealous of me, because she knows I'm prettier."

"You may be prettier, but he picked me," Emma said pointedly. "Now go away. I'm tired of sharing, after all."

"Okay, okay, we can take a hint," Lauren said, sliding back out of the booth.

Only after they were all gone did Emma meet Ford's gaze. "Are you sure you're ready to be a part of this crowd?"

"I think the five of you will keep me in stories for years to come," he teased.

Emma grinned. "We probably will. Too bad you won't be able to print any of them."

"I'm counting on you to find some way to compensate for that."

Emma felt her heart flip over. "Oh, I can definitely do that."

"Want to start now?"

She hesitated, thought of all she'd planned to do today to get ready for court, then dismissed it. After all, how often did a woman get engaged?

"Your place in ten minutes?" she asked.

"Make it five."

Emma made it in four and then put every single second she'd saved to very good use. It was absolutely amazing how inventive a highly motivated woman could be.

Epilogue

Ford and Emma were married in a ceremony at the Clayton ranch two weeks before Sue Ellen's trial was scheduled to begin. Because of the timing, they kept the ceremony small, just the Calamity Janes and their guys, along with Ryan, Teddy and family. Ford's parents came from Georgia and fell in love with Emma and Caitlyn, and with Winding River.

Because Emma couldn't choose only one bridesmaid from among all of her friends, she had Caitlyn stand up for her. Ryan served as Ford's best man.

Three weeks later Emma stood in a courtroom with Sue Ellen beside her awaiting the jury's reading of its verdict. Ford sat in the front row right behind her. Just before the foreman stood to speak, she glanced at him.

"I love you," he mouthed silently.

That gave her the strength to face the solemn jurors.

"We the jury find the defendant, Sue Ellen Carter, not guilty," the foreman read.

Sue Ellen stared at the man, her expression blank, then slowly turned to Emma.

"I'm free?" she whispered.

Emma hugged her. "You are free."

Tears streamed down Sue Ellen's face. "I can't believe it." Her gaze sought out Ryan in the back of the courtroom. He was already making his way toward her.

Suddenly Sue Ellen stiffened. Emma turned and saw Kate standing in the aisle. Ford was about to intercept her, but she said, "Please, I need to see Sue Ellen. I'm not here to cause a problem."

Emma glanced at Sue Ellen, who nodded. "It's okay."

Ryan moved to stand protectively beside Sue Ellen as Kate came closer.

"I'm sorry," Donny's mother said, her expression anguished. "I loved my boy. I've listened in this courtroom the last few days and I've learned a lot. I'm ashamed to admit it, but part of the blame for what happened rests with me. I stayed with Donny's daddy for a lot of the same reasons you stayed with my son. By doing that, I told Donny what his daddy was doing was all right, that it was what I deserved."

Sue Ellen regarded her with pity and understanding. "It's hard when you love someone to have the courage to leave, isn't it?"

Kate nodded, tears streaming down her face. "Forgive me."

"That's easy," Sue Ellen said. "The hard part will be forgiving ourselves." She looked at Ryan, her heart in her eyes. "But I'm going to try. I really am."

A few days after the trial ended, Emma helped Sue Ellen pack. She was determined to leave Winding River to live closer to her sister in Montana and start a new life where she could build happier memories.

In the weeks after that, Ryan spent a lot of time

commuting north to try to convince Sue Ellen that they could have a future together.

"I think I'm getting through to her," he told Ford and Emma when he stopped by their house after his latest visit.

"But will she ever want to come back here?" Emma asked, concerned that he might still get his heart broken.

Ryan grinned. "That's just it. She won't have to. I've been talking to the sheriff up there. He's got an opening."

Ford's gaze narrowed. "For a deputy? Will you be happy with that?"

"I'd be happy being dogcatcher if it meant having Sue Ellen in my life, but the truth is, the sheriff's going to retire in two years. He says with my experience, I'll be the best candidate to take over."

The thought of Ryan leaving Winding River filled Emma with sorrow, but she reminded herself of how selfish she was being. All he'd ever wanted was the chance to love Sue Ellen. If he was finally getting that, who was she to start listing objections? Even so, she couldn't help crying just a little at the prospect of losing him from her life.

"I'm happy for you," she said finally.

"No, you're not," Ryan said, grinning. "You don't like letting go. You never did."

"Then it's a good thing I'm not going anywhere, isn't it?" Ford said, squeezing her hand as she fought the salty sting of tears.

"Will you invite us to the wedding?" she asked Ryan.

"I expect the two of you to be our witnesses," Ryan

said. "Without you, who knows if we ever would have gotten this chance?"

He stood up then. "Well, it looks to me as if Emma has something on her mind, so I'll get out of here and leave you two alone."

She frowned at him. "You can't read my mind."

"Of course, I can. Always could," he said, then leaned in close. "Congratulations, by the way."

She shot a startled look at him, but he merely winked. "If it's a boy, Ryan's a nice name."

"Get out of here before you spoil my surprise."

After he'd gone, Ford studied her intently. "Okay, spill it. What surprise?"

"We're going to have a baby," she said, watching his face to gauge his reaction. It had only been a couple of weeks since they'd stopped using birth control. Apparently they'd slipped up before that, because the doctor estimated she was at least six weeks' pregnant.

"A baby," he echoed, looking stunned. "Already? Are you sure?"

"Very sure. I took a home pregnancy test, then because I couldn't believe it had happened so fast, I had the doctor check it out, too."

"How long have you known?"

"For sure, since I saw the doctor this afternoon."

"How did Ryan know?"

"Lucky guess. He knew I wouldn't cry over the thought of him leaving. It had to be my hormones acting up."

"Oh, I suspect a few of those tears were for him, but it's not like you'll never see him again," Ford said. "People from Winding River have a way of coming home again."

Emma gave him a watery smile. "They do, don't they?" she said happily, already anticipating Lauren's permanent return the following week. Then all of the Calamity Janes would be close by.

"When will we know if this baby's a boy or a girl?" Ford asked.

"Not for quite a while yet. Do you want to know ahead of time?" she asked him.

"I already know it's going to be a boy," he said with confidence. "I don't need a sonogram to tell me that."

"It's another girl," Emma declared, just as convinced. "Caitlyn has been pleading for a sister, and you give her everything she asks for."

"Are we going to fight about this, too?" Ford asked, regarding her with amusement.

Emma grinned. "Right up until the day I deliver. Since I married you, I've discovered that there's nothing quite as stimulating as a good, heated test of wills."

"I'll show you heated, darlin'."

And he did.

* * * * *

Get 2 Free Books,
Plus 2 Free Gifts -
just for trying the Reader Service!

SHERRYL WOODS

32979	MOONLIGHT COVE	___$7.99 U.S.	___$9.99 CAN.
32976	ALONG CAME TROUBLE	___$7.99 U.S.	___$9.99 CAN.
32975	ABOUT THAT MAN	___$7.99 U.S.	___$9.99 CAN.
32947	DRIFTWOOD COTTAGE	___$7.99 U.S.	___$9.99 CAN.
32927	THE BACKUP PLAN	___$7.99 U.S.	___$9.99 CAN.
32895	MENDING FENCES	___$7.99 U.S.	___$9.99 CAN.
32845	SWEET TEA AT SUNRISE	___$7.99 U.S.	___$9.99 CAN.
32814	RETURN TO ROSE COTTAGE	___$7.99 U.S.	___$9.99 CAN.
32641	HARBOR LIGHTS	___$7.99 U.S.	___$9.99 CAN.
32634	FLOWERS ON MAIN	___$7.99 U.S.	___$9.99 CAN.
32626	THE INN AT EAGLE POINT	___$7.99 U.S.	___$7.99 CAN.
31791	THE CALAMITY JANES: CASSIE & KAREN	___$7.99 U.S.	___$8.99 CAN.
31732	DOGWOOD HILL	___$8.99 U.S.	___$9.99 CAN.
31679	THE DEVANEY BROTHERS: DANIEL	___$7.99 U.S.	___$9.99 CAN.
31668	A SEASIDE CHRISTMAS	___$7.99 U.S.	___$8.99 CAN.
31630	THE DEVANEY BROTHERS: MICHAEL AND PATRICK	___$7.99 U.S.	___$8.99 CAN.
31607	THE DEVANEY BROTHERS: RYAN AND SEAN	___$7.99 U.S.	___$8.99 CAN.
31589	HOME TO SEAVIEW KEY	___$7.99 U.S.	___$8.99 CAN.
31581	SEAVIEW INN	___$7.99 U.S.	___$8.99 CAN.
31466	AFTER TEX	___$7.99 U.S.	___$9.99 CAN.
31442	WIND CHIME POINT	___$7.99 U.S.	___$9.99 CAN.
31414	TEMPTATION	___$7.99 U.S.	___$9.99 CAN.
31391	AN O'BRIEN FAMILY CHRISTMAS	___$7.99 U.S.	___$9.99 CAN.
31348	MIDNIGHT PROMISES	___$7.99 U.S.	___$9.99 CAN.
31326	WAKING UP IN CHARLESTON	___$7.99 U.S.	___$9.99 CAN.
31262	A CHESAPEAKE SHORES CHRISTMAS	___$7.99 U.S.	___$9.99 CAN.

(limited quantities available)

TOTAL AMOUNT	$ _____
POSTAGE & HANDLING	$ _____
($1.00 for 1 book, 50¢ for each additional)	
APPLICABLE TAXES*	$ _____
TOTAL PAYABLE	$ _____

(check or money order—please do not send cash)

To order, complete this form and send it, along with a check or money order for the total above, payable to MIRA Books, to: **In the U.S.:** 3010 Walden Avenue, P.O. Box 9077, Buffalo, NY 14269-9077; **In Canada:** P.O. Box 636, Fort Erie, Ontario, L2A 5X3.

Name: _____

Address: _____ City: _____

State/Prov.: _____ Zip/Postal Code: _____

Account Number (if applicable): _____

075 CSAS

*New York residents remit applicable sales taxes.
*Canadian residents remit applicable GST and provincial taxes.

MIRA®

www.MIRABooks.com

MSHW0615BL